Gilles stared through th
this man was indeed [illegible]
shit storm of trouble. And yet— "Did you see the marks on him?"

"Yeah," Houston said. "The neck wound was impressive. Damn near tore his head off."

"Yes. So tell me, if Deacon had done that to you, how would you feel about it?"

"I guess I wouldn't be too happy. Even so, it's no guarantee of trust. There's still nothing stopping him from walking right out of here, straight back to Deacon and betraying us all."

Gilles had to agree, and said as much. "It could, however, be a moot point," he added. "He should have awakened by now."

"There's something wrong with him?"

"I—" he stopped. They both turned and looked down the corridor. Eleanor was approaching. She clutched a brown cashmere wrap close around her shoulders, and her gray hair was loose. She looked stronger, refreshed, and Gilles gave a sigh of relief. Maybe now there'd be some answers.

"You tied him up," she said, joining them at the window. She looked at them, bemused, like they'd lost their minds.

Houston stuck out his jaw. "Damn right we tied him up."

Gilles sought to diffuse the conflict between the two. "Eleanor, I need you to tell me why he won't wake up."

"Well, that's easy enough." She pulled the wrap a little closer. "He doesn't want to."

I want to thank David Wilson and David Dodd at Crossroad Press, particularly David Dodd, who provided his expertise and helped me knock this little rascal out of the park. I'd also like to thank David Smithson, Tony Tremblay, and Cheryl Jones, who forged bravely through earlier stages of the book and helped me figure out what worked, and what didn't. And to all at Necon, Horror World, and the Los Angeles Chapter of the HWA, this lonely business is made infinitely more bearable by your light of friendship and inspiration.

Macabre Ink is an imprint of Crossroad Press Publishing

Cover by Dave Dodd
Design by Aaron Rosenberg
ISBN 978-1-941408-67-4

For information address Crossroad Press at 141 Brayden Dr., Hertford, NC 27944
www.crossroadpress.com

First edition

[redacted]

BLOOD PATERNAL

BOOK I OF THE ORIGINS OF BLOOD SERIES

Fancy a bite?

JANET JOYCE HOLDEN

Janet

Macabre Ink

To my husband, Tony.

PROLOGUE

To my beloved sons and daughters, to my family,

Many years ago I left you. I embarked upon a journey of discovery none of you understood, and have been gone so long that many of you question my very existence.

And what of it, then—this journey of mine?

Alas, it ends in despair.

I have struggled for many days, hoping I might instill some grace, some compassion in what I am about to impart, but I have never been a graceful man, and besides, the details are pointless.

The truth, then.

We do not belong here. We have never belonged here.

And so, make peace and prepare, my children, and heed my resolve.

For I hereby return to you.

And I will slay you all.

Anton Weiss

CHAPTER 1
GILLES

The wind danced across the valley, pulling the dust along in carefree streamers, and despite Gilles' temporary shelter beneath the branches of a spare-limbed oleander, the sunlight weighed heavy and oppressive on his shoulders. To his left, Eleanor was crouched alongside a similar shrub, making full use of the dismal shade it offered while sand and grit swirled at their feet, looking for ways to sneak in through multiple layers of protection and make their lives an even bigger misery.

There was movement ahead. It was Houston, giving the all clear. Gilles glanced toward his companion, and after a mutual acknowledgement, they left their shelter and dashed toward thick adobe walls. Once they were beyond the squat building's threshold, under the shelter of darkness, Gilles joined the others in throwing back hoods and removing protective goggles.

Houston's broad shoulders filled the hallway. "Delacour was right. We're a couple of days too late. Consequently, it doesn't smell too good in there."

Eleanor pushed ahead and entered the gloom.

"Stay here," Gilles told his male companion, "and keep your eyes open." He followed the woman inside, and wished just this one time Delacour had gotten it wrong. Houston was correct—it did smell bad and it got worse as they moved, slowly and carefully from one room to the next. He counted sixteen bodies, all of them torched and unrecognizable. In some cases, all that remained were slivers of charred bone; their killers, efficient and thorough, had known exactly what needed to be done.

Eleanor appeared alongside him. Her gloves were off and tucked in her belt, leaving her pale fingers free to touch the remains. It was the only way she could identify them. "Four upstairs," she said. "They're all accounted for except one. And there's no sign of the donors, as if they've simply disappeared."

Gilles glanced at the immediate surroundings. Shattered glass and charred flesh lay scattered amongst splintered furniture and spent cartridges. There were six bodies in this one room alone. "We'd better let Houston take a detailed look, and find out exactly how it happened. You and I will keep watch. We'll do what we can and attempt to find the other when it gets dark. We can't leave everything like this."

She nodded, her face etched with lines of sorrow and bitterness."He's fulfilling his promise, isn't he? Just like he said he would."

Gilles grasped her shoulder, and attempted to sound reassuring. "Try not to worry. Delacour will know what to do."

He spent the rest of the afternoon outside, uncomfortable but aware of the necessity, and stayed in minimal contact with their driver. From his viewpoint under the protective shade of the porch, he could see the full length of the valley and the only road in and out. And while his eyes shifted back and forth across sand and desiccated vegetation, he wallowed in a pit of bitter reproach.

They had been fools, thinking this place was safe. Up to now it had been considered a sanctuary, a haven, with the inhabitants well out of reach of the bitter politics that occasionally erupted between members of their society. But now their Grand Father, if this was indeed the work of Weiss, had unleashed hell and everything had changed.

The sun was low on the horizon, the sky a gaudy splash of pink and orange by the time Houston emerged from the house. "They didn't use the tunnel," the man said, looking out toward the East. "I don't know why. I'm guessing it was blocked somehow. I'll check at the other end when it gets dark. Still haven't found any sign of the donors."

It was time to clean up, catalog the dead, and sweep the entire massacre under the desert's vast, forgiving carpet. By the time they were done and heading home, a dull glow emerged from the hills, where a fire burned. By morning, the house, a sanctuary no longer, would be a smoldering ruin, dry and barren as the land surrounding it. As for the donors and their missing person, there was still no sign, as if the desert had simply swallowed them up.

They reached the airstrip about an hour before dawn and climbed aboard a small jet prepped and ready for takeoff. Once they were airborne, Gilles settled at the far end of the cabin and ruminated on everything he'd witnessed. After a while, he raised his head and glanced at his companions. Houston was at the front of the plane, his eyes closed and his feet propped up across the aisle, looking easy and rested. Eleanor was in between, curled up tight in one of the leather seats, her face drawn, her thoughts haunted by the dead. It pained Gilles to see her like that, but he knew there was nothing he could do. He knew the plight of the missing girl, Dimitra, was clawing at her too. For a long while back there, she had objected strongly to them razing the building and destroying a good source of shelter. But they'd looked everywhere and had surmised she was either in the hands of their mysterious enemy, or dead. Either way, Dimitra was gone, and curse his sense of relief, but he was secretly glad this particular young lady was now out of their hands.

Disgusted, he attempted to shed his mind of pain and selfishness, lest it spill over and infect the others. They were all tainted, spoiled and torn apart by what they had just witnessed, and by what they'd had to do. Dust, scent, and faint particles of the dead still clung to all three of them and it would be a while before they could cleanse themselves of it. And it wasn't over. There would be a debriefing, and a discussion on who might have done such a thing, whether it was indeed Weiss —their Grand Father gone mad —or someone else, closer to home.

He knew Houston's opinion and despite the apparent nonchalance, the man was bleeding vengeance. Gilles looked at his watch. Another hour and they'd be starting their descent. He settled back, took a slow, deep breath. Delacour would be expecting him to be the voice of reason once they returned. Better calm himself then, become objective, and start practicing that voice.

CHAPTER 2
MARK

Almost there.

He could see the car, a beacon of hope, a shiny, black sedan waiting to sweep him away from the madness. Mark smiled firmly and pulled away from the gathering of giddy, delighted teenagers and their moms who'd wanted their picture taken alongside him. He felt the hand of his publicist on his shoulder, and let her steer him along the line at the side of the theater, away from the crowd and toward the curb.

"Had enough?"

He nodded, trying not to look desperate.

She shrugged. "They've had you for thirty minutes, give or take. It's more than some would give their adoring public. Come, you'll be late for the party and Molly wants to talk to you." She pushed him toward the car.

The cameras were still flashing, the crowd still watching his every move, and he worked hard at keeping the smile on his face. "You know, for a minute there I thought you were rescuing me."

"I'm sorry, darling, but she said it was urgent."

A valet opened the car door, he stepped inside the vehicle, sank into the black leather upholstery and, despite present company, he let out a long sigh of relief when the door slammed shut, blocking out the flash and clamor of the crowd. The driver pulled into traffic and he glanced to his left. "Hello, Molly."

She launched straight into business. "I have to be at LAX in an hour but I needed to talk to you first. I'll drop you off at the party." Typical Molly, no preamble, she wasn't even looking at him. Instead, her smartphone had her attention, and he watched her finger slide authoritatively across the screen. After all the adoration out there on the sidewalk, right now it felt like he'd been magically transported and was now back in high school, outside the principal's office awaiting detention. He smiled at the absurdity of it, leaned back, closed his eyes, and rubbed the bridge of his nose. He was used to this. She'd been his manager for nearly five years, but despite her brusque, acerbic manner, he could hardly complain. His career had assumed a steady, lucrative climb since she had taken him under her wing and so he took it, tried to relax, and waited.

The car turned south and then west onto Sunset. It was Tuesday night, busy, but the vehicle made good progress.

"So."

He opened his eyes and saw the phone resting on her lap and her hands clasped alongside it. She was staring at him, dressed in her usual immaculate uniform—black pant suit and a plain, slashed neck blouse, her hair gathered severely at the nape of her neck. She was in her early forties, narrow-framed and lithe. Mark continued to find her very attractive, when she wasn't treating him like her whipping boy. And yeah, wouldn't he like to perform a little role reversal on that.

"So," he answered, and flashed her a picture-perfect grin.

"Did you read the script?"

Ah, crap. "Yes, I did."

"It's perfect for you."

"It is, or it was, until I discovered who was directing. And you hid it from me. I had to find out for myself."

"Mark—"

"I'm not working with Strang again. I'm not doing it. I thought we'd been through this." A day with only four cups of coffee, two Advil, half a pack of cigarettes, and a belly full of anxiety for sustenance, not to mention an inexplicable sense of foreboding that had been accumulating all afternoon; he was feeling weak, lightheaded, and nausea beckoned. He wasn't up for this and she knew it. He watched her eyes get all narrow and mean as he prepared himself for the verbal tsunami.

"We *have* been through this, Mark, and I've already told you, you're not big enough to start calling the shots. Not yet."

"I don't care."

"And I guess you don't care that the last time you pig-headed bastards worked together it got you the fucking Globe nomination." Her voice was getting a familiar edge to it. She was just warming up.

He sank into the leather seat and stared up at the vehicle's ceiling. "Molly—"

"It's a done deal. Or it will be if you get your head out of your ass. Do you realize how much work I had to put in? The shit I had to wade through? You're not the only prima donna in this fucking town."

He turned away and looked out of the window. Armin Strang. A brilliant director, highly acclaimed, box office gold, and, as it turned out, a sexual predator. Mark had spent the best part of eleven weeks avoiding the guy's repeated aggressive advances. No way did he want to go through that again. "Molly, you don't underst—"

"Understand what—how you're going to fuck up your career? It's just three months in Baja, for God's sake. And the script has Oscar written all over it. Oss-Kerr, get it?"

He looked back at her. The smile on her face was evil and triumphant, making him feel trapped, like he was sinking in quicksand. The attendant disquiet also increased, and unconsciously his fingers began rapping on the sill of the window. "Let me out of the car."

But she wasn't done. "What the hell is wrong with you? I didn't force you into this line of work. You knew what was involved. You knew how much broken glass you'd have to crawl through. Remember that little talk we had? Right at the beginning, about keeping our heads down and getting the work done, about keeping our noses clean and not getting all—"

"Molly, let me out of the car." He tried to stay calm and keep his voice down. Quicksand. Past his shoulders. Up to his neck. Escape became mandatory.

"I won't take no for an answer, Mark."

"Let me out of the fucking car!"

She laughed, just one hard, single bark that held no humor in it whatsoever. "What, just dump you, the mighty Mark Niels Gannon, out onto the sidewalk? Make you walk down to Wilshire? Don't tempt me."

He tried the door handle. Rattled it frantically. It wouldn't budge. He heard her talk to the driver and soon after the car pulled over and stopped. He heard the lock click and he fumbled with the handle, desperately trying to wrench the door open. He heard her give out an overly patient sigh.

"You're going to do this picture, you arrogant prick," she purred. "You know why? Because you're hungry. You want this. So, go on. Off you go. Have this little tantrum. I'll talk to you when I get to New York. Tough love, honey."

Moments later he was standing on the sidewalk watching the car move into the center lane. "Sure," he muttered. His head spun, and a well of nausea rose inside his throat. He blinked, looked around, and raked fingers through perfectly coiffed hair. She'd dropped him off on one of the quieter sections of Sunset, and after a break in traffic, his surroundings had become unnaturally quiet. Shadows thickened and became a threat, and the resultant atmosphere gave him the chills. It was a sensation he was entirely unfamiliar with, and feeling stupid and disoriented, he looked left and right for a place to cross the street.

He began to walk. As a distraction, he started going over everything she'd said. Three months in Baja, with Strang's overactive libido and the lure of a potential Oscar win. He was twenty-seven years old, still in the ascendant, still caught up in that heady, intoxicating mix of fame and fortune, fully aware of how lucky he'd been so far, and how far removed he was from that dumb, provincial kid who'd only dreamt of making it big. Oh yeah. He wanted this. He wasn't done yet. Molly was right. And he was already regretting his half of their conversation. She'd probably put up with a ton of shit from Strang's people, and now he was throwing it at her from his side of the deal. Good thing she was tough. Time to step up and show he was made of the same material. And yeah, he could handle Strang. He'd done it before. Truth of the matter, it had been easy.

So what was all that in the back of the car, huh? His turn to wield the whip? Decision made, he smiled as he headed east, in the hope of finding a crossing at the next light. Yeah, he'd do it.

Do it and be damned.

He'd walked maybe twenty paces when he heard footsteps behind him. He glanced over his shoulder. There was another man on the sidewalk, walking toward him, walking fast. The guy looked formally dressed, in a dark suit, maybe a tuxedo, and Mark wondered where he'd come from. He could have sworn he was alone only moments before.

"Do it and be damned," the man said, smiling as he approached.

Mark came to a halt, stunned, and not only because the guy had repeated one of his very last thoughts. In fact, he discovered he had no choice. He stood perfectly still and stared like an idiot as the man walked right up to him and stopped. Similar build, slightly taller, a little older, pale skin and blonde hair. In the dim light offered by a nearby street lamp, they could have been mistaken for brothers.

"Take off your jacket."

Mark shrugged the jacket past his shoulders and let it drop onto the dusty sidewalk. Five thousand dollars of fine wool, supremely tailored Burberry, just like that. His earlier apprehension came back with a vengeance, and jagged like lightning in his skull. The stranger reached forward and rested his hand on Mark's shoulder, before letting it sweep across his collarbone and up toward his throat. Cold fingers pushed upward against his chin and tilted back his head. In his peripheral vision, Mark saw car headlights flashing by in both directions. It all looked distant, part of a world he didn't belong to right now. *I should make a run for it,* he thought. But he didn't move. Instead, he just stood there, helpless.

A vehicle—a black stretch limousine—pulled in at the curb. The hand released him. The examination was over. The car door swung wide and he felt other hands on him now, sliding effortlessly around his limbs and torso, fingers locking gently into his hair. They pulled him inside and laid him down on the carpeted floor. He thought he saw a number of faces above him but he could no longer focus. He felt drunk, out of control, terrified, and completely at their mercy.

Hands continued to roam over him, eager now, pulling at his belt, his shoes. He felt fingers cold as ice scrape across his abdomen and slide across his chest. He tried to stop them but he still couldn't move a muscle. Not one. He heard his shirt tear, and inside, way down, he heard a voice yelling at him. It reminded him of Molly. *Move. Scream. Throw a punch. Anything, you idiot.* Instead, he lay there utterly compliant while those hands kept busy, pulling and tearing at his clothes, stripping him clean, revealing every inch of flesh.

He felt the soft vibration of the car engine beneath him, revving gently, and the pull as it accelerated forward. *Help me,* he thought. *Somebody, please help me.* Panic churned inside him but ultimately it lay there hog-tied, unable to summon the necessary adrenalin that would mobilize him.

He was lifted. One of the other passengers cradled his head and he heard a woman's voice. Again he thought about Molly, his manager, and how he'd desperately tried to escape her, and had succeeded, only to leap out of the frying pan and into a considerably hotter fire. Now here he lay, helpless, terrified, his mind telling him in no uncertain terms he was about to be torn apart by wolves or worse.

A second ticked by. Followed by another. And the first stab of pain came from his lower leg—hot, startling. It traveled upward and spiked hard in his brain. A scream was imminent. He even drew in the requisite amount of breath. But the fully intentioned howl of agony came out instead in the form of a gentle, barely audible gasp. He felt the moisture from it brush past his lips while inside he silently screamed blue murder.

The first, piercing arrow of pain was joined by another, this time at his forearm. Another followed, and another, and another. His thigh, his abdomen, his shoulder, they all joined in and became a cacophony of agony. They connected, becoming a terrible web that tortured and tormented him, and he could do nothing to stop it. Horror raged through him unchecked, hammering relentlessly at his sanity until it lay fractured and broken, and even then it didn't stop. All outlets for his terror and anguish had been completely sealed. It seemed particularly cruel, like his tormentors had thrown him alive into an acid bath, slammed down the lid, and left him to burn.

Some time later—minutes, hours, he couldn't tell—his head was shifted slightly and he heard a female voice again. A pale blur hovered above him, a face like the moon in fog. "You're so pretty," she whispered. "Please don't cry." He tried to answer her, to tell her that he didn't know he was crying, but if he was, then he couldn't help it; that he was scared and in pain and he couldn't move, but it was useless.

He began to tell himself he should be grateful, that amidst the agony and the horror there was at least one voice of compassion. And for a while he clung to that voice as the web continued its hold on him, kept the pain flowing steadily, relentlessly, on and on until gradually it began to weaken.

I'm dying, he thought. *Finally.*

He closed his eyes. He felt stripped to the bone. His life, all twenty-seven years of it, every second, every breath, everything he'd worked for, everything he'd gained and lost, all gone. He started to pray inside, to beg for oblivion. He couldn't take any more.

The pain lessened considerably, and he felt a sudden jolt as the lower half of his body was dropped back onto the carpeted floor of the car. He let out a sharp gasp, the first real sound he'd made since being pulled into the vehicle. Strong hands were now supporting his shoulders, while another gripped his hair and pushed his head sharply forward.

"Had enough?"

A male voice. He remembered. It belonged to the man he'd met out on the sidewalk. He also recalled the question, asked of him a million years ago amidst a glorious backdrop of camera flash. He struggled, and attempted to give the same answer and nod in the affirmative. Despite the effort, he failed.

"Open your eyes. Look at yourself."

No choice. He did as he was told. His body, musculature chiseled and defined after months and months at the gym, now lay extended before him in glorious ruin, as pale as a ghost, like a statue of tainted marble. Everything seemed drained of color. He could see puncture wounds on his chest and lower torso—black, deep holes that seeped liquid that looked more like oil than blood. There were more of them on his upper thighs, on his arms and lower limbs. He took it all in before his head was wrenched away, and thankfully, he lost sight of himself.

"Are you afraid?"

He was now looking at the man's face, and he marveled at the clarity of it after being in a fog for so long. He was particularly drawn to the eyes, pale and cool like an icy cavern, eyes that lessened their grip on him slightly, allowing him to slowly shake his head.

"Good."

His head was pulled further back, his neck exposed and extended until he could no longer see anything but the dim upholstery of the vehicle. He knew what was coming, so when the pain began again, this time at his throat, it was agonizing but expected. He let out another gasp, but that was all he could manage. This time the agony burrowed in further, awakening new terrors that flailed wildly inside him. But he was weak and all he could do was lie there and suffer, and wait. It couldn't go on forever, he knew that. As the pain coursed through him once again, he began to sink into an odd complacency, knowing everything inside was already broken, that they couldn't possibly do him any more harm, until abruptly the terror lurched forward and shattered something deeper.

There was a burst of color, a strange and compelling vista that swam before his eyes. He clawed desperately toward it because he knew if he could reach it, the pain would go away and he'd be free, then he could hide and become strong again. But despite being tantalized by that flowing kaleidoscope, something managed to reach in and give him an almighty push, one that sent him reeling and clawing back toward his shattered psyche, the mind-numbing, terrible agony, and the man who was steadily, relentlessly, killing him.

A faint battle of wills began, but he didn't have the strength to last for long. He was dying, and after a little while he felt the pain lessen and dwindle. He heard a groan, a sound of satiety, of hunger satisfied, or an absurd culmination of sexual gratification. *Glad to be of service,* he thought bitterly. He began to drift, but not too far. He still felt shackled, helpless. And death was coming.

The car door opened and fresh air poured in. He could smell the sea and his tortured heart leapt for joy. He was being pulled, dragged from the car. Cool air, grass, sea salt. He heard the snap of a flag in the wind and the faint crash of surf on rocks. The air was moist and warm on his bare skin. He felt someone lean close, and cold fingers were touching him, raking over him like claws. He couldn't see, and so he listened.

"Is he still breathing?"

"Yes, barely."

"But not for long."

He was dragged, kicked, and rolled. He attempted to rise, to float away, but invisible chains still bound him, still tethered him to his body. He could now see it lying there in the dark, pale and battered directly beneath him, and further below, beyond the cliff edge, he saw the sea, breaking and foaming on rocks the color of oblivion.

"This should do it. The dawn will see him dead."

Another kick, and another, and he saw his body roll and drop over the edge. It began to pull him with it, tugging, insistent, gathering momentum. He looked back toward the voices, their owners dwindling shadows in the dark.

You're too late, he told them, as he began to fall.

I'm already gone.

CHAPTER 3
GILLES

Preoccupied, he didn't notice it at first. Baggage from the trip—heavy thoughts of sorrow and anger—did much to hide the anticipation, and it wasn't until they were in the elevator and Eleanor had remarked upon it, that he was able to tune in.

Houston cast him a glance. "Now what?"

Their Elder, Delacour, still had to join them, so that left Christina and Saleem and the rest of the staff upstairs, holding the fort and dealing with whatever *this* was. Gilles focused his senses on a corkscrew trail of fear and cautious optimism. An odd combination. The fear, borne of the unknown, he discounted. As for the optimism—

"We have a stranger in the house," he told them. "A newcomer."

In some respects, Gilles felt relieved. Their new guest fought for everyone's attention and offered a good amount of distraction while they waited for their Elder to arrive. A little self-centered perhaps, and dangerously complacent, but it gave his team a little breathing space, gave them chance to distance themselves from the horror of the last twenty-four hours and think on something else. As for their guest—

"Where did you find him, Christina?" He looked down at the woman alongside him—tiny, dark haired, and fragile as a bird, there were many who misjudged Christina at first sight. Gilles knew better.

"Palos Verdes," she said. "Saleem says he's seen him before. On television."

Television. Gilles glanced toward the other side of the room where Saleem was crouched over his laptop, typing furiously while a glowering Houston looked on.

"And the circumstances?"

"I was following some of Deacon's people. Just a precaution, with everything that's happening right now, I wanted to see what they were up to. I think Deacon was among them, but I couldn't be sure." She shrugged. "Anyway, they kicked him out of the car, and pushed him over the cliff edge."

He frowned, raised an admonishing finger, a gesture she certainly wouldn't appreciate, but still… "Following Deacon is dangerous." He stepped a little closer so he could examine their guest, who lay in repose, either unconscious, or sleeping. The man looked fairly young—mid-twenties, or a well-preserved thirty-year-old, certainly no more than that. Fair hair and skin, around six feet tall.

"I was careful," she told him, deadpan, with a dismissive flick of her wrist.

Gilles smiled, crouched alongside the bed, and refocused on the stranger. There were signs of trauma on the torso, bruises—probably from the fall—and faded puncture wounds. Similar marks lay on his arms, and he was willing to bet the legs, currently hidden beneath a thin layer of cotton pajamas, would be adorned with more of the same. Each wound told of the indignity and brutality of his death. He'd been feasted upon, had become a human smorgasbord to a party of killers. The coup de grâce, however, had been performed at the throat. The skin there was crumpled, ravaged, and surrounded a jagged scar that was still healing, while the color of ruin pulsed slightly beneath the epidermis. The wreckage of the throat sang of greed and lust, of hunger that knew no restraint. They probably didn't care if they'd re-birthed him or not. Drunk, giddy, they'd be under the careless assumption that if they cast him out in the open air, he would have died when dawn arrived, not knowing a savior was close by. He looked at Christina. She was still staring at this man, mesmerized, enthralled, and he wondered if she had considered the implications.

"Got it," Saleem announced from across the room. The computer screen lit up the triumphant grin on his youthful features. "That's his profile." He and Houston were both staring at the laptop.

"Slight resemblance, maybe," the other man said, "but if you're right—" he approached. "We need to take him back out there and leave him."

"No." Christina shot Houston a defiant look.

Gilles stood calmly between them, waiting for them to arrive at the same conclusion he had, after they'd had their usual push and shove battle for dominance. Houston was standing his ground. The two were evenly matched, despite their physical differences, and seeing as they constantly disagreed on just about everything—this, for them, was tantamount to a normal conversation.

"If he's famous, he'll be a news item. Somebody, somewhere, will give a shit. And we don't need that. Especially now."

"We can hide him."

Houston let out a derisive snort. "What if he doesn't want to hide? And what if—" he jabbed an accusing finger toward the man lying on the bed "—it was Deacon who did this?"

Gilles smiled. There. He stepped between them, looked down at Christina, and waited.

"I said I wasn't sure Deacon was with them. I didn't see him."

"Nonetheless," Gilles said.

Saleem had joined them, and was staring at each one of them in turn. "You want to kill him? Haven't we had enough of that already?" His voice wavered. Two of his closest friends had been at the desert sanctuary and were now reduced to charred bone and memory.

Christina sensed a personal triumph and appeared to grow a little in stature. Houston threw up his hands.

"No killing," Gilles told them. "However, we'll need to place him in more secure surroundings, at least until Eleanor's taken a look at him, and preferably until Delacour arrives."

"Hey, I'm all for that." Houston grinned.

"Lock him up. Like a prisoner." Christina was outraged.

Gilles nodded. "We'll make sure he's comfortable. Call it a compromise." He looked around at the others. No more arguments were forthcoming. It wouldn't be the most hospitable welcome, but the precautions were necessary. Personally he'd feel a whole lot better when Eleanor had dived in and established the facts.

But that wouldn't be for a while.

He gave orders to be awakened if their new guest began to stir, which, under normal circumstances could well be in the next few hours. Until then, the man was to be restrained, locked up, and guarded. And it would be done, despite Christina's protests. The fact that she'd even brought up Deacon's name told Gilles the monster had been inside the vehicle, partaking of the feast. As for why Deacon would be so careless, it was unprecedented. But, he already had enough to think on and lament over, and so that little conundrum would have to wait.

Eighteen hours. The sun had set beyond the horizon once more, and still their guest hadn't awakened. Gilles stood out on the balcony, his eyes taking in the view beyond the bluffs, past the shoreline, out toward the faint, indigo line that split sea and sky. There were lights out there in the far distance, winking in the dark; ships and planes passing by, wholly indifferent to what lay ashore.

Up until now, he'd felt safe here. The house was completely new, a modern, grand affair, purpose built, nestled cozily under a high-level security blanket. In some neighborhoods the sheer, sweeping glamour of its design would have raised eyebrows. But here on the coast, south of Los Angeles, it was one of many such places, all of them competing for a medal of grandiosity, where immediate neighbors on all sides preferred their privacy and assumed the inhabitants of this particular dwelling were much like themselves: film industry, sports, finance, medicine, mostly retired and unwilling to be disturbed, thank you very much.

He looked over his shoulder, back toward the door. Saleem was standing there. He hadn't noticed the younger man's approach but then, like Christina, he was good at that. Gilles beckoned him forward.

"So, tell me who he is."

Saleem pushed his hands in his pockets, stepped alongside, and joined him looking out to sea. "Mark Niels Gannon, he's an actor. Not A-list, or anything fancy like that. Up and coming. He was in a TV show that had two Emmy nominations before it was cancelled, and he was nominated for a Golden Globe last year."

"Nominations, but no actual awards?"

"No. Not yet anyway."

"Family?"

"Single. No kids. Parents back east and a younger brother who lives in New Zealand. No scandal. No arrests."

"So. How much heat are we going to have to take?"

Saleem shrugged. "Some. I haven't seen anything on TV yet, but it's only been a couple of days. He might become local news if there's nothing else happening."

Gilles focused on the horizon. "Very well. Find out what else is going on. Maybe there's something we can use as a smoke screen."

"Does this mean we get to keep him?"

"You'd like that."

Saleem's broad grin shone and he nodded. "I saw his last film, read a couple of interviews. He seems like a cool guy."

"Seemed," Gilles corrected. Things would be very different now for this man named Gannon. "Now, go find me something."

When Saleem had gone, Gilles stepped away from the balcony and descended a set of concrete steps that led toward the lower environs of the building. He entered the interior via a solid metal door and continued down until he was in a section of the house that lay dug into the hillside. At the end of a gray, featureless corridor, he spied Houston. The man was standing with his meaty arms folded across his chest, his entire posture one of immovable stone. Light shone through an interior window and Houston's attention lay on whatever was beyond it.

"Still sleeping?" Gilles joined the other man, and now both of them stared into a small, square room lit by an overhead lantern. Its only contents were a bed and its occupant—one of them strapped very firmly to the other.

Houston grunted. "You remember the night we got into a fight with Deacon? You and I, and Delacour. All three of us. Do you remember that?"

Gilles nodded, knowing exactly the point Houston was about to make, but he kept silent, continued to listen.

"I mean—as a team I'd say we're pretty strong, formidable in fact. And yet he brushed past us like we were nothing. You got hit pretty bad if I remember it right."

Oh, he remembered, all right. He gave Houston a weak smile.

It hadn't been their finest hour, up against Weiss's powerful, immediate progeny, and by the time it was over, they'd all had plenty of wounds to lick. And not because of their foe's superior physical strength. Had it been merely down to that, they would have won the day. Gilles stared through the glass toward the body on the bed. If this man was indeed Deacon's creation, they could be in for a shit storm of trouble. And yet—

He pointed. "Did you see the marks on him?"

"Yeah. The neck wound was impressive. Damn near tore his head off."

"Yes. So tell me, if Deacon had done that to you, how would you feel about it?"

"I guess I wouldn't be too happy. Even so, it's no guarantee of trust. There's still nothing stopping him from walking right out of here, straight back to Deacon and betraying us all."

Gilles had to agree, and said as much. "It could, however, be a moot point," he added. "He should have awakened by now."

"There's something wrong with him?"

"I—" he stopped. They both turned and looked down the corridor. Eleanor was approaching. She clutched a brown cashmere wrap close around her shoulders, and her gray hair was loose, falling down her back. She looked stronger, refreshed, and Gilles gave a sigh of relief. Maybe now there'd be some answers.

"You tied him up," she said, joining them at the window. She looked at them, bemused, like they'd lost their minds.

Houston stuck out his jaw. "Damn right we tied him up."

Gilles sought to diffuse the conflict between the two. "Eleanor, I need you to tell me why he won't wake up."

"Well, that's easy enough." She pulled the wrap a little closer. "He doesn't want to."

He shared a puzzled glance with Houston, and while both of them were rendered speechless, Eleanor pulled back the bolt. Houston snapped out of his stupor, stepped forward, and slammed his fist against the door.

"I can't let you in there."

She let out a sigh of exaggerated patience. "Well, if you really want to know who created him, I need to go in there and touch him."

Gilles caught Houston's eye and nodded. Knowing for sure was crucial.

"Okay," the big man said, "but I'm going in first."

She stepped aside and waited. Had she been Christina, there would be a big, loud war of words going on right now. So Gilles silently thanked the gods for the peace and quiet, and followed them inside. Despite the apprehension, his mind leapt, a bubbling pond of curiosity while he weighed the pros and cons. As they approached, he saw the man's throat had now healed significantly, and only a deep gray shadow now traced the area where the scar had been. The mark would likely remain for some weeks. What had Saleem called him—Gannon? An actor? He wondered if the duplicity of that profession was likely to be a factor in trying to determine where he stood, when he woke up.

If he woke up.

Houston, as usual, seemed to catch his train of thought. "Careful, he might be faking it."

"It's okay," Gilles said. "He isn't." He saw Eleanor nodding in agreement, watched Houston give a shrug and back off. Now they had to be patient and wait while Eleanor had a look at him. It might take no time at all, or it might be a long and drawn out—

"Oh," she said. She was sitting on the bed, holding the man's hand in one of her own, like he was her grandson lying ill in hospital. All that was missing was the beep of a heart monitor, an intravenous drip, and a vase of flowers, although it would be a stretch to suggest he and Houston were standing in for concerned relatives. Gilles flexed his fingers, realizing he was becoming tense. Out of the corner of his eye, he saw Houston had already pulled his pistol.

"They enhanced his pain receptors," she told them. "Stimulated his mental distress."

"Pain *and* suffering." He nodded, his face grim. Yes. That would shift the taste, giving it the necessary appeal for a particular palate. "For how long?"

"Five, six hours. It's hard to say." She let go of the man's hand, tilted her head, and reached forward to stroke his face. There was no reaction. Their guest remained stubbornly dormant.

After an infuriating pause, "Eleanor. Is he Deacon's?"

She nodded, and Houston stepped forward. The barrel of the pistol was now about six inches from the man's head.

"I can make this real quick. Finish it while he's still like this."

Gilles had prepared for this, and was about to suggest a few, less deadly alternatives when a single, external thought stopped him in his tracks.

Wait.

The shift in atmosphere, a growing tension that danced in the air, made everyone hesitate, and moments later, footsteps rang on the corridor. Eleanor stood as a dark-haired, sallow-skinned man entered the room. Gilles leaned forward and offered a solemn bow.

Delacour.

Houston had backed off, but the business end of his pistol was still pointed at their sleeping guest's head.

Their Elder smiled affably at each one of them in turn, then focused on the man strapped to the bed. "Is he *that* dangerous?" His face crinkled, the beginnings of a smirk.

Gilles struggled to answer. There was real power in the room now, power that affected all thought and judgment, that rendered their fears highly questionable and ultimately without foundation. He saw Houston lower the weapon. Eleanor was smiling.

Delacour nodded, seemed satisfied. "Very well then," he said. "Let's wake him up."

CHAPTER 4
MARK

The faces reappeared. He thought he'd escaped them, thought he'd managed to sink to a depth even they could not reach. He thought he was dead. And yet, here they were, a hazy collection of blurred images and voices. Back for more, to tear at his flesh, to feast on the marrow of his bones, to devour all that remained. And so, in defiance, he swam deeper. No longer would he offer that pretty little side dish of terror they craved. It was gone, he was gone, and they could suck on his bones for as long as they wanted.

He hung there in the dark, having nothing better to do, until curiosity pulled him in another direction and he drifted, called out, entertained the notion he wasn't alone. He came across a shape in the gloom, a solid core of strength and rage that hovered in the air, wound tight into a Gordian knot. It was fascinating, unexpected, and it lured him close. He began to ask questions and found himself rebuffed. The thing was busy, had work to do, but perhaps it would pay him to sit around and watch for a while. Watch and learn. And so he did.

There had been opportunities over the years, to think about death and any number of consequences, but he'd also considered himself way too young to give the subject any serious thought. During the first fifteen years of his life, the priest at the local church had told him he was destined for Heaven or Hell, and lately he had entertained the whimsical assumption that Hell was more likely. But it was abstract. He still had years of living to do. On a practical level, he didn't give a shit.

So now, as he hovered in the gloom, he felt ill-prepared. According to his scant knowledge on the subject, this wasn't how death was supposed to be. For one thing, this strange, hovering core was alive. That much was evident--a burning cluster the size of a fist, giving off heat like a furnace, and it appeared to be growing, gathering in strength while he hung there and watched.

He remembered a girlfriend. Ex-girlfriend. When they'd split up, she'd written him a letter, telling him in his next life he'd be reincarnated as a worm, and she a bird, and that one morning, nice and early, when it rained and he popped his head out of the ground, she'd be there waiting, and she'd rip him out of the soil and eat him. He remembered showing the letter to a friend, who'd told him he'd also received threats on a similar theme, that it was a cliché, and they'd sat there and laughed.

But now it seemed eerily prophetic. In fact, it suggested a pattern that threaded through his entire adult life, of being consumed, of being cannibalized; the girlfriend, his career, and now this. And it brought a bemused smile to his face.

Still, she might have had a point. About the reincarnation, at least. There had been no sign of Heaven or Hell. At one point he thought he'd seen the light everyone talked about, but it wasn't there anymore. Instead, he had the core, giving off dry, intense heat like a small, dark sun.

So, if it was reincarnation, what was he becoming? The core looked strong, powerful. Maybe he would return to life as a bull. Spend a few years rutting in the fields before being led to the slaughterhouse. Hell, that fit right into the current cycle, didn't it?

Becoming bold, he reached and pressed his fingers lightly against its surface and attempted to discern the mystery of it. After all, if it was part of him, he figured he had a right to know. And what he sensed through his fingertips was power—raw, aggressive, arrogant, and greedy—but this was no mere bull, and there was a recent familiarity about it that he couldn't quite place. Touch brought discomfort, made his hand recoil, and he backed off.

He stopped a short distance away, baffled and alarmed, and it was a while before he could approach once more and re-engage. And when he did, it sang to him, taunted him, declared an appetite rampant and insatiable. What was he becoming, then? And if this *was* to be a part of him, how was he supposed to control it?

Tired of the mystery, he looked up. In the far distance, way above his head, everything seemed quiet. Had they already finished their feast? Or had they deemed it unworthy and finally left him alone? Movement caught his eye. It was a rope—thin, dangling, being lowered from above. And in the darkness it shone red, it was beautiful, and he was sorely tempted to swim toward it, his hands outstretched.

There's no need, the core declared.

Mark frowned, and sensed a battle of wills. The red rope was still on the approach, and both he and the entity alongside him watched and waited, until it was almost within reach.

Now, it said. It reached out, pulled hard on the rope, while at the same time it drew him in, where it surrounded and smothered him so he couldn't escape. It had swallowed the rope too, which had split apart and become many-limbed, like a head of snakes, like a medusa. Some of the limbs entered him, plunging straight through his chest and he cried out, for they brought pain—new, fresh, and stabbing—and he began to flail and gasp, until some deep, dark, overly patient memory reminded him that he'd been through all this once before, many, many years ago.

You're being born, it told him.

Remember?

The memory sank back before he had time to argue with it, and he discovered he needed every bit of his energy to stay whole. They had begun to rise, and the core was trying to absorb him, consume him before they reached the surface. But he'd had enough of that. If this was new life, then it was time to turn things around. It was time for him to be the consumer. And on that thought, oddly enough, the smothering stopped and the thing backed off, as though it seemed quite satisfied that he'd reached that conclusion.

A truce then, and they bore the pain together and continued to rise.

The breath of an ocean breeze on his skin, and flowers in the room, their scent sharp and tingling, pulling his senses from the pit of oblivion. Dim light on opening his eyes. It was more than adequate. A light, fluffy caramel bedcover, his fingers dallied along its smooth, satin-bound edges. Windows, open, telling him it was dark outside.

Rich, heavy drapes. And men. He counted three. One sitting in the chair next to his bed—shoulder-length hair, olive-skinned, narrow build, relaxed, one foot raised and resting on the opposite knee. This man gave him an easy smile. The other two—a tall black guy with high cheekbones, and his blocky, heavily muscled, pale companion—both wary, despite their efforts to hide it.

He looked down. There. The needle in his arm. And a long, thin pipe of red leading up to a reservoir of blood. The rope. The lifeline, such a thin and slender thing that had hauled him out of the abyss and back into the land of the living. His eyes flicked back toward the men. The two standing were expecting something. Was he in danger, then? Were they? He was confused, for these were not the ones he'd imagined were fighting over his carcass, tearing at leftover gristle and bone.

The seated man leaned forward, and held out his hand. "Welcome back, Mr. Gannon."

Mark pushed himself into an upright position. It was a firm handshake, but the real test of strength lay beyond it, a light but nonetheless insistent mental push. He looked down, stared for a moment at their hands, at the contact. Touch. He'd need to remember that. "I have questions," he said.

The other man let go and nodded, still smiling. "I'm sure you do. But let me introduce myself first. My name is Delacour. This is my House, and these two gentlemen are my friends and colleagues, Gilles and Houston."

The other men nodded warily. Mark stared at them for a moment, realizing they thought he should be bound, shackled, and restrained for their own safety. It seemed absurd and it brought an unexpected smile to his face. "Please, call me Mark."

Patiently, they told him what he had become. What it would mean from now on. Told him what he already knew, deep down, in that dark cavern where the core lurked. No longer human, that was all stripped and gone. He was something else, something new. Not the worm, not the bull. Something else.

Part of him wanted to disbelieve—the distraught, flailing part that still remembered a life that had ended so ignominiously on the floor of that limousine. *Don't be stupid,* the core told him. *And pay attention. They're asking questions.*

They were asking about the man who'd murdered him. His killer, his creator; their nemesis. He began to understand why two of these men were wary of him, and he wanted to tell them it was okay, that he was different. But the core laughed at him and continued to pull at the blood coming through the drip, inspiring another inner struggle that left him confused and drained.

In the end he held up a hand. "Please." He'd had enough.

The man sitting alongside him named Delacour nodded and smiled. "Of course." He stood up. "You need more rest. I'm sorry if we've exhausted you." He glanced toward the window. "Dawn will be upon us, soon. Get some sleep."

They left him alone, and he lay back and listened to the strange, slow thud of his heart, and ran his tongue over and over the slight, twin deformities behind his upper row of teeth, then he turned on his side, curled up, and waited. For a little while, his eyes remained open, staring at the window. He saw the light gradually shift, and with it, the windows take on a darker hue. A short time later, he heard the sound of a small motor, and saw the grand drapes sweep gradually together, shutting out the dawn, shutting out everything he remembered about being alive, and instead opening up a well of despair.

Vampire.

No more sunlight. Not anymore.

He slept.

CHAPTER 5
MINA

Three long flights of concrete steps beneath the streets of Manhattan and she arrived at a door unmarked but for a few scuffs that spoiled the matte gray paintwork. She knocked, and glanced up toward the camera. While she waited for the click of the lock, unease reached out and stroked playfully at the nape of her neck.

Once through the door, she hesitated. The atmosphere shifted, became stronger and more disturbing, enough to make her skin prickle with discomfort. Ahead in the gloom, a man dressed in a sleeveless vest, his skin half bathed in weak yellow light, waited alongside an open doorway. He inclined his head for a moment, and his face registered relief.

"I'm glad you're here." He ducked back into a room at the end of the passageway.

She followed, pulled off her coat, and entered a cube illuminated by a desk lamp and a TV bracketed to the wall. "How is he, Hector?" *Not good,* her thoughts insisted.

"Fitful, restless, not feeding. And I can't get him to tell me what's wrong." He scraped narrow, splayed fingers over his shaved head. Their resident's mood was infecting Hector, too, despite his natural resilience. His shoulders were hunched and his eyes danced, barely glancing at her before settling on a heavy metal door at the rear of the room.

"I'd better go in there and talk to him." Hector's guitar lay across the table so she threw her coat on the back of a battered, leather-covered swivel chair instead.

"Are you sure that's a good idea?"

She smiled. "It's okay. And someone has to."

The man walked to the door and threw back two heavy bolts. "Just be careful, okay?"

"I will." Mina approached, reached up, and caressed the man's jaw, saw his eyes close briefly at the touch. "I'm glad you're here for him, Hector. Danny isn't the easiest person to take care of."

"I won't leave him," he told her.

"I know." She stepped past, crossed the threshold, and entered Danny's prison.

Beyond the open door, despair oozed thick, accompanied by a faint scent of blood coagulated, dried, discarded, gone to waste. She paused for a moment, heard the door close behind her, then continued along a short passage and emerged into an underground apartment of, by New York standards, reasonable size. She rolled her shoulders, smoothed back her hair, and walked through.

"Danny?" She kept the timbre of her voice low. All the lights were turned off, and although he sometimes forgot, on this occasion she suspected he'd left himself in darkness on purpose. Unhindered by the gloom, she walked by furniture that was comfortable and expensive, to Danny's taste when he could be bothered with such things. However, right now it all sat there forgotten and useless and she discovered him lying on the floor. He'd sunk low, gone deep into depression.

She kicked off her pumps and lay alongside him, shifting slowly, deliberately until she was molded against the base of his spine. She slid her arm around his upper torso and pulled him gently against her chest, just the thin barrier of their clothing between them. "Hey…"

"Time to die." He let out a shuddering sigh that vibrated through her entire body. "Every one of us."

"Shh, it's okay." He felt fragile and light as a feather. He was getting worse, so much so it was beginning to frighten her, because right now she couldn't feel the depth of the pit he'd dug and wondered if the day would come when she could no longer pull him out of it.

After a while he rolled over, his hand came up and he began to stroke her hair. "We could do it, you know," he told her. "We could do it right now. Just wait for dawn, and—"

"No."

"—walk out into the sun." His voice picked up, took on some urgency. "It'll be quick—"

"Danny. Please."

"It's better than what's coming, Mina." And for a moment, he pulled her down, into a confusing morass of imagery that tore mercilessly at her sanity. His voice sank. "I'm frightening you. I'm sorry."

"Yes, but it doesn't matter." She tried hard to make light of it.

"It does, but I want you to remember." He leaned in and kissed her. "When it comes, I won't let you do it alone."

In his current state, she figured it would do little to argue with him, so she didn't. "Okay," she answered, hoping the word hadn't become a pact between them, signed in blood and promise. It was time to change the subject. "You're hungry."

"Blood belongs to the living."

"Just a little. Just for me?"

Danny sat up, long limbs bending awkwardly, hair disheveled, his shirt a mass of concertinaed wrinkles, telling her he'd been scrunched up and sleeping like this for hours, maybe days. And she made a mental note, not to leave it so long between visits. Not when he was like this.

He looked to the door. "Hector," he said.

"If you don't like Hector, I can bring someone else."

"Another of your meek and willing lambs?" He smiled and shook his head. "No. Hector it is. Do you think he'll play his guitar for me?"

Back home on the Upper West Side, staring into the mirror, it felt as if he was still with her, his melancholy bleeding into the upper layers of her skin, making them heavy as lead. She shifted her focus, saw the look of concern on the face of the man standing directly behind her, and she attempted a smile.

"You're tense," Martin said. "You usually enjoy this."

She lowered shoulders that had gradually crept up toward her ears. "I know. I'm sorry."

His deft fingers were still tangled in her hair, but he'd ceased massaging and moments later he withdrew. "Something else, then?"

She stood and faced him, lingered on wavy, bright russet hair and eyes full of playful challenge. Heat radiated from his skin like a warm fire and she reached up and kissed him. "Not now. Later," she said. "Sleep with me."

"Sure." He nodded. "I have some work to finish."

She watched him go. Dr. Martin Morris. Hardly a meek and willing lamb. Not that one. She closed her eyes, spent a few moments trying to slip out from under Danny's umbrella of doom, then, having done her best, faced the mirror once more, ran a brush in long, slow sweeps through her hair, then tied it back neatly, made sure she looked presentable and went in search of her Elder.

It was late, an hour before dawn, and already she could feel the House beginning to wind down for the day. Goran wouldn't have retired, though. Not yet, and downstairs he proved to be in his usual spot, in his study, surrounded by a miasma of cigarette smoke and talking on the phone.

She hung around outside until he was done with the call, then entered and gave him the requisite bow. He was already on his feet, shirtsleeves rolled up, pouring large measures of whisky into two crystal tumblers. He pushed one of them into her hand.

"Sit down, Mina."

She did as she was told, cradled the glass in two hands, watched him light another cigarette, and retake his seat behind the desk.

After a long exhalation of smoke, "So, you went to see Danny."

"Yes."

"And he's no better, is he?"

"No. I found him lying on the floor in the dark."

Goran took a large swig from his glass and leaned back. "Tell me what's on your mind."

She looked at him. *Like you don't already know.* She could feel her thoughts, palpable and raw, bleeding out. Even Martin had sensed something. "It's just—" she hesitated "— keeping him in there, locked up. We're not helping him."

Her Elder shrugged. Eyes bored into her, black as night. "He's insane, Mina. Let him go and he'll be dead within a week, if that. He can't take care of himself. You know this."

She nodded. "I just want to alleviate some of his despair. It's unbearable."

"Unbearable for you because you are his direct progeny. You feel his pain acutely. And he'll use that to manipulate you."

Her fingers gripped the crystal tumbler in her hands. Danny wanted out. He wanted to walk into sunlight. He wanted to die. And here she was, trying to persuade their Elder to loosen his bonds a little, so he could slip out and do just that. She felt like a fool, and saw for the first time what lay within the invisible shroud Danny had draped around her shoulders. Had she still been human, she would probably have wept. Instead, she took a strong pull of the whisky and felt it burn down the back of her throat.

Goran was smiling at her, not unkindly. "I've no wish for him to suffer, Mina. But I can't let him go. If I do that, I might as well pour gasoline over his head and set him on fire. Then what would you think of me?"

A bitter laugh escaped her. "We can't win."

"No, we cannot. Tell me, what does he speak of?"

She leaned back in her chair and took a smaller sip of the whisky. "It's still the same thing. About the end, and how we're doomed. It's almost as if he's read our Grand Father's letter word for word."

"Maybe he has, one way or another." Her Elder hesitated. "Actually, now the subject has arisen. Something may have happened in that regard."

"Oh?"

"About a month ago, there was an attack on House Delacour in California. There were a few deaths. Quite a few."

Mina stared, speechless.

"So," he continued. "I'd like you to go out there. See what you can see. It may well be an escalated spat, with someone like Deacon. However, if it was Weiss..."

He didn't need to finish. If it was Weiss, it meant the letter was all too real and they were in big trouble. She nodded. "I'll go." It would take her mind off Danny, she decided, and get her out from under his gloomy, manipulative spell.

Goran smiled. "Good. I'll have everything arranged. You'll leave at sundown."

"Yes, Sir." She stood, placed the empty whisky tumbler on a side table, and gave him another formal bow. As she left the study, her mind raced on ahead. What did she know about House Delacour, other than it containing misfit members of their vampire society: strays, orphans—and assassins for hire? A smile flicked briefly across her features. Danny would probably love it there, for a little while, at least.

She headed upstairs. Martin was in her room, already undressed and waiting, and she smiled at him, basked in his presence, such a beautiful distraction. She walked by him and flung herself on the bed. "Undress me," she told him.

He laughed, and got to work. She let him pull off her boots, her jeans, watched him take time with the buttons on her shirt until he was able to slide the smooth fabric over her shoulders. And by the time he began on her undergarments, she was up on her knees, her hand wrapped tight around the hilt of his stiffening cock and her teeth embedded in his throat. Just a taste, not enough to tire him, she let his blood trickle down inside, let a gentle moan escape as she savored the heat, and the iron flavor of it, while her free hand roamed the scorching muscles of his torso until she felt as if she might burst into flame.

She withdrew, licked her lips, let him lower her onto her back, and luxuriated in his body heat as he leaned in and kissed her. And all the despair Danny had heaped on her shoulders began to melt away, and the trepidation of her upcoming journey was resolutely pushed aside. All that talk, of sunlight and fire, of killing and death. Not for her. Not yet. Instead, she succumbed to another kind of fire, wrapped her limbs around the man in her bed, and let it burn and burn.

CHAPTER 6
GILLES

"No progeny of Deacon would respond well to aggression and imprisonment. Neither would the rest of us for that matter. So let's try a little common courtesy. Mr. Gannon is entitled to that."

Delacour had been correct, of course, so they had opened their arms, let down their guard, and welcomed Gannon into the House. Their Elder had also considered him enough of a priority to give Gilles and Christina the task of mentoring him. It had stuck in Gilles' craw a little, but, with the exception of a few minor difficulties, so far, so good.

It was still early evening, and from his position on the corner balcony, Gilles was able to look down onto the beach where a gathering of five sat around a small, flickering pit fire. Christina was there, teaching Gannon control. There were also three donors in attendance—two women and one man—all three completely under the man's spell despite the fact that he had almost killed one of them a week ago.

The man's appetite had emerged aggressive, bold, and rapacious, right from the very beginning, and it was accompanied by an aristocratic aloofness and blasé sense of entitlement that had some of their staff fussing, over-accommodating his needs, and running up into Beverly Hills for his clothes. Oh, he was Deacon's progeny all right. He had more than the usual charisma, too. All their donors were quite smitten.

He watched as Gannon moved onto the male. He always kissed the donors first, regardless of gender, touched and caressed them, and not in a perfunctory manner, either. It was all part of an emerging ritual and right now that young man in Gannon's arms would give him his last drop. Christina was there to make sure he didn't.

Gilles looked away—and saw Saleem hovering at the door. "What?" he said, with a little more irritation than he intended. It was unsettling watching Gannon, bordering on voyeuristic.

Saleem stepped outside. "I just wanted to report that there's nothing to report. Oh…" The young man hesitated as he looked down toward the shore.

Gilles had had enough. He beckoned and they re-entered the house. "And?"

"Nothing on TV, not even the gossip shows. Internet traffic is minimal. A few die-hard fans maybe, but that's all."

Five weeks. That's all it had taken before the media had moved onto the next best thing. They had got lucky. Two abrupt, simultaneous celebrity divorces and bye, bye Mark Gannon. Naturally, there was his immediate family to consider, but that would be handled, if and when it became a problem.

They moved further into the house, Saleem chattering about various nuggets of celebrity gossip he'd found. "—and you'll never guess who got busted for—"

Gilles raised a forefinger. "I don't want to know." His companion grinned and fell silent.

They joined Houston and Delacour in the main lounge. Gilles took a seat opposite the two men on one of the low couches. Saleem joined him and began to fidget as soon as he sat down.

"So, how is he doing?"

"Better, I think," he told Delacour. He heard Houston mutter something unpalatable under his breath.

"Good. I want him to go with Eleanor tonight. Saleem, tell Christina, would you?"

Gilles leaned forward. "The sanctuary?" he asked, once Saleem had dashed out of the room. He shared a glance with Houston.

"Yes. So far, we've got nothing on exactly who perpetrated the massacre. He'll have different senses."

Houston glowered. "He'll have Deacon's senses."

"That's what I'm counting on," Delacour replied. "And yes, I know it's a risk, but it's one I've already discussed with Eleanor."

Gilles sat back and thought on it. So far they had come up empty. Their first visit, right after the attack, had been so full of horror it had bled over and obfuscated everything. They'd had no choice but to wait until the noise had died down, until their own emotions no longer clashed with residual echoes and psychic imprints. Nothing a live human could see, nothing a fire could destroy. However, both Delacour and Eleanor had since been back twice and found nothing, so yes, on the face of it Gannon was a good choice. After all, as Deacon's progeny, he was third generation.

Third.

And that made him, as Houston had put it a few days ago, one powerful son of a bitch.

And yet, so far, with the exception of appetite, much of Gannon's impressive blood lineage remained hidden. Mentally, there was no doubt the man was an expert blocker. Gilles couldn't read him at all. He made it look natural, like there wasn't anything to see. Five weeks out of the gate and he was catching on pretty quick. And there lay the problem. Right now, what lay behind that thick curtain was anyone's guess, and maybe this would be an opportunity to find out a little more.

Also, there was still the matter of the missing girl, Dimitra, to consider. Gilles allowed his face a wry twist. None of them seemed eager to talk about that particular subject, least of all Houston who had always been reluctant and unsettled around the girl, his behavior hinting at some insight he always refused to discuss. Better to let that particular subject lie then, for now. Leave it to Eleanor, who wouldn't forget. And if there was still a clue out there to Dimitra's current whereabouts, then he felt sure she'd persuade Gannon to unearth it, if he proved capable of such.

It was odd how she and Christina seemed perfectly at ease with their intriguing newcomer, while he and Houston prowled like wary tigers. Even Saleem, totally smitten, danced on the edges, too awestruck perhaps to get close to the man. Gannon had told them all repeatedly he wasn't Deacon, and maybe the women had seen some truth in that, whereas Gilles still didn't believe it.

"In the meantime—"

Gilles shut off his line of thought, and brought his full attention back to the other men in the room.

"—if this is indeed what we believe it to be," Delacour continued, "then we have to start thinking about our financial arrangements and come up with a few alternatives."

"Weiss could get at the Foundation?" Houston asked.

"Of course. He set it up. It's supposed to be an irrevocable trust, wholly in the hands of trustees, but we'd be fools to rely on that premise."

Gilles looked at his Elder. "You don't think he truly disappeared, do you."

Delacour laughed. "No. If there's one thing a vampire excels at, it's hiding in plain sight. If I know Weiss like I think I do, then no, I don't think he dropped out completely. He's always taken an interest. We're his children."

"Children he now wants to destroy. Let's not forget about that," Houston growled. He shifted awkwardly. "See, none of this makes sense."

"You still think Deacon is behind the sanctuary massacre."

"Sure. What is it he told us once—he doesn't like the anarchy we represent? I think he used Weiss's letter as an excuse. Hell, I'm still not convinced that letter came from—"

Gilles watched Houston falter, entirely glad that he'd at least stopped there and not full out called their Elder a liar. Delacour merely grinned.

"I wish that were true," the man said. "At least we'd know where we stood. And I'm not discounting everything you're telling me, Houston. There is a chance he used the letter to his advantage. However, if Deacon was the offender, I'm inclined to believe another possibility."

"That Weiss ordered him to do it," Gilles said. Deacon was Weiss's immediate progeny. There had to be an immeasurable bond between them, and there lay a whole other can of worms.

Houston was shaking his head. "If Deacon is working on Weiss's orders, then ultimately, if we take the letter at face value, at some point Deacon has to destroy himself. That's not the Deacon I know."

Delacour leaned back, folded his arms. His smile widened. "So, if you were Deacon, what would you do?"

"Well, I sure as hell wouldn't fall on my sword willingly. I'd stall—"

"Maybe start on those I want out of the way anyway, be seen doing what Weiss wants me to do," Gilles interjected, "use it to buy some time until I've figured out a way of saving myself."

"Exactly," said Delacour.

"So, is that what we're talking about?" asked Houston.

"We don't know, until we get some more answers from the sanctuary."

"On Weiss's orders or not. If he did this, we have to go after him with everything we've got."

Gilles watched the two men nod, agreeing on what amounted to all-out war, and he felt his heart sink.

Saleem bounced back into the room. "He's getting dressed." He looked around. "What? What did I miss?"

Gilles stood up. He smiled. "Nothing." His attention shifted toward his Elder. "I'll make sure he's dressed properly."

"Yes. Thanks, Gilles."

He left the room, eager to be out from under Delacour and Houston's thundercloud, although now Saleem had returned, it would no doubt dissipate and the subject would be changed.

He found a bemused Gannon in one of the utility rooms, being dressed by two of the donors.

"So this—" the man flexed glove-clad hands, then pointed to a pile of dark clothing folded neatly on the table "—all this, will protect me?"

Gilles nodded. He watched Gannon puzzle over it, then relax and let one of the donors pull a black shirt over his head, not in the least bit self-conscious, as though others had been dressing him since birth. "The main thing is not to forget you're exposed. You stay covered, and you'll be fine."

Gannon nodded. "This is..." he hesitated, "where we're going. This is about Deacon, isn't it?"

"We're not sure, but it might be. How do you feel about that, Mark?" He watched, looked for the smallest detail that would inform him that sending this man out alone with Eleanor was a bad idea.

Cool, gray-blue eyes flashed him a look, along with a sharp stab of thought, a mental dagger of reproach. "He murdered me, Gilles. How do you think I feel?"

It was a badge of reassurance. *I'm on your side.* No conflict of interest. It made him wonder if Gannon realized exactly what his relationship with Deacon was, and what would happen, if and when they finally re-united.

"Just keep an open mind, and discover what you can," he told him.

And I will try and do the same.

CHAPTER 7
MARK

"Your first time in sunlight."

Mark nodded, and attempted to appear relaxed. The diminutive woman alongside him in the rear of the vehicle was behaving as if it was the most natural thing in the world. Vampires, walking around in daylight. Sure, no problem. With some difficulty, he attempted to parry the lurid and spectacular images inside his head, of bodies exploding at dawn, and changed the subject.

"I'm still not sure why you wanted me to come here." A quick look through tinted windows gave him a view of the desert—hard, featureless ground but for the occasional crop of shrubs and a jagged line of rock in the distance. He felt the heat and the imminent threat of incineration coming through the glass and wished he were back at the House, back in his room, anywhere but here.

Eleanor was adjusting the glove on her left hand, its cuff rolled all the way up to her elbow. "I just need your thoughts, Mark. Your perception."

"On something that happened weeks ago," he reminded her. Even the others, with the sole exceptions of Delacour and Eleanor, had doubted the efficacy of another trip.

"Five minutes," said one of their accompanying donors.

Almost there.

Mark checked his gear and looked toward the front seats. The two men in front, both human, were dressed in much lighter clothing; he and Eleanor were distinctly more vulnerable out here. Even so, Mark discovered he was concerned about the donors' safety. "Are you both armed?"

One of them turned and nodded, and so he sat back and tried to relax. It was impossible. He felt on edge and imagined hidden demons out there, just waiting for them to stop and the doors to open, enabling the hideous creatures to pounce and tear them all to shreds.

A few minutes later, the driver brought the vehicle to a halt.

"Ready?"

He reached beneath his cowl, adjusted the balaclava. "I guess."

The door locks clicked and sprang back. Time to stop quivering with anxiety and go for it.

He stepped out, gave a curt nod to the rifle-wielding donor holding the door, and immediately he felt the full weight of the sun's heat land on his head and shoulders. It was unbearable and he wanted nothing more than to scramble back inside the shelter of the vehicle and slam shut the door. He thought Deacon had cured him of all his terrors. Apparently not.

Eleanor was already on the move and he had no choice but to follow. It took him a few strides, but eventually the fear lessened, dwindling from a white-knuckled, crawling horror into something more manageable. His clothes moved easily around him, the outer garments comfortable, long and flowing. He felt like a comic book character. He smiled at the absurdity of it under his cowl, settled into his stride, and began to pay more attention to his surroundings.

Just don't forget you're exposed, Gilles had told him. *Never forget.* Right. No chance of that.

The road they traversed wasn't all that different from the land surrounding it. Just a line of packed earth and gravel that in this particular instance ended at a shallow wall. In the near distance lay the remains of a burned-out building—their destination. Eleanor had told him to keep his mind open, and as they passed the wall and headed toward a small courtyard, he frowned and wondered exactly what he was going to find. Their small party stopped at the door. The roof had collapsed, making further egress difficult.

"What do you want me to do?"

"I want you to go inside."

He nodded, and paid careful attention to the next few steps. The interior was compromised, but a large part of it still looked relatively cool—and more to the point, dark. Inside was shadow upon shadow, everything blackened by the fire. But it hadn't always been like this he realized, as one step followed another. No windows, but there had been lanterns. When he looked down, he caught the outline of what remained of them, shattered on the floor.

He stopped. In his mind's eye he saw blue mosaic tiles that presumably still lay there beneath the soot. His perception had shifted, resulting in a sharp disorientation. He heard soft footfalls behind him and reached out.

"Eleanor—"

"It's all right, Mark."

Yeah, sure it was. He grabbed hold of her gloved hand and steadied himself while struggling with a recollection of something he'd never seen before. He felt stupid, like a child, and knew that would have to change. He made sure his feet were planted firmly amidst the debris, squared his shoulders, let go of her hand, and continued further inside. Whatever ghosts lay ahead, he'd simply have to meet them head-on and deal with them, just like he'd had to deal with being sucked dry, murdered, and brought back to life again. Yeah, just like all of that.

The core inside him began to swell and burn in his gut. He felt it pushing at the boundaries of the makeshift corral he'd constructed, eager to burst out and display its growing belligerence.

He swallowed it down, knowing Eleanor might well pick up his mood. Hopefully she'd put it down to his apprehension, real enough despite the fact that he knew there was nothing here that could really hurt him—not unless he stepped into one of those pools of sunlight ahead and pulled off his protective gear.

Onward then, through an arch, where he had to squeeze past a pile of smashed tiles and broken crossbeams, and beyond a column of daylight that poured in through a gap in the roof. "Careful," he told those behind him. Blackened furniture, some of it burned to unrecognizable stumps, jutted from the floor like stalagmites pushing their way upward inside a hellish cave, all of it caked in soot that crumbled and flaked as he brushed past.

It was the aftermath of an inferno and it left a bitter, exotic, multilayered scent that caught in his throat. Nevertheless, it had failed to cleanse all the memories that dwelled in this place, memories that bled from the walls or lay scattered and thrown amongst the black soot, along with wails of pain and betrayal, horror and disbelief, panic, and suffering. They hung in the shadows, hiding as whispers, or they splattered gaudy and loud across the carbon-dusted tiles.

He gasped, and had to fight hard to bring the noise of it down. He knew what Eleanor wanted. She wanted access to those memories, but the more his mind stretched out, the more unstable and unsure he became of them. What was truth, and what was merely a result of fanciful guesswork powered by his fertile imagination—and more to the point, how would he be able to tell the difference?

"These footsteps—are yours and Gilles'," he said, pointing to the ground. "And Houston's, over there."

"Yes."

Okay. That was too easy, even in the aftermath of the fire. Having been prepped for the journey, he already knew they'd been here. He paused for a moment, imagined Gilles stood in the very same spot, looking at something on the ground. "Bodies," he muttered. Sad and indignant remains. No physical signs of them now. They'd been picked up or dragged off. But she didn't want that. They already knew all of that. He shook his head, frustrated, fought through the clamor, still unsure of how he was supposed to tap into it.

A solid frown now dwelled beneath his balaclava as he continued further through the wreckage, until he reached another area open to daylight. Here was a jagged gap in the exterior wall, and the ground was an uneven mound of blasted stucco, rebar, and concrete. One of Houston's munitions. He turned around, a question on his lips.

"Why did he—" He held up his hand. "No matter." The less he knew the better. Too much clutter in his head already. He crouched low and laid his hand on the charred debris. Here was something relevant, but it was elusive, appearing in the mental equivalent of his peripheral vision, only to disappear when he tried to focus on it. There was a passageway under the rubble, blocked now. It had been a means of escape. One that had failed. Another memory from his briefing back at the house.

He took a deep breath, tried to empty his mind of all else, and waited. He waited until he knew it was futile. Whatever gift Eleanor thought he might have, it wasn't this. He stood up slowly, and prepared to give her the bad news. And by the time he had risen to his full height, his mind had switched, frantic and chattering, now latched onto something his senses *were* tuned to.

"We've got company."

"Are you sure?" she asked.

"Yes, I'm sure."

It took another full minute before she was able to concur, and by that time he had both donors posted outside, on the lookout.

"If it's Weiss—or Deacon—"

Mark shook his head. "If it's Deacon, don't worry. I'm his son, remember?" His voice swelled with cocky assurances. It was the core talking, and he was glad she couldn't see his face—crestfallen at the possibility of a violent end, and instilled with a bitterness that simmered with thoughts of meeting the man who'd killed him. Despair crept behind a single door. All he had to do was open it.

One of the donors got their attention. A vehicle was coming in cross-country, and Mark shook off his acrimony. One vehicle meant there wouldn't be many visitors, so if it did come down to it—

"Five," Eleanor said quietly.

He agreed. And presumably they wouldn't all be vampire. Closer and his perception gave him more. "They're not Deacon's people either," he added. *And how the hell did he know that?* "Any ideas on who else it could be?"

"I really don't know," she answered, distracted. "There. Three vampire, two human. We'd better put ourselves in plain sight."

"Is that a good—?" But she had already stepped out into the open and so, with no choice, he followed, and saw dust rising along with the flash of headlights off to the left. Moments later, a heavy off-road vehicle rolled to a halt and its occupants spilled out—three clad in heavy, head-to-toe garments and four of the five appeared to be armed.

Too late to stop her, he watched Eleanor walk forward to greet them. Unsure of his own particular role, he fell back on proximity, silence, and a tough, square-shouldered stance, laughable in this instance as two of the vampires he faced were built like Houston, were armed with rifles, and he wasn't fooling anybody.

He felt a mental push—inquisitive, intrusive, then another. They were attempting to read him. It was easily handled and he smiled beneath his cowl. This was a game he could play.

"Eleanor?" The unarmed one, a female voice.

"Mina."

So, despite the fact they were covered completely from head to toe, the women knew one another. Maybe this wouldn't be so bad after all. He saw weapons being lowered all round, but he kept up his stance—bluff, bluster and his stubborn mental block. Right now it was all he had.

One of the donors arrived to stand alongside him, and together they watched the two women greet one another. Mark tried visually to size up the male vampires. No easy task when everyone was wrapped up in protective gear. He was also still under mental scrutiny, it was beginning to tick him off, and so he did some pushing of his own.

They were wary, he discovered, uncertain but not overly hostile. And there was enough, after a small, easily won battle of wills, to let him know why they were here. He tried scent, too, but anything distinctive was dulled by distance and the balaclava pulled tight over his face. He managed to catch a hint of moss and cold, and traffic; everything seemed stale, like they had been on the road too long. Not local, then. On a disjointed, remote level, he found this exercise instructive. These were the first strangers he'd encountered outside the Delacour House.

Eleanor was addressing the newcomers, so he broke off his analysis and listened.

"What are you doing here, Mina?"

"There were rumors. Bad ones. We thought we'd come and see for ourselves." The woman's covered face shifted slightly toward Mark.

Eleanor turned and beckoned. "Mark, come say hello."

He stepped forward, inclined his head toward a vague shape dressed in similar garments. He expected to receive a nod by way of exchange. Instead the woman took a sharp step back, enough for her rear foot to skid on gravel. It was quickly followed by an awkward bow.

"Eleanor, I wasn't aware—"

"It's all right, Mina. He's just a new member of our House."

"Really." Disbelief fluttered like a moth in the air between them.

Mark frowned. "What does she see?"

"She sees better than most," Eleanor said.

"In that case," he held out his hand, "Mina, I want you to come with me."

The two women looked at one another.

"Now," he said. He reached out, took the stranger's gloved hand, and felt the slight, delicate fingers beneath the rough, opaque fabric. He stared at the shielded connection between them, and wondered if he would get the chance to take that glove off, once they were in the dark.

But now weapons were raised, on both sides. He didn't care. He ignored them and began to pull the woman into the building. Maybe it was the fact they were out in the sun, he reasoned, or that he just wanted to get this whole charade over with. And nothing whatsoever to do with a growing longing to touch her, to pull open those robes—

"Where are we going?" There was fear in her voice.

"Trust me," he told her, and added, "watch your step. You'll see." He felt a slight tug on his arm as she hesitated. Just a second or two of resistance before she followed him back into the ruined interior. At one point he heard her gasp.

"It's the dead," he told her.

"If you can see them, why do you need me?"

He ignored her, stepped carefully, and continued to pull her inexorably through the ruin toward the pile of rubble created by Houston's bomb. "Here. Right here." He pushed her down, made her crouch amongst the debris at the edge of the light, just as he had.

She stumbled, tried to pull away. "I don't know, I can't—who are you?"

"Later, right now I want you to tell me what you see."

The others were approaching. He heard one of the men. "He needs to let her go. Right now."

"Don't listen to them," Mark urged. "Just concentrate. There's something here. Something important." He gripped her arm. "I can't do this. So, it's down to you."

"Okay." She pulled away from him. "Please, just give me a moment."

Mark let her go, settled on his haunches, and did as she asked. In the meantime, the core was hammering on his skull from the inside. *You can control them. All of them. Just reach out—* He ignored it, and kept his eyes on the female.

"There's a tunnel—right below us—it was sealed."

"I know. But what happened before that?"

Her voice wavered. "Screaming. There was ultraviolet. Everyone... came running through... they were shot, and burned... and then later, there was a man, a human standing here."

He swallowed, shared her distaste. "Focus on him."

"He's—he's just standing there." She gave a snort of disgust. "As if it was nothing."

"What else?"

"Conviction... so single-minded."

"He's being controlled?" offered Eleanor. "Compelled?"

The other woman shrugged. "I think so, and—my God they're all human. The attackers are human." She drew in a breath, began to rise.

Mark reached across, lay a hand on her shoulder, pushed her back down. "Not yet. Controlled by whom? Tell me." He heard Eleanor and the two men whispering rapidly amongst themselves. No one was for stopping them now. They wanted to know, too.

The objection coming at him from beneath Mina's hood felt like an iron spike digging inside his skull. Her other thoughts were similarly barbed. "It's important," he added, not letting go, rebuffing her anger. "Who is it?" *Is it Deacon,* he wanted to ask. Somehow, right now, it mattered. Oh, yes, it mattered. So important it was making his head spin.

"Dark hair. Narrow face. Just a shadow. It's all I can see."

Not Deacon, then. A sense of relief appeared, so profound, so strong, and at odds with his rancor, it startled him.

"That could well be Anton Weiss," said Eleanor.

Mark fought hard to relax, and he let Mina go. He stood up and looked toward his companion. "That's what you were looking for, wasn't it."

He received a curt nod. "Any sign of our missing donors? And the girl?"

The stranger shook her head in reply to Eleanor's questions. "A girl? No. I'm sorry, I can't see any more."

Mark looked at the two women, wondered how, between them, they were able to figure all this out. But he was still confused, only half paying attention, still feeling guilty at the relief he felt, despite his hatred, that the perpetrator ultimately wasn't Deacon. It was an unwieldy combination of emotion and he pushed it back, swallowed it before it drove him crazy.

The stranger had risen now. Her thoughts offered him a tangled drift of confusion and reproach. She wanted very much to be offended, to express her outrage, but didn't dare. Didn't want to. She was curious about him, despite the fact he'd acted like a jerk. "I'm sorry," he told her. "I'm not usually so rude." He looked toward Eleanor. Maybe she'd help him out.

"We need to warn everyone," was all she said.

Back outside, the others said their goodbyes, turned to leave, and he envied them as they got into their vehicle. Doors slammed, tires crunched on gravel, and when they were gone—

"Who were they?"

"House Goran. East Coast. An ally for the moment, I think." Eleanor was staring out toward the rapidly dissipating trail of dust.

The name meant nothing. He was still getting used to all the Houses, their hierarchies, their hostilities and alliances, and where Delacour's House fit in. He was disappointed to see the woman go, baffled by her over-polite farewell bow, but he also felt relieved at having retained his anonymity. No startling revelations about his immediate ancestor, not out here with five armed and wary strangers for company. "So, we got everything we came for?"

"Not everything."

He looked longingly out toward the West. He dearly wanted to go home. But at least it would be dark soon. "The missing girl."

"How much do you know about her, Mark?"

"Nothing." He shook his head. "Well, almost nothing. I know that when her name comes up, everyone seems to wish it hadn't."

"She was here, with the others. During the attack. We never found a body."

Mark pointed out beyond the wall. "If she ran out there, if she was caught in daylight—"

"She wasn't among the dead, Mark. I see the dead. I can't see the living."

He stared at the dark cowl covering her face. "You destroyed this place. You, Houston, and Gilles. You must have been sure she wasn't here, still around, still in need of shelter."

"At the time, yes. We searched everywhere—"

"But now you're not so sure."

"No."

"There's no one alive here, Eleanor. I'm sorry."

"So, what keeps bringing me back?"

He gave her a hard look, and realized she wouldn't see the gesture. In the end, he gave up and headed back inside, and once they were back at the pile of debris, he waited.

"I'm beginning to wonder why Houston set off the incendiary, here of all places," she said after a few moments.

Mark shrugged. "Security, maybe? He did it to block the tunnel, didn't he?"

"But why? What would be the point?"

"Because guys like him like to blow shit—excuse me, blow stuff up?" He heard her laugh. "What was underneath all this," he added after a moment, "can you remember? I'm not seeing anything unusual.".

He watched Eleanor crouch low, and place both her hands amidst the tumble of charred stucco and dust. "Do you think there might be something buried underneath?"

"Well, I could pull away a few of these larger pieces," he offered. He looked out through the hole in the wall. The sky was beginning to darken. Not long now.

And so he began, carefully, making sure he didn't disturb any part of his clothing and expose himself to the remnants of daylight. He had no idea what Eleanor expected to find. Certainly the girl wasn't buried here. They'd already hauled off the bodies before they started torching the place. He thought about reaching out, trying to imagine what he might find, but he didn't trust himself to come up with anything honest, so instead he just kept quiet and kept on working.

He moved maybe thirty chunks of debris, until he had opened up a gap about three feet in diameter and had gotten below floor level. The blast had blown through the tiles, right into the concrete slab. So far, nothing, but at least it was now dark outside. No big deal if either of them tore a hole in their gloves. He pulled back his hood and pulled the woven mask off his face, and she took over, drawing powdered concrete back with her fingers.

A moment later— "Oh," she said.

"What is it?"

She was pulling at something, momentarily stuck until it came abruptly loose. She drew back her hood and mask, and held the item up in front of her. It looked like a small leather drawstring bag, it could have been black or dark brown but right now it was covered in light gray dust. She pulled at the drawstring, peered inside. "I knew it."

"Eleanor, what—"

"It's her cards."

"Cards?" He tried not to look or sound as dumb as he felt.

"Dimitra's tarot cards." She stared at the bag, a triumphant smile on her face, before tucking them under her cloak and giving him an apologetic shrug.

"Does this mean we can go home now?" he asked hopefully.

"Yes," she beamed.

"Good." He looked on, puzzled as she stepped past him. Tarot cards. Were they the reason why Houston had set off the incendiary? If so, he didn't understand why. Why go to all that trouble? But no matter, it was a pile of stupid cards and there were more important matters to consider.

He brought up the rear, followed her back outside and toward the vehicle, his spirits already buoyed by the prospect of leaving. As for their other discovery, if followed to its logical conclusion, Weiss, their so-called Grand Father, their ancient ancestor, had sent out his army of human killers, and had begun what he'd promised.

And everyone had to be warned.

CHAPTER 8
GILLES

A three-hour flight, followed by another hour by road. They had plenty of time before dawn arrived and were perfectly insulated inside the vehicle, but Gilles decided he would be glad when they finally reached their destination.

Gannon leaned forward. "Looks like Vancouver," he said after a glance out of the window, his first words since they'd left California. He had been utterly silent aboard the jet, inanimate save for fingers rapping idly on the armrest of his airplane seat, and so introspective that Gilles was beginning to worry.

"It is," Gilles replied. "You've been here before?"

The other man nodded. " Two years ago. I was…" He shrugged. "It doesn't matter." He turned back toward the window, but not before Gilles had caught the look in his eye. They'd all held that look, once. One foot still in a past life, struggling to accept it was gone, for better or worse.

This last few weeks he'd expected Gannon to be more vocal, to express some form of outrage or anguish or even joy, once everything—his death, this new life—had sunk in. Instead in their place was a guarded resignation, a near-silent acceptance. Nor had the man asked any questions, or seemed the slightest bit interested beyond the immediacies of appetite. Gilles wasn't buying it, and occasionally when Gannon was distracted, he had pushed, quietly, surreptitiously, looked for the brewing, torrential storm that just had to be there, all bottled up, vying for blessed release. But so far, he'd simply run into that mental roadblock. The man was a little more forthcoming with Eleanor and Christina when he chose to be, but by all accounts, and barring appetite, his formidable blood heritage had yet to show its true colors.

The car swept past downtown, crossed the bridge and headed into West Vancouver. It was raining and the streets glittered like jewels. Trees hung low, their branches strewn with diamonds, while water scattered and danced on pavements and poured into drains.

A short climb up a narrow tarmac road, before the driver stopped the vehicle outside a tall, wooden gate. Another moment passed and the gate opened, then they began a slow approach toward a two-story house surrounded by a cluster of protective evergreens. Straight ahead, light spilled boldly from an open door in the dark, where men waited with raised umbrellas and stepped forward as soon as the car drew to a halt.

Houston was out first—quick, on the alert, giving everything the once-over before nodding toward Delacour who then headed out, exiting the vehicle and assuming a relaxed stride beneath the phalanx of temporary shelter. Gilles told Gannon to step out next while he took up the rear, and they both dashed the short distance through the rain toward the door, their umbrella wielders admirably keeping pace.

At the threshold, sheltered from the downpour, Gannon stopped and closed his eyes. He was looking back toward the night, breathing deep. "The trees."

Gilles followed his gaze. Yes, their scent was quite beautiful. Pity it had taken a newcomer to remind him.

Inside, a log fire burned in the hearth at the rear of the hall and helped light the dark surround of polished, floor-to-ceiling mahogany. An elaborate, carved stairway led upward, partially illuminated by the rich multicolored hues of stained glass lamps, and the air hung rich with the scent of lacquer, furniture polish, and wood smoke. Near the front door, Houston was fighting off a glower of disapproval while checking in his pistol with one of the staff, and Delacour was already engaged in small talk with Tobias, one of two pale, fragile grandsons of their formidable host, Violet Marsh.

In the meantime, Gannon had walked over to one of the stairway balustrades, his hand reaching up to caress the griffin carved there on top of the rail, distracted, eyes wandering beyond the carving, taking in the décor, and was by all accounts oblivious to the glances heading his way, particularly from Tobias Marsh.

"So much for secrecy," Houston mumbled, now alongside.

Gilles turned away, fell into the barely audible murmur that was necessary to avoid being overheard. "He's just curious. Mark's new." They were still keeping Gannon's identity under wraps, for now. But if one of the Marshes figured out exactly who he was, well now, that would be something, wouldn't it.

Houston appeared to be reading his mind. "Yeah, right. Just be ready if the shit hits the fan. Violet is no fan of Deacon."

Moments later they were being ushered through an elaborate, carved architrave toward the library. In passing, there was a mutual and polite nod between Gilles and the young Marsh, although the term young was a misnomer, for the fragile, apparent twenty-two-year-old standing before him was in fact well over three hundred years old. However, what followed gave him a slight twist of apprehension as the man gave Gannon a formal bow—one afforded, quite correctly, to an Elder. Bringing up the rear, Houston was practically ignored altogether.

Gannon had offered a smile but seemed a little perplexed and Gilles had to tug on his arm in order to get him to move through the doorway. He saw Houston roll his eyes and suddenly he had to work hard at keeping back a grin.

The library had always doubled as a reception room for as long as Gilles could remember. The entire house was crammed to the gills with books, stacks of papers, scrolls, illustrations, and paintings, everything concerning their kind. If it existed, then it, or at least a copy of it, was filed here, lined in regimental rows, or stacked high, or bundled carefully together, every room, every passageway akin to a repository. At least, in this particular room, there was space enough to mingle and at this late hour of the night, the Marsh family—Violet, her son Robert, his daughters Lily and Rose and sons Tobias and William—played host.

And as usual on such an occasion, everyone was formally dressed. Gilles had forsaken his decidedly more comfortable garb for a well-cut, charcoal gray suit that sat easily on his lean, muscular shoulders. Delacour looked less like a renaissance artisan and more like a corporate big shot, immaculate in navy wool, his hair scraped back, tied and lacquered, while Gannon looked every inch Deacon's progeny, not a blond hair out of place, dark suit sharply tailored, tie ever so slightly, aristocratically crooked. Even Houston looked civilized, sporting a suit, shirt, and tie in a manner that, surprisingly enough, suggested he was more than comfortable. Everyone, including the staff, looked about ready to attend either a wedding, a funeral, or at the very least a high-powered business meeting.

And with the formality came the usual rituals; the slight, mutual bow between Elders, between peers, and a deeper one reserved for the host. Violet Marsh accepted the accolade with a smile and a regal nod. She was clad in dark red, a dropped waist 1920's gown embroidered with tiny black beads that to Gilles' perception glittered like birds' eyes. Her steel-gray hair was immaculately coiffed, her eyes were alive, taking in every aspect of these visitors to her House. If Gannon's presence gave her pause, she didn't show it. Standing alongside the rest of her family, she looked as strong as an oak. Her son, tall and spindly, and his four adult children looked frail, like shadows alongside her. Gilles knew a little of their history, of how the Plague had ravaged them, nearly taken them all, until Violet had taken matters into her own hands. He'd always wondered if *grandmother* was the correct term, and whether she was in fact an older relative. He figured it would be an interesting story if he ever got the chance to hear it.

So close to dawn, there would be little time for small talk and pleasantries. They would all need to retire soon, leaving the formal introductions and serious business for the following sundown, and while Delacour was commandeered by their host, Gilles became aware of the gentle push of thought in the room, perhaps a little more than was normally polite. Gannon was now looking around, bemused, a smile growing on his face. Someone was trying to read him, and getting nowhere by the looks of it.

Gilles let it go. Despite the distractions, he had work to do, even at this late hour.

A girl arrived carrying a tray of filled crystal. He took one of the glasses, and bade Gannon do the same, then saw him wince after taking a sip. Gilles tried his best not to smile. Blood, a few days old, with an anti-coagulant. Marsh House rules. No blood taken directly from the source. In contrast, Houston had taken and downed his glass in one gulp, wholly indifferent to age and temperature, and appeared perfectly content to level his hard gaze at the other unfortunate recipients in the room.

The blood cleared Gilles' head, and not a moment too soon, for they were immediately approached by two young women, both immune to Houston's glower.

"Lily, Rose," he inclined his head. This close they looked pale as porcelain and fashioned from pared, slender bird bones. Both around eighteen going on three hundred and fifty, the smooth skin of their faces suggesting the former, eyes gray as their grandmother's hair telling of the latter. It was a spooky combination, one seen to varying degrees in their society, but never so profound as here.

"You've brought someone new," said Rose, her doll face and ancient eyes shifting toward Gannon.

The man smiled, gave both girls a polite nod, and after a sideways glance at Gilles, deliberately extended his hand toward Rose. The girl took it, straight off, like she'd been waiting, like this had been a pre-arranged challenge. What passed between that handshake, Gilles could only imagine, but after an unobtrusive examination of the surrounding ether he decided to let it go. Gannon needed the practice. There'd be other occasions such as these, and the sooner he was accustomed to them the better.

Houston, who'd also drawn in a breath, barked out a laugh, slapped Gilles hard on the shoulder, and set off toward Delacour who was beckoning him. After a short period of small talk, Gilles began to relax. Gannon had laid aside his introspection and now appeared controlled and comfortable enough in the company of strangers, chatting and being utterly charming to Lily and Rose.

And while they talked and socialized, the Marshes' human staff and companions glided between them, deftly balancing trays of elaborate crystal and attending to any other needs they might have. He saw Gannon reach for another glass despite his earlier distaste, and reasoning he could leave him safely in the girls' clutches, he turned his attention to the hovering William, the eldest grandson and spitting image of his willowy father.

He received an affable smile. "It's good to see you, Gilles, despite the circumstances."

"Likewise. How is everything, Will?"

The man's eyes flitted toward Violet. "Tense. Grandmother's moods have been worse than the recent storms."

Gilles smiled. He could well imagine. "With more storms to come, I suspect." He was reaching, pushing, they both were, trying to gauge one another, uncover answers to the same questions. Obviously they'd been given the same brief. And once that was established, they both broke into a grin. There was a mutual backing off. He had no qualms about being in any of the Marshes' company.

"My sisters seem enamored by your companion. He's new, isn't he?"

Gilles nodded. "Yes. And a bit of a mystery. Christina rescued him from a watery grave."

"Hmm," the other man cocked his head slightly, and lowered his voice. "Mind if I offer some insight?"

"Not at all." *And here we go,* he thought.

"Well, you've probably got most of it already. Strength, and I see trauma during his rebirth, it's quite significant."

"He says he doesn't know who did this to him. Says it's a complete blank." There. Shift the lie toward Gannon.

William Marsh nodded. "Trauma will do that. Keep your eye on him. I'm not saying he'll become unstable, but—"

"I'll do that," he answered, maybe a little too quickly.

"I'm sorry, Gilles. I'm far too blunt. Comes with age I'm afraid."

"That's quite all right, Will." Saved. By the other man's conjecture. "It's good advice."

Another smile passed between them, but before Gilles could field another question, this time regarding the Marshes' position on Weiss, the conversation was interrupted, and William's younger brother, Tobias, informed them their rooms were ready. No matter. Having got the gist of a few undercurrents, he reasoned he'd done what he could, for now.

As for their new addition, Gannon appeared to be on his best behavior, and keeping an eye on him hadn't proven too traumatic. In fact, although the man had cast a few predatory glances toward some of the human staff, he had behaved impeccably. A short while later, when they were led upstairs through the sprawling house, along passageways narrowed by teetering stacks of books, where they were all offered separate guest rooms, Gilles retired to his own room with only a mild sense of unease at having to leave Gannon on his own. The man still needed a lot of sleep, and would probably be out cold for the entire day. There were, after all, other issues to gnaw upon. And so, as he got ready for bed, he cast his mind toward sundown and the reason they were here in the first place.

Violet and her family were in danger and they needed to be warned, but he also knew his Elder had something else in mind. As for what that was, Delacour hadn't been absolutely clear. Gilles wondered how much Violet Marsh wanted to get involved, and where her mind was on this whole affair. No one had believed Weiss would carry out his threat, maybe some of the Houses, including Violet, still didn't believe it. There had been a cull of Delacour's little band of waifs and strays. So, what? Perhaps it wasn't a bad thing in the eyes of those like the Marshes, their family all part of the grand scheme, where ancestries were proudly catalogued and heritages carefully marked. Where deviations were swept under the carpet quickly, coldly, surreptitiously. No room for those who didn't fit, whose ancestors were unknown or dead and the lines of succession broken and lost—the likes of him, or Eleanor, or Christina, or those other poor unfortunates that had died in the desert.

Gilles wondered if the Marsh family would prefer to hide their heads beneath the sand, behave as though the massacre was part of a local dispute, between Deacon and Delacour, yet another deadly spat between long-term mutual antagonists and of no consequence to the remaining Houses.

Was he being a little disingenuous? Pre-judging them? Perhaps. They had all been complacent, let the warnings slip through their fingers, and had frittered away the opportunity to do something before it was too late. And now it was here, now it was upon them in the form of Delacour telling them they should prepare, maybe run for their lives. Weiss had struck when no one believed he ever would, and the reality, that it would be just a matter of time before it arrived unannounced on this particular doorstep, might very well prove too much. He found it hard to imagine those three-hundred-and-fifty-year-old fragile children doing anything proactive to protect themselves.

And yet—he'd sensed a certain level of anticipation while talking to William. So, maybe he was wrong. He knew it was always a bad move to second-guess the likes of Violet, or Delacour, or any Elder for that matter. It was as if they moved in their own circles of logic that ran counter to everyone else's. And in this particular instance, he fervently hoped it was so, providing it didn't adversely affect the rest of them.

Sleep then. For whatever happened, come sundown, he'd need to be well rested and alert.

CHAPTER 9
MARK

Mark stared at the bedroom door. He was alone, at last, and a wry grin twisted his features before it disappeared and revealed a more despondent expression. He began to pace. In his present state, he felt hemmed in, imprisoned, overcrowded by the room's low ceiling, the overstuffed bookcase, and the ancient, bulky furniture. Heavy velvet drapes covered the window, a necessary layer of protection and yet, instead of providing reassurance, they simply added to the claustrophobia. It all amounted to a reflection of his embattled insides and he longed desperately for Christina, or Eleanor, who'd always kept him talking during moments like this, when the core was a demanding, treacherous beast, filling him up, intent and particularly determined to master him.

He realized now, it had been too easy back at the House. He'd been hoodwinked, fooled by the core and his own overconfidence, lulled into the belief that he could handle it. And when Delacour had asked him to play his part on this trip, naturally he'd agreed.

He stopped pacing and raked fingers through his hair. Control of the core. Sometimes he had the measure of it, had that bullish monster in a firm, confident grip. Ah, but not now. Every once in a while the bastard sensed a weak spot and picked a fight, and tonight he'd been wrestling with it ever since they'd boarded the plane. Right now he was on a losing streak. The core wanted blood, for starters, and not that ice-cold dreck served earlier. Hell, no.

It was a battle he'd already secretly lost. He'd been distracted. All those strangers in that room downstairs, all of them curious, all sending forth a barrage of silent questions that demanded the same answers. *Who are you? Where do you come from?* Easily handled when the core wasn't being rambunctious. Not so easy when the thing was howling and ebullient, grasping and greedy.

He slid off his jacket, hung it carefully on the back of a chair. He went through the motions of kicking off his shoes, pulling off his socks, sliding loose his tie, and twisting open the buttons on his shirt, while his mind recognized similar acts taking place elsewhere in the house, a collective response to dawn and the need for sleep.

But not yet, not for him. Instead, the core had taken Delacour's request, had concocted and put into action an additional plan that wouldn't leave him alone for very much longer. So simple, so horrifyingly easy, he was appalled. Just a slight touch as he'd taken the glass from one of the female members of staff, with just a glance in her direction. And now all he had to do was wait. Wait and fight some more with the monster inside. He felt like a cheat, a liar, and there was a good chance he'd be able to add the word rapist on the back of all that, too, going off the current demands of his appetites. No way that girl would appear on his doorstep of her own accord. The honorable thing would be to step outside, go find Gilles, and tell him what he'd done.

But the core wouldn't allow it. And already it was seducing him, stoking his hunger, extolling the delights in store, persuading him to stay put, leave it alone… and wait.

Minutes passed, agonizing and slow, until finally he sensed her out there on the corridor, picking her way quietly along, being careful, just as he'd told her to. And all of a sudden, he was hovering there by the door, his fingers inches away from the handle, knowing he should wrench it open and tell her to go away. But instead he gripped gently, and pulled.

He felt the heat radiating from her, caught the scent of trees in the rain, of red wine and lilies, printer ink, and shoe polish moments before she came into view. Upon her arrival he reached out, took her hand, and pulled her gently into the room. She was beautiful, her hair like silk falling down her back, her face upturned, displaying a warm, delightful smile.

He pushed the door until it clicked shut. "Put your arms around me," he whispered, and he gasped as her hands slid beneath his unbuttoned shirt and encircled his torso. So close now, he buried his face in her hair and breathed deep, drew in layer upon layer of scent. Given time he reckoned he'd be able to retrace all her steps for the past week. He looked down at her. "Take off my shirt." He stood still, and tried to relax as she slid the garment down past his shoulders and let it drop at his feet.

Inside, the core spun slow, authoritative, utterly confident of his next move, and right now he was too mesmerized to fight back. The girl wore a pale blue nightgown, just three buttons, and he was able to slip it over her shoulders, where it joined his shirt on the floor. He leaned in and kissed her, luxuriated in her response, the warmth of her lips, and pulled her into an embrace. Her chin was already raised and he began to assure himself this was no different than what he did with the donors back in California.

Oh, but it was. This was a different House, with a different set of rules, and he was damned sure this girl hadn't signed on for this. Her permission had not been granted, her compliance was fully down to his control of her. He brushed his lips behind her ear, let them travel down to her throat, the tip of his tongue searching, finding the right spot. Her body pressed close, he'd already felt the beat of her heart, so quick and strong it reverberated through to his bones. A moment later, he sank his teeth into her flesh and connected, his eyes closed, all inhibitions and rights and wrongs pushed aside, his mind already dancing with hers, stimulating her senses, stroking her desire, picking the locks on her memories as Delacour had asked, with consummate ease.

With the first taste it felt like being alive all over again. The pounding, urgent thrill of it drew him in and increased his need. Somewhere, above or below, he could hear Christina, telling him not too much, never too much; he could hear himself screaming to stop, a voice torn and ragged, becoming desperate, having to fight now on two fronts. For along with the bloodlust, the usual roaring tide of sexual urgency wasn't far behind, and one of his hands slid below her ass and pulled at her thigh, urging her to lift her leg and wrap it around him. Now it felt as if they were welded together, his impatient and eager cock stiff as an iron rod between them.

Another long moment, and he withdrew indolently from the girl's flesh, half-dragged, half-carried her over to the bed. He felt drunk, euphoric—yet another blow to his conscience, yelling away in the background. He lay her down, straddled her, let his splayed hand slide up her torso, cup her right breast, thumb and forefinger gently squeezing. "So beautiful," he whispered. "You're so—" He stopped and looked down to where a drop of blood—from his lips, just a tiny drop—had landed just below her ribcage. He stared at it, red on flesh so pale, so vulnerable. He felt her hands at his waist, pulling, tugging at his belt, felt it loosen. They had both crested a rise and were about to hurtle downhill. When he looked at her face, he saw her eyes had darkened, her lips had parted, and now they let forth a gasp of determination as she struggled with the belt.

"What—what's your name?"

"Megan." She grinned, hungry. Oh, he'd done a masterful job on her.

"Megan." He swallowed. "I want you to scream." It came out sharp, an urgent hiss the core tried desperately to mollify.

She paused, gave him a frown.

"Scream, damn it." Louder now, as he fought hard to find a voice. "Do it! Do it, before it's too late."

And she did. He watched her chest rise, and broke into a grin as she let forth an ear-piercing yell.

"Again!" He shook his head, delirious, tried to shake off the vision of her throat, already violated and smeared with glorious red. He failed miserably at preventing his knee from forcing her thighs apart.

It happened fast, and he had to give Houston his due, who somehow managed to storm into the room and get enough leverage to throw him right across the bed and hard against the bookcase before he had time to react.

Mark bounced off, ended up on the floor, and a cascade of books, rudely jolted from their resting place, flew down to join him. He was hauled roughly to his feet. He felt gloved hands twisting his arm, and he found another grin on his face, this time born of unmitigated, blessed relief, now that he couldn't do any more damage. "Gloves, Houston?" he teased. "What's the matter, you don't trust me?"

That got him another hard slam against the bookcase that knocked all the wind out of him and left him pinned there.

"I knew it was too soon," growled his attacker.

He relaxed, took in a slow breath, absorbed the smell of ancient parchment, dust, binding, and leather, part of him coldly taking in the measure of the other man. He heard the girl, Megan, sobbing. The room seemed crowded all of a sudden, other voices, some registering affront, others apologetic. As expected, he'd caused quite a stir.

"Houston." Gilles' voice. "Let him go."

Released, he gathered himself, stood slowly upright. "I'm sorry," he said. Robert Marsh held the girl. Someone had wrapped her in a blanket. Beyond the hulking form of Houston, Gilles was shaking his head, while Delacour was standing in the doorway, giving him an even look. As soon as Houston glanced away, he gave the Elder a barely perceptible nod. There. Job done. Badly, but it was done.

There were long minutes of abject apology and contrition, and the door closed once more. He was alone again. This time it took longer for the House to settle. Sickened, he lay back, and tried to calm himself. Now came another difficulty as he prepared for repose, this time with no distractions. Now it was time to wrestle with his demons, alone and unaided, when he couldn't pretend and he couldn't put on a mask, because a mask didn't do any good.

He was cold, and that short dalliance with the girl had done nothing but increase his appetite for heat. Heat meant life, and he had neither of those things. Not any more. Now all he could do was stand on the outside and look in, like a child locked out of the house, only able to see the roaring fire in the hearth, and feel its heat by leaning close to the glass in the window.

Temporary respite came in the form of the living, like the girl just now. Just a glimpse of what he had possessed a mere few weeks ago, but it was far better than nothing. Blood cooled and died when it entered him, but while he was connected, he could pretend he was still one of them. And when he couldn't feel it any more, when he could no longer touch and caress the rich, warm flesh of its donor, he became hollow, dead—nothing.

Inside he felt tattered, rotten, and adrift from everything he'd ever known. Life, his family. Just thinking about Mom, Dad, and his brother Matthew made him twist and panic, like he was drowning. They were still out there. He presumed they still thought he was alive, and they were probably worried about him. What the hell was he supposed to do about that?

He laid his head on the pillow, using the recent memory of the girl as a lifeline, her naked body pressed against him, beautiful, a fleeting pleasure—one he could have prolonged had he been prepared to give in. He realized his hands were trembling. He was shivering for no practical reason, for the cold he felt wasn't a physical thing. Beyond extremes, temperature didn't seem to matter. It was just his body, clinging to the same old memories. Stupid, but there they were.

On the periphery of his thoughts he could feel Gilles, out there somewhere, still fretting, pacing. He felt unworthy of the man, of his cautious acceptance and courteous attempts to help him despite considering Mark to be nothing more than a ticking time bomb, just waiting to go off in everyone's faces. No doubt he would consider tonight a precursor, and maybe he was right. He would have to explain at some point what his actions were initially all about, but now wasn't the time.

He shifted onto his side, curled up into a fetal position. No life, no heat, no looking through the window. Not today. And today it seemed only fair that he should suffer. He felt pathetic, and for a moment he thought tears might well in his eyes, despite knowing they never would.

Disgusted, he fought back the self-pity and tried to sink into the oblivion of sleep, and eventually, unnoticed, his hands resumed their trembling.

"Megan is held in high regard. A deliberate choice, or did you just get lucky?"

They were standing in the hallway next to the crackling fire, their voices hushed. Mark had his head bowed slightly, and his eyes were downcast as if he was being scolded like a ten-year-old boy who'd just broken a vase. "Both, I guess."

Delacour nodded. "And?"

He suppressed a cold grin. "They don't trust you, but they trust Deacon less. Weiss is still venerated, worshipped, almost. I get the impression Violet hates Deacon nearly half as much as I do." He sensed a smile on the other man's face and raised his head. "Mind if I ask why this is so important?" He figured he had a right to know after being pushed out on a limb, made to wallow in his own stinking pond of rape and gluttony and make a complete fool of himself.

"Once all this sinks in, once they start taking this threat seriously, we'll start to see some polarity," Delacour began. "Houses will break old alliances, flock toward new ones purely based on survival. It's happened before. It has to be done. None of us can survive on our own. And I need to know which way Violet is likely to go."

"Friends become enemies, enemies become friends."

"Yes. For the duration, until it's over."

Mark shrugged. The politics didn't really interest him. Violet Marsh's dislike of Deacon however— "Do you think she—" He halted mid-sentence as they were approached. Delacour didn't skip a beat.

"So, you're not in on this meeting, Mark. It would be too disruptive."

That was news, and he tried hard not to look stunned. Gilles and Houston had arrived and they were accompanied by both of Violet's grandsons, and so he lowered his head again. "Yes, Sir," he muttered.

"It's all right." A voice to his right. "I'll look after him."

He turned and looked down upon the pale, fragile face of Tobias Marsh.

"So, I guess you drew the short straw, huh, Toby?"

They were standing at the far end of a sweeping lawn that led downhill away from the house. Straight ahead lay a wide stretch of water, and in the distance to the far left, Downtown Vancouver glittered like a beautiful and unreachable Valhalla. Mark's ill mood had returned, the core indignant, poisoning him with outrage. Delacour had done the wise thing, of course. Right now he was definitely persona non grata in the Marsh House.

"Actually—" Marsh hesitated for a moment. "I volunteered."

Mark snorted. "What, to stand out here in the cold? Wouldn't you rather know what's going on in there?"

"I know what's going on in there, and quite frankly—"

"You'd rather not?"

The other man let out a sigh. He seemed edgy, nervous. "I take it you read the letter from our Grand Father?"

"You mean Weiss, and that 'My beloved children, ah, screw it, I'm going to kill you all' memo he sent out? Yeah, I read it." He looked down, saw that Marsh was staring at him, astonished. He grinned. "Oh, come on, Toby, how can he kill us when we're already dead?" The last two words came out bitter and he attempted to calm down. Bad enough he'd been out of control once on this trip. "My apologies," he added. "I'm being a jerk."

"It's—it's all right. The situation is affecting us all."

"Yeah. And I guess I picked a real good time to join the club." He worked on his smile, softened it a little, put his hands in his tailored woolen coat pockets and started to walk slowly along the periphery of the lawn. "So, tell me, Tobias. How did you become a vampire?"

"Nobody told you?"

"Don't forget, I'm new. Something about a plague, wasn't it?"

Toby nodded, keeping pace. "In 1665. It took Mother first. Then my sister's husband and their child. And when we all started to get sick..."

"That must have been a bad time."

"It was."

Mark glanced up toward a starlit sky. So much for trying to lighten things up. He began to wish fervently he was back in California.

"Do you—do you mind if I ask you something?"

Caught off guard, distracted, he shook his head. "Not at all. Ask away."

"What do *you* remember, about your becoming?"

He stopped walking because the core was now knocking hard on the inside of his skull. Time to pay attention. He cocked his head, stared hard at Marsh. "Not much," he lied, "other than... it was traumatic. I remember that."

"I could help you," Tobias said. "If you're able to remember a little, where it happened, a face—"

"And what if I don't want to remember?" He spotted a short flight of stone steps leading down toward another patch of lawn, and the water. He took his hands out of his pockets and started to walk again.

"Mark, you mustn't be afraid. Surely it would be better if you knew."

It's not fear, Toby. Hell, no. Try howling, catastrophic rage, instead. Try that.

He smiled. The man was following him down the steps, out of sight of the house. "You think so?" He kept his voice light. Inside, the core had already told him how to kill the man in six different ways. Look at his eyes. Read him. He knows who you are. *He knows.* "And how could you help me any better than the others, Toby?" He reached the bottom of the steps and waited.

"Well, some things I already see. Your strength, for instance—"

Told you.

Mark closed his eyes while Tobias, still on the approach, continued, utterly oblivious and warming to his subject, still intent on yanking his chain.

"—it's quite incredible. Like you had an encounter with an Elder. In fact, I'm certain of it."

See? Told you.

"An Elder, huh?" The other man had reached the base of the steps. Mark stepped close, and looked down at a pair of eyes that shone like polished black coals. Inside, he was flailing on a tide of anger, pushed forward by an indignant core, and was attempting to bargain desperately with an unrecognizable currency. "How do you know that?" he whispered.

Toby was staring at him, his face narrow and pale, and his posture changed slightly, shoulders squared, tensed. Physically and mentally braced. Yeah. Like he fucking knew.

"I'm—I'm empathic."

And whatever leash Mark had been able to muster internally, finally snapped. The core had had enough. He reached up quickly, grabbed Toby's collar at the neck, his knuckles now pressed against the flesh of the man's throat. Touch. He didn't care. "Then it's time to stop playing games." His voice was brittle and hard, and so full of menace he barely recognized it. Malevolence rose like bile in his throat, bitter and murderous and bullying, rejoicing at the fragility of the one he now held in his grasp.

"Mark—"

He dragged the man over to the steps and pushed him down, slid his hand past the collar until he reached the nape of the neck, then gripped and locked his fingers in thick strands of jet-black hair, while his inner battle with the core had become a bloody, knock-down drag-out fight. "Tell me what you see," he growled. "Tell me."

"You're stronger than grandmother, and you're afraid—"

He shook Toby once, twice, like a rag doll it was so easy. "No, Tobias, I am not." The fire roared. The big secret he was supposed to keep, about his ancestry, he felt the wall around it dissolve while his fury grew. He was tired of hiding, sick of lying, exhausted by holding it all back. "It isn't fear, it's hate. Do you see?" It felt good, to do this. It was a release.

"Mark—" the voice seemed so far away. "Please don't—"

"You wanted to know." He shook him again. "Didn't you."

"Yes—"

He was out of control. Completely. And the chaos was seductive, willing him to let go and give the core more of his rage, empowering it toward an act of terrible violence. Flailing, near helpless and grasping at straws, he made a desperate deal, and came up with the only possible alternative that was acceptable to the raging monster inside. Blood, he needed blood. He pushed the other man down against the steps, attempted to gauge his resistance, and saw a mind that lay wide open. He leaned in and gripped Toby's shoulders. He'd never kissed a male vampire before, and this time the skin, the flesh of the lips, yielding, responsive, felt cold. So delightfully cold.

He met no resistance. None. His fingers slid deftly to the collar, worked loose and slid apart the knot of the silk tie. *Not the throat,* the core instructed him. So he began on the shirt buttons, expertly opening them one by one, revealing the pale flesh beneath. Still no resistance. It was his way in, and it would be Toby's downfall. He pulled away from the kiss. Toby began to tremble and was now gazing at him with rapt adoration. It was a look that astonished Mark, stopping him in his tracks and making him fight desperately for calm. And after a long moment, "I'm going to show you who did this to me," he whispered, his lips brushing light as a feather against Toby's ear. "I'm going to show you everything."

Fear, excitement, hunger, and arousal, a miasma that hung between them as he slowly pushed Toby's head away from him until his back arched, and Mark leaned in, settling on an area of flesh just below the collarbone. He heard the man gasp. Still no resistance, while the bite connected with the somnolent heartbeat, the slight catch of breath, the tension in the musculature and the dizzy mix of terror and delight. The pathway to bind the will lay there as promised, wholly recognizable and so the core leapt eagerly for it, proud of its own role in this terrible act.

Now, he felt resistance.

"Mark, no—"

He felt the mental push, intensified and panicked, and so he pushed back. He felt a hand on his shoulder, attempting to fend him off.

"Mark. Please, there's no need—"

Too late. No longer a push, he wielded a mental spike, and drove it in hard, felt the will collapse, heard Toby cry out. There was no pleasure in it, none, and Mark knew he'd stepped over a line. Way over. And the full weight of three hundred and fifty years of scattered thought and memory slammed into his head like a wrecking ball. In shock, he withdrew and dropped Toby like a hot brick onto the steps. Watched him crumple at his feet. Wanted to weep and laugh, all at the same time, giddy like a madman. Instead, he fell into a silence bound tight with barbed wires of guilt, while the core got busy, rounding up the mirror of Toby's psyche and pushing it into the confines of a small box, all nice and tidy, something it could peruse at a later date. But he'd almost killed him. Just like that. Oh God. Instead, he wondered if he might have done something worse.

Toby was struggling on the ground, so he reached down and took his hand. There were no big secrets between them now. Not any more. "I shouldn't have done that," he said, pulling the man to his feet.

Those same eyes regarded him, now full of hurt and reproach. "I would have done anything, anything you asked."

"I know that now." The core had backed off, bloated and satisfied, leaving him with the bitter aftermath and ashes on his tongue. "And you're going to have to tell me exactly what I've done to you, and what this means," he said, and even though he knew, he wanted Toby to spell it out. Supporting him with one arm, he reached forward and idly brushed dust from the man's shoulder.

"What you did—it means I'm bound to you. It's enforced loyalty, a form of slavery, and it's irrevocable. It's usually offered as a punishment." The man looked away. "I didn't know it was Deacon."

Mark winced. "Toby, I'm sorry."

"No. I put myself in danger."

Yes. You did. "It isn't your fault."

The man wavered, took a deep, slow breath. "He tortured you. I felt some of the pain. Why did he do that? It's forbidden."

Mark shook his head. "I don't know. But this does not go in your records. Neither does it reach the ears of your grandmother." He watched the man struggle with his shirt buttons and straighten his tie into a neat Windsor knot despite his shaking hands. "And I'm sorry you had no choice."

Toby appeared able to stand on his own two feet, so Mark let him go. "I chose to be here," the man said.

"Even so." He looked back up the steps toward the house for a moment, and then down at his feet. "I was… I was going to kill you. And this was the only other response I could think of."

A nervous flick of a smile. "I know. Mark, your fear—" he held up his hand as Mark protested. "Wait. Hear me out. Your fear isn't borne of Deacon. I understand that now. It's something more important. It's about what you're becoming."

"And what am I becoming, Toby?" He felt the irritation of the core in his voice. Fear. Such a pathetic word. It could be nothing but a weakness.

"I don't know."

Mark stared out over the water. "So, what happens now?" Up above, he could see stars. It all looked so calm and serene out there, making what he'd just done seem all the more obscene.

"Whatever you want."

Mark nodded. Bound. Unquestionable loyalty. He was responsible for Toby now. "Right now, you stay here, then," he said, "with your family." He turned away from the bay, kept his face bland as he headed toward the steps, practice for the mask he'd soon have to wear. At the top he gestured toward a gap in the trees, toward the lit windows of the house. "And you need to start paying attention. You're in danger. We all are."

Toby followed him, his posture and voice now carrying an easy deference. "No more shying away from meetings."

Mark snorted. "Exactly." *Look where* that *got you.* "What about Violet? Is she going to start taking all this seriously?"

"That'll depend on how persuasive Delacour is."

He shrugged. "Well, she doesn't strike me as being stupid." The other man gave him a look that assured him the old lady was anything but. It made him wonder how long Toby would be able to keep hidden what had happened between them, not to mention how she'd react. Somewhere down the line there'd be a reckoning. Delacour and the others thought he was in the hole just because of the girl, whereas instead he might have messed up this entire trip, for all concerned.

He felt exhausted all of a sudden. But at least the core had settled, was content, no longer at war. This was the first peaceful moment he'd had since they'd set out yesterday. He took a deep breath, let all the scents of the surroundings—ozone, pine trees, distant smog, and sea salt—lull him into a state of calm. He looked down at his three-hundred-and-fifty-year-old companion, reached forward, swept away a lock of hair and kissed him lightly on the forehead. "Walk with me." He offered his arm. "I want you to tell me what it was like for you. In the beginning."

CHAPTER 10
GILLES

They emerged around 3 a.m. to a sky that was heavy with clouds lit faintly by the city across the water. The air was crisp, cold. It felt good to be outside, away from that cloistered room full of people and the attendant mental tug of war. Barely half of Gilles' attention had been on the meeting anyway, while the other half puzzled over the disgraced Gannon. That early morning behavior yesterday had left Violet fuming and had shocked him, until he told himself it shouldn't have. It was only five weeks and the man had the appetite of a T. rex. What did they expect? They were getting sloppy, complacent, and that was worrying, especially now. Delacour's attitude toward the man was also continuing to confound, by keeping the immediate progeny of a long-term antagonist on a very loose leash.

As for the meeting, they'd had a hard time convincing Violet that Weiss's threat had teeth, and the sanctuary massacre wasn't a local dispute. Once again, he suspected the deaths in the desert would have held more impact had they belonged to an older, more established house—Goran's or Nakamura's, and not Delacour's rag tag assembly of loose and untidy connections.

He also figured he now had a better idea of what Delacour sought to gain, but perhaps the whole thing had been a complete waste of time. Houston had complained as such, already ill at ease about being here and not on guard at home. And although Delacour had told them a direct attack on their House right now was unlikely, Gilles wasn't Delacour and didn't have his protective brand of self-assurance.

At the far end of a huge, sweeping lawn, he spied the errant, new addition to their motley group of outcasts, gradually walking toward the house in the company of Tobias Marsh. He studied the body language—at ease, like two old friends taking a stroll in the garden. Warm laughter drifted toward him and he frowned. The Gannon natural charm had been busy. Still, he considered a vampire as old as Marsh should be able to take care of himself; he'd at least be partially aware of the webs their troublesome newcomer was spinning. In some ways it was a pity the Marshes didn't know Mark's pedigree. He would have liked to see the looks on their faces.

Movement behind him interrupted his thoughts.

"Pity she doesn't know."

Gilles glanced back over his shoulder. Houston was a short distance away, looking down toward the lawn. He smiled. "I was thinking the same thing."

The other man gestured toward the two figures walking toward them and narrowed his eyes. "I'm wondering why he didn't try anything yesterday. Why he didn't fight back."

Gilles nodded. "When you hit him? Well, we both know he rolled with the punches. Maybe he figured you were getting him out of trouble."

Houston stepped up alongside him. His frown deepened. "Yeah, and there'll be more where that came from, I can feel it. And what about that cloud of gloom, right after? It permeated the entire house."

"You felt that, too?"

The other man nodded. "Never piss off an Elder, right?"

He was about to answer until he looked out toward the garden. Gannon and Marsh were still quite a distance away, but close enough to be within earshot, and so conversation ceased. Gilles glanced at his colleague, whose troubled features lay at odds with his usual easy, pragmatic approach to everything. Dealing with Gannon was something they could both do without right now, in the light of the gathering storm. At the end of the day, Gilles was all for a quiet life, one that was afforded him every now and then, but apparently, right now, it was not to be.

By the time the two men on the lawn had reached the steps, Delacour was outside and saying goodbye to their hosts. It was time to leave. He watched Gannon and Tobias Marsh clasp hands and say their farewells, and he took careful note of the touch—Gannon was getting bolder, more accomplished in that respect—and he found himself dearly wanting to know what they had been talking about, out there in the dark.

Back in the limousine, they sat in silence.

Houston bore equal amounts of relief and anticipation on his features now that they were going back home, Delacour appeared deep in thought, and Gannon was staring out the window, his mental brick wall a mile high. The storm had swept in once again and rain was hammering hard on the roof of the vehicle as their driver picked his way along streets awash with runoff.

"Well, gentlemen," Delacour said eventually, as they were crossing the bridge into Downtown. "Do you think we have an ally?"

"Hard to say," Gilles offered. "The Marshes have always liked their neutrality. I can't see Violet readily wanting to get her hands dirty."

"Let's take Violet out of the equation for a moment. What about the others?"

"William had the same M.O. as I did. We spent both nights trying to sound one another out," Gilles said. "But he seemed positive, willing to be proactive. The girls are wary, and Robert—"

"That stuffy old bastard is mad as a hornet," interrupted Houston, "thanks to him." He shot a hard look toward Gannon alongside him. It got the man's attention, and tore him away from his studious examination of the window.

Gilles glanced toward the ceiling of the vehicle for a moment. This had been brewing for a while. He shifted his weight forward and sat upright.

"Something on your mind, Houston?" Gannon sounded irritated. "Still pissed off I unearthed those cards you thought you'd buried?"

Gilles raised an eyebrow at that. The other man barked out a laugh. "Sure. It has nothing to do with bursting into your room and finding that girl naked, and you tearing at her throat and ready to rape her."

"But I didn't get that far. I wouldn't." The voice had shifted, sarcastic, smooth as silk. "Not when I have you to stop me."

"Oh, and that makes everything excusable—I should have put that bullet in your skull the night you arrived."

Gannon laughed. "You were going to kill me? While I was helpless?"

"Damn right I was. You really don't give a shit. You might have endangered this entire—"

"Gentlemen," Delacour said.

Houston stabbed a finger in Gannon's direction. "He shouldn't have come with us. He—"

Gilles reached forward and brushed his fingertips against Houston's forearm. He gave him a warning look once he'd got his attention, and the big man leaned back in his seat. "Sorry," he muttered.

And that was it. The end of it. At least while they were in the car. Gilles settled back, realizing he'd been about to spring forward and disrupt a physical altercation. Opposite him, anger was shimmering off Gannon and Houston like heat off a desert highway. But neither man was about to push it. Not after Delacour had given the word.

He sighed. They were bickering like street urchins. Things were beginning to speed up, get out of control, and the cloistered, stuffy Marshes were going to be part of the chaos, whether they liked it or not. Still, as far as Gilles could see, there was nothing to be done other than step up and try and keep pace.

On arriving home, it was a relief to find everything as they had left it. Neither Christina nor Saleem had anything earth shattering or terrible to report, and Eleanor was still out looking for Dimitra, so they all collapsed into their beds as dawn began to rise.

However, respite was brief, and sundown had Houston up close and pecking at his heels.

"He'll betray us all. Just you watch."

"If there's a remote chance he does, I don't think it will be on purpose," Gilles told him, trying to stay unruffled. He'd had an unsettling day of sleep and had a sour sensation in his belly that had so far refused to disappear. For Houston it seemed, Gannon was beginning to assume the role of super nemesis. They were outside, and he was at least thankful for that. He took a few steps along the concrete path that led to the beach, just to allow himself a little more personal space. "And do you really think Delacour would let him stay here if he thought that might happen?"

Footsteps rang on the path around the corner, and both men turned. Strong as he was, Gannon wasn't Saleem. A few moments and he came into view. He had one of the donors with him, and the look she was offering him was akin to worship. He heard his colleague mumble a curse, and then another as Gannon joined them after dismissing the girl.

After an awkward moment of silence, "Look, I'm not Deacon."

So, nothing wrong with his hearing. Gilles realized he was making a mental checklist, looking for weaknesses. That told him he had misgivings of his own. Trust lay like a baton between them and he was wary about picking it up, despite already having had a conversation with Delacour about that. About how important trust would be with this man. "I'm sorry, Mark," he said. He attempted a smile, but honesty also had its part to play. "I suppose we were a little taken aback by what happened at the Marshes'."

Houston, imperious as a block of granite, jabbed a finger. "I don't trust you." That word again.

Gannon gave him a flat look. "I know."

Anger rose like steam from the taller man, his thoughts stabbed forth, spiky and bitter. "Well, if you'll excuse me, *gentlemen,* I have work to do."

Gilles watched Houston storm off and then beckoned. "Come. Walk with me." He led Gannon down onto the beach, hoping the wide expanse of the shoreline and the gentle hiss of the sea would diffuse the situation. Soon, both pairs of boots were sinking in wet sand as the men strode along just short of the water's edge, and for a long while neither of them spoke. Gannon was the first to break the silence. His head was bowed, as though he was intent on watching every step he took.

"About what happened…"

Gilles looked at him. "Mark, confirm something for me. Delacour asked you to read the donors, didn't he?"

The other man nodded. "He wanted something on Robert, or Violet, indirectly. And I didn't expect—I didn't *realize* how easily it could get out of control. A strange place, people I didn't know. Every single one of them trying to get inside my head."

"Then I apologize," Gilles offered. "I feel I should be able to help you, but I don't know how."

Gannon threw him a glance. "Well, that makes two of us." He settled his gaze on the horizon. "You know, sometimes I think I have it. Control. But then it finds a way of slipping through my fingers."

"It'll come, with time."

"Christina doesn't know about this. She's going to be pissed."

Gilles grinned. "She'll know about it soon enough."

"You think I'm a screw-up."

"No, Mark. You're just new to this." And for a moment he thought he sensed a crack in the façade, as though the man was on the verge of telling him something new, something vital. But it came and went, and was replaced by an aura of despondency.

"I don't want this, Gilles. I want my life back."

"You know that isn't possible." He'd been waiting for this conversation. It was natural, inevitable, and Gilles wondered what had finally brought it to the surface. Obviously the trip to Vancouver had been more traumatic than he thought.

"I know. It's just… my Dad, we used to talk. I miss Mom, and Matthew…"

"Your younger brother."

"Yes. And the worst thing is, I could just pick up the phone and—" He'd stopped walking. He was spiraling down, Gilles could feel it like a poison cloud, swirling and enveloping them both.

"Mark."

"I know. I know I can't do that, and I'm sounding like some whiny, homesick little brat." The man took a deep breath, rammed his hands in his pockets and they began to walk again. Then, a little way further along the beach—

"So, what is all this, Gilles? What am I?"

"I wish I could tell you. Unfortunately, vampire or human, we're still left with the same existential questions. In short, I don't know any more than you do."

"Okay—so how about Deacon and Delacour? Why the animosity?"

"Deacon doesn't like loose ends."

After a snort of derision, "All that hierarchy and ancestry?"

Gilles nodded. "Essentially. Most of us here have no clue about our ancestry. Some of us were created in error. Without Delacour's protection, we'd all be hunted down and destroyed."

"And when he finds me, he's going to kill me all over again."

What to say? The conversation appeared hell bent on heading for despair at every turn. "Mark, before you died, did Deacon tell you why—"

"No."

It came out abrupt and cut him off. Now he was completely at a loss. They walked on in silence, and to give the man his due, Gannon appeared determined not to sink any further into his desultory mood. Thoughts flared occasionally from behind the wall, and Gilles perceived the man was giving himself quite a talking to.

Eventually, "Where are you from, Gilles? Mind if I ask?" The question arrived not long after they turned back toward the house.

"Marseilles, I was born in 1921. I became a vampire just after World War Two."

"In France? You don't have much of an accent. You speak French?"

"Yes. And some German and Italian, although they're a little rusty these days."

Gannon looked at him. "Danish Irish, by way of Michigan. No second languages."

"You don't have an accent, either." It got him a brief smile, and he thought perhaps they were making some headway, until—

"I want to destroy him, Gilles, and I've never wanted anything so much in my entire life."

That was the trouble with Gannon's blocking ability. One never knew what was coming. He kept his voice calm and firm. "You're angry, about your rebirth and how it was done. That may pass."

Gannon snorted. "It won't."

No point in arguing about that. Not right now. "Well," he said instead. "At least it's something you and Houston have in common." It got him another smile, and the thundercloud lifted a little as they continued to walk back to the house.

Over the next few nights, everything shifted into an uncomfortably high gear. It began with news that some of the independents were either dead or missing, followed by catastrophic news about Amsterdam. Now the Europeans were taking notice. Net traffic was infused with panic, phone calls were hysterical and angry, all of it culminating in a frightened call for help so much closer to home.

And now Gilles was standing inside Delacour's office. He'd waited until Saleem and Houston had moved into the next room to hammer out the logistics. They didn't have much time.

"All right, Gilles, what's on your mind?"

After a moment's hesitation, "I think taking Gannon along is a mistake."

"Your reasoning?"

"It might well be a trap, and as for Gannon, he struggled at the Marshes'. At the club he'll be coming up against vampires far more worldly, some of whom might recognize him for who he is. Also, we still don't know Deacon's position on all this. And some of his people frequent that place."

Delacour nodded. "Agreed. But if Miles's premonition is correct, assuming these are Weiss's assassins, they'll come here sooner or later and we need to make them think twice."

"The numbers haven't been verified. There might be more than we can deal with—"

"We can't ignore Miles's call for help. This is what we do. As for House Deacon, I really don't care if they get caught in the crossfire. As you say, we don't know where Deacon stands right now. Come on, Gilles, we've already discussed this."

"If—if this ends up in a war," Gilles winced, "won't we be doing precisely what Weiss wants us to do? Killing one another would save him a lot of time and trouble, wouldn't it?"

Delacour leaned back in his chair and stared at the ceiling. "I appreciate the bitter irony of this, but right now we don't have a choice. And—" the Elder added "—I don't see anyone else offering to help. Do you?"

Gilles reluctantly shook his head. "What about Gannon? Why can't he stay here?"

"No, he comes with us. We need his perception, he's backup for Christina and he'll be able to recognize his own kind. Maybe he'll be able to stop them from sticking their nose in and doing something they'll regret."

"You intend to use him, against his own House."

Delacour looked straight at him. "Right now, against Deacon and Weiss, he's the best weapon we've got."

CHAPTER 11
MARK

Mark stood by and watched as the others loaded up, still not one hundred percent sure of what was expected of him or how much influence he'd have.

"Hey." The voice belonged to Houston, who was scowling at him as usual. "You remember what you're supposed to be doing?"

He stepped forward. "Yes. Don't I get a weapon? I can use a rifle, and I had some sidearm training. Two weeks with some ex-military guys, when—"

A derisive laugh cut him off. "Actor boy. A whole two weeks, huh? And where are you going to hide it, in that fancy suit?"

Mark swallowed back a retort and looked down at the narrow cut of his jacket. Good point.

Houston shook his head. "You shouldn't need one. Remember, tonight you're just observing, and you're backup for Christina. First sign of trouble, you get her out of there, understand?"

He nodded and backed off. He had more than enough to think about: exit strategies, his role in this entire, crazy business. What they were planning was illegal, wasn't it? Killing people? But he wasn't part of that world any more. As for whom they might run into, the core was spinning like a carousel over the possibility of meeting up with his own killers—those who'd pulled him inside that limousine and set about draining him, who'd reveled in it, who'd cared nothing for how he suffered. So yeah, fuck illegal.

Once outside, he slid into the passenger seat of the rear vehicle on the driveway. Christina was alongside him, and one of their donors was at the wheel, all set to follow the car in front containing Delacour, Gilles, and Houston.

"You ready?" she asked him.

"I guess. You ever done this before?"

Christina shook her head. "Nope."

"Scared?"

"Yes."

"And where we're going, you've been there before?"

She nodded. "It's where we get some of our donors. There'll be vampires from all over. It won't just be Deacon's people. There are quite a few independents in Los Angeles." She smiled. "Don't worry. I'll look after you."

He cracked a grin. "Thanks." He kept his eyes on her as she looked out the window. Based on her reaction a few days ago, that business at the Marsh House hadn't come as a surprise to her, like she'd expected him to misbehave, and her attitude suggested she thought the others were at fault for not sharing her misgivings. It made him wonder what would have happened, or not, in this particular instance, if she had been with him on that journey. She certainly hadn't given him any grief over it, hadn't judged him, unless he had already been pre-judged. Then again, she didn't know about Toby. None of them did.

"What?" She'd caught him staring.

He gave her one of his camera smiles. "Nothing." He received a gentle prod in the ribs before she went back to gazing through the tinted glass. After that, everything seemed to speed up and they reached their destination far too soon. Not enough time to process everything, even though he'd gone through it with the others, again and again. Just not enough time.

Downtown Los Angeles, off Broadway. A side street containing a mismatch of medium and tall buildings of indiscriminate age, that hugged the sidewalk and closed out a sky that glowed with city lights, the line of windows and doorways broken up by the occasional patch of ground reserved for all day, eight dollar car parks. They drove past a dimly lit canopied entrance, but didn't stop until they were an entire block away. They got out of the car and he watched Christina smooth down the short skirt of her dress. She looked markedly different in high heels, bared shoulders, and draped silk crepe—beautiful, like a tiny, porcelain doll. *She shouldn't be here,* he thought.

The others climbed out of their vehicle a few yards ahead. A quick nod, a quiet word with the drivers, and they began to walk. The other three men disappeared, leaving Mark and Christina alone on the sidewalk. He offered his arm, she smiled, and they set off across the street in no particular hurry. Christina assumed a slight sway, not her usual gait. It would have brought a smile to his face if they weren't about such deadly business.

After a few paces, "Hey, I can feel something." He looked down, briefly disoriented.

His companion laughed. "Don't worry, it's not an earthquake. It's just the city." The rumble of a passing tram, voices, cars, hammering and demolition—history—all hushed into a whisper that oozed from the pavement and permeated every step. "You look good," she whispered.

"So do you."

Traffic was minimal, and they encountered only one pedestrian, a down-and-out, his head lowered, a skinny frame bundled in enough layers of clothing to protect him from a Michigan winter, a distinct contrast to Mark's dark, narrow cut, John Varvatos suit. He began to feel overdressed, but that changed when he looked ahead toward the canopied doorway. There, foot traffic was a little busier, and looked sharp.

"What if we can't get past the velvet rope?"

"You're so funny," she told him, her face like stone.

There was a short line at the door—two couples, and then a group of three women and two men. He tried not to look, but he could feel their eyes on him, hungry and wanting. He slowed, couldn't help it, looked at them and smiled. Christina had to drag him toward the door. "This isn't going to be a problem, is it?" Her voice was like the jab in the ribs in the car, earlier. It got his attention.

"I'm sorry. It's just, they want…"

"I know. It's why they're here. But you should be used to this level of crowd adoration."

"This is different." And it was. This was nothing like when he was alive, when he'd needed, craved the attention. Sure, it had pandered to his narcissism and stroked his ego. Yet there was still a level of intrusion that had made him uncomfortable. Whereas here, this new hunger, and what these people were offering, rode over everything.

He glanced back along the line. A girl, looking at him as if he was a god, whose dark hair shone like satin and who smelled of Chanel Cristalle, laundry detergent, moss, lilies, carnations, cigarette smoke, and gasoline. Yes, her. And then maybe her boyfriend, oh yeah—In-N-Out Burger, the tang of Thousand Island dressing, and Heineken, wood shavings, and engine oil. Hell, yeah. And that was just for starters. He turned back around and grinned. "I'll behave. I swear." Christina rolled her eyes.

The usual two obligatory, broad-shouldered men flanked the door, but there was no security check. Mark gave them a nod as he passed by them. They knew. All these humans knew what he was. And inside there were more. It had been difficult at the Marshes', but this—he was hit by a myriad of scents in the low-ceilinged hallway and he paused, taking in a breath. But only for a moment, before he shook it off and the mask came down, then he assumed a demeanor that would hopefully enable Christina to relax a little. What had Toby said, that he had the aura of an Elder? Well, now it was time to act like one, whatever that meant. And having only Violet Marsh and Delacour as a benchmark, he opted for a version of Delacour's relaxed insouciance.

He followed Christina as they worked their way around the periphery of the club. He heard music—percussive and loud—and laughter; he smelled sweat and cognac and whisky, and more poignant, blood.

"I hope Delacour knows what he's doing. You're going to attract a lot of attention here."

"I'll try and keep a low profile." *Try* being the operative word. He was having limited success on that score so far, although tonight he felt more assured, more in control than during the trip to Vancouver, while the monster inside, in its current guise of attention whore, was proving to be a little more benevolent.

They headed for a curved flight of carpeted stairs. Mark kept his eyes on the back of Christina's head as they passed others. He could feel the attention through the ebullient wash of thought directed at him, and via the core, basking like a bloated lizard behind his eyes.

As they moved, he tried to keep his mind open and pick up any sense of trouble. It proved a baffling exercise, as he had no clue of what he was looking for.

At the top of the stairs, a short distance away, stood another doorman. The VIP area.

"Are you ready for this?"

"Of course." He pushed his hands together slowly, trying to calm down.

"What about the humans we're looking for?"

He shrugged. "Right now, I've got nothing."

The doorman bowed and opened the door as they approached. The blood scent was stronger now. Cold for the most part, but there were suggestions that more personal, intimate ingestion was being enjoyed somewhere inside. Mark steeled himself for even more sensation. He was way out of his depth and sinking fast.

Four steps, through the doors and into the room beyond, and he breathed a sigh of relief. Downstairs he had sensed a crowd. Up here it was less congested—a mixture of hot and cold, human and vampire, in groups according to the seating arrangements—sets of low, dark leather couches around large, flat tables of a similar height. There was a bar straight ahead, and to the left, he saw people standing next to a glass-paneled wall, looking down at whatever lay below. He smiled. Funny how all meeting places looked the same when you boiled it down. This place reminded him of some of the clubs he'd frequented in West Hollywood.

His eyes did a quick sweep, and he saw a few of the room's inhabitants abruptly turning away, feigning disinterest. He frowned. "Female to the left, over by the window," he began. "Strapless red dress, the man standing next to her, dark suit, dark hair. They're Deacon's. And there are two more." He spoke as loudly as he dared. It was barely a whisper. The woman in red was staring at him openly. Something in her eyes wanted him to stop and change direction toward her, toward *kin*. As for the man alongside her—

"Four," Christina said.

"Yes." It became difficult to follow her, to keep his face impassive. His head felt like an ocean churning beneath the forces of a hurricane.

"Are you okay?"

Oh, she knew, his tiny little guardian. "I'm fine." He looked down at her and smiled. "And you said you'd protect me."

"No, I said I'd look after you. You don't need protecting."

"You don't think so?" He glanced back over his shoulder. The man and the woman were both staring at him, now. He raised an eyebrow. The man inclined his head, barely perceptible, but it was there. The core inside him demanded more, but he decided to quit while he was ahead. Christina was facing the bar, leading him by the arm. Hopefully she hadn't noticed that little interaction. They'd acknowledged him, and the man in particular had tagged him as a superior. The evening was becoming more complicated by the minute.

At the bar he declined. "I'm not hungry," he told his companion. In truth, his appetite was raw, tugging at him mercilessly, and of its own accord had already picked out a likely donor. However, he could hardly tell her he wasn't about to drink cold blood from a glass because Deacon would never do that, and therefore neither would he. He was playing a number of games here, he realized. He looked down at her, wondered exactly how much of his inner turmoil she could see. Gilles had told him never to underestimate Christina.

"Who are the other two?" she asked.

He told her. A tall, older guy, and another woman, with a group of other vampires in the far corner of the room, all of them trying to pretend he wasn't here. They were confounded and confused, and now something was lodged in the back of his throat. A whole array of emotions, ones he never expected to stick in his craw. Loyalty? Ownership? Family…

He needed something to clear his head. He shifted his attention and allowed the young man standing a few feet away with a group of donors to catch his eye. There followed a slight nod, a reciprocal acceptance, and a brief gesture toward the end of the bar.

"Would you excuse me?" he asked Christina.

"Why, what—" she stopped, seeing the donor already on the move. "Mark—"

"I won't be long. I promise."

"Make it quick," she growled. "Five minutes."

"You'll be okay?"

She snorted. "Just don't get into any trouble."

He nodded, and set off after a scent trail of paper, ink, Irish Spring soap, Marlboros, chicken Alfredo and white wine, and something cold, tart, like frozen cranberries.

Around the corner from the bar, an alcove, and within it a faint mix, a residue of scents. Others had been here.

"I knew you were hungry." The donor stepped back into shadow and slipped off his jacket.

"You can tell?" He pushed the man gently against the wall. Felt the body beneath his fingers shiver and let his hand linger, splayed across the man's chest while it absorbed the idyllic heat through the thin, smooth cotton of his shirt. Alive, that's how it felt. Even the faint smell of burned tobacco was a delicious reminder.

"Yes," the man whispered.

"Tell me your name." Mark raised his other hand, and his fingers began to weave through soft, jet-black hair. More beautiful heat, this time from the scalp.

"Angel."

"You a regular here, Angel?"

"I'm here twice a month, maybe. It depends—"

"On how much we take."

"Yes."

He looked yearningly into a pair of dark eyes, pupils wide in the gloom. "And you're trembling," he leaned forward, brushing his lips along the side of the man's jaw, "because you've just figured out how hungry I am. How much I want you."

"Yeah." The voice came out cracked and hoarse. "But it's okay. Take what you want. I don't care."

Fingers locked in the hair at the nape of the neck, and he pulled back the head. "Oh… I will." He drifted, already inside the man's head, stroking the pleasure sensors, but not too far. This wasn't the time to be greedy. "Is this really better than sex with your girlfriend?"

"It's different."

"Put your arms around me." Mark felt the other man's limbs slide around his torso and let out a soft gasp at the sudden increase in body heat. He wasted no more time. A thin, precise puncture, access to a crimson well of life. Angel relaxed, like they all did, utterly compliant. The core swelled, became needy, but not incessantly and he pushed back, easily. *Never too much,* he told it. *Never too much.* Christina's mantra. Fifteen seconds or thereabouts, the differing tempo of their heartbeats counted it out. He felt giddy and dazed from the pleasure of it, and pulled away reluctantly. "Thank you," he whispered.

Angel grinned, short of breath. "My pleasure."

Mark's arms were heavy and recalcitrant; they didn't want to let the man go.

"Hey—haven't I seen you before, on TV?"

It broke the spell. "A lot of people say that."

"Just one of those faces, huh?"

He nodded. "Yeah, I guess."

They shared another grin, then slowly disconnected. Mark stood back, leaned against the wall, and let the other man walk away while he chose to savor the moment and the rippling thrum of energy inside him. Five minutes, Christina had told him. Another deep breath and he moved out to rejoin her, but someone was standing there, partially blocking the way. The woman in the red dress. She inclined her head; it was awkward, like she wasn't sure if the gesture was required or not.

"He's one of my favorites," she said. "Did you know that?"

"Yes," he realized, and forced back a proprietary smile. He stepped closer, looked down at a pale, elegant face and brown eyes that carried the weight of decades. As old as Gilles. At least.

The eyes narrowed. Not anger—fear. "Who are you?"

He was only partially aware of the question, insignificant compared to whatever else was rattling inside his head. Why so easy in her presence? Where was that bitter hatred for all things connected to Deacon, so vigorously nurtured these past few weeks? Where was all his righteous anger? And where the hell was the woman's male companion? Mark's eyes flitted left and right. Saw nothing. Felt no imminent threat. Not to him.

He spoke quietly. "You need to go, you're in danger. And take the rest of the family with you. Now."

He stepped past her and re-entered the room. Confusion ripped through him as he made his way back toward Christina who was more or less where he'd left her, only now she wasn't alone. Four others were standing there with her, all equally cold-blooded. A rapid but hushed conversation ceased as he approached and he mentally chided himself for not paying attention and trying to pick up the gist of it. Not that he was in any state of mind to concentrate. The blood was meant to clear his head. Instead he was more adrift than ever.

Three of Christina's companions immediately melted away as he arrived. Unease shimmered in their wake. That left the slender, older man, who looked him in the eye, and gave him a slow, gracious bow, before rejoining his companions further along the bar.

"What was all that about?" he asked.

She gave him a tight, humorless smile. "Oh, they all want to know about you, Mark."

"I scare them," he realized.

"Despite their pretence, yes."

He frowned. *Not as much as I'm scaring myself right now.* He looked down at her, wondering if she'd seen anything of his encounter with the other woman.

"We need to find Miles." She appeared uncomfortable, annoyed. "If he's mistaken and we've picked the wrong night, we need to get you out of here."

He held back a tell-tale sigh of relief. He'd be out the door right now if he had his way. He focused on her, blocked out everything else, everyone else—the continuing distractions of nearby donors, and especially thoughts of his encounter with the female. That warning. Like he'd actually cared.

"Mark? What's wrong?" Christina was so dangerously perceptive and he had absolutely no idea what to say. Then, abruptly she drained her glass. "I see Miles. Let's go."

The office was uncluttered, and looked like a showcase: art on the walls, contemporary furniture, and certainly not the kind of place where any work got done. In fact, Mark sensed the opposite. There were traces of human sweat on the wide, polished desk, the scent of blood everywhere—some of it tainted, drawn via pain and struggle. Just that alone made him dislike the man now standing before them, who'd almost genuflected when he and Christina had approached and whose eyes, when he thought Mark wasn't paying attention, kept darting toward Christina accompanied by a barely hidden 'Who the fuck is this guy?' expression.

The man looked to be in his forties, medium height, narrow frame, sharp dresser, handsome—dark hair beginning to recede and cropped close to his head. He had predator written all over him. He was the kind of guy Mark had run into occasionally in his former occupation—a producer, or one of the bigger agents, someone used to calling the shots. So it felt odd and childishly gratifying to see this guy bowing his head.

He decided to opt for distance, and walked over toward the window while Christina dealt with him. Through tinted glass he could see the floor below, feel the muffled bass thud of music. He focused on the crowd, face by face. Where was this mysterious enemy they'd been promised? He was getting nothing, and the core, heavy as lead inside, appeared similarly baffled.

"I hope you didn't bring us here on a wild goose chase, Miles." Christina was also unimpressed.

Mark turned, saw the man smile.

"Hey, come on, premonition isn't an exact science—" Miles quickly shut off the charm, and thoughts in the room abruptly jagged with tension. "They're here. Don't you feel it?" He joined Mark at the window. "Down there. They have to be."

Mark narrowed his eyes, attempted to concentrate and not let the other man's anxiety drive him crazy, until finally he was drawn to a particular section of the club. "Some guys, and a woman, over by the billiard tables," he muttered. "I don't see..." There was no sense of hostility or foreboding, no inner alarm going off, and yet—

"What is it?" Christina asked.

Miles was staring into the room, sharing Mark's view. "There's something missing."

Of course. Mark felt like kicking himself. "Desire."

When he'd arrived at the club, desire had flicked out its forked tongue like a huge, fat snake, had gotten a taste of him and made its intentions perfectly clear. He'd felt it before they'd entered the building, while walking past that line of young men and women. They'd all displayed some form of it—want, desire, need, and the anticipation that went with it.

"They're not here for us," Christina said.

Miles nodded. "And yet I don't sense any actual intent."

Humans. It should have been easy. "I want to go down there," Mark told them. "Get closer." He looked at Christina.

She held up a hand. "Wait, I need to tell Delacour. Mark, wait—"

But he was already on the move, out of the office, back into the VIP room and heading for the stairs. Why the rush? Anything that distracted him and drew him away from the other storm brewing in his head, and if it turned out to be dangerous, then fuck it. He didn't care. And he almost reached the door to the floor below when someone blocked his path.

"Where are you going?" The question was asked pleasantly enough. It was the dark-haired vampire. Red Dress's male companion. So close, the recognition, the blood tie, his own kind, it was stunning.

Mark blinked. "Downstairs," he answered. "Excuse me." He stepped to the left, found his path blocked once more.

"No. You're coming with me." Matter of fact, not in the least bit threatening, like it was a given. The man even wore the beginnings of a smile. Same height, similar build, he looked a little older but not by much. As for his generation—somewhat lower, and yet still not giving an inch when Mark brought his will to bear.

"Mark!" yelled Christina, arriving behind him.

And while the other man was momentarily distracted, Mark ducked back to the right, slipped out the door, past the doorman, and a smile crept across his face as he descended the carpeted stairs.

CHAPTER 12
GILLES

An endless stream of concrete ribbons that connected and pulled together a thousand communities, the mighty city of Los Angeles had barely laid claim to the land it rested on, and its recent, sun-baked history lay thin, a polite whisper beneath his feet. Profoundly grateful this wasn't an ancient city ebullient with echoes, he tried desperately to focus on what was happening across the street… until everything he'd been afraid of, every misgiving he'd had, began to coalesce. It began with a vague sense of unease, and ended with a hushed staccato conversation between Houston and Delacour on the radio.

Six men, one woman inside. Gannon had jumped the gun, but had somehow managed to verify their targets and now one of them was heading out front.

"Now," Delacour whispered.

Gilles turned, but not toward the front of the building. Instead he took a step back and pushed—sideways, until the air shifted, became cold, and the surrounding walls took on the appearance of faded bones. Alongside him, out in the real world, Delacour's iridescent edges dazzled and shimmered.

Ghosting, his Elder called it, a trick only Gilles could perform—stepping through a twilight boundary and traveling within the extremities of his past, rendering him quite invisible but utterly at the mercy of his memories. It took a couple of paces to re-orient himself, and once done he headed out unseen. He wondered what would follow in his shadow on this occasion, for something always did.

As he approached the street corner, he caught the smell of goatskin and whispered a sigh of relief. Not the war this time or the heart-wrenching death of his mother. This time the memory choosing to stalk him was innocuous and mundane, borne on the scent of animal skin, vegetable dyes, and hot dust pushed through the cracks in the windows by the Mistral. It was Marseilles; the bookbinder. He glanced down at his hands—they looked younger, the palms now pigment-stained, and he smiled. A fond memory. Still, it wouldn't pay to linger and let it get too firm a grip.

Across the street, his quarry was in sharp relief—a flare of orange and red against a broad wash of gray, so Gilles headed in that direction. The man strode purposefully, turned the corner of the building that housed the club, and walked diagonally across a narrow side street toward a line of vehicles tucked and hidden between high walls. The dark heat of another human oozed from the window of one of the cars, accompanied by the stomach-lurching scent of gasoline. "Now?"

The quarry's voice was distorted through the veil. "No. It's too late. Start her up, take her around the front."

Only two paces away, Gilles watched the vehicle ease out of its parking space. He then shifted his attention to the shimmering glow of the man in front of him. Houston could pick off the man in the car at some point, but this one—this one would be down to him. Had the man committed murder already? At the sanctuary? A positive answer would allow for justification, but this was hardly the time for polite questions and attacks of conscience. Instead, it was time for speed, and the need for it overrode everything else.

He turned and pushed, emerging from his gray sanctuary into the alley as the car headed toward the street. He saw the man before him turn slightly and register surprise. But it was too late. Gilles' back leg sweep knocked him off his feet and slammed his shoulder hard on the pavement. A fist followed, plunging downward and embedding in the man's throat, crushing the windpipe. Gilles backed off, left the man to choke. Not a pleasant way to die, but this was far from a pleasant business.

He watched the car, now turning onto the main street. He whispered into his radio, told the others about the gasoline, then reached down and dragged the still-dying man along the concrete and pushed him behind a small, overflowing dumpster. He counted three other vehicles and made sure they were empty before heading toward the rear of the building. He tried to imagine how Gannon and Christina were faring inside. So far, no obvious alarms had been raised, but that didn't mean a thing.

Around the corner, he found two exits, one from the kitchen, and another a few yards further along—a back entrance to the club proper. He kept his distance, found some cover, and waited. No point in ghosting unless it was absolutely necessary. He'd gotten lucky with that last memory. Odds were that something more sinister would be waiting to latch onto him next time, and the hooks would be deeper. So instead he settled in amongst the available shadow, where he had a clear view of the back of the club, and waited for more instruction. There was a sour taste at the back of his throat. This was deadly business they were about, and the sooner it was over, the better he would feel.

Another minute and Delacour began to rattle out descriptions of six others, then told Gilles they were going in. With at least three exits to cover, he ran through variants of what might happen next. Some of his thoughts ran to the mayhem Gannon might be causing, but he did his best to shut it off. It was a distraction he could ill afford.

He heard gunfire and the screeching of tires. Movement. The door to the kitchen. A male vampire, dark-haired, with a face that looked very familiar, walking with a purpose, followed a few moments later by a male human that fit one of the descriptions. They both headed for the parked vehicles around the side of the building. Together? He didn't think so, despite the vampire's identity. The human paused, was pulling a weapon, but Gilles had already removed two throwing daggers from his vest and had taken a step forward. The man went down before he could get a shot off, blades hammered in to the hilt.

The other vampire didn't break his stride until he reached the corner. "Do you ever miss, Gilles?" The man offered him a smile before stepping quickly out of sight.

"Wait—" he began, but now a verbal cue came quietly through his earpiece, and the prickling feeling at the base of his skull was telling him things were heating up inside, too.

He grabbed the fallen man, collected his firearm, and retrieved his own weapons. He had managed to hide the second body just before a fast, high wall of black and chrome bore down on him, the vehicle's engine roaring, giving him one split second to dive out of the way. The vehicle, a black Escalade, swept past, tires squealing as it turned and disappeared around the far corner of the club.

Gilles scrambled to his feet, telling the others about the escapee. "Deacon's man—it was Rory."

"Nice of him to stick around and help out," grumbled Houston.

"All right, move in," ordered Delacour. "We managed to lure them out front. Mark and Christina are out, and they're safe. I think we've accounted for everyone, but watch your step."

Gilles moved toward the rear door and hugged the wall as patrons began to spill out. The atmosphere jumped with fear, chatter, and confusion, a heady mix of vampire and human. He kept close to the doorway and watched. No one was paying him the slightest bit of attention. And taking that as his cue, he slipped inside the building.

He'd been to the club before and had a reasonable sense of the interior layout. He picked another spot close to the wall as people pushed past, and his eyes took in human faces and body language. They'd have to be quick, before the cops arrived. Two dead bodies out the back already, no doubt some inside, and whatever mess lay out front.

As the crowd thinned, he moved further in. The evacuation appeared to have been orderly, going off the tidiness of the interior. Just the one overturned table, and broken glass by one of the interior doors. However, panic and uncertainty hung there like a cloud. He peered inside the cavernous dancehall, then headed toward the front door. No sign of anyone, donor or otherwise, until he arrived at the foyer, where a small crowd had gathered, all vampire: Delacour and Miles, the club manager, among them.

"You assured me you'd be discreet." Miles was staring down at the body of a female human. A pale gray pistol lay alongside her, and the sight and scent of blood was overpowering, mesmerizing. None of those standing witness could take their eyes off it.

Gilles frowned. "It looks like she pulled the trigger." He leaned forward to get a better look, while shaking off the pull of hunger and thirst.

"She did. I saw it," said a slender, blonde girl alongside Miles. He caught the look on her face, shock and yearning, both at odds with one another.

"Anyone touch anything?" Delacour asked. After a few shakes of the head from those surrounding him, "Good." He crouched alongside Gilles, performed a quick search on the body, his fingers light and careful. "Miles, you need to let the police see this one, and the three outside by the truck. We'll take care of the one upstairs. That way it'll keep all the action at the front door. Give you an easier yarn to spin."

"There are two dead out back," Gilles said.

Miles offered him a grimace of distaste. He then nodded toward two male vampires standing nearby and immediately they set off for the rear door.

Gilles' attention returned to the corpse. One shot to the head, it had taken the back of her skull clean off and splattered blood and brains all over the carpet. Suicide? After everything had started to head south? Eleanor would know perhaps, but Eleanor wasn't here. It was one hell of a mess.

Houston arrived through an interior door. He carried the body of a man over his shoulder. Delacour set off after him, but not before telling Gilles to take an alternate route back to their vehicle, just in case. "Keep your radio on."

He acceded and was about to set off. Instead, he stalled. "Miles." He beckoned the man away from the siren song of the dead woman's blood. "What was Rory doing here?" And when the other man's eyes shifted away, "Well?"

"I don't know. Look, I don't want to get involved—"

"This isn't about us and Deacon, Miles. And don't tell me he was here socializing."

Miles looked at him. "He said—he told me he was here to meet someone."

"Who?"

"He didn't say. You know him. He isn't exactly the talkative type."

Gilles nodded. He also knew Miles wasn't being completely forthcoming. But there wasn't time, not now, when the sirens were howling and getting closer by the second.

"Go on. I'll handle it," said the other man.

"You sure?"

"Yes. You're not one of my staff, or a customer for that matter. You don't fit, so get the hell out of here."

Gilles couldn't argue with that. He backed off and retraced his steps toward the rear exit. Outside, he saw the two henchmen slamming the doors shut on a dark blue Chevy van before sliding into the driver and passenger seats up front. Miles's clean-up crew. Their casual attitude made him wonder exactly how often they engaged in body disposal. And yet it was Delacour's group who had the so-called reputation. He let out an exclamation of disgust. Miles hadn't exactly been oozing gratitude, either.

He set off toward the southeast, away from the sirens, away from their rendezvous point until he felt it safe to backtrack and activate the radio. He experienced a strong sense of relief as he heard Houston telling him they were clear of the scene, and that Christina and Gannon's driver had reported in.

As for what they'd achieved, it appeared difficult to quantify. Their enemy had been woefully ill-equipped. What was it then, a test of strength? It was an inefficient and callous use of manpower if that was the case. None of it felt right, and he was sure the others would share his misgivings. Something to discuss, then, back at the House.

He left a dark side street and crossed a wide, tree-lined thoroughfare under the flat, pale orange light of street lamps. A man shuffled past, a hobo, dressed in so many layers he seemed misshapen. He was accompanied by a familiar stench—sweat, booze, urine, and age. Age that, for a moment, seemed to step beyond the boundaries of the city itself.

But who could be older than the city? Having already passed by the man, Gilles stopped and turned.

The man was gone.

CHAPTER 13
MARK

"Shit."

Mark braced himself as the car lurched around a corner, while his mind reeled with sensation from the recent staccato punch of a bullet through glass and the hot splatter of blood on the sidewalk as he and Christina had dashed out of the club and raced toward their vehicle. He looked back through the rear window at the rapidly diminishing towers of Downtown.

Christina was giving rapid instructions to their driver. "Continue west. We'll turn south farther on."

Mark kept his eyes on the road behind them. Inside, his mind churned, horrified at what he'd just done. He'd been right in the middle of it, his own hands dirtier than Christina realized, and it didn't seem right that they were able to speed away from it, just like that. Not when he had identified the targets. Not when the core had stepped up and done something he hadn't thought possible.

"Christina, I think I killed the woman with the gun."

They were moving west along one of the less-populated roads south of Wilshire. Traffic was intermittent, just as well with the speed they were traveling. Twice, his head brushed the roof lining of the car as they bounced over drainage dips in the uneven pavement.

"What do you mean, you think you did?"

"I told her to do it. It was easy. I didn't want her to shoot you." He faltered as the car went over another bump. "We might want to slow down," he offered. "We don't need to get pulled over and I don't think—"

He stopped, then shifted his attention to Christina's side of the car. Too late.

Something large and heavy slammed into them and all at once Mark's entire world consisted of the sound of punctured metal and broken glass. The momentum threw him sideways, then around and backward as the front passenger door buckled sharply inward.

Everything stopped. He felt pinned, imprisoned, while the damaged vehicle popped and cracked all around him. He struggled with his seat belt. "Christina!" She was pushed against him, showered in glass, her limbs and shoulder partially hidden in the folds of split, tortured metal. He looked into the front. Their donor's head was at an odd angle in the driver's seat, the seat itself pushed into the center of the car. The airbags had deployed and the interior was full of dust. Free of the belt, Mark attempted to move. He thought he could hear something, or someone, outside. There was a crack of a pistol and Christina's body jumped.

He turned around and began to hammer at the back window. Already damaged, it shattered easily and he began crawl out of the tight confines of the car. He smelled oil, gas, and blood. Almost free, he felt a sharp punch on the back of his shoulder, and the momentum of it pushed him off the trunk of the car and sent him sprawling onto the pavement. The accompanying sound told him he'd just been shot. The pain was excruciating. He tried desperately to block it, but in the end there was no need. The core had taken over.

He crawled toward Christina. He couldn't get to her. There was a huge vehicle, a black SUV, its front end all crunched up and partially imbedded in her side of the car. On the opposite side, a light pole had proved immovable and the sedan had partially wrapped itself around it.

Movement. He ducked, and the pistol cracked once more. He dashed around the other side of the larger vehicle and saw a man standing there, braced, gun at the ready.

"You *are* coming with me," the man said.

Mark didn't stop. He ran headlong into the guy and drove him down onto the sidewalk. The weapon clattered on concrete. Up close, he recognized the dark hair and the lean face of Red Dress's companion. He didn't hesitate. He rose up and brought his knee sharply down onto the man's ribcage, then scrabbled for the gun. And he didn't stop until he'd fired every remaining bullet into the man's torso.

"The fuck I am," he gasped.

Sirens.

He dropped the weapon. Smoke was coming from beneath the buckled hood of the car and he stepped on top of it, then kicked his way through the windscreen. The donor's eyes stared out at him, lifeless.

"Christina!" He heard a groan. He crawled inside the vehicle and began to extract her from the wreckage. Parts of the car were embedded in her flesh and he had no time to be gentle. Finally, he managed to haul her out the back window. "I'm sorry," he whispered. "I'm sorry." He saw a distant flash of blue and red. He picked her up; she felt light, like a doll, and he began to move, found the nearest cross street, and with no means of contacting any of the others, he headed north with his precious, injured burden, away from the crash.

By the time he'd reached his intended destination, he reckoned it was too close to dawn for comfort. He was north of Wilshire, on a quiet street tucked away from the city hustle and bustle, inside a hallway in a hacienda-style block of apartments. If he'd made the wrong choice—

He tried the bell one more time and waited, while Christina stirred uneasily on his shoulder. His nostrils flared, caught a faint whiff of Issey Miyake perfume, and he let out a sigh of relief.

Muffled, from the other side of the door, "Who the fuck is it?"

"Molly. It's Mark. Mark Gannon. Please. You have to let me in."

There was a rattle of chains and locks. The door began to open. "You have to be kidding me. Where the hell have you—"

She stepped back.

Mark pushed his way in. He had no choice. "I'm sorry, Molly. I had nowhere else to go."

She hovered a few feet away, her arms folded across a navy blue silk robe, shocked into silence and pale as a ghost while he gently lowered Christina onto the rug in the hallway.

He frowned. Needed blood. He reached into his jacket and

pulled out his wallet. It felt damp. He opened it, pulled out a card, and handed it to Molly who took it with trembling fingers. He'd never seen her tremble. Ever.

"You need to get to a hospital," she began.

"No." He stared at her. "Molly, I need you to do this for me. I need you to get dressed, go outside, find a payphone, and dial that number. Give them the address but not the apartment number, okay? Then I need you to wait out there for a delivery. They don't need any cash, and there'll be no questions asked."

"This card. It's got blood on it."

"Yeah. It's probably mine. Please, Molly. No questions, don't call the cops. And hurry."

When she'd gone, he dashed around her apartment, closing every blind and curtain he could find. Then all he could do was make Christina comfortable, and wait.

"Blood," his companion whispered.

"On its way, but you can have some of mine," he said. She shook her head. He knew her reasons. His blood was Deacon's blood. She'd risk dying before taking any of that. Not to mention it might well make her feel worse, not better. They'd talked about that once—if the generation gap was too big, how it could be fatal.

He sat back in the dark, on the floor of Molly's hallway, Christina's head cradled in his lap, exhausted, dejected, feeling useless, going over his botched-up rescue while they waited. He could have grabbed the donor's radio. The guy might have had a smartphone, too. Right now, unless Christina was able to communicate somehow with Delacour, they had no discreet way of letting the others know they were safe, and he wasn't about to pick up Molly's landline. Even the call Molly was making out on the street was risky.

And then there was Molly. Could he trust her? What if she decided to call the cops instead? What if—?

Footsteps on the passageway outside. A key in the lock. He braced himself, got ready to move.

"So. What *is* this?" Molly shut the door, and held up a medium-sized, padded cool bag. "Have I just broken the law?" She appeared to have recovered a little.

Mark reached for the bag and opened it, then counted a dozen pouches stacked neatly inside. "It's blood." He gestured toward the interior of the apartment. "I closed all the blinds. They need to stay closed."

She hesitated for a moment, then crouched alongside as he fed one of the pouches to Christina. Her words came out fast, edgy. "Is she going to be okay? What happened tonight, Mark? Where have you been? We've all been worried—me, your family—and apart from the fact you look like you've been in a car accident, you look—you look ill."

"I have been in a car accident." He frowned, opened another of the pouches, and focused on feeding Christina for a moment. "Remember that night you dropped me off? On Sunset?"

She nodded.

"Something bad happened." Just looking at her brought it all back. That night. He'd been so full of it. Even when she'd thrown him out of the car, he'd still wanted to pin her against a wall and slide his hands underneath the silk shirt she was wearing. So cocksure and full of himself. Until he'd met Deacon.

"No shit. And that's it? That's all you can tell me?"

"It's difficult."

"And this girl. Doesn't she need a doctor?"

"No. Just this." He opened a third pouch.

Molly sat down, her back against the opposite wall. "Blood. Out of that bag there."

He nodded. They both watched Christina struggle to ingest. Mark made sure she took it all in, and whispered words of encouragement. "You mentioned my family," he said eventually. Christina was resting now and had curled up on her side. His senses told him she was starting to recover.

Molly shrugged, and narrowed her eyes. "I've had calls from your parents, your brother—"

"Matthew."

"Yeah, Matthew. Did you know he sounds just like you on the phone? But I'm guessing he's better looking."

"Baby brother, huh?" Mark shifted, trying to relax without disturbing Christina. "No way he's better looking." He attempted a smile. She didn't reciprocate.

"Why didn't you contact them? At least let them know you're okay."

He leaned back against the wall. "Molly, I am not, as you put it, okay."

"So, tell me about it. You always were a stubborn bastard, you know that?"

"Yeah." He smiled again, defeated. "Help me take off my jacket."

He reached forward and she moved to help him. He heard her gasp. "Oh, God, you're as cold as ice and there's blood all over your shirt."

"Yes. I got shot."

"Mark—"

He held up a hand. "Just bear with me." Reaching into the cool bag, he retrieved one of the pouches and pulled it open. His voice became dull, and matter of fact. "Let's start putting the pieces together." He took a swig from the pouch. "I look cold, as you put it. I am cold." He gestured along the hall. "I can't stand daylight any longer. Neither can Christina. We don't eat. We drink blood. We get shot and survive, same thing with car crashes."

A pause.

"What, you're vampires?"

"Sounds stupid, doesn't it?"

Molly backed off, returned to her crouched position on the opposite wall, and began to laugh. But her mirth was forced and it didn't last long. "What is it, Mark? Drugs? I shouldn't have thrown you out of the car—"

"Yes, you should. I was being an asshole. And no, it's not drugs."

She glared at him in the dark.

He swallowed. Remembered watching her car disappear in traffic. Remembered walking, and Deacon coming up behind him. All so fast. He felt a lump at the back of his throat. "Look, it's hard to explain," he stumbled over the words, "but I can't just call up and tell my parents—Hey, Mom, Dad, I'm okay…" He saw tears glistening, rolling down her face. "Molly, don't—"

"Fuck you, Mark. I shouldn't have kicked you out of the goddamned car!" She drew up her knees, pulled them under her chin.

Christina stirred on the floor. Her hand reached up, came between them, and rested on one of Molly's arms. "It's okay," she whispered. She sounded delirious. "I'll look after him."

He thought Molly would pull away, but she didn't. And for a while they all sat together in the dark, in silence. In the quiet, Mark felt the blood pulsing through him, restorative and invigorating, and despite the initial distaste of having to drink cold, he also felt proud of the restraint he'd shown. Deacon would have spilled Molly's blood without a second thought. He stole a glance at the woman who sat opposite him, realizing his own appetites had been pushed away, memories of his old life proving the stronger, holding back all thoughts of feasting.

He looked away. No. Not all thoughts.

"I need to rest," he told them both. "Right here." *No danger of any natural light here in the hallway,* he figured, frying him while he lay sleeping. Molly fetched him a pillow and a blanket, and he lay down. "Delacour," he said quietly to Christina.

"He knows," she told him.

Temporary oblivion beckoned.

On waking, he stretched, sat up, felt disoriented. He heard female voices, saw artificial light spilling through a crack in the door. He felt something hard on the floor beneath his hand; he picked it up, and held it in front of him between thumb and forefinger. A spent bullet. He grinned, rolled his shoulder, tested its mobility. Blood was dry and crusted down the front of his shirt. He probably should have taken it off, he realized. Soaked it in water. Too late.

He regained his feet, and pushed open the door. Beyond it, Christina and Molly were huddled together on the couch, watching TV like two eight-year-olds on a sleepover, Christina so pale and deceptively fragile next to his tanned, slender former manager. He gave Christina a hard look. She shrugged. He shook his head and went looking for the bathroom.

A few minutes later, he had finished washing the remnants of dried blood from his face and torso. He checked his shoulder in the mirror. With the exception of a slight discoloration, there was nothing to suggest his flesh had ever been pierced, and once he'd cleaned up, all other traces of last night's damage were completely gone. It made him wonder about the other guy. He'd gotten lucky, he knew that much. The man hadn't expected him to bull rush him like that. Had he killed him? It was doubtful. There hadn't been time to check, and—

You didn't want to.

A slight knock and the door opened. Molly stepped inside. She didn't look at him. Instead, she picked up his shirt, and checked the nametag on the collar.

"Expensive. And it's ruined. Your jacket, too."

He turned to face her. "Molly, did she force—"

"No." Now she looked at him. "I offered." Her eyes wandered lower, over his shoulders and torso.

Heat shimmered off her and his appetite leapt. He stepped closer so he could bask in it. He caught the faint notes of her perfume again, as well as toothpaste and a trace of cigarette smoke and coffee—two scents in particular he fondly remembered. He reached up, and gently traced the line of her chin. "You need to be more careful around us, Molly."

"I guess. But damn it, you're both so alluring."

His hand reached out, and explored the length of her collarbone. He could feel the tantalizing heat through his fingertips, and imagined the gesture a mere precursor before lifting her up and pressing her gently against the wall, the same hand slipping upward beneath her T-shirt, and cupping one of her breasts while he nuzzled at her throat—tongue, teeth searching, determining the perfect spot—

He stepped back, realized what he was doing, and turned away. "Don't come too close," he ordered. He watched her frown at him in the mirror.

"Whatever," she said, dropping the ruined shirt. "Christina told me to tell you, some guy called Houston will be here in ten minutes."

CHAPTER 14
GILLES

"So, what's our next move?" Houston rubbed his hands together, had a gleam in his eye.

Gilles let out an exaggerated sigh.

"Oh yeah, you, the reluctant assassin." The other man laughed.

"For now, we need to be on our guard," stated Delacour.

They were sitting on the sunken couches in the living room. Saleem was to his left, huddled over his laptop, a bundle of twitching energy, and at his right, Gannon and Christina were curled up together, inseparable since the attack on the club.

"We should be okay here," offered Saleem. "We're very well protected."

Delacour nodded. "It's when we're out in the open, that's where we're vulnerable. If I were in their shoes, I'd start picking us off, one by one. It's bound to be a tactic these people will use."

"So, when we leave the compound, from now on it's in twos," Gilles said.

"At least," added Delacour.

Houston folded his arms. "That's going to cramp my style."

"You don't have any style," Gilles remarked. They shared a grin.

"In the meantime," Delacour continued, "we need to find a way of getting Weiss to call off the hounds, or at least discover why he's so intent on destroying us."

"What's the point in knowing?" asked Houston. "I thought he'd just lost his mind?"

Saleem shot him a look. "Don't you *want* to know? Aren't you in the least bit curious?"

"What I'm curious about is Deacon, how he fits into all this," the big man answered. "Gilles said he thought he saw someone. Out on the street. But my money is still on Deacon pulling off this shit on his own. Let's face it. No one has seen Weiss for years. For all we know, Weiss is dead."

"Houston, I didn't know who or what that was." Gilles settled back. "It could well have been one of my memory flashbacks." He shrugged. "It happens sometimes."

"Weiss isn't dead." Delacour got to his feet, and went to stand at the window. "I'd know. And so would he."

All eyes turned to Gannon, and Gilles saw the man shift awkwardly, uncomfortable at being under scrutiny. Christina was stroking his hair idly, and a flick of her eyes told everyone she was guarding him like a mother bear would guard her cubs. That aside, Gilles sensed something between Gannon and Delacour. A tangled web of complicity and contention that hadn't been there before, that now drifted in the ether between them. The two had taken residence in Delacour's office yesterday evening, the night after the raid, and they'd been there for hours, locked in a conversation none of the others had been privy to, but one Gilles was determined to get to the bottom of, one way or another.

"All right," announced Delacour. "Eleanor is returning tonight. Houston, I want you to make sure her travel security is more than adequate. Christina, make sure she knows about everything that happened. Don't leave anything out." He frowned. "We're on high alert, everyone, so let's keep it that way. Everyone has their responsibilities, so let's all go double-check, make sure we're prepared."

Everyone nodded and murmured their assent, and the meeting was over.

He found Christina in one of the corridors, talking to a member of staff, making sure Eleanor's room was ready. "A word?"

"This sounds ominous, Gilles." She led him into her room. "What is it?"

"The meeting last night. Between Mark and Delacour. Any idea what it was about?"

"Ah." She sat down on the edge of her bed and gestured to an armchair close by.

Gilles folded himself into an overstuffed little monstrosity covered in pink chintz and waited.

"I don't know the outcome," she began, "but I have a good idea what it was about."

"Mark didn't discuss it?"

She shook her head. "We're close, but there are some things he just won't talk about."

He nodded. Maybe Delacour had told him to keep his mouth shut. "So, what are we looking at?"

"A couple of things. I could be wrong about the first, but not the second."

"I'll take that into account."

Christina leaned back, brought her feet up onto the bed. "Do you remember when he first came to us, Gilles? How full of hate he was?"

"Toward those who killed him, yes, I remember. And he told me quite recently that wouldn't change any time soon."

"But that was before we went to the club."

Gilles raised an eyebrow. "What changed?"

"Everything."

Unease crawled through his gut. "He met some of Deacon's people. That was to be expected."

Christina sat up. "Yes, but it wasn't what *he* expected."

It should hardly have come as a surprise. "So, he *does* feel kinship."

"Yes. Very much so. He feels… a sense of responsibility."

"As an Elder should, misplaced as it may be in this particular case." He frowned.

"He won't do anything to harm us, Gilles."

"Are you sure?"

"I'd stake my life on it."

"You might have to," he shot back, sharper than he intended. He was rewarded with one of her withering looks, the kind usually reserved for Houston.

"He's conflicted," she continued. "And I'm pretty sure it's why he asked Delacour if they could talk."

Gilles nodded. "Well, at least he's being honest." He let out a breath, thinking it was over.

"As for the other thing—"

Oh, here it comes. "What?"

"Promise me you'll keep it just between us?"

"Christina—"

"Delacour knows, but promise me all the same."

Curiosity getting the better of him, he sat up straight. "Very well, I promise."

She cleared her throat. "The woman you found dead, inside the club."

He nodded.

"Mark did that." She bit her lip. "He compelled her."

So, now he was a killer, too? "I thought Delacour told you both not to engage, to get out as fast as you could?"

"Oh, we were running, Gilles. We'd reached the foyer. She was chasing us. I heard a shot, it was close, and then I heard another. Mark was right behind me and he didn't even break his stride."

"You're absolutely sure it was him?"

"Yes." She looked away for a moment. "He told me it was easy."

"Like it was a game?" The idea rattled him.

"No, no. He was appalled. I think."

"You think."

"Hey, we got hit, right after he told me about it." Raised voice. Not good.

Gilles backed down. "Okay, I'm sorry." In the quiet moment that followed, he wondered just how much they were underestimating the man. Christina broke the silence.

"When we were in the club, before everything started, people were looking at him, Gilles. And it wasn't just because he was a stranger."

"They sensed his strength."

She nodded. "I thought he'd be a little nervous. We're all that way, at first."

Gilles attempted a smile. "But not him?"

"No. He walked in there like he belonged, like he owned the place and had done for centuries. His mannerisms, the look on his face, just the way he carried himself."

"And they all took notice."

"I felt like I was on the arm of a prince."

"Maybe you were."

Christina laughed, but then her face fell. "One of Deacon's people, not the man who attacked us, a woman. I thought I saw Mark talking to her."

Gilles couldn't keep the suspicion from flooding back. "I thought you both stayed together?"

She shook her head. "I let him go. Only for a few minutes. He hooked up with a donor."

"Did he, now."

"Yes. The donors were all over him, staring at him, they all had that look in their eyes. And it was on his way back toward me. I saw the woman intercept him. They may have passed a couple of sentences back and forth, no more than that."

"Hmm." He tried to stay objective. "It could have been nothing. Let's face it, if you were one of Deacon's people, wouldn't you be curious? And while I wouldn't have been quite so gauche to stride up and ask him who he was, someone like Houston, who can't bear the slightest bit of intrigue, would have for certain."

They both smiled.

"Maybe you should ask him about it," he continued. "It doesn't have to be a big deal, it probably wasn't." *Ask him, and then tell me.*

Christina nodded. "I will." She appeared conflicted.

"You trust him, and yet—" Gilles stood up, ready to leave. "You're a little afraid of him."

"Does that seem stupid?"

"No," he said. "The truth of the matter is, I think we all are."

He'd stripped off his boots, dropped them nearby, and now seawater oozed and swirled between his toes. The sea was calm, the waves slid lazily across the sand, and he wished he was in a similar state of tranquility. If Christina was right, about the meeting between Gannon and Delacour, it would certainly explain the prevailing mood. Gannon was no longer Delacour's puppet or avenging angel, and after what else she'd told him, it meant he was continuing to be impulsive and dangerous, too.

The family connection. It had to happen sooner or later. The individual strands of kinship were strong, or so he'd been informed. It was hard to think that way when their own small group was such a mismatch of bloodlines.

But Gannon was different. He was third generation, and where he stood in the grand scheme of things, everything was profoundly simple. Weiss, Deacon, then him. He was damned near royalty. Delacour must have been out of his mind to even consider using him. Although he had to have known this moment would come. Sixth generation, hundreds of years old, Delacour hadn't lasted this long by being stupid or delusional. So, obviously there was another game being played here.

Gilles took a deep breath, let his chest slowly expand, while his mind went over the conversation he'd had with Christina. She was a good judge of character, and she'd told him they could trust Gannon not to hurt them. But that was now. What would happen over time, once he'd had the opportunity to rub shoulders with more of his direct kin? And what would happen, gods forbid, if he ever ran into Deacon?

He collected his boots and began to walk, not liking where this particular train of thought was going, and it chased him all the way along the beach. That night, when he'd narrowly avoided being struck by Rory, Deacon's right-hand man, Gilles hadn't known until later that he'd been in pursuit of Gannon. He'd gone to extremes, too, which highly suggested he, or another, would try again. Deacon wanted his boy, and he was betting that Delacour wasn't about to hand him over on a plate. That left Gannon, and the rest of them for that matter, in one hell of a predicament.

CHAPTER 15
MINA

She walked along streets glittering with the aftermath of rain. She was immune to the chill in the air, but her hunched shoulders, hurried gait, and inexpensive, bulky woolen garment suggested otherwise. Her hair was scraped back and hidden under a cap, her face partially covered by plain, non-prescription lenses and unfashionable frames. And thus, she was invisible. Only the lack of condensation when she breathed was a giveaway, while others out on the street exhaled clouds of breath like frost dragons.

In midtown Manhattan, a few streets away from the billboards and bright lights, she crossed a tree-lined avenue, descended a short flight of steps, and pushed open a glass-paneled door. It was a quiet night—only a few patrons at the bar—and she walked toward a row of booths hunkered beneath blood-red walls covered in old photographs, their subjects smiling, brandishing various wind and brass instruments, their scrawled signatures decorating the immediate foreground.

At the fifth booth along the row, she stopped, inclined her head briefly, then slid inside, still unbuttoning her coat.

"Mina, you're late."

She didn't answer immediately. Instead, she pulled off the cap, let her hair slip past her shoulders, took off the glasses, and placed them carefully on the table. No more need for pretence. Not here, not now. "I apologize," she offered, once it was done.

The couple sitting at the other side of the table, a man and a woman, both vampire, stared for a moment. The man blinked like an owl, until nudged in the ribs by his companion. The woman leaned forward. She appeared to be in her early forties, bore an elegant, narrow face, chic hair, and manicured fingernails. "So, it's true then."

Mina nodded. There didn't seem the need to elaborate. Not yet.

The man shifted uncomfortably, and ran a bony hand through unruly, salt-and-pepper hair. "Christ," he muttered, decidedly unhappy. "So, what are we supposed to do, now?"

"Come to the House," she told them.

"No," said the woman.

The man turned to his companion. "You know, maybe it would be better if—"

"Charles, I said no."

Mina sat back in her seat, and felt the beginnings of a mental tug of war. A waiter stopped by and she asked for a scotch, then she waited.

"There's no persuading her," Charles declared eventually. He reached for his glass of wine and downed half its contents—a dry red, a house Merlot, if he was drinking his usual. It would have been a fine, rebellious gesture, if one were to ignore the refined metabolism that allowed him to ingest an entire barrel of it and not feel a thing. But he played it out anyway, presumably for Irena's benefit, with all the louche arrogance of an aging trust fund kid, which, in some respects, he was.

Of course, there was no way Irena would come back to the House, not of her own volition, Mina knew that, but she felt obliged to offer the suggestion, purely because of the circumstances. What she'd witnessed out there in the desert had frightened her. All those rumors, all that talk, and now more disappearances; suddenly the worst aspects of that visit had become all too real, written by ghosts in dust, fire, and blood.

"Irena, what if it was just for a short while? Until we knew exactly what we're up against? " She stopped. Her drink had arrived, and once the waiter had departed, "What I saw out there..." But the other woman was staring at her, giving her *that* look, and so she gave up. Irena was Goran's immediate progeny, and there was bad history between them. Bad enough that Irena had stormed out of the House many, many years ago, never to return, preferring to live as an independent. Bitter enough that if it came down to it, Goran would not force her to return home, even though he had the power to do so. Any trouble and he'd stand back and let her burn. It was a sorry state of affairs, but at least Irena had Charles to look after her.

"So, what can we do?" Charles. Attempting to be practical.

Mina shrugged, took a sip of her whisky. "Stay on your guard, watch out for any humans that—"

"Humans?" he chuckled.

"Yes. All the attackers in the desert were human."

He smiled lazily, gestured out into the room. "That rather pleasant young man who brought your drink, I could get him to strip naked and do handstands on the bar in about three seconds." He leaned out of the booth for a moment. "That goes for the rest of them sitting there, too."

She saw Irena's mouth curl into a smile, watched them join hands and look at one another, their mutual irritation dissolved, the earlier spat forgiven. So utterly sure of themselves, they were both high generation and many years old, and they'd somehow managed to settle and live quite well in this big city. Their early, immediate, dangerous appetites had dulled, had long been replaced by idyllic nights of wine drinking and duets—he the violin, she the cello—along with the occasional foray into light-hearted mischief. They were financially secure, had loyal staff, were extremely enviable, and they knew it.

"We don't all have your particular gifts, Charles," Mina shot back sourly. She winced as she got that look again, this time from both of them. "I apologize," she said, and lowered her gaze momentarily, "but you need to start taking this seriously."

Irena frowned. "Living at that mausoleum is no good for Mina, Charles. Pretty soon her sense of humor will be gone and she'll be as dull as the rest of them." The woman leaned forward, formidable, her eyes sharp chips of emerald. "Please give us some more light-hearted news," she said. "Have you managed to find a companion, yet? And that doesn't include your donors, despite the scandalous behavior I keep hearing about."

She sat back, feeling pinned to the wall, while the other two looked on like an indulgent but overbearing uncle and aunt.

"I think she's found someone already," Charles said after

a moment. The corner of his mouth twitched. "Someone she's thinking about."

Mina took a deliberate, long pull of the scotch in her tumbler and put the glass down a little too hard. He'd been wandering around inside her head and she hadn't even noticed.

"Charles, please don't be rude, and stop prying," Irena purred. Her eyes were still on Mina, and her face lit up. "Who is he?"

She looked away, couldn't bare the scrutiny any longer. "I don't know." And when their attention on her failed to diminish. "I haven't even seen his face." Inside, she railed at herself. Was it so obvious? That voice, that veiled touch, that irresistible aura of raw power. She saw her companions share a glance. "Can we change the subject? Please?" *To something more important, like keeping you two alive?* She shouldn't have mentioned the House, she realized. It had thrown things off track, brought out Irena's stubbornness, and had waylaid Charles's initial doubts until he'd become his usual assured, invincible self. But if anything happened to these two, she'd never forgive herself.

"Oh, very well," Charles relented. "We should talk more about this Weiss business, I suppose. It's just—I sort of expected you to tell us Deacon was involved in all of this."

"If Weiss is true to his letter, then Deacon's life is at stake," Irena interrupted. "He'll be under threat like the rest of us."

"That's all very well, my darling, but don't forget who Deacon is. And let's not forget our ancestors' rather nasty habit of manipulating us when it suits them."

"Even if that were true, you don't know Deacon like I do."

Mina watched Irena shoot her partner a nasty look, and for a moment they were at odds again. She took the opportunity and waded back into the fray. "We should come up with a plan. Make sure we keep in touch, at the very least. We should establish a rallying point, and if anything happens—"

"If it does, what does Goran intend to do about Danny?" Irena's eyebrows were raised.

Mina faltered. "I—I don't know. We either hunker down, hope he'll be below the radar, or we move him."

"And good luck with that," Charles snorted, followed by a mumbled "Sorry," after getting another elbow in the ribs.

"How is he?" Irena's question carried genuine concern.

Mina shook her head. "Not good. All this Weiss business. It's filtered through somehow and it's upsetting him."

"Ah, poor Danny." The other woman let out a sigh, sat back in her seat. "It's like he knew this would happen all along."

"Or—he's simply mad as a brush," added Charles. That got him another jab.

Mina had had enough. "Look, I have to get back." She wriggled into her coat, pulled on her glasses, picked up the hat. "Just promise me you'll stay in touch, come up with a plan, and if you sense even the slightest thing, you call for help, yes?"

They both stared at her, reluctant children, like she was the Elder at that particular moment.

"Of course we will," Irena told her after a moment. "And likewise, if you find yourself in trouble, consider us a place to run. You know where we are."

She stood up and buttoned her coat. "I'll let you know if there's news."

Charles nodded. "Have a safe journey home, darling."

"I will." She gave them both a quick bob of the head, turned, and walked outside.

At the base of the steps she paused, pulled on the hat, and spent some time tucking her hair beneath it while inside the conversation continued.

"Such a beautiful girl. A pity."

"About what?"

"About Danny."

"Danny is a tortured soul, Charles. And did you really have to be so rude? He's her Father, and he wasn't always like this."

"The man's insane. Goran should have let him go years ago."

"And let him kill himself? Can you imagine how distraught Mina would be?"

"Yes, I know. It would be painful. But not for long. And then she'd be free."

"Would she? Would it stop her from thinking the way she does about herself?"

"It might. If he wasn't around, drooling like an imbecile, reminding her… ah, she's still here, outside, listening to us."

"Then we should do the polite thing and stop, wouldn't you say?"

"Yes, darling, I suppose we should."

Mina pulled up the collar of her coat and climbed the steps to the sidewalk. Perhaps, she thought in the bitter gloom of the night, there would come a time when she was not so transparent, when those two old harpies could glean nothing from her. However, until that time arrived, the road stretching ahead promised nothing but mortification, harsh truths, and embarrassment.

She headed back in the direction of Broadway before turning north, and for a while she hated those two back there, family, and such dear, beloved friends. Wished they'd mind their own business, wished they'd stop skinning her alive every chance they got.

It was barely past midnight, more than enough time to walk home, so she settled into an even stride while her mind drifted. When it sought to latch onto any particular subject, she deliberately pushed it away and continued to skim the surface, unwilling to delve too deep, certainly not after the conversation she'd had with those two.

The temperature was dropping and pedestrian traffic became thin as she headed north toward the park. People walked past, ignoring her, intent on their own business, all of them lit up and giving off heat like a passing procession of medieval torches, flickering and billowing in a sharp breeze. On another night she would have enjoyed this. She loved the city, the anonymity it provided, the energy that saturated everything, the thrum of history beneath her feet, and especially the people who walked its streets, each one of them a life story just waiting to be read, a heady mixture of joy, pain, happiness, contentment, and disappointment. But tonight their allure was minimal, dampened by her poor appetite this evening and safe knowledge that hunger would be satisfied when she was finally, and thankfully, through those thick oak doors and into the formal sanctuary of the House.

She was, therefore, in no state to deal with the unexpected, and the girl took her by surprise.

Some young kid, out on the street after midnight, her lank hair and ragged clothes already telling the tale—a beggar—easily dismissed, except for the fact she was giving off no heat. None. She was standing as a beggar might, too, her back to the wall, looking outward, hoping to catch a generous eye.

Instead, she caught Mina.

Switched off and drifting, she hadn't expected the encounter. The juxtaposition of child and vampire startled her, and stopped her in her tracks. The kid looked barely in her teens, skinny, frail, and immediately she took pity and stepped closer. "Hey," she began.

The girl, ignoring all protocols, reached out lightning fast and grabbed her hand. Mina instinctively tried to pull away but the grip was strong as steel. This close she could now look into the girl's eyes, and right there she realized that any attempt to break free was pointless.

Images flooded her mind, and the entire carpet of the city became translucent—bricks and steel, weeds and concrete, tunnels and dust, earth and water. She could feel it ripple and breathe, ponderous and immense. And she wasn't afraid, she discovered. She was simply a part of it; her feet had spread roots, had delved below, directly into the heart below the city, and for a moment she felt completely, utterly grounded.

But now the girl was pulling her toward a window. Her anchored feet dragged the weight of the earth along the sidewalk. Worms, rats, pollution, slivers of moisture, were inherent in every step. A storefront loomed and the girl pointed, wanted her to see what lay beyond the glass. There was a flat screen TV, part of a display, a company logo that flickered and died, replaced abruptly by an old black-and-white TV show. Puzzled, she looked back at the girl, but the eyes were insistent and forced her to pay attention.

An image of two men, both wearing dark suits, they were facing one another in the midst of an animated discussion. The younger man was blond, cute; the older man stern, as hard as stone. Curious, she strained to hear what was being said. But the image shifted, and with it, the actors on screen. They became tall and distorted, such a profound change that it startled her and made her take a step back. But it was too late. As she watched, their faces curled and hardened into masks of bronze, and now the screen was swelling, filling the entire window, pushing farther, pushing outward until the men were standing right there, out onto the street, part of the sidewalk, part of her world.

She discovered sand beneath her, soft under her bare toes, and her heavy coat had been replaced by crumpled silk pajamas, while the men—oh, not men, not any longer—had taken her by the arms and were pulling her like dogs fighting over a bone.

Terrified, she began to scream. She looked at the girl, who stood by while the monsters kept on hauling until her shoulders cracked with the strain, her flesh so taut it was about ready to rip apart. "Please stop," she begged, her voice high-pitched and raw. "Please."

"Wait," said the girl. On the horizon, the thin line of dawn appeared below a layer of cloud, and the horror of being torn to pieces was supplanted by the sun's golden promise of annihilation. The monsters relented and ceased their tug of war, and their bronze-plated hands drew away from her limbs, allowing her to fall to her knees in terrible agony. The respite was brief. The sun's rays appeared over a glittering horizon, and for the first time she could see water out there, flat and expansive as the sand she was kneeling on.

But the growing fan of light obliterated everything. It pierced her eyes and lanced through her chest. All of a sudden, she lay on the ground in a million tiny pieces, nothing more than dust, while the ones who'd sought to split her in two hung overhead, looking down, curious and hungry.

Quickly she began to shift and roll, burrow and blend in with the sand, hell bent on escape. One of the monsters reached down and frantically sought to scoop her up with cruel, hooked fingers. It was the younger of the two and it let out a growl of distress. But it didn't matter. She was safe, scattered across the ground where she belonged, just tiny pieces of a grander design, spread out across a beach already warming in the rising sun.

The girl was close by. "Remember this," she said. "Remember all of it."

The air abruptly felt cold. It was dark when Mina opened her eyes and finally realized where she was, and that she lay crouched, huddled beneath the window. She looked around, terrified. No sign of the girl any longer, instead—a passing pedestrian.

"Hey," he said. "You okay?"

The heat shimmered off him, warm and inviting, and not the blistering, terrible heat belonging to her premonition. Instead, it served as a beacon in the cool air; she was shivering, she realized, and not from the cold. Raw and exposed, her allure had drawn him in, and he stepped closer, offered a hand. She reached out, used him to re-attain her balance and claw her way back to reality. "I'm fine," she whispered. On regaining her feet, her hand briefly rested on his shoulder. Inside she fought to stay calm, and not let the panic spread. "You go home, now."

He smiled, saying, "Yes, ma'am," and did as he was told.

When he'd gone, her eyes frantically searched the street. Still no sign of the girl, and the images in her head were a flock of shimmering, horrific birds, flying distant, getting smaller and smaller while her body still shook with dread. She looked down at the sidewalk—concrete, not sand any longer. Scared out of her wits, she broke into run. She hit the park and crossed Columbus Circle, ran like the wind and didn't stop until she'd reached the gates of home.

CHAPTER 16
GILLES

Two chairs were now pulled up alongside the desk. Their current occupants were huddled over Saleem's laptop, and were presently conspiring in a foreign language. Or so it seemed to Gilles. Toby Marsh had arrived abruptly two nights ago, accompanied by a female donor he thought he recognized, along with two portable hard drives that were now plugged into the House system. Toby and Saleem had been sitting there for hours, talking animatedly while drives whirred and screens flickered, busy with sliding indicators and status bars.

The Marsh Annals. Everything. Files, blueprints, documents, photographs.

In the midst of dealing with the club repercussions and Miles's bitter complaints, the slender, diminutive Tobias Marsh had arrived quietly and unannounced on their doorstep, while his grandmother Violet had, by all accounts, taken the initiative and swept the rest of the family north to an undisclosed location. How much farther north, Tobias wasn't saying, although Gilles couldn't exactly see Violet living in Alaska. Still, strange times called for strange measures, and the woman, presumably having taken heed of Delacour's warning, was proving to be a survivor.

As for why she had risked sending one of her beloved grandsons in the opposite direction, right into the heat of it, into one of the few Houses taking a more proactive stand, he could only imagine. Delacour had been overjoyed. It was quite a coup to get one's hands on a copy of the entire archive. Strange times indeed.

Christina arrived and slid her hands around him. "What are

they doing?" She squinted and looked through the open door.

Gilles laughed. "You're asking me?" He followed her gaze. "Backing up, reorganizing files—I assume." He felt her shiver. "Everything all right?" he asked.

"I don't know. *Is* everything all right?"

He turned so he could face her. "What troubles you, Christina?"

"I don't know. It's just—two, three months ago—we seemed so settled here. Safe." She tightened her grip on him. "And now..."

"It's all right to be afraid," he offered gently.

An uneasy smile broke across her face. "Afraid? I'm scared shitless. Will we need to go on the run, too? Leave our home? Like the Marshes?"

Uncertainty. That's what was gnawing at her. Christina was tough, but she had succeeded in avoiding chaos during both her lives so far, whereas it had been quite the opposite for Gilles. And speaking of chaos—

"Where's Gannon?"

"With Delacour, I think." Her smile brightened, as it always did on this particular subject.

He was about to voice his suspicions, that a discussion was taking place with House Goran on the East Coast, when Houston rounded the corner.

"Meeting. Five minutes. Delacour's office." The man poked his head into the room beyond and slapped his hand twice against the door. "Hey. That means you two weirdoes. Five minutes. Get your shit together."

Gilles rolled his eyes while Christina burst into a fit of giggles.

"What?" asked Houston, oblivious.

While Christina chased the man down the corridor, Gilles stepped inside the room and joined Saleem and Toby.

"Apologies for Houston," Saleem exclaimed. "He's a Neanderthal."

Gilles regarded them both. "He can be a little brusque. But he's a good man to have alongside you in a firefight, or any other fight for that matter."

Their new guest nodded, his face solemn. "I hope it doesn't come to that." He stood, and began to roll down his sleeves and button up his shirt cuffs. Gilles caught the tremor of thought, of feathers ruffled, of vague unease. This man was a glorified librarian, out of his comfort zone, away from the iron protection of his Grandmother. What in God's name was he doing here, accompanied by a treasure trove of family secrets? It was unprecedented. "If you'll excuse me," Toby continued. "I'll go get my jacket."

The informality of House Delacour obviously hadn't rubbed off on him yet, and when he'd gone, Gilles repeated his concerns to Saleem. "Has he said anything to you? About why he's here?"

"He told me it was his decision. I could be wrong, but between you and me, I think he's here because of Mark."

Gilles stared at him for a moment before his eyes shifted to middle distance. Vancouver. He attempted to put two and two together, came up with a few answers, and felt a hand tugging at his sleeve.

"Go easy on Tobias, Gilles," Saleem implored. "He's not used to this. And if we're going to survive, we'll need him."

Hours after the meeting, where Gilles had been informed he had a plane to catch, he got another call to meet Delacour in his office. When he arrived, he found his Elder in his usual position, leaning back in his chair, feet up on the desk, while Saleem perched in an adjacent seat.

"Close the door, Gilles."

He did so. "Trouble?"

Delacour gave him a quick smile. "Please, sit down. Saleem, tell him what we've been doing."

Gilles took a seat.

"The woman who gave refuge to Christina and Mark, after what happened at the club. We've had her under surveillance." Saleem raised a finger as Gilles began to object. "It was for her own protection. She was connected to Mark, to his work. She was his manager."

"I see. If he's keeping tabs on Mark, Deacon will know who she is."

"Exactly," said Delacour. "Continue, Saleem."

"We thought we'd give it a few days, make sure she was still under the radar. Then, two things happened yesterday."

Delacour sat up and pushed an envelope toward Gilles, who

took it and pulled out the contents. There were three photographs. The first two were similar—a man sitting inside a car parked on the side of a street. "One of Deacon's men? Is this outside the woman's apartment?" He stared at the photos, but didn't recognize anything. He hadn't been there when Houston had collected Gannon and Christina.

"Maybe, and yes," Delacour told him. "Now, take a look at the next one."

Gilles pushed the first two photographs behind the third and looked down at the image. He frowned. "It looks like Mark." And it did. Gannon, in daylight, dressed in jeans and a T-shirt, entering the building with a carryall hefted over one shoulder.

Delacour grinned. "It does, doesn't it."

"It's his brother," Saleem told him.

"Ah, shit." His curse caught him by surprise. "Are you saying these two arrived simultaneously?" He flicked through the photographs once more.

Delacour shrugged, leaned back, and his boots arrived back on the desktop. "Your opinions, gentlemen."

"Could be coincidence," offered Saleem.

Gilles shook his head. "Could be, or Deacon already has tabs on the brother, and he's led them unwittingly to these apartments."

"A long shot though, wouldn't you say?" asked Delacour.

"Admittedly it seems a little far-fetched. Especially since this guy lives in—Australia?"

"New Zealand," Saleem and Delacour corrected him in unison.

"Well, he isn't in New Zealand now."

There was a short silence. Gilles placed the photos back in the envelope and returned them to the desk. He leaned forward, looked at the other two men. "So—what do you want me to do?"

"I need you to find out who's watching the apartment. And we need to be careful."

"And if it *is* Deacon's man? Or Weiss's?"

"Then our Mr. Gannon needs to tell his brother to get on the next plane home. For his own safety."

The meeting was adjourned. Saleem ducked past him, in all probability wanting to get back to his beloved computers and Toby.

"Before you go, Gilles—"

He stopped in the doorway. Delacour was now standing at his desk, fingering the envelope. "We need to put this to bed quickly," his Elder said, "before you go to London."

"That doesn't give me much time."

"Three days to wrap it up, one way or another. We can't afford to miss that meeting." The man frowned. "Funny, I expected Deacon to have made a move against Weiss by now. Despite our mutual dislike, I figured I'd have heard something. But as yet, as far as I know he's had no contact with anyone. Not even with Nakamura in San Francisco, who'd be his closest ally."

"Unless Nakamura is lying. Do you still think Mark has something to do with all of this? Can we trust him enough to go to London?"

Delacour shrugged. "Right now we don't have a lot of choice. If the Foundation has called a meeting, then I need to send a representative. I don't want the Trustees using their discretionary powers to strike us off the list of beneficiaries, simply because we didn't turn up. That's always been part of the deal, and—before you say anything else, yes—I have a bad feeling about it, too. Not about Mark, though. About the Foundation. There's no way I'm sending you alone into that vipers nest."

"It's just a meeting."

"Yes, but aside from keeping your eyes and ears open, you need to be on your guard. It's the only source of income most of us have. And despite never showing up at these events, Deacon still manages to keep his name on the beneficiary list. And that by the way, is something most of the others aren't aware of."

Gilles nodded. "I'm starting to hate the idea of taking Merrill."

"We always take a donor on long trips, Gilles, you know that."

He acceded, fully aware of the practicalities and protocols. "Anything else I need to know? About the trip?"

Delacour shrugged. "A couple of things you ought to be aware of regarding Mark. They're certain to figure out he's high generation and defer to him. He won't betray us, but try to keep him out of situations where he might get a little trigger happy."

"And we're not talking about guns, are we?" Gannon's dominant nature. The dead female in the foyer of the club.

His Elder smiled. "I know Christina told you what happened.

Also, something she doesn't know—at the Marshes', he panicked and bound Violet's grandson."

"Toby?" Gilles rubbed the bridge of his nose and tried to accept this information as if it was all perfectly normal.

"I don't know what Tobias did while we were up there, but I suspect he cornered Mark with too many questions."

"Couldn't he have just walked away?" He fought hard to keep the incredulity out of his voice.

"He's third generation, Gilles. Fresh out of the gate, has no idea of his capabilities and obviously, neither do we. We're failing him badly in that respect."

"It's hardly our fault if—"

"I know. I'm not assigning blame. I've talked to him about it. We've discussed this trip in particular, and what to expect. He's being reasonable."

Gilles closed his eyes for a long moment, then, "Okay. What do you want me to do?"

"Just stay with him, advise him, look after him, and—I do know what I'm asking of you. I realize it's not going to be easy."

He kept his face blank. "And what about his connection to Deacon?"

"We'll cross that bridge, if and when we come to it. Despite the fact I don't trust that wily old bastard, a connection between us might not be a bad thing, ultimately." And there it was, Delacour's reason for keeping Gannon close. Not as a weapon, as a way to forge an alliance.

"So—does this make Deacon our enemy or our friend?"

Delacour spread his hands. "Both, I'm afraid. We're going to have to be very careful."

He nodded. "And Goran?" Members of the New York House would be their traveling companions for the London trip.

"An ally, for now. We go back a long way, but everything could change, depending on circumstance. Just be on your guard."

It was all heaped up, a teetering pile of mistrust and potential betrayal, so he shoved it unceremoniously to the back of his mind. "I'd better set things in motion for this other business. I'll be ready to move as soon as the sun goes down."

Delacour nodded. "I'm sorry to push all this on you, Gilles. But you're the only one I trust. If I gave it to Houston, he'd probably just kill everything on two feet for simplicity's sake."

He smiled. "Don't worry. I'll handle it."

A formal bow, and Gilles set off. He had Saleem, Gannon, Houston, and some of the donors to talk to before he settled in to sleep for the day. Inside, his head was spinning. Trust. That word. It had been bandied about so often lately, he wondered if he really knew the meaning of it anymore. And now Tobias Marsh was here, bound and eating out of Gannon's hand, plugged into their databases, privy to all their secrets, and Gilles felt a shiver run down the length of his spine.

CHAPTER 17
MARK

The driver, Adrian, drew the car to a halt about a block away from Molly's apartment. Mark laid back his head and stared at the upholstered ceiling. This was not something he was looking forward to.

"Give me ten minutes," Gilles told him.

Mark watched him get out of the vehicle and disappear quickly down a side street. After a few minutes—

"You got family, Adrian? Siblings?"

"Yes, Sir. Three brothers and a sister."

"You get along?"

"Most of the time." And after a grin, "But I guess we fight a lot, too."

"They have any idea what you do?"

"No. And I'm trying to keep it that way."

Mark nodded, lapsed into silence.

After another minute, "Course, if they got into trouble," the driver added. "What I'm trying to say is—I think you're doing the right thing."

Doing the right thing. Yeah, like he'd done the right thing with Toby. But at least the word had got around about that now, and he'd been able to acknowledge the connection between them and assuage some of his guilt. "I guess so," he said. He looked out the window, watched passing traffic. The donor knew the score. If Matthew saw the sense of it, it would be Adrian that drove him to the airport, and the sooner the better. That's if everything went to plan and they got out of this in one piece. He started to worry about

Gilles, out there in the dark, stalking the guy who was watching the building. What if something went wrong? What if something had already gone wrong?

He felt dismayed at this latest turn of events. They'd known about Matthew for a couple of days and hadn't told him about it until tonight. Gilles had already been here the night before, to determine who was watching Molly's apartment, and the discovery, that it was one of Deacon's men, was making Mark's stomach curdle. He tried to shut it out and concentrate on what he had to do—but failed miserably. He checked his watch. Time. He opened the door.

"Good luck, Sir."

"Thanks." Mark forced a brief smile, left the vehicle, and began to walk.

"Who is it?" Molly's muffled voice.

"It's me." A door chain rattled, a lock slid back. When she opened the door and he saw her, the first thing he wanted to do was sweep her into his arms. Part of his old life, standing there, radiating heat and the scents he craved. He wanted to bury his face in her shoulder and breathe deep. Instead, he stepped over the threshold and watched her deliberately back off. Distance. She had remembered. Good.

"You told him," he said. He tried not to sound accusatory.

"Yes. He called again, and yes, I told him."

He nodded, inhaled slowly. "Where is he?" There was movement to his left.

"I'm right here, you fuck—" His brother Matthew stopped in his tracks and was now staring at him. Mark tried to choke down the emotion welling up inside him, tried to ignore the remnants of sea salt and acrylic airline seat covers and shower gel and a more recent smell of white wine and clam chowder. She had been feeding him, at least.

Molly hovered on the periphery. "Holy shit, you two look alike."

He saw his brother take a step forward. He held up his hand. "That's far enough, Matthew. You don't touch our kind, and you never get too close. In fact, the further you stay away from us the better."

"Our kind? Us? What the fuck are you talking about?" Despite the outburst, Matthew remained where he was.

He felt an all-too-familiar rancor growing inside. "Just pay attention. I'm trying to make sure you live longer than I did."

"Live longer? What the hell?" His brother looked desperately toward Molly.

"I think we all need a drink," she announced. "Can you drink, Mark?"

"Red wine, if you have it." He saw her nod before disappearing into the kitchen, leaving him alone with Matthew, tantalizingly alive, stirring up bold yearnings of hunger and longing. The core inside wanted him, wanted Molly, too. Heat, blood, it didn't care about anything else.

Matthew took another step back, held his hands slightly forward, like he was ready to throw a punch if he needed to. He appeared shaken. "You don't look good, Mark. You look... cold. What happened to you?"

He had to smile at that, and he tried hard to keep a bitter twist from appearing on his lips. "I was murdered."

A nervous laugh. "You're not making any sense, big brother."

"What did Molly tell you?"

"She said it was complicated."

"She got that right."

Matthew took a deep breath. "So, you got into some kind of trouble, but couldn't you have let our parents know you're okay at least? They might have forgotten about you in Hollywood, but Mom and Dad haven't, you selfish prick."

Mark snorted. Felt his temper rise. "Just stop. You're starting to sound like her." He stabbed a finger toward the kitchen. "And like I told her, I am not *okay*."

His brother clenched his fists for a moment and then released them. He slowly backed up and sat down, then gestured for Mark to do likewise. "Look, I'm not getting it, so you'd better explain."

Reluctantly, he took a seat opposite. Molly returned, handed him a glass, gave another to Matthew, and then retrieved her own. She approached.

"Sit over there, Molly," he ordered.

She gave him a sour look, but went to sit next to his brother. She appeared to be handling this pretty well, considering the circumstances. There was a hard shell of stubborn protection surrounding her, one he was sure she'd honed over the years, one that served her well, one he didn't even consider breaking.

Matthew took a long pull from his wineglass. "So?"

"Okay." He cleared his throat, paused for a second. "The night I disappeared, I was on Sunset. It was around ten o' clock. I was walking toward the crossing and I was approached. By a man. I'm going to describe him to you, and I want you to promise me, that if you ever see this guy, you'll run like the fucking wind. Are we clear?"

They nodded and he watched them carefully as he ran through Deacon's description. Both were leaning forward, looking to be paying attention. And he thought about what happened in Vancouver, when he'd fallen to pieces, and wondered if that would happen all over again. But he couldn't allow it. Not tonight.

He continued. "This man—he walked up to me and started talking. He made me do everything he commanded. Everything. He made me take off my jacket, and then a car, a limo, drew up to the curb. There were people inside and they pulled me in there. They took off my clothes, and they started to bite me, drink my blood, and they made it hurt. I couldn't do anything to stop it. They drove around for hours, while I lay there dying, and then they dumped my body over a cliff."

A pause.

"Christina rescued him," Molly said. He saw her hand shaking a little.

Matthew looked at her. He seemed dazed. "Who's Christina?"

"Why isn't she with you, Mark?"

"Gilles is with me tonight," he told her. "He has some business to take care of before he comes here. Tall. Black guy. A gentleman, you'll like him." He switched his attention back to Matthew, and looked for a reaction. He'd tried hard to be human, tried not to let the aura of command take over and exert its usual influence, but he wasn't sure how successful he'd been. Right now his brother was sitting there, silently watching him. Under normal circumstances he'd be on his feet, yelling at him and calling bullshit.

"Matthew?"

His brother stood up, drained his wine glass. He seemed to be struggling, searching for the right words. "So you're supposed to be dead?" he said eventually. "Is that what you're saying?"

Mark nodded.

"And yet—you're here. Talking, breathing, drinking wine, and telling me some fucking stupid story about—hell, I don't know what the fuck you're trying to tell me."

There. That was more like it. Mark slowly got to his feet. "Matthew, look at me." He saw his brother shake his head. Felt the core inside, edging forward, eager to grasp the reins. "Look at me." And there were tears in his brother's eyes when he finally did. The sight cut him to the marrow. He wanted nothing more than to turn and walk out of the door. "What does your gut tell you?"

"I don't know."

"But you know there's something wrong." He received a curt nod and breathed a mild sigh of relief. Maybe they were starting to get somewhere.

Molly shifted in her seat, still cradling her wine glass. "Since neither of you are going to say it—Matthew, he's a vampire. I didn't believe it, either. But when he came here, he'd been shot. He left the bullet on a shelf in the bathroom and Christina showed me…" She gave up, offered Mark a withering glance, and he replied with a helpless shrug.

His brother was looking on, horrified. "Shot. Oh God…"

"Matthew—" Mark began. His sibling held up a hand to stop him and walked off into the kitchen.

Molly leaned back on the couch. "I'm sorry. He just sounded so distressed on the phone, I couldn't lie to him."

"You used to lie to me."

That got him a whiplash taste of the old Molly. "That was business, you miserable fuck."

"I'm sorry. I deserved that."

"Damn right you did."

He stared at her for a moment, and he realized in an odd, perverse way he was enjoying this. In fact, he was reveling in it. Right here, right now, he was Mark Gannon, the live version, the human, arguing on equal terms with his manager, his brother, just like old times. It was an illusion, one that was about to break into a million pieces, but just for a moment he basked in it, unwilling to let it go.

He put down his glass. "I need to warn him, Molly. He could be in danger."

"Seriously? From whom, those people who shot you?"

"Maybe. I don't know." He walked into the kitchen. Matthew was leaning against a counter top, his arms folded in front of him, left hand rubbing his chin. He looked deep in thought. Mark stopped a short distance away and waited.

"A vampire?" His brother's voice came out cracked and torn, still rippled with disbelief. "You have… fangs and everything?"

"Yes. If you want I can show—"

"No!" Matthew took a sharp step away from him. "Fuck—no. Get away from me."

He felt the need to retort, to keep pushing his little brother like he always did. It felt right. Felt human. And it was hard to draw back. But eventually, "I need you to leave," Mark began. "Someone's been watching the apartment. You could be in trouble."

"Why—what have I done?"

"You haven't done anything. But they might be trying to get to me."

His brother let out a bitter laugh. "Oh sure, that's right, Mark. It's all about you. Always has been."

"Look, you obviously don't—"

"What are we going to say to Mom and Dad? What are going to tell them?"

Stopped in his tracks, Mark looked away. After a long moment of silence, "I don't know." He swallowed, hard. "What's the official word?"

"That you're a missing person. Not presumed dead. Not yet, because it's too soon and no one's found a body yet. Word on the street is that you had some kind of breakdown and you're in fucking Cancun or somewhere."

"Then maybe that's how it should stay."

"Are you kidding me? Have you any idea what our parents are going through right now—"

"That's enough." Fury. It welled up inside, burning and vitriolic; he could barely control it. "Just what the fuck *are* we supposed to tell them, you idiot? The truth? That—"

A knock on the door silenced them both. Mark moved quickly,

out of the kitchen. Molly was almost at the door.

"It's Gilles," he told her.

"You can see through doors?" she asked, her eyebrows arched.

"Something like that."

He stayed where he was and fought his temper while Molly let Gilles in. He sensed his brother alongside, on edge, curious, still angry, still in shock. They weren't done yet. Not by a long stretch.

Gilles walked in exuding an ocean of calm. He introduced himself and appeared a little bemused. "Are they giving you any trouble?" he asked Molly, who smiled and seemed quite enamored.

Her expression quickly soured as she looked toward Mark. "Just the usual family shit," she answered. "And my parents wonder why I won't go home for Thanksgiving."

Mark tried not to get all ruffled under Gilles' subsequent scrutiny. He was fired up, as was Matthew, and if anyone could calm things down —

"Have you expressed our concerns about your brother's safety?" Gilles asked.

"I've been trying, but right now he's not listening." He turned and looked at his brother. "You need to leave. You're in danger."

"I'm not going anywhere."

Gilles cleared his throat. "Mr. Gannon. There have been some fairly unscrupulous people following you. It might be for the best."

"I don't care."

Mark rounded on him. "Will you listen to the man?"

"No—fuck that, Mark, you listen to me. She told me you got shot. You're in trouble. Let me stay and help you."

"You'd be helping me by getting on the next flight home."

"We have a car outside," Gilles added calmly, "for whenever you're ready."

"It's not happening. You think I'm just going to walk away and then hear about you being found dead in an alley somewhere in a few weeks' time?"

Mark closed his eyes. Down in the pit he saw an image of himself, naked, pale as a ghost and covered in puncture wounds. "Matthew, I'm already *dead*." He opened his eyes, saw Molly wince. An awkward silence followed. Matthew was the first to break it.

"Sure," he said quietly, he appeared to be struggling to get the words out. "But I'm not going. You guys put me on a plane. I'll come straight back."

"And what about Molly?" Mark asked. "If you stay here, won't she be in danger, too?" He was down to his final round of ammunition, and not to be outdone, Molly linked arms with his brother. "I don't care," she said. "I want to help, too."

Mark took a step back and turned away, defeated, saw himself spiraling down, the black pit calling his name. After a few moments he felt Gilles' presence alongside him. "I don't know what to do," he confessed.

"Actually, we do have a contingency plan. Delacour anticipated this."

"And?"

"We keep the apartment under surveillance. Take a few more security measures. Some have already been taken. It's not ideal, but it's better than nothing."

"Think it will work? Think it will keep them safe?"

Gilles shrugged. "Like I said, it's better than nothing. Let me talk to them."

Mark hung back, stayed out of the way while Gilles sat with Molly and Matthew and talked everything through. Now that the heated flush of his humanity was beginning to cool, he felt another energy tugging at him, urgent, rapidly trying to reassert itself. When it came time for him to leave, he used it and became distant, protected by a shell of false indifference. It was the only way he could leave his younger brother back there in that apartment without breaking down. No physical contact, no embrace, not even a handshake—things he remembered them doing when they weren't bickering like rats. That would have been the human thing to do, and it was all gone.

Back in the car, on the way home, "If there was any disrespect, whatever Matthew said, it was all aimed at me."

"I know. It wasn't a problem."

He leaned back. His head was spinning. "I just—I wish I could have persuaded him. And Molly must be out of her mind."

"They stay because they love you. It's just that you don't see it, or you choose not to."

"So, I really am an asshole, huh?"

Gilles looked at him. "Perhaps, but you're also tired and not thinking clearly. Calm yourself, we'll be home soon."

Mark turned away, folded his arms across his chest, and looked out of the window. After a while he realized he was sulking. "I'm sorry," he said.

"It's all right. You're upset."

"Even so, I apologize, and I'm glad you were with me. It could have gotten out of hand."

"You wouldn't have harmed your brother."

"You sure?"

"Yes."

Mark laughed half-heartedly. "You know, I've tried looking out for him. Always, when we were kids. But he was so fucking independent. Always pulling away. I guess we're not much alike." He caught Gilles' grin and he smiled. He couldn't help it, but it was bittersweet, and it was really starting to hit, how much he missed his family. "You know, I almost felt human, tonight."

"You miss your humanity. It's still with you."

He nodded. "How did you handle it, Gilles? At first, I mean."

"It wasn't the best of times. Everyone I'd ever known was either dead or missing. This was a relief. A new beginning."

"I sound ungrateful."

"No, not at all. Your rebirth involved torture and murder. Time heals, but you still have a long way to go."

Mark frowned. "I guess I should just learn to live with it. The sooner the better."

"You will."

He took another glance out of the window. They were almost back at the House. "What happened to the guy who was watching the apartment?" He sat up straight. "Did you kill him?"

"Unfortunately, I had no other choice."

"One of Deacon's men."

"Yes. And not one who could be warned off. He took a rather belligerent exception to my suggestions, in fact."

"You okay?"

A smile. "Yes, and thank you for asking."

He'd been so preoccupied. Mark stared. The other man was

wounded. He could smell it and he cursed himself. "How bad?"

"After a few hours and some blood, I'll be fine."

Mark shook his head, mortified. "Gilles—"

"Don't worry about it."

He sank back in his seat. The man sitting next to him had been injured, badly. Matthew was right. He was a selfish prick. And on that note, a new set of questions reared their ugly heads. Anyone who could take a bite out of Gilles had to be tough. In terms of resources, Deacon was committing a hell of a lot to watching over his little brother. And to think, Mark had told him he *might* be in danger.

"Our security will be adequate," added Gilles.

Mark nodded. Preoccupied, he'd let his own mental guard down, and he suspected Gilles was quietly discovering new ways to get in. He focused, closed a few mental doors, and began to feel contrite all over again.

Injured, and he hadn't even noticed.

CHAPTER 18
GILLES

"So, you're recovered?" Houston didn't lift his head as Gilles entered the room. He was busy, checking provisions that Gilles and Gannon would need for the trip.

"More or less." Just under twenty four hours and the ragged tear in his flesh, just beneath his ribcage, had pulled together, leaving an impressive scar that would no doubt fade, given time.

"Good job you can handle yourself. That kid's a liability. I still think Delacour is out of his mind sending him with you."

Gilles leaned against the counter, folded his arms, and watched the other man place a set of volatile incendiary spikes into their protective containers. "Don't forget—that kid, as you call him, is a third generation Elder."

"Yeah, and he's still fresh off the boat. It's not like he's a Green Beret. He told me he had two weeks of sidearm training up in Canada for some TV show a couple of years back. Two weeks." Houston rolled his eyes.

Gilles smiled. "It doesn't always come down to guns."

The other man pushed the now sealed containers slowly into a small rucksack. "For the likes of me it does." He grinned like a shark. "Not all of us have your education, Gilles. What's that thing you do with your feet again?"

"Savate. And I wouldn't exactly call it an education. As for Gannon, his weapon is inside his head."

"Right. Which makes him one hell of a loose cannon. Him being screwed up and conflicted and all. Especially now that his younger brother is in the picture."

"Ah." Gilles couldn't argue with that.

"And speaking of the brother, guess who's in charge of keeping him in one piece?"

He leaned over the counter, picked up the rucksack, and peered inside. Four narrow spikes of death and destruction. He hoped very much that he didn't have to use them. He placed them back where he'd found them, then looked straight at Houston. "You're not in the best of moods this evening."

"Nope. And neither would you be, after getting your head chewed off."

Gilles raised an eyebrow.

"Oh, it took Delacour a while, but I knew it was coming."

"Ah. The sanctuary. Dimitra's cards?"

Houston nodded. "Apparently I shouldn't have dumped half a ton of rubble on top of that little witch's trick bag." He shrugged. "I would have gotten away with it, too, if it hadn't been for Eleanor's persistence."

"I didn't even know it was there. I didn't feel anything at all."

"Neither did Eleanor. Dimitra had hidden it pretty good. And as you know, it took another trip, with Golden Boy in attendance, before she figured it out." Houston's frown became incredulous. "He should have backed off when he got the first hint and kept his mouth shut."

"They're just cards, Houston." Unable to help it, he added a slight smirk.

"Yeah, yeah, you laugh it up. Now that the cards are here, she won't be far behind."

Both their faces fell.

"So, which bags are mine?"

Houston pointed. "That one, and those two over there. And you'd better get Actor Boy down here. There are a few things I need to go over with him before you leave."

Gilles picked up his belongings. "Thanks," he said. He meant it. Houston's spikes, blood pouches, and carefully compiled bundles of thick, protective garb had saved his life more than once.

The other man nodded. "Just be careful, okay? And watch out for those English and European bastards. Sooner I see your miserable hide back here the better."

"I will."

Loaded up, he left the room and headed back toward the main house. On this trip, it seemed he'd have to watch out for just about everything.

A few hours later, Gilles, Gannon, two donors, and four flight staff were wrapped in the safe cocoon of the cabin, while the aircraft, a 737 business jet, waited on the taxiway for permission to take off. There'd be more crossing the Atlantic when they picked up the East Coast crew, but for now there was plenty of room.

Gannon was sitting across the aisle with his donor. The man seemed at ease, certainly enough to suggest that he and Houston hadn't gotten into a verbal skirmish before they left. It came as a surprise to Gilles, however, that he'd brought the girl who'd arrived with Tobias from Vancouver, Robert Marsh's favorite, whom he'd attacked during their ignominious visit. Right now she was alongside him, her head resting on his shoulder, and their hands were locked together in the manner of a couple of honeymooners as they waited for takeoff. Gilles shielded his thoughts. The less said about it the better.

A few more minutes and the jet turned onto the runway and accelerated. There followed a slight disorientation as they took off and became airborne. This was always the best part of the flight as far as Gilles was concerned, before they gained altitude and the monotony settled in, and he always regretted not being able to look out the window during daytime flights, absolutely sure that he'd relish the sight. Alas—

A wistful glance toward the screened windows brought him into eye contact with his own donor. They smiled at one another, content and familiar in one another's company, before retreating back into the net of their own thoughts. With Merrill he'd committed the cardinal sin of exclusivity. Staying with one donor was inadvisable, he knew that, purely on the basis of their relative longevity and the tendency to become attached—a human trait that led toward a string of rather painful emotions, as one was forced to watch a donor gradually wither and die, ravaged by time, a fate not shared by his own kind. One was supposed to keep a certain distance. It was better for all concerned. But this one, she'd been at his side now for almost twenty years. He enjoyed her company, her quiet sense of humor, her stoicism; they were well matched.

He cast another glance toward Gannon, who doggedly continued to hold a tight grip on his humanity at all costs. Gilles wondered if he was doing the same thing, in his own way. He let out a sigh, determined now to let go of the chaotic merry-go-round of thoughts that always accompanied the presence of the man across the aisle. Instead, he turned his attention toward the trip and tried to recall what he remembered about the Foundation. He'd been there twice already, but only in a limited capacity. This time it would be different. As a full representative he would be treated differently, although his lack of documented lineage would no doubt be a factor, especially among the more ancient members. Old habits and traits died hard. Well, this time attitudes would be interesting. Especially with Gannon in tow.

He slept.

Until he felt another's thoughts tugging at his sleeve.

Gannon. Alongside him, jumpy as a faun.

"Can we talk?"

Gilles shifted into a sitting position, took a few moments to collect himself. A quick look around told him they were alone. "What is it, Mark?"

"I sent the donors to the rear of the cabin." The man let out a long breath, laid his head back against the seat. "I just had the weirdest dream."

"Are you certain? Because we don't—" Gilles hesitated. *We don't dream.*

Gannon became animated, looked confused. "I know. But it was daylight, and I saw her. Then it got dark and she changed. And she pushed me, so strong, and I fell—" It was coming out rapidly, with broad strokes of unease tightening his voice until it became almost childlike. He'd seen Gannon in various states of distress before, but not like this. "—and she sat on my chest, just a girl. Dark hair. She told me I had to kill myself. And she meant it, too."

Gilles' first thought was to instill calm until he heard the last part of it. "Describe the girl once more, in detail," he said.

"In daylight, she's so bright I can't tell." A look of embarrassment, an attempt to slow it down. "But in darkness it's like all the life has gone out of her. She's skinny and drawn, a gray dress that's all tattered. And her eyes just draw you in and drain all the life..." Gannon paused, leaned forward, began to massage his temples. "Who the hell is she?"

It didn't make any sense. "Have any of us described Dimitra to you? Christina? Eleanor, or Delacour?"

"The missing girl? Nope. No one seems to want to talk about her."

"Did you touch those cards? At any time?"

Gannon shook his head again. "I didn't go anywhere close."

"What about Houston? While you were getting ready this morning?"

"We talked about the cards. I apologized about finding them. I didn't want him to think I'd gotten him in trouble on purpose. But he never described her."

"She's—an unusual child. Not a child at all, in fact."

"She's vampire though, right?"

"Yes."

"So, what's she doing inside my head?"

"I don't know." He shrugged, tried to make it look nice and easy. Like it didn't matter. One thing he'd discovered about Gannon, when he was self absorbed and looking inward, his needle-sharp perception fell apart, and right now that was a definite advantage as Gilles began to spin a yarn and tell a lie. "It could be you picked up some of Houston's thoughts. There isn't much that scares Houston, but she does."

Gannon seemed to be chewing over his explanation. "It's possible. Maybe I didn't realize..."

Gilles nodded. "Don't trouble yourself over it. It's probably nothing."

"Okay." He could tell Gannon wanted to believe it, but didn't seem wholly convinced.

He tried a different tack, one of diversion. "Not long now before the others board."

"I guess..."

Gilles kept digging. "And you've already met Mina, I gather?"

Gannon looked at him, brightened. "Yes, and I've no idea what she looks like."

There, a more-than-adequate distraction. "I'd warn you about her, but somehow I get the feeling I won't need to."

A smile became a grin. "Is she cute?"

Gilles laughed. "Yes—and she knows it."

"I'm about to meet my match, huh?"

This time they both laughed.

Gilles kept him talking, and by the time they had landed in New York, Gannon was in a lighter mood. An Elder, the man's overall mental state was of legitimate concern. Delacour had asked him again to keep an eye on it as everything started to pile up. The younger brother, Matthew, was a problem, but this latest revelation had caught Gilles by surprise.

Dimitra.

And that lie he'd told, pure guesswork, the one about Houston's thoughts kicking around in Gannon's head, oh how he wished that were true. What was it Houston had said back at the house, about those cards and their appearance heralding the girl's return? The man wasn't a natural prophet, but on this occasion…

They were on the ground, still taxiing, heading toward a hangar and out of the sun. It gave Gilles time to collect himself. Gannon had assumed a mask and looked suitably bored, as if the journey was already proving tiresome. Right now he looked so much like Deacon it was uncanny. Another little dilemma, waiting in the wings, for when someone else on this trip put two and two together on Gannon's heritage and got the right answer. A risk they knew they'd have to take, but right now it felt nowhere near as troubling as that disturbing young girl appearing in Gannon's head while he was sleeping. A premonition? It was the only viable explanation.

"Stay as you are," Gilles told him as the jet came to a standstill and the cabin crew began to open the door. He rose and stepped forward, the official host. Beyond the doorway the hangar lights were bright and he could see movement—a slender figure dashing up the steps, long legs and a sweep of chestnut hair.

"Gilles!"

He smiled and waited for the inevitable, and half a second later she was in his arms, embracing him deftly, wildly, expertly avoiding even the slightest touch of bare flesh. Over her shoulder he saw three men ascending the steps, all carrying bags and not one of them human. Two more than expected, and no doubt their donors would be next.

"It's good to see you, Mina." He cast another glance outside. "Extra passengers?" He told himself not to be alarmed, they were hardly outmatched with Gannon on board.

"Yes." She gave him a smile most men yearned for. "Goran figured we'd need a bigger presence against the Europeans."

He nodded and concurred. Goran, most certainly a European, probably had it figured better than most. The strings of treachery on that continent were entrenched deep and connected every hierarchal map and bloodline, and like the bloodlines they went back centuries. Not that it was any better on this side of the Atlantic. The New World was a little out of practice, but it was catching up nicely and had been ever since Deacon had arrived on her pristine shores.

He and Mina stood by the door while the other men embarked, and Gilles watched as all three gave Gannon a clipped, formal bow as they passed by on their way to the middle cabin. It was reciprocated, barely. Gannon had assumed the pretense of reading a magazine and had barely looked up as they filed by. He wanted to smile and wondered perhaps if the man was overdoing it. He also watched that bored look change as the donors arrived, whereupon the man's expression briefly shifted to that of a hungry bear looking at a picnic basket. That was more true to form. Gilles mentally steeled himself. This was going to be some trip.

"Come," he said to Mina. "I'll introduce you, although I believe you two have already met." He touched her elbow, felt her go a little tense. Well, well.

"Mark, this is Mina."

Gannon had put down his magazine and decided to pay attention. There was a half-smile on his face, and the eyebrows were raised just a little. Curious, but not overly much. "Hello again."

She gave him a bow. Gilles couldn't see her face for the fall of her hair, but her voice carried a barely perceptible tremor.

"Hello, Mark. It's good to see you at last."

"Likewise."

After an awkward pause, "Shall I sit—?"

"In here, by all means," Gannon told her.

Gilles watched the man give a regal wave of his hand, gesturing toward Gilles' side of the cabin before picking up his magazine once more. And that was that. Mina appeared both confused and relieved.

"I'll check on the others. I'll be right back."

Gilles nodded, smiled reassuringly. When she'd gone, he stared across at Gannon who was struggling hard not to laugh. He sat down, closed his eyes. There would be another seven hours of this, and on top of that, the crew still had refueling and their flight checks to do. Hopefully Gannon had got over his fears of the young girl and would settle down and fall asleep once more. Perhaps Mina would do the same.

And camels might fly.

CHAPTER 19
MARK

He'd been thinking about Matthew.

Everything else—what he'd become, his hatred of Deacon—had faded and become insignificant. Oh yeah, and Molly, she'd been dragged into this, too. He should never have gone to her place with Christina, and he should have contacted his brother as soon as he'd gotten the chance and told him sure, he was in Cancun, living it up, and to tell Mom and Dad everything was cool.

Thankfully, partial salvation had arrived during his latest conversation with Houston. They'd squared things between them about what happened in the desert, in a matter of a few sentences. Mark hadn't known, hadn't realized about the cards. Houston knew that. They were cool. They'd discussed Matthew, and Mark had left knowing the guy would do his very best to keep his impetuous younger brother safe. He couldn't have asked for more and the relief he felt was palpable. And on that note, he'd drifted off to sleep not long after they'd taken off.

He didn't dream, Gilles was right about that. Not in the normal sense. However, sleep wasn't total oblivion, not for him, for he still carried a subconscious awareness, enabling him to swim down into the depths, and pay a visit to the core, to say hello, to pass the time of day and maybe check on its unscrupulous progress.

Only on this occasion he hadn't been the sole visitor. And what he'd attempted to describe to Gilles later hadn't covered the half of it, simply because it had been so difficult to describe. He'd seen her in daylight first of all, her face shifting and unrecognizable, and every step she had taken had invigorated the entire world. He'd felt the thrum of power in the ground beneath his feet. It was beautiful, and he'd even reached out, because he'd wanted her blessing, too. But when she had finally stepped toward him, everything around him had shifted and her steps were no longer a bounty—they were a blight. When she'd pushed him, she was made of steel and he couldn't move. That's how she had forced him to listen.

Death. By his own hand. She'd showed him endless means, all of them cruel, all of them heartless and final. He'd felt the core diminish somewhere deep in his consciousness, and he knew then, as it withered, so would he. He'd remembered Toby's words about his fear of what he might become, and now here *she* was, a dark avenger in the depths of his soul, determined to ensure that becoming would never take place.

He had awakened with a jolt. He'd felt sick, delirious, and he'd panicked and gone to waken Gilles. Only instead of the expected reassurance, he'd upset the other man, too, no matter how hard he'd tried to hide it.

Dimitra. Just a girl. But who the hell was she? What was she? Even now, remnants of her still lay there in the depths. She wasn't completely gone. Tiny pieces like shattered glass that made his heart ache and poisoned his insides. Alongside her the core quailed in her presence.

But thank the gods for Gilles, who'd kept him talking, who'd pulled him inch by inch out of those shriveled depths and away from her steel clutches—in the nick of time, too, for they had landed soon after and Mark had had to ready himself for an entirely new charade.

They had been aloft for less than an hour and he was listening to the small talk going back and forth across the aisle between Gilles and Mina. Some of it roused his interest; he hadn't realized there were Houses in Austria and France and Peru, and that some were already independent of the Foundation while others, like themselves, depended upon it utterly. News also, was the fifty-fifty split between those who considered Deacon to be the devil incarnate, while others believed he was a savior who would protect them from their Grand Father's madness.

He tried to keep track. Occasionally he asked a question, one that hopefully didn't make him sound stupid, all the while struggling to keep up his veneer of aristocratic irreverence. On the whole it worked enough to stop him from brooding and kept him from revisiting that deadly child inside his head.

He also sensed a game developing. More than once he caught Mina glancing in his direction when she thought he wasn't paying attention, and he wondered if she might be looking for any cracks in his façade. He certainly didn't mind, it added to the distraction. If there was some kind of challenge being thrown his way, then he liked that even more. He'd jokingly asked Gilles if she was cute, but she had turned out to be far more than that. She was exceptionally beautiful. One of those long-legged, gorgeous girls he just might have had a chance with in Hollywood, relying purely on his own looks and charm, providing there were no A-listers sniffing around.

But things were different now. Amongst this crowd he was about as A-list as he could get, and just the mere thought of what he'd like to do to her was becoming a very effective tool in shutting out all the darkness and dread. Completely. Utterly. Absolutely. Temporary salvation beckoned and he fought to keep the smile off his face while he considered the possibilities.

Would she let him?

Touch, it would be inevitable and intimate, but this was no mere human donor and potentially she was a considerable risk. Could be she was simply a lure, fish bait for her Elder, what was his name—Goran? There to break him apart so they'd know everything about him. Or maybe not. Did they even care? And was she even the *slightest* bit interested?

She was interested. He was sure of it.

He looked down, noticed his left hand on the armrest, fingers tap, tap, tapping, over and over. He clenched his fist, slowly released. Every move could be a giveaway. He went back to his bored expression. For all of half a minute. Then he deliberately set his eyes on her.

Look at me.

She was still talking to Gilles who was commanding all her attention. Come on. Look at me.

Look at me.

There. She faltered mid-sentence, her eyes shifted toward him and he held them, just a couple of seconds before he broke off. He settled back, waited another minute, then he stood up and stepped into the aisle.

"Everything okay, Mark?" Gilles asked.

He nodded, pointed toward the back of the plane. "I need some rest." He headed off into the middle cabin before any more conversation was forthcoming. He saw the donors had gathered together under a cluster of light and were playing cards. Every one of them raised their head as he entered. He ignored them and continued on until he reached the three men, Mina's companions, sitting alongside one another. He gave them a little more attention this time, paused, nodded, and a calculating note floated to the surface to give these men some of his time before they arrived at their destination.

Then a short corridor past a small kitchen and a bathroom and he entered the dimly lit rear cabin. His face broke into a grin. Two wide leather seats on either side of a polished table, cupboards and drawers lining the rear bulkhead—and a bed.

He sat on the corner of the bed, took off his shirt, pulled off his loafers, and dug his toes into the carpet. He'd told Gilles he needed rest, and this, if it came down to it, was as good a place as any. But rest meant sleep, and that meant another horrific trip into the bowels of his psyche, unless of course the girl had gone. Maybe now would be a good time to—

A soft tap at the door.

He leapt to his feet, flicked the latch, then retreated and was back on the bed when Mina entered the cabin. She looked tense, apprehensive, and remained standing just inside the door. He stood up. "Hi."

A pause. "Did I come here by choice?"

"I don't know. Did you?" He backed off and smiled, gave her a little more space. He watched her take a step further into the cabin, saw her eyes flick toward the door as it clicked shut behind her. "It was a request," he assured her. "You don't have to stay."

"Really?"

"Really. Your choice. Although I have to warn you, I'd very much like you to stay and I can be quite persuasive." That got him a smile.

"Oh, I can imagine," she answered. He saw her eyes move down over his shoulders and torso.

He held out his hand, saw her hesitate. "Come on," he whispered. "Don't be afraid."

"I'm not." She tossed her hair back over her shoulder and he watched it glisten in the light. Oh, yeah, he liked that.

He reached out quickly and took her hand. "Let's get this over with." He tried to keep the grip light, inconsequential, and felt the pushing and pulling of thought between them, establishing boundaries. They were close now, so close he caught a myriad of scents—smoke, jet fuel, blood, fallen leaves, rain and concrete and moss on stone—and he closed his eyes, all the better to take them all in, take them apart and discover everything about her.

"Oh…" she whispered.

"What?" He kept his eyes closed, still focused while his other hand brushed back her hair and he leaned in, gently grazing the area of skin just below her ear. He felt the pulse, not the blinding, overpowering hammer of a donor, but steady, somnolent, hypnotic. But he wouldn't bite her there. Not yet.

"You're built like a Greek statue."

"By-product of a former career." He could feel her other hand now, roaming over his chest, sliding down over his abdomen. He opened his eyes and gave her that smile. "So, are you staying or leaving?"

"Oh, I'm staying."

"Good." He let go of her hand and started on her shirt, his fingers expertly twisting tiny buttons that felt smooth, cold, like pearls. His mind was already three, four steps ahead, planning as he always did, establishing a path of control. He kissed her gently and withdrew, backed off just a millimeter, became aware of her leaning forward, eager, pushing to reestablish the contact.

One thing that had astonished and delighted him from the very beginning—how easily the donors had capitulated and opened themselves to him, how they had placed themselves completely and utterly at his mercy. His growing sexual ambiguity had been another revelation, as he drew in both genders to feed his appetite. Because it wasn't just about the blood. Not for him. Their delicious surrender, how they shuddered and trembled to his slightest touch, it excited him beyond measure and made sex more enjoyable than it ever had been while he was alive.

Of course, with a fellow vampire this would be different. He'd come close, on maybe two occasions, with Christina. But both times he'd felt her hesitate and he'd backed off. When she'd found him right at the very beginning, out there on the shore in the dark, he'd been left to die, ruined and comatose, still wrapped up in the horror of his passing and rebirth. He didn't know what she had seen inside him, how deep she'd been able to look, but he'd wondered. As for Mina—

She'd already undone the button on his jeans, and despite their generation differences she thought she was on equal ground right now, and maybe even had the upper hand. So he played along, gave her a little room while his hand rose and cupped her breast, still encased in her bra, pinched and teased her nipple gently through delicate lace, then gasped as he felt her hand slide down into the confines of his clothing and take a good, firm grip along the length of his cock. It was already engorged, pushing, looking for a means of escape. It eagerly conspired with her and he had to fight hard the urge to let her go further. But then he slowly, inexorably pulled her hand away and lifted her until she was sitting on the table. He pushed her knees apart, looked down at her, and smiled. Her eyes were bright, alive with challenge and mischief. He slid the shirt from her shoulders while he kissed her again and let it fall below her elbows. Then he pulled. "I can see," he whispered as he twisted the fabric behind her, pulling it taut and catching her wrists together, "I'll have to restrain you."

He pressed his hand against the flat of her belly, unfastened and worked his fingers slowly down the front of her low-rise jeans. He trailed the tip of his tongue beneath her ear. "And now it's my turn."

CHAPTER 20
GILLES

Five hours into the flight, Gilles became aware of a presence alongside him. He opened his eyes and found Mina curled there in the next seat. She was wearing a toweling robe, her hair was wet, her face was clear of makeup, and she was staring at him. She looked fragile, vulnerable. He caught the glimpse of a faint shadow on her throat. He sat up. "Is everything okay?" He glanced over his shoulder. No sign of Gannon.

She smiled. It warmed her entire face, and he breathed a sigh of relief.

"Where did you find him, Gilles?"

Ah. Where to begin. "He's just an orphan, Mina. Like everyone else in our House, either lost or cast aside."

Mina hugged her knees close under her chin. "A mistake on someone's part, don't you think?"

He didn't know what to say, didn't know what had passed between them, but the fact that she was asking questions—"Yes, and somewhat of a mystery."

Her smile broke into a grin. "He's high generation, certainly—frightening, greedy, a control freak, and I can't take my eyes off him."

Gilles barked out a good-natured laugh. "But you obviously managed to break away at some point."

"Barely."

He grew serious for a moment. "He didn't hurt you."

"Oh, no." Another smile flashed across her face. "But he likes to play games."

"Is a word of caution likely to fall on deaf ears, Mina?"

She shrugged. "Probably. What are you going to tell me, Gilles? Don't break his heart or don't get too close?"

"Something like that."

She shot him another grin. He gave up and lay back. He hadn't known what to think when they'd both disappeared, but in the end, he'd settled, got some rest and to hell with it. If there was any trouble he figured he'd hear all about it. By the looks of things, they'd both survived the encounter and that was that, unless she'd managed to tear off his head at some point. But, no, he sensed the man resting, somewhere at the rear of the jet.

Mina shifted closer.

"Tired?" He raised his arm and she moved into the crook of his shoulder. Once she'd settled, he attempted the same. This flight had turned out to be more peaceful than expected. For some, at least.

An hour before they were due to arrive, Mina had disappeared and Merrill brought his suit. When he looked toward the middle cabin he saw Gannon, already dressed in formal pants and shirt, standing in the aisle and talking to Mina's male colleagues. Their body language looked relaxed, like they'd been gathered like that for some time. Gilles was impressed. The man was doing his job. And by the time the jet was on its final approach, both Gannon and Mina were in their respective seats, buckled in, eyes forward, all business.

It was still dark when they landed and the air carried a bitter chill as Gilles stepped nimbly down from the jet toward one of three waiting vehicles. The airfield looked deserted, just a few admin buildings, their windows in darkness, the control tower, and two larger hangars in the distance. To the far left he caught sight of a sparse, moving snake of vehicle headlights traveling along a distant highway. Looking back he saw Gannon paused at the top of the steps, his eyes closed, allowing his heightened olfactory senses to go to work.

Shortly afterwards, they were together in the rear of the middle vehicle, a black limousine. Gannon looked uncomfortable. They were alone. Mina, the other three men, and their donors were in the other vehicles. Somehow, Gannon was being afforded special treatment, right from the get-go. A pity then, their host wasn't aware of Gannon's aversion to limousines, stretch or otherwise.

"What do we know about Mina's team?" Gilles asked.

"Ryan, Powell, and Gage." Gannon rhymed them off. "Gage, brown hair, he's the computer guy, and knows finance. The other two, like Houston. Ryan is the taller one. They're okay."

"And do you have them under your spell?"

Gannon smiled. "I'm working on it."

"Good. We'll need to provide a united front, with you at the helm. The Europeans are old, and they're bound to pick up a strong sense of your generation. As Delacour mentioned, everyone we meet is likely to defer to you and they will insist on formal protocols."

"No pressure, huh?"

"Well, as we discussed back at the house, there may be times when I can't be with you."

"Unless I insist. I'm third gen. That counts for something, doesn't it?"

"Yes." He tried to keep a level tone. "And if I'm not mistaken, that will be four generations higher than the Foundation president. But we don't want them to know that. Don't underestimate these people, Mark."

Gannon laughed, his mood appeared lighter. "I know. I'm just kidding." A pause. "But what if someone figures it out?"

"It shouldn't happen, provided we keep a low profile. As far as we can tell, no one over here has been in regular contact with Deacon's people for a very long time. I'm assuming Mina still doesn't know?" He raised an eyebrow.

Gannon shook his head. "No, she doesn't."

"Good."

In the silence that followed, Gilles took the time to get an assessment of the other vehicles. The one behind was lagging, but soon caught up. He realized he was slightly on edge, that he would be glad when they'd all arrived at their destination. Then, out of the blue—

"You'll stay with me, though. You won't just turn me loose."

His thoughts interrupted, he didn't say anything for a moment.

"Gilles?"

"Yes. Yes, of course. As much as I possibly can."

The cars swept, then crawled into London. A glance out of the window gave Gilles a view of low, heavy clouds colored an all-too-familiar dull orange by city lights. It wasn't raining and yet the pavement still shone with the aftermath of a recent downpour. After a while, the streets narrowed and the buildings closed in. When the vista suddenly opened up and the car swept onto a bridge over the Thames, he heard Gannon let out a soft exclamation.

"Wow..."

"First time in London?"

"Yes."

"If we get time for a walk while we're here, then we should."

"A walk by this river?"

"Yes, if you like."

Gannon nodded. "Can we stop the car, get out?"

"No."

"Just for a—"

"No. Third generation or not."

The man sat back, but not quite as relaxed as before. Gilles saw his foot tapping, his fingers running along the cuffs of his sober, navy Armani suit. The city was already having an effect, as all old places did, and it would be so much more profound for a vampire of Gannon's caliber. Layer upon layer of history, tugging and pulling at his senses, telling him its stories, revealing all its glories and miseries.

Across the river, along streets lined with blocky, imposing buildings, and then into a square filled with slender trees and ornate, wrought-iron fencing. The vehicle slowed dramatically and turned, crept through a narrow arch into a private mews, and came to a halt alongside a row of carriage houses adjoining their much grander counterparts.

"Is this it?"

Gilles nodded. The door opened. He got out first, spied a small reception committee, then gave a quick hand signal to Gannon. They were the first out, as protocol demanded. Gannon appeared to have gotten a grip and the mask was now firmly on. Gilles followed him as they walked toward stone steps and an open doorway. There was a formal bow afforded Gannon and polite instructions to enter. Up the steps, they entered a stone-floored corridor that led straight into the interior. At one point Gilles spotted a row of bells near the ceiling. This was the old servants quarter he reasoned, adapted precariously for the twenty-first century by way of long, anachronistic ropes of electrical cable that ran high along the walls. He heard the others, their footsteps a short distance behind him.

Through another doorway, a right turn onto thick blue carpeting, and into a wide, grand hallway where a huge, glittering chandelier hung above light oak-paneled walls. And directly below it, one of the Foundation bigwigs, waiting to greet them. A mutual bow between him and Gannon, while Gilles remained a few paces behind, completely ignored.

Mina appeared in his peripheral vision and he felt a slight tug at his sleeve. Her eyes shifted upward as he glanced toward her. After a moment, he looked up and slightly to the left, where a wide, cantilever staircase curled toward the upper floors. Partway up, a man was standing there, looking down, watching the formalities. Pale skin and close-cropped blond hair, he had a look of physical strength about him. He became aware of Gilles' scrutiny and they exchanged a brief, barely perceptible nod.

Gilles took note and switched his attention back to Gannon. So close to dawn, it appeared they were about to be led to their respective sleeping quarters. They were, apparently, the last ones to arrive, and Gannon was being informed there would be a meeting, promptly, at sundown.

Moments later, they were surrounded by human members of the Foundation staff, who picked up their bags and began to lead them up the steps toward their sleeping quarters. Gilles stayed close to his charge, who had assumed a proper measure of lofty arrogance and was allowing everyone else to mill and fuss around him, until they arrived at their quarters, where he insisted that Gilles have an adjoining room.

He watched Gannon and Mina share a glance before they separated, before Gannon took his donor Megan's hand and retired to his suite. Once he had Merrill settled into their quarters, Gilles left and knocked quietly on Gannon's door.

"Who was the guy on the stairs?"

Gilles was in the midst of checking Gannon's accommodation. "Security. I haven't seen him before. But Mina has."

"He's perceptive."

He stepped out of the bathroom, satisfied everything looked secure. "Anything we should be worried about?"

Gannon shrugged carelessly. Megan was pulling off his jacket. "Probably not."

"You're sure?"

"Yes." The man's fingers were fumbling with the cufflinks of his shirt. The mask had dropped and he was showing all the signs of being overtired and hungry, having not rested when he was supposed to on the plane. "So, I take it—" more tugging and pulling at his shirt "—there's no one hiding in the bathtub?" An insolent grin spread languidly across his face.

"No," Gilles replied flatly. "Get some sleep, Mark."

"Yes, sir." A mock salute. And now Gannon had taken hold of his donor, was already nuzzling at her throat and mumbling, "—fuck these fucking cuff links—"

Gilles rolled his eyes and left them to it. A quick look left and right along the corridor, beyond intermittent pairs of shoes, all laid neatly outside their owners doors, waiting to be polished; it all seemed orderly and quiet, so he entered his own room and reluctantly had Merrill get him ready for sleep.

"You're tense, distracted," she told him.

"It's like dealing with a child."

"Just as well he has you, then. He *is* young, Gilles, and he has a lot to bear."

He took her hand, brushed his lips against her wrist, felt the seductive warmth that lay pulsing beneath her skin, its promise and vitality plucking at his attention. "I just hope Delacour knows what he's doing."

"Too late to worry about that now, love."

"Agreed." He sank back and curled around her. Blood and sleep. He probably needed it as much as Gannon did.

And as for security, right now he knew it was time to rely on precedence, protocols, and other centuries-old forms of behavior. Predictable and therefore safe, or so everyone in this house thought. But times were changing, were being changed, their lives now thrown to the vagaries of the wind. They were uneasy thoughts that curdled his stomach and threatened to keep him awake.

Fortunately, solace lay in his arms. Merrill felt soft and warm, and as his hand drifted across her stomach, she arched her back and pressed herself against him. He moved lower, felt her pulse quicken and the beginnings of his own arousal. He kissed her shoulder, then her neck, heard her let out the faintest whisper of a sigh as his fangs slid forth and pressed gently, teasing against tender flesh. But not yet. Not yet. Blood and sleep, yes. But they could wait a little while longer.

CHAPTER 21
MINA

"Sit down, Mina. I'll take care of it."

Celia dragged both their travel bags over to one side of the room, and a knowing smile appeared as the woman began to unpack.

"Is it that obvious?" She sat down on the edge of the bed and pulled off her boots.

The other woman laughed. "Yes, but he *is* captivating." She pulled out a jacket wrapped in tissue and shook it out.

Mina certainly couldn't argue with that. And the disturbing, butterfly-in-the-stomach feeling she'd experienced out in the desert was now magnified tenfold. She fell back across the canopy, and stared up at the ceiling. It was ridiculous and unprecedented how she felt right now, and it had begun as soon as she'd stepped aboard the jet. Oh, how Irena and Charles would laugh at her, caught up in her own nets of infatuation. She sat up again, her body disjointed, on edge and tingly, and felt the mattress shift as Celia crawled up behind her.

"Don't worry, it wasn't overly noticeable."

Mina let out a long, protracted sigh as the woman began to massage the knotted muscles along her shoulders. "You have no idea how hard I had to work at that."

"I can imagine." Celia's hands shifted to the back of her neck. "Who's the other man accompanying him?"

"Oh, that's Gilles."

Fingers paused for a moment. "Delacour's assassin? Well, that's surprising. Not whom I had imagined at all."

She nodded, beginning to unwind, physically at least. "Yeah, he's a nice guy. Despite his reputation."

"This is turning out to be quite a trip. Just as well you didn't bring Martin with you."

Mina snorted out a laugh. "Gods, can you imagine?"

"Yes," the other woman joined her in laughter. "Unfortunately, I can. Although I suspect he would have dashed off to the British Museum or somewhere equally stuffy at the earliest opportunity."

And yes, maybe he would have, but then again, there was no predicting what Martin would do, which is why she had asked—begged—Goran, once she'd discovered who would be on that jet, to allow Celia, one of his favorites, to accompany her instead. The woman was levelheaded, in her mid-thirties now, and had been one of Goran's donors since the age of twenty. She and Mina had become good friends.

There was also another player in this tangled mess of attraction and longing. Oliver Bryant. Perched like an eagle on the stairs, watching her. It was perhaps unfortunate that some of the men she attracted were more dominant, less compliant and accepting of whom and what she was. She suspected, no—*knew* her choices were also partly to blame. But she had discovered, quite early on, as her extraordinary allure had emerged, that the sexual battleground was infinitely more interesting when up against someone of Bryant's nature. She enjoyed sex, always had an appetite for it, and it was something she fully embraced and refused to hide or apologize for. And when circumstances shifted, she had always been able to let go, but she also accepted that not all her partners over the years had been willing to do the same. Bryant certainly hadn't, and in truth she had missed him, and wondered if her current choice of donor, the intense Dr. Morris, was an unconscious effort to replace what they'd had.

But now everything was different. Her confidence and aplomb in such matters were cracked and in danger of breaking into a million pieces.

So, who was Mark Gannon?

She had felt the attraction back in the desert like a blow to the gut, despite being unable to see or touch him. His allure had radiated like a blinding sun, had burned away her own and made her feel like a silly, bashful, *human* girl. Ah, and that wretched moment before she'd boarded the jet, knowing they would likely meet face to face, wondering if he'd be indifferent, or derisive, whether he would simply dismiss her, because surely, with an allure this strong, he'd have women, and men, literally throwing themselves at him. And there she was, a siren, a heartbreaker in her own right, about to be given a taste of her own medicine.

The first hour aboard the jet had been agonizing, and she'd tried so, so hard not to stare at him every chance she got, had clung desperately to Gilles as a distraction, right up to the point when he'd looked at her. Really looked at her.

After that it had been a delicious and terrifying blur. Unused to being the submissive partner, she'd gone all out and ended up in a wrestling match, the result of which had seen her tied up in her own clothing. That beginning had been contentious and exhilarating, and as for the rest, his touch had been deft, practiced, strong, and yet wickedly gentle in the right places. The only truly fearful moment had arrived when he'd bitten her.

She had never allowed that before and there had been a moment of panic, while he'd crouched low over her spread thighs like a predatory leopard. His hand had traveled upward, between her breasts, over her chin, and two of his fingers had slid invasively inside her mouth. And it was at that moment of distraction that his teeth had pierced her inner thigh, and she'd felt that first wave of blistering ecstasy as he slipped so easily inside her head. Yet somehow, toward the end, the physicality had drifted into something different and the attentions of his fingers, his tongue, and his cock were akin to a ritual of worship that had left her begging. And he'd bitten her, again and again. She didn't care.

In the end…

Her head lolled and she snapped open her eyes.

"Shh, you're tired," whispered Celia directly behind her. "And you need to feed." Her voice sounded hollow, distant.

Mina blinked, hadn't realized she'd fallen into a daze. She shifted and curled around Celia's warmth. "You'll stay with me?" she asked.

"Of course. Now come on, let's get those clothes off."

A short while later, satiated and curled in the arms of her donor, she began to drop toward sleep, fully expecting to sink back into her earlier, erotic torpor. But instead, she kept on falling. Until she hit the ground hard, bounced, and shattered into fragments so tiny a slight breeze was able to pick her up and carry her this way and that. Until she blended entirely with sand the consistency of fine powder.

Looking up, she could see them towering above her. Their copper hides glistening in startling daylight. And again, one of them reached down, as if to capture all her pieces in his long metal fingers. She felt them dig into the sand, the creature's grasp eventually becoming desperate and ultimately futile.

It was the same vision as before, but this time—

The one now crouched and digging, so frantic, so terribly distraught. It now bore a face. It was the face of Mark Gannon.

CHAPTER 22
MARK

He waited for what he considered long enough. Then, after a conspiring wink at Megan, he slipped out the door, hoping fervently he wasn't too late. No one around, and there it lay, across the corridor, two doors down. Plain, solid, and the thin draught creeping from under it as they'd passed by earlier and the scents it bore had told him exactly where it led.

Still undiscovered, he crept along, opened the door, entered the stairwell, and looked up. Gilles would never have allowed this, which is why he'd behaved like such an asshole and thrown up a smokescreen. No doubt there was a humble, crawl-on-his-belly apology in the cards for this evening. But right now—

Around him and below him he sensed movement, members of staff going about their business, and those like him, satiated and slow, on the verge of sleep. But not for him. Not yet. Instead, he took the steps two at a time, hesitated in front of the door at the top, placed his hand against it—and pushed.

Cold air whistled through the gap and he let out a grin. He slipped off his shoe and used it to jam open the door. After all, it would be no good if the thing slammed shut and locked him out. Not at this time of day.

Stepping out onto the roof, he breathed deep and let the wind whip at his shirt and riff through his hair while his eyes checked out the horizon. The sky was still choked with clouds but the dawn was already emerging. He could feel its might behind the storm and could see the earth rolling inexorably toward it. Its power, and his utter helplessness before it were beyond exhilarating.

But now something else clawed for his attention, drawing him away from all notions of danger and his inner alarms; it was the siren song of the city and the reason why he was up here in the first place. It howled and cried and he took it all in. He sensed the river flowing, just streets away, and all the blood and sweat and death and life drenching the buildings and the land below, echoed on and on and on in every street, as far as he could see. He felt the hammer of endless feet walking and running, vehicles and carts and horses, and the relentless roll of day after day after day as life continued, leaving its mark smeared indiscriminate and everywhere. Steam trains and black curls of smoke from chimneys seventy years old and the stench from the river and fire and parades and bombs dropped from the sky and murder and joy. Flowers and fish, sorrow and marching bands and glittering towers, the horror of the gibbet and church bells. It all came in a rush, and when a thin sliver of dawn sprang like a dart through the clouds, he was both mesmerized and unprepared.

"Sir!"

He gasped, impaled. It was a piercing lance, a cruel arrow already slammed deep in his chest, forcing him backward, until he faltered and dropped to one knee.

"Sir!"

Someone had him by the arm, was pulling him back toward the door. He couldn't breathe, it was so hot, and he struggled, scrambled, searched desperately for cover. There was a man, hauling him inside, into the shadow of the stairwell, and he crouched against the wall while his rescuer, jacket flapping in the wind, struggled with his trapped shoe. Mark felt completely helpless, still delirious from the heady delights of the city, and now knocked stupid by the pain. It was utterly glorious and when the door finally closed, he began to laugh.

Now all the sounds and scents were dimmed and that awful sunlight was banished. The man pulled him to his feet, and slid his shoulders up the smooth, painted wall.

"Are you all right, Sir?"

"Shh," Mark told him, grinning like an idiot. "If he finds out, I'll be in trouble, but I'm so glad you rescued me." His senses were beginning to sharpen now, latching on to the more immediate, the heat radiating from his rescuer, and the accompanying scent of car polish, apples, and brake dust. Upright now, he pushed the man toward the adjacent wall, and watched him relax.

"It was the door alarm. I was sent to check it."

"And you saved my life." Green eyes, skin almost as pale as his own, freckles around the nose, a few wrinkles around the eyes, thick, wavy brown hair, cropped short and so beautiful that he reached up and ran his fingers through it, then gripped gently, at the back of the head, near the scalp. He felt the man catch his breath. "You're one of the staff here."

"Yes, Sir."

Mark pulled him closer, felt the man's body heat, tasted the sharp tang of an alcohol-based aftershave and the skin of the throat, slightly rough on the tip of his tongue. "Don't be afraid," he whispered. "I can make this quite pleasurable."

Back in his room. Flat on his back, in bed, staring at nothing. If only it was always like this. His mind was awash with sensation—the respect, the deference, the private jets, and everyone calling him Sir; all those scents and tastes, the hidden secrets of cities, unraveling and revealing themselves right before his eyes. Blood, sex, body heat. Mina's skin against his fingertips, the way she closed her eyes and arched her back. And no hate, no pain, no Deacon, no worry, no longing for something he couldn't have. Just this, and only this.

He was still overwhelmed, still reeling and drunk with it, and he knew he had to slow it down and acknowledge he needed rest. He rolled over and curled up against Megan, settled against her soft skin and comforting heat, while the storm inside him raged on.

Sundown. And by the time Gilles knocked on his door he was sober, contrite, and ashamed. He'd acted like a pain in the ass in front of a man he considered a friend, he'd gone off on some risky escapade, out on the roof, set off the alarms, almost gotten himself killed and—lets not forget—taken blood from someone other than his donor that, in all probability, had broken every rule in the book.

"I'm sorry." Those were his first words. "About this morning."

"You were tired." Giles stepped past him, and entered the suite.

He closed the door. "No. It was the city." He stared at his shoes for a moment. There was a slight scuff on the left one that hadn't quite polished out. "I went out on the roof."

The other man flashed him a look of astonishment. "The roof. At dawn."

"Yes, I just had to get out there to take a look and I almost got fried. I set off an alarm and some guy rescued me, dragged me back inside, and I pushed him against the wall and I drank—" He stopped. Gilles wasn't looking at him any more. He'd turned away, had slipped his hands in his pockets, and was shaking his head like he always did when Mark pissed him off. "Like I said," he finished, "I'm sorry."

"And is that it? The extent of it?"

"Yes. Swear to God."

That got him a snort of derision. There was an awkward pause. He opened his mouth once more, about to say something else, when Gilles raised his hand.

"Two things," the man said.

Mark settled back on his heels, stayed silent, and grudgingly prepared himself to take what was coming.

"Number one. You leave the safety of your room. You go out alone. You climb out onto the roof—at dawn—and almost get yourself killed."

Mark nodded, tried not to wince as Gilles' eyes now bored into him.

"Number two—all that cufflink bullshit. You were lying to me."

"I didn't say any—"

"You were lying, Mark."

"I'm sorry."

"Oh, and let's not get into the impropriety of it all. Triggering alarms, compromising their security. What about the man, your rescuer? A Foundation staff member?"

"I didn't take too much." His hackles were on the rise, he was becoming annoyed, angry; he heard it in his voice. Unreasonable on his part, but there it was. Gilles sensed it, he saw his face change, saw it grow cold.

"Mark, I can't help you if you lie to me."

"I know. And I can't promise I won't do it again."

"So where does that leave us?"

"You need to learn to read me better."

Another silence, so much worse this time. He watched Gilles take a slow breath, noted the stiffness in his shoulders. "Are we ready?" the man said.

Mark nodded, fought his temper, and tugged irritably on those infernal shirt cuffs.

"Then we'd better go, Mr. Gannon. Or we'll be late."

With his new eyes, it had become a simple matter to perceive the differences between light reflected off the window and light passing through it. Despite the glare of the room's interior, he still had a good view of the square outside. He was on the second floor and was currently looking out into the street toward a wrought-iron fence and the trees beyond it. It looked dark and peaceful out there, with just a slight breeze barely shifting the topmost branches.

Behind him he could hear Gage, huddled over a table discussing the finer points of asset liquidation with someone from the London group. So far, the meeting had been a dismal affair. By all accounts, Weiss was in the process of revoking all his trusts, while Deacon was contesting his validity to do so, and the fact that Deacon's name had cropped up at all had thrown a lot of the attendees into a panic.

Mark was using this break in the proceedings to steal a little time alone and acquire some breathing space. As soon as he had set foot in the room in the earlier part of the evening, the mental rush of thought had begun. Far stronger than he'd ever encountered before, while those present, some of them hundreds of years old, appeared determined to settle the mystery of him, even as they outwardly acknowledged, and in some cases openly deferred to, the high generation aura that surrounded him.

There was deft, well-practiced use in that mental barrage, too. It came at him from all sides, both subtle and bold, ending in a myriad of attitudes—bemusement, suspicion, and in some cases anger when they came up against what Gilles like to call the Gannon brick wall. All of it layered beneath a veneer of polite greeting and easy conversation, comments about travel and the weather, commiseration on the amnesia surrounding his rebirth, and it didn't stop, even as the meeting had progressed, while they sought to get to the bottom of this mystery he represented. It had been tough, distracting, and its deflection had taken up a lot of his energy.

As for the meeting's purpose and subject matter, he was completely out of his depth. Luckily, Gage wasn't. Thankful he'd made a point of discovering Mina's colleagues' talents before they'd landed, it had been an easy thing to refer the technical aspects of the meeting to Gage and let him take the lead. He'd also had Gilles' help, talking quietly on the sidelines when matters of general protocol came up, determined not to let Mark sink like a stone, despite their earlier exchange.

But one thing was becoming clear. With the exception of a number of smaller properties, bank accounts, and commodity reserves, all the big money was in Weiss's hands and locked in a power struggle with his direct progeny, Deacon. So, why were they here? To try and steal away some of the scraps before it all came tumbling down? That appeared to be the summation of it so far. They were all about to get their finances severely curtailed, and could do absolutely nothing about it. He glanced down at his expensive suit and felt like some trust fund kid about to be cut off by a disgruntled father. The absurdity of it made his face twitch.

He continued to bask in the moment and attempted to reaffirm some modicum of sanity. A short while later, he sensed a man on the approach. He frowned. He was in no mood to hold a civilized conversation with a stranger, but neither was he about to make a run for it. Mark kept his mouth shut and offered no acknowledgment as the man, who initially seemed content to remain silent and share the view out of the window, arrived.

Eventually, "You gave my man quite a scare." A quiet voice, deep timbre, English accent.

"I'm sorry." Two words that were becoming annoying and repetitive. "The city. I couldn't resist."

"So I gather. It's understandable. London takes some getting used to."

Mark looked over his new companion. Blond hair, a couple of inches shorter in height, a face that suggested late thirties or early forties—no guessing how old he really was. There was a faint glimmer of a smile there, on a face he recognized from the night before, watching him like a hawk from the stairs.

"Forgive my presumption, Mr. Gannon," the man continued, "but someone of that name disappeared from your approximate location on the west coast of North America not too long ago." He paused, held out his hand. "My name is Bryant."

Mark stared at the hand, didn't reciprocate, and returned his eyes to the window. "I think you know enough about me already, Bryant." A bland smile escaped him. "And call me Mark."

The man let his hand fall. "Not many would risk what you did this morning."

Lacking patience, he threw caution to the wind. "Crazy, huh? But this isn't Los Angeles." He looked across at Bryant. "She sings."

A barely perceptible nod. "That, she does."

"Do you get used to it?"

"Yes and no. Sometimes..." Bryant shrugged. "Paris is much the same."

"Then I have to go there, too." Mark looked over his shoulder and saw Mina and Gilles across the room. He caught their eye, gave them a helpless look, hoping to illicit a feeling of guilt, after leaving him in this man's clutches. He saw a look of concern flash across Mina's face, mirrored by Gilles for a moment, before the man registered a knowing smile and pulled Mina away. Mark grinned, turned back to Bryant, and gave him his full attention. He noticed the other man had followed his gaze and saw his eyes had tightened momentarily.

"So, I'm guessing we're talking because you don't like mysteries, Bryant."

The man shrugged, his easier expression now fully regained. "There's always a story to tell, Mark. Especially by those taken under Delacour's wing."

"And the fact that I don't remember, that I'm not forthcoming?"

"Let's just say it's my business to know."

"Ah." Mark closed his eyes for a moment. "And yet, you don't think I'm lying. No, wait—you don't know whether I'm lying or not. And it's beginning to yank your chain."

Bryant glanced briefly across the room. "Everyone is guessing. Most are putting you at seventh generation, sixth at the most. I think you're higher than that."

Mark shrugged helplessly. "And what are the odds of that?"

"Slim." Bryant's lips narrowed. "These days our Elders are pillars of discretion. Closeted, secretive. They're also jealous, covetous, and protective of their status. The last thing they want is—"

"Someone like me."

They both smiled. It was Bryant's turn to shrug. "They like everything kept in order. Lineage, hierarchies, ancestry, everyone knowing to whom they belong."

"They don't appear to like me very much."

"You're an Elder. That counts for quite a lot, hence the deference you've received."

Mark stared at the floor, noticed the edge of the carpet was slightly frayed next to the window. He felt the other man staring at him. "What if I'm a mistake, an error in someone's judgment?"

"They don't like mistakes, Mark."

"So, what is this? A warning, to watch my back?"

Bryant nodded. "Maybe..."

"But, what?"

"Your death is still with you, the pain of it is written in your eyes, on your face. I'm betting the others can't see it, the barbarity—"

Mark held up his hand for silence. He felt as if he was being peeled apart like an onion. "So, my creator was a monster." Inside the core was laughing. But he had to stop thinking about it. He had to block it out, shut it out, to deny it. He looked at the man standing before him, so able to pry him apart, and wondered if he'd have to do something about that.

Bryant grew a little wary. Nevertheless, he continued. "There's something else."

"Oh?"

"I think what was done had a purpose. I don't think you're a mistake at all."

Mark stared at him, eyes boring in hard until he saw the man falter. The core wanted his head on a platter.

Bryant took a step back, offered him a slight bow. "I have offended and I apologize," he said. "I'll take my leave. Please be careful, Mr. Gannon. No more trips out onto the roof."

Mark watched him go, and fought to bring the core, all spite and vitriol, under control. He stared out of the window, and let the view outside take him away. He wanted to be out there, he realized. Out there, lost in the city. Anywhere but here.

CHAPTER 23
GILLES

"Something's wrong."

That was an understatement. Gilles saw the guy Mark had been talking to leave the room. A quick look around and he saw the others, on alert after that unnerving ripple of ire had swept through and cloaked everyone in disquiet.

"Bryant," Mina said. "I'll go after him—"

"No," Gilles told her. "Go to Mark. Distract him, calm him down." *Stop him from blowing apart his entire façade.*

He watched her go then set off calmly toward the door, and tried to ignore Gannon's mood, bitter and unhappy, tapping on every vertebra along the length of his spine.

Outside, a wide corridor led back to the grand staircase in the hallway. He spotted Bryant approaching the far end. The man stopped after realizing he was being followed and turned. Gilles slowed his approach but drew close, giving them the opportunity to talk without being overhead.

"Gilles."

He nodded by way of reply.

"I upset your boy."

"Would you mind telling me what it was about?" They had already begun a mental tug of war, and it took a few moments to subside. There would be no handshake on this particular occasion, no veneer of politeness. Generations, he'd put them about the same, and yet somehow, this man had got through to Gannon, past that implacable wall.

Bryant had stopped short of the stairway, had glanced over his shoulder, presumably checking to see if anyone was around. Gilles did the same. "I was trying to fill in a few blank spaces," the man said.

"His lineage."

"Whoever it was—"

Gilles' voice came out flat. "They tortured him. Did he tell you that much?"

The man looked away for a moment, appeared embarrassed. "The pain is obvious. It runs through him like veins in a slab of marble."

Gilles cocked his head. He'd never seen that in Gannon. It made him consider further the man standing before him, and what he could see. "And your summation?"

"That he fell victim to one of our, admittedly rare, high generation undocumented."

"And you told him this?"

"I told him to be careful." He glanced back toward the room they'd just left. "That the others' attitudes could be—unsympathetic. But that wasn't what upset him."

"I see." He waited, made it clear he wanted a further explanation.

"I also told him I didn't really believe he was just the random progeny of a sadistic wild card."

"Oh?" He wasn't quite sure where this was going, but had the man guessed? Out of all the vampires gathered here, this one, decidedly low on the food chain, had ultimately cracked the code? His thoughts moved quickly toward damage control.

"There's a purpose, Gilles. Some grand design."

Another, like Delacour, who didn't consider this a simple matter of sadism? Gilles frowned.

Bryant was staring at him. "And this would make a whole lot more sense if we knew who did this."

Would it? "His current welfare is all that concerns me, Mr. Bryant."

The man nodded. "You're looking after him?"

"Yes."

"It's commendable. And the fact that he's an Elder—I'd say he needs to know where he stands," the man once again glanced back down the hallway.

"So, now you're looking after him, too."

Bryant shrugged. "Let's just say I'm intrigued. The grand design, as it were."

"Right now," Gilles told him, "all I'm looking to do is keep him out of trouble."

The man stood up straight, offered him a solemn bow. "Then I apologize if I did anything to prevent that. It won't happen again."

Gilles folded his arms across his chest and stared at the man. "Well, then."

He watched Bryant turn and leave, head down the stairs toward the main hall. Then he retraced his steps, back toward a much calmer atmosphere. He found Gannon sitting on a couch, Mina alongside him, close, regarding him exactly like Christina did, her manner protective, almost maternal. Everything appeared to be fine, and he took a seat opposite. But it was like sitting next to a volcano, never knowing if the next eruption was minutes or years away.

Gannon's fingers were tapping lightly against the stuffed arm of the couch. "You promised me a walk."

Gilles nodded. "I did. Along the Embankment. When the meeting is done, providing there is time."

"Good. I'd like that."

Ryan approached the group. "Looks like we're reconvening," he said.

The conversation had shifted.

"We should take matters into our own hands." Gevani tapped the ash from his cigarette into a small, elaborate crystal ashtray.

"What, go on the offensive?" someone asked further down the table. "Against Anton Weiss?"

The meeting was in a long, narrow dining room, just off the salon. Twin chandeliers hung low from the ceiling over the table but neither had been illuminated. Instead, low light came from a series of gilded, baroque wall sconces that left most of the room in shadow and yet picked out random aspects, such as the vertical curl of Gevani's cigarette smoke. Gilles saw that Gannon couldn't take his eyes off it as it trailed like a thin ribbon, upward from the table.

Most of the vampires here appeared to be clinging to at least some of their old, human habits. There were tumblers of brandy, a lit cigar that Gilles found particularly cloying, and veiled glances of longing toward Mina, who appeared to be basking quite happily in the glow of worship. Sex, booze, and smokes. By all accounts there were just some things one never lost the appetite for.

"What are you afraid of, Beronne? A little excitement?" Gevani laughed.

"I just don't want to get hit, like Los Angeles and Amsterdam."

"You think keeping your head down will make a difference?"

There was a murmur around the table. Gilles knew they still didn't want to believe, despite the evidence. And even if they did—

"We should try and strike a deal," one of the other women said.

Gevani stubbed out his cigarette. "With whom, Deacon? Forget it. This financial battle between them is a smoke screen. He's Weiss's direct progeny. Ultimately, he'll do as Weiss tells him. How is it none of you are willing to acknowledge that?" He stared at each one of his colleagues in turn. "The only reason we're sitting here, trying to figure out a way of staying alive, and not calmly laying our heads on the chopping block, is because we're all at least a couple of generations removed. We *think* we're independent, that we can make our own decisions. Most of our immediate ancestors are dead. That doesn't apply to Deacon."

"Deacon's hardly a puppet," the woman said.

Gilles saw Gannon smile briefly, but other than that, he was keeping his mouth shut, taking it all in.

"And have you considered," she continued, "that he's unlikely to enjoy the idea of laying his own head on the block, as you put it?" There were murmurs of agreement at that.

He became aware of movement in his peripheral vision. The door. He acknowledged Bryant as he returned and quietly sat at the table, as did some of the others. Gannon kept his eyes straight ahead. And so it went on.

"Do we have time?"

The meeting was at an end. "Two hours before we leave for the jet, and it's not far, so yes," Gilles said. He had wanted to stick around, but he also felt that getting Gannon out of the building wouldn't be a bad idea. The man was still attracting attention no matter how low key he was, and Gilles didn't want a repeat of the earlier situation. Especially now. He'd already figured out who was likely to make a deal with whom, the usual rift between Europe and the Americas had opened up, and if there had been a way to get out of there and take off early, it would have been entirely preferable as far as he was concerned.

Mina was hovering. "I'll stay with the others." She was obviously unwilling to leave Gage, Ryan, and Powell in the clutches of the Europeans.

Gannon took her hand for a moment. "Be careful. We won't be long."

Out in the hallway at the base of the stairs, Bryant was hovering. "We'll be about an hour," Gilles told him.

Bryant smiled. "The city."

He nodded, saw Bryant step aside with an easy smile as they headed for the door. Or, as it turned out, three doors: an inner, etched beveled glass door, followed by a solid wood and metal affair, then down some steps through an ornamental wrought-iron gate that swung easy and slow on its hinges.

Gannon was ahead of him. "Which way?"

"We need to cross the square. That way."

The man seemed to be in a hurry, already lost, drawn by the siren song of the city, the events of this night temporarily forgotten. And so they headed southeast, crossed the square, its streets entirely devoid of traffic. Around the corner were faint sounds of life, an occasional vehicle, and through a gap between buildings, trees and the river.

"Do you feel it?" Gannon asked him quietly.

Gilles hesitated, until it dawned on him. Not the city. "We're being followed."

Gannon nodded. "Not easy to detect in a place like this."

He was right. So much dazzle and chatter, memory oozing from every brick, drifting up from the gutter, permeating the soles of their shoes with every step. One of Bryant's men he assumed. Just keeping tabs, being careful. Not a bad move under the circumstances. Something he would have done, especially if—

"We need to get rid of him, and circle back." Gannon was looking left and right.

Not the river, then. Gilles hesitated, surprised.

You need to learn to read me better.

No shit.

Aware of his body language, he increased his stride a little and tried to stay relaxed. "Halfway down the block, cross the street, take a right." The route was still vaguely heading toward their destination.

And when they'd turned the corner—

"Some of Deacon's people are here. I can feel it," Gannon said. In the shadow between two high stone walls, the man's face had changed utterly. He'd dropped one mask and assumed another. He looked angry, dangerous. It was astonishing.

"You know what I can do," Gilles told him.

"Your disappearing act? Delacour told me... Look, can you do it without killing him?"

"Yes."

"Okay, so long as it's fast. We have to reach Mina and the others."

"Why?"

"They're in trouble."

"From Deacon?"

"No. Something else."

He frowned, was confused. But this was hardly the time to stop and have a discussion about it. Instead, he'd just have to go with his gut, and right now, away from the mental clamor at the Foundation, it was agreeing soundly with Gannon.

They continued to walk toward the end of a narrow back street. Beyond the faint scent of rotting garbage he could hear a radio playing, while up ahead to the left, light shone from a window and steam drifted from a vent and clouded the pavement. Someone up early, getting ready for the dawn and all the chaos it brought. And just before the vent, deeper shadow and the hint of a doorway. He glanced to his right, saw Gannon had already disappeared into a similar hideaway.

He ghosted. A sharp turn and black shadow twisted to gray. Kelp, rotting fish, the cry of gulls arrived, as part of his vision took in a sketch of the quayside in Marseilles. He emerged from his hiding place, saw the outline of a man at the end of the street, hesitant, making tentative steps forward into the gloom, aware that his quarry was here, somewhere. He saw Gannon step out, bold, hands in the pockets of his wool coat. Time to move.

"What did you do?"

"Broke his neck." Gilles moved to the fallen man's shoulders after checking him for weapons. "Take his legs. We need to get him into the dumpster over there. Otherwise, come the morning, he'll fry."

Gannon moved to comply. And once it was done, "A pity he wasn't armed," Gilles said. "All our weapons are back at the Foundation."

"Hang on, wait here." Gannon began to walk toward the illuminated window down the street where music still played, his stride almost jaunty, in time with the beat. A sharp crack of breaking glass. A muffled yell. It must have been all of twenty seconds and Gannon was back with a broad grin and a cleaver in his hand. A meat cleaver. "What do you think?" Looking at the man's face wasn't like looking at Gannon at all. Something had changed. "It was all I could find."

Gilles frowned. "Do you know how to—never mind. Come on."

They retraced their steps until they came upon the square, this time staying to the south side until they reached the tall row of houses that contained, among others, the Foundation. He had no idea what they were going to do, or what they were up against, but after Gannon's comment back there, he feared the worst. Weiss. His own sense of preservation was telling him it was pointless, that if they were to survive at all then they had to get away, and fast. But Gannon was now looking toward the roof.

They found a way around the back, involving trash cans, a knuckle-scraping scramble over a wall or two, and upward, until they were on the slate roof of the carriage houses. Gannon was surprisingly limber and light on his feet, or at least right now he was. Gilles followed, equally surefooted, and considered at this moment the man would have survived Marseilles in the 1940s quite well.

There were vehicles, a large van and a truck, parked down in the Mews that hadn't been there before. Early morning deliveries perhaps, but Gilles didn't think so. And he didn't need Gannon anymore to tell him something was terribly wrong.

Gunfire.

Faint, intermittent.

"Shit," Gannon said.

They had to smash a window to get inside. There was no alternative, and he steeled himself for what was coming as they slipped inside a dark, empty bedroom. This close he had a better idea of what they were up against. Somewhere below, people were dying. Another rattle of gunfire. It was blatant, uncaring of the attention it would bring in a neighborhood such as this, and pretty soon Gilles reckoned they'd be fighting on two fronts. And then dawn would arrive and there'd be no place to go. He wondered if Gannon had figured that out. That it was a distinct possibility they were already dead, and the only variant available to them was how.

The other man had quickly pulled off his coat and was already dashing across the room. "Wait," he hissed, but Gannon had opened the door of the bedroom they'd broken into and Gilles had no choice but to follow. "Mark, wait—"

As soon as he emerged, there was a sharp crack and a flash in the gloom, closely followed by another and another. Gannon had taken at least two bullets in the chest and had gone down, but not before he'd hurled the cleaver.

It missed, landed on its blunt edge with a muffled thud, then bounced and slid along the carpet.

The gun went off again and Gilles felt pain rip through his shoulder. He rolled away with the momentum given to him by the bullet and made a dive back inside the room, back into his shadow world. The landing felt hard, jarred his senses, and the walls were abruptly all shades of gray. There was smoke, screams, and footsteps and above all, the cloying sense of being trapped. A cellar. He scrambled to his feet, shook it off. A poignant memory, this one. He stepped back outside. In the corridor, a man was striding along the carpet toward Gannon while slapping another magazine into his sidearm. Gilles walked alongside, stepped by, pushed out of the memory, acquired the necessary leverage, and twisted.

The assailant, a human, dropped. He kicked the man's weapon toward Gannon who was scrambling awkwardly to regain his feet, jacket torn, dark blood staining the shirt beneath. "You okay?"

"I got it," the man croaked. "Go. I'm right behind you. Do whatever you do. Disappear. Find Mina and the others. Don't forget the donors. We have to get them out." And when Gilles hesitated, "Do it."

There was no point in arguing about it. He tapped his left temple. "Use your head, Mark. Remember, it's your best weapon." He ducked back into shadow, and now it seemed as if the entire corridor was on fire and he instinctively ducked. From bad to worse, but he kept moving. Down a stairwell, past two human males with determination and murder written all over their faces. He couldn't warn Gannon, but at least the man had a gun now, and hopefully he'd taken his advice.

Down another set of stairs, the surrounding walls dancing with greedy, hot curls of flame, so real that he had to struggle hard to remind himself the fire wasn't there. But the memory of it was chasing him down, literally hot on his heels. He reached the hallway. There were bodies and blood on the floor and on the stairs, accompanied by the acrid scent of incendiaries. Some vampire, some human, the killers had been indiscriminate in matters of choice, effective and thorough in their methods.

He heard the firefight, somewhere toward the rear of the house, and so he headed for that. He dashed across the elaborate hallway and its glittering chandelier, down a corridor, and approached another group of men, vampires this time. He didn't recognize them. Guns. Reinforcements? From where? He watched as they met up with three men including Bryant. He almost quit the protection of his memories and joined them until he realized they appeared to be making no effort to join the fight still blazing down the hall.

He frowned and pressed on; he rounded a corner and came upon the source of all the noise. He slipped past, catching his breath. His other world sensations were beginning to feel too real. It was time to get out while he still could, and so, quickly through a doorway into the kitchen, he dived behind a polished steel cabinet and emerged. He sensed his clothes about to catch fire and smelled the stench of burning, and fought hard to push it all away. He was out of the memory now. Nevertheless, remnants of it clung to him like soot.

"Where the hell did you come from?" Gevani was crouched

nearby, staring at him, eyebrows knitted together. A clatter of bullets. They both ducked.

Movement, further down the aisle. "Gilles?" He saw Mina, also under cover. "Where is he?"

"Coming. I think," he replied. He thought he heard Ryan cursing somewhere ahead, but there was no way he was going to stick his head out and look. A quick mental roundup, now that he had all his senses, told him there were five of them holed up in here, in various stages of disrepair. He'd seen the firepower outside and it wasn't looking good. He told the others, gave Ryan the enemy positions, and prepared to dive back into the shadows once more.

Abruptly, the firing stopped.

CHAPTER 24
MARK

He waited, gun in one hand, cleaver in the other, while he continued his fight with the core, a rampaging monster, thick in his gut and growing exponentially, feeding off the pain in his chest and putting him at risk with bold exhortation. The gunman in the corridor had taken him by surprise while he'd been distracted, and it had become essential to gain at least some modicum of control.

He looked down at the weapons in his hands, and acknowledged that Deacon wouldn't need them. That particular thought brought more inner turmoil when he remembered Bryant returning to the meeting hours earlier. There had been some manner of contact between them, and right now Deacon, his murderer, was somehow involved in this.

Two men appeared at the top of the stairwell. Human. Both armed, minds fully intent on their purpose. But in the end it didn't matter and Mark kept the smile on his face. "Take me downstairs," he commanded, and watched with some relief as the barrels of their weapons fell. A step forward and his body registered its acute displeasure. Two of the three bullets were still lodged inside, one was in his heart and he knew, at some point, it would be a problem.

It became an effort to walk and not stagger down the stairs, while his mind stayed with the men accompanying him. He managed to collect and cow three more when they reached the entrance hall, and as they ventured toward the sound of gunfire, he had to step over the bodies of the fallen. Amongst them, he saw Powell. A chemical incendiary had been used on him and he was barely recognizable. Megan was also gone; he could feel her death like the bullet in his heart. Anger boiled inside, and threatened to break his focus.

More armed men were stationed along a hallway leading to the rear of the house. A bullet arrived from the opposite direction; it zipped by and shattered a nearby mirror. The noise was deafening and fought with his concentration. "Stop," he said, attempting to sound authoritative, determined not to slur. "Just stop." He had to bite his lip, close his eyes, and shut everything out until he was certain he had control.

It was a good minute before he saw Ryan emerge, followed by Gevani, Gage, and thankfully Gilles and Mina. Bryant appeared, behind the group with more men—Deacon's men. Mark couldn't sway them all. And those he did have in thrall, he wouldn't have for long. His heart was failing. He knew that now.

A nasty jag of pain rose in his chest. His voice became urgent. "Disarm them, quickly." He watched, near helpless, while the traitorous Bryant rounded up and disarmed the shooters.

A voice. "What the hell is going on?" He recalled Gevani's name through the dull throb of agony.

"Weiss's men." He pointed with the core's beloved cleaver, and nearly overbalanced. "But Bryant is here to make sure Deacon gets what he wants." He trailed off. It hurt so bad he was going blind.

The hallway became distorted with a roar of sound and muzzle flash. Weiss's humans dropped and twitched. He grinned, delirious. "That takes care of that, I guess." But the gun barrels were still up, this time aimed at Gevani, Gilles, and the others.

"Bryant, what's going on?" Mina's voice.

Mark took a step forward. He wanted desperately to close in on the owner of that voice. But he was becoming more disoriented by the second. He could hear sirens, streets away but they didn't have much time. "They have to take me," he said. He looked toward Bryant, or whom he thought might be Bryant. He held up the meat cleaver, waved it comically. "You let the others go, and I'll come quietly. Gilles, you hear that? Stay with her…" The pain was unbearable and he wondered if this was how it felt, to have a heart attack.

He dropped the cleaver.

"Mark!" Mina again.

He fell to his knees, sank to the floor and the room began to spin.

He felt hands on him, disarming him and hauling him upright. Someone punched him hard in the gut. He doubled over and went down again. He heard Bryant giving orders as the hallway faded. Something about a van. But the pain began to obliterate everything and the deep pit beckoned. Two more solid kicks to his midsection and he began a majestic dive toward it.

However, part way on his journey the agony abruptly ceased. Bryant had him by the collar. "I've given you morphine," the man said. *Now you listen to me. You listen.*

And so he listened.

The truck's rear door opened and men hauled him unceremoniously to his feet. He was still drugged, and they'd bound his arms to his torso with wide nylon strapping and shackled his wrists. At least he'd managed to push out the bullets. He was also mighty glad of the morphine, regardless that it slowed his heart rate and kept him subdued. He could feel it inside, colder than the shackles that bound him. It made him stumble, and encouraged his head to spin if he moved it around too much.

Everything, inside and out, appeared slowed down, at half speed. He smelled jet fuel as he was dragged across a shiny floor. He looked down, noticed he'd lost his jacket somewhere along the way, and saw blood spattered on his shirt. His feet snagged and they had to haul him none too gently up a set of metal steps. He caught a glimpse of a cockpit to his left, prior to being pushed and strapped into an airline seat.

A voice, female, "Please be more careful and make him comfortable."

Family.

He smiled, and drifted into oblivion.

They were airborne by the time he awoke. Air friction roared softly through his ears, it lulled him and kept him calm. He looked down. The shackles were off and someone had done a reasonable job of cleaning him up. He glanced to his left and saw her standing alongside. "Where are we going?" he drawled.

"We're taking you home."

Home. Of course. He felt the needle in his arm.

"There's no need for that."

"I'm sorry, Mr. Gannon." She had a narrow face, and cold eyes that softened a little as his mind clawed for her attention. "This is the last, I promise. You'll be clear of it by the time you arrive."

He wanted to say *oh, sure, that's perfectly okay then,* but he didn't have the strength. He tried to stay awake for as long as he could. He sensed the warm heat of donors, somewhere close. But there were other vampires, too. His own, his family. *They'll do as I say,* he thought. *They'll take me back.*

Another minute, maybe more, and he fell asleep again.

I'll keep them safe. All you have to do is promise me, that purpose we talked about—assure me you'll fulfill it.

There were drops of blood on the sheets and his fingers reached out and stroked them; they reminded him of poppy petals, strewn there for no apparent reason other than to fascinate and keep his mind off the last two hours. But he'd enjoyed the last two hours, hadn't he? And now he felt guilty. Once his body had fully metabolized the drug, he had awakened ravenous and his mind had possessed no other thought than to satisfy an overpowering hunger and thirst.

Beyond the droplets of blood—a long strand of hair, its owner laid silently on her stomach, asleep or unconscious. Asleep, he hoped. She had a companion, also quiescent, eyes closed, lying on her side. Both of them he'd had sex with, both of them he had bitten. He sat up and let his eyes roam over them. They were beautiful and their scents were complicated and electrifying, and despite his guilt he wanted to waken them and go at it all over again. He could still taste raw hunger on the tip of his tongue and yet he knew he'd probably taken too much. His senses buzzed. Another girl. Maybe he could have another. The prospect sickened and excited him and he thought of Megan, how he would never have touched her this way, and how she had died, had been murdered, and all because of him.

He stood up, looked in the mirror, and failed to recognize anything on his face. The eyes were the worst. Hungry, arrogant, it was the core, changing him, poisoning him. Bryant's words still hung there in his head, regarding his purpose. But what was his purpose other than to become a monster?

He cast his eyes over the two donors. No bruises, and their chests rose and fell, regularly, slowly. He breathed a sigh of relief. He looked at the cabin door, closed, allowing him privacy and complete discretion. What had been the motivation behind such generosity? Family or not they were taking him to Deacon, and what was Deacon about to do, other than rectify his little mistake and murder him all over again? So what was this—his last supper? Was this how you treated an Elder before you killed him?

He sat down again, confused and contrite, his head in his hands. Mina and Gilles. What had become of them? Should he be in mourning? If so, he'd had an odd way of showing it, so far. He stood up, paced, sat down again. One of the girls shifted and moaned. He crawled over there and lay alongside. She opened her eyes, smiled languidly.

"Shh," he told her, and buried himself amongst warm flesh. "It's okay. It's going to be okay..."

They touched down, refueled, took off again. He slept, awoke hours later, and began to feel the descent toward their final destination just as the girls finished dressing him. His clothes, a dark, tailored suit and gray cotton shirt were a perfect fit and to his liking; it was as if they instinctively knew his tastes and had been expecting him. *A waste,* he thought, seeing as he was about to get his head ripped off or his entire body pushed into daylight. But at least he wasn't afraid of that. He'd died before.

Instead his mind languished in a well of regret. He should have been up front with Gilles, told him he'd had a bad feeling, and shouldn't have insisted on that walk when he knew the other man would follow him without question. He shouldn't have gone out there, despite not really knowing what was wrong until he was away from that cacophony of thought. Had he been there when the firing started he might have—

The cabin door opened. He let out a sigh. Now he had a whole new game to play.

They were standing, waiting for him, at their seats or in the aisle—seven male vampires, two female, and a number of humans, all of them inclining their heads as he approached. One of the men beckoned. "Sir, if you'd like to take your seat, we're on final approach."

Back to Sir, was it? The core preened.

He sat down, buckled in. Someone asked if he'd like a drink. He declined. He was horribly confused but damned sure he wasn't about to show it. "Where's our destination?"

"Las Vegas, Sir."

Of course. He wanted to laugh. Instead, he leaned back and closed his eyes. His final hours in a place he fondly remembered. It could be worse.

On approach, as the jet pitched and rolled through the desert air, he thought about Deacon. Would he meet him here in Las Vegas? He thought about that for a while, and what he'd do when they finally came face to face. The desire to kill the man still burned, but not so bright as before. He felt numb about himself, and still feared for the others. Bryant said he'd protect them. Mark didn't believe him and Megan was already gone. He should have taken care of her, and instead he'd slipped out and left her undefended. She was dead and it was his fault.

It was still light when they arrived. In the closed hangar Mark saw two vehicles waiting, a stretch and a sedan. He headed straight for the sedan, confusing his newfound entourage, but he reckoned if they were going to treat him like a rock star for the moment, then they'd have to put up with a few minor proclivities. No fucking way was he sitting in a stretch limo with these people. Been there, done that.

Once inside, he felt the heat bear down on the exterior of the vehicle and it became instinctive to lean slightly away from the passenger door despite the tinted glass. With his head still stuffed with the events of the last twenty four hours, he didn't pay attention to where they were going until the light abruptly disappeared and the car swept down a ramp into an underground car park.

They stopped and the door was opened for him. He got out, feet landing on ridged gray concrete, a ceiling of similar material hanging low over his head. It felt like a tomb. It felt safe, this row upon row of cars, shiny and glittering, parked as far as he could see while people—human—strolled idly back and forth among them. He could hear noise, sounds of all kinds as he was escorted toward an elevator. Scents of dust, heat, sand, car exhaust fumes, the sticky residue of something spilled on the ground nearby, and more people. He kept up his façade but inside he was reeling. And when they emerged from the elevator into the casino, the sound hit him like a wall. Chatter, yelling over by the craps tables, and the near unbearable jangle of slots. He remembered loving that sound when he'd been alive, but now it felt like the volume had been turned up to the max and then some.

They moved along the periphery of the gambling hall. He considered making a break for it but soon gave up on the idea. It wasn't because he had nowhere to go. Deacon. He wanted to meet him. He had waited long enough. As for the casino, he had no idea which one it was. One of the new ones, going off a carpet that still bore a considerable amount of pile. It felt soft, cushioned and luxurious beneath his feet while they waited for another elevator.

A member of his escort cursed softly. He turned.

"Are you Mark Niels Gannon?"

Two kids, a boy and a girl, twelve or thirteen years old. Just a few paces away, smiling at Mister On The Brink of Film and TV Stardom.

"Hi," he said, and grinned. He held up his hand as two of his companions stepped forward. He approached.

"Can we take a picture?" Both kids eagerly brandished their phones.

He sensed the level of unease around him, gathering like a storm. "Sure," he said softly. And he went through the motions, posed with one, and then the other, and then both. He had one of women take the pictures, her face like stone.

The girl touched his hand. "You're so cold," she said, her expression full of concern, the heat and vibrant waves of life flowing from her, filling him with longing. He looked at their faces, realized it wasn't just his identity, his fame that was holding them in thrall. And he wanted to be sick.

"Rehab," he told them, his face solemn. "It's part of the treatment."

He backed off and watched them nod sagely. Even twelve-year-olds knew about rehab nowadays. Others were looking at him now, wondering why two kids wanted their picture taken with some guy who stood waiting for an elevator. His fellow vampires moved in and soon he was surrounded, pushed forward, and the doors were closing.

"Your past life." It was the woman who'd injected him on the plane.

"Yes. And if any of you even think about touching those two, I'll rip your fucking hearts out."

They began to rise. Now he was angry, furious, in fact. He could feel the core inside swell, and he had to fight hard to get it under control, while the rest of him felt hollow and empty, disjointed and out of step. And why? Because he wasn't alive any more. He had died at the hands of these people surrounding him, shoulder to shoulder, trapping him in the confined space of the elevator. Everything was gone, and by the grace of those two young kids, he'd just been given a most poignant reminder.

CHAPTER 25

GILLES

The van swayed as it took a ninety-degree turn and Gevani cursed bitterly in its dark interior. "All they have to do," he added, determined to hammer home the obvious, "is open the door while it's still daylight."

Gilles stayed silent, his mind busy in recovery mode, desperately trying to pull a few pieces of sanity out of the whole shattered mess of the last few hours. Merrill was gone. He was going to kill Bryant for that. As for Gannon, the way they'd dragged him off, after using him as a punching bag. Dead? Highly likely. However, he was still alive, and unlike Gevani, he was unwilling to give up. Not yet. Even though they were weaponless, had all sustained injuries and were struggling to recover, having no current access to a blood supply.

The van slowed, everyone glanced uneasily at one another, until the vehicle picked up speed once more. Gilles wondered where Bryant was taking them. They'd been traveling for quite a while and were presumably out of the city by now, heading for some remote site, a place where no one could witness their abrupt and no doubt messy demise. And yet—

He'd caught a few stray thoughts from their captor. A feeling of uncertainty coming through the tangled chaos, as if there had been a radical shift and things were not going as planned. The Gannon effect perhaps, pulling destiny in another direction, oblivious to everything except its own course. Now he felt a lump rising in his throat. He'd promised Delacour he'd look after him, and he had failed, spectacularly. That thought gave birth to another, about how attached he'd become, to what essentially was Deacon's fledgling hell spawn. But there was much more to Gannon, he knew that, now. And now he was gone.

However, this wasn't the time for ruminating on his current failures. He placed his hand once more against the wall of the van. The heat of the sun conducted warm against his fingertips, promising doom. He looked at his comrades, his eyes fully accustomed and attuned to the dark. None of them had been originally dressed in a manner that would protect them from daylight, and now they were less so, after Bryant's men had partially divested them of their clothing. There was no breaking out of the van and making a run for it; they'd be dead in seconds. So, that left Gilles' gut reaction, telling him there might be a way to wriggle out of this mess after all. Pity it wasn't giving him any of the finer details.

He looked across at Mina, sheltered between Ryan and Gage, and she lifted her head once she'd become aware of his scrutiny. "Is he dead?"

"I don't know," he replied honestly. "And perhaps we should leave it at that." He attempted to absorb his own words of false comfort, but it proved difficult when he held a few more pieces of the puzzle. He had a good idea what was lying in store for Gannon—if he was still alive. He was supposed to have died, out there on the rocks, and it was perfectly reasonable to assume that Deacon, with his strict, bordering on fanatical sense of hierarchy and propriety, would consider Gannon to be a loose, untidy end that needed trimming, with extreme prejudice. He hadn't offered the young man any particular mercies while he was killing him, so a change of heart was unlikely. Gilles just hoped the man's second demise would not be as bad as the first. He realized Mina was continuing to stare at him.

"But why would they take him away like that?" she asked. "Why not put him with the rest of us? He said something before he collapsed—"

"Yeah. About Deacon's men?" Gevani interrupted. "Why would they be concerned about him?"

Both were now regarding him, and pretty soon they were joined by Ryan and Gage. But what should he say? Was there any point in keeping Gannon's identity a secret any longer?

The van lurched, slowed considerably, took a sharp turn to the left, and ground to a halt. Gilles felt relieved, temporarily off the hook, despite fears of what might happen next. He heard one of the vehicle's front doors open, followed by the crunch of boots on gravel, receding, presumably one of Bryant's human lackeys. Two other vehicles pulled up behind. Then the driver was back and the van edged forward again, and now the engine took on a new sound, a reverberation—they were inside a building. More doors opened and slammed shut.

"Here it comes," Gevani growled.

Gilles could see the man had both fists balled tight, had shifted his position slightly so he could pounce upright. Ryan had assumed a similar posture while Gage was pushing Mina further behind him. Out of the three, he reckoned Gevani would pack the most devastating punch; he had street brawler written all over him, a character Gilles was utterly familiar with. In contrast, he loosened up, stayed relaxed, pushed all his fear and doubts out of the way. They would only slow him down.

A fist slammed hard against the door from the outside, making his companions jump.

"Shit," muttered Gage.

"Can you all hear me in there?" Bryant's voice.

"If you're going to kill us, why don't you just get it over with," said Gevani.

"I'll take that as a yes, then." A pause, and then, "Okay, here's the deal. We're sheltered in here, no one's about to get toasted. So, you all step out nice and slow, and my men won't shoot you. How about that?"

Gilles still had a hand on the wall of the van. "We're out of the sun," he assured the others.

"Let's do it," said Mina, pushing forward, "this is ridiculous."

"All right, you bastard, let us out," called Gevani.

The door popped open. There was light beyond and none of it natural. Gilles watched Gevani go first, still poised and ready to spring at a moment's provocation, followed by Ryan and Gage. Gilles stepped quickly in front of Mina. "Wait," he whispered. He wanted something from the other men, a nod of reassurance that told him they were not about to be gunned down and slaughtered on the spot before he'd let her step outside. Ryan glanced back, gave him what he was looking for, and he let Mina climb out next, while he came last.

Thought coiled between both parties like thick, venomous snakes. One quick glance told him they were in an empty airplane hangar. Behind him, about thirty feet away from the front of the van, sunlight pushed through a hairline crack beneath the hangar door, dazzling and beautiful, and his eyes were immediately drawn to it. Luckily, it was too far away to be of any threat, and he shifted his viewpoint toward the kidnappers. Bryant and three of his men were standing before them. All were armed, same with another two men, one on either side of the van. All were dressed in thick sun garb. There was another, a human, their van driver presumably, but he didn't count. Not unless he was going to make a run for the door and push the opener. The two cars following them presumably had drivers, too. That meant two more humans. Gilles took in everyone's positions and calculated. A pity he didn't have a couple of Houston's incendiaries on him, it would have made the odds so much easier.

"So, now what?" demanded Gevani, outrage shimmering from him like heat.

Bryant shrugged. "I'll tell you now what, Gevani. You keep that temper of yours in check and I let you all go."

"Just like that, huh?"

"Just like that. But I have… a few questions, before we take our leave."

"You're leaving us in here?" Mina looked around, and frowned at Bryant.

"Oh, you'll be quite safe. Your own hangar is only half a mile away. Just a few fences to climb, and I know you're capable of that."

Gilles watched her eyes narrow as she advanced. "You knew Weiss was coming, so did Deacon, and you all stood by and let it happen. Why did you do it? Powell, our donors, they—"

"I did what I could to help you," Bryant snapped. "And you could try being a little more gracious." He'd partially lowered his weapon, but it snapped back up once more as both Ryan and Gage stepped forward. "Get back, all three of you."

A glance from Mina and they took a reluctant step away from their captor. Mina wasn't done, however. "Since when did you become Deacon's puppet?"

Bryant laughed loud. "We are all Deacon's puppets, my darling. Perhaps you should take a moment and remind yourself exactly who he is."

Outrage made her eyes glitter. "You betrayed us all. And what about Mark?"

"Ah." A humorless grin slowly appeared on Bryant's face. "Our mysterious Mr. Gannon. I assume you've slept with him. Pining for him already?"

Mina's face twisted. "Where did they take him? Is he dead?"

Gilles heard the emotion in that last question. Bryant had also caught the inflection in her voice and reacted with a slight flinching at the corner of his eyes. It was barely noticeable, as though he'd been inflicted by the tiniest of wounds. Gannon wasn't the only one able to cast spells of infatuation. Mina was an expert at it.

The man looked down for a moment. "I don't know," he said finally. "On both counts."

"Who the hell is that guy, anyway?" interrupted Gevani.

Bryant smiled tightly. "That's a good question. One I've been asking myself for the last two days."

"Well, he was obviously big enough to warrant special treatment." Gevani cackled derisively. "Deacon figured you couldn't handle an Elder, huh? Figured he'd have to do the dirty work himself?"

"Actually, my money's on something different." Bryant shifted his attention toward Gilles. "You see, I know something you people don't. They wanted him alive. In fact they wanted him alive so much they didn't care if the rest of you survived at all."

Gilles kept his features relaxed. "We were expendable? There to keep Weiss's goons busy, while you made sure Deacon's people got away with Gannon."

Bryant shrugged. "That's about the size of it. Deacon wants him alive, and the question is, why? The man's a natural dominant. That makes him dangerous. So, how about it, Gilles? Are you going to tell us who he really is?"

"But he doesn't know—" Mina stopped. She was also looking at him, now. So were the others. It was an identical scene to the one back in the van, only this time Bryant and his men had joined the crowd.

He stared back. Under normal circumstances he would have

said nothing, and Gannon's secret would have gone with him to his grave, but Bryant's trail of thought was tugging at him. There were revelations there, and the only way Gilles would get to them was if he handed Gannon's identity over on a platter. Ah, gods. Mark, forgive me.

"He's third generation," he said, and waited for them to do the math.

Gevani whistled, but it would be another second or two before it dawned on the man as to what exactly that meant. In the meantime, Gilles watched Mina's face gather in comprehension and struggle with the enormity of the revelation.

"Holy shit," blurted Gage. "He's Deacon's progeny? He's been our enemy all along?"

Gilles shook his head. "No. He is *not* our enemy."

"The hell he isn't," muttered Ryan, face like thunder, reminding Gilles entirely of Houston.

Mina was stunned, and Bryant obviously couldn't resist the sucker punch. "Well now, that's quite a notch on your belt, sweetheart," he purred, laying on honey and vitriol in equal measure.

"He is *not* our enemy," Gilles repeated, frowning at the man.

"Well, they did kick the living crap out of him," Gage offered with a shrug. "They pumped him full of morphine, too. I could smell it."

"Could be a cover," Ryan told him.

"But—" Mina was struggling for words. "He saved us, didn't he? He stopped Weiss's men. And I remember what he said." She pointed a finger at Bryant. "He was attempting to strike a bargain with you."

Bryant lifted his chin. Now all the attention had swung back around. He cleared his throat. "All right, now listen. If you're wise, you'll return home and keep your mouths shut."

"You want our discretion," Ryan said. "After what you did. After you stood by while they killed all the others."

"Consider it collateral damage. This is the best I could have done."

Gilles smiled, just a faint twitch. Merrill was far from collateral damage, and one day, Bryant was going to pay. But not yet. "Let the man talk," he said.

Bryant acknowledged him, under the impression he'd acquired Gilles' support. "I went along with this because I believe Gannon is important to our survival."

"But how?" Gevani scowled. "He's Deacon's boy. That puts him close to Weiss, too."

"I don't know how," Bryant replied, "but it's important that he stays alive."

"Wait," interrupted Gilles. "Gannon shouldn't have happened. He was left for dead and we rescued him. What if Deacon is about to rectify that mistake? What if it's already been done?"

"He's not going to destroy him, Gilles. I'll stake my life on it." Bryant stared at him. *And if you get your hands on him again, you take better care of him. Understand?*

Gilles kept his face straight. Bryant was a telepath?

"This isn't making any sense," Gevani said.

Bryant wheeled on the other vampire. "I don't care if it makes sense or not. Now, if you'll excuse us, we need to leave. We have our own hides to protect." His men began to head toward the sedans. "I'd ah—think seriously about returning to the van," he added. "Shelter, for when we open the door."

Ryan dashed off toward the rear of the vehicle. "Mina," he called.

Gilles saw her hesitate. "You really didn't care? You were prepared to let the rest of us die." She sounded bitter, angry.

The man nodded tightly. "Just get in the bloody van, Mina."

Gilles pulled her away, gave her to Ryan, watched as Gage and Gevani stepped up into the van's interior. "You really think he's going to save us?" he asked Bryant.

"Like I said," Bryant's face twisted. "I'd stake my life on it. I *have* staked my life on it."

"But you don't know how."

The other man shook his head. "No. Not yet. Now if you'll excuse me."

Gilles watched him head for one of the waiting sedans while he tried desperately to make sense of it.

"Gilles." It was Ryan, calling from the van.

He turned, walked over, and stepped into the safety of the vehicle's interior, then watched Ryan shut the doors from the inside, blocking out the light. Mina was huddled at the rear, her face blank.

As soon as he took a seat, she scooted over and clung to him, having no care that their flesh touched, enabling him to fully comprehend the reason why her entire body was shaking. They'd all had a brush with death. It was understandable. But he discovered that it wasn't Bryant's treachery that had her trembling like a leaf. It was Gannon she was afraid of.

He blocked out his own misgivings so they wouldn't add to the feeding frenzy of fear coursing through her. And in doing so he found himself strangely confident. There was a chance, if Bryant's intuition was correct, that Gannon might make it through, after all.

CHAPTER 26
MARK

House Deacon, he discovered, was a two-floor penthouse that swallowed up the entire upper levels of the casino tower. The female vampire who'd kept him sedated during the first leg of the flight home, Alice, gave him a quick tour along wide passageways laid with sumptuous carpet, past walls displaying contemporary art, through lounges decorated with polished wood. Everywhere he walked, people turned and looked; vampires gave him a respectful bow, donors gathered in clusters, astonished and overawed as he passed them by, and every one of them oozed the same easy familiarity as those who'd kicked the living crap out of him and dragged him onto the plane. Family. The duality of their welcome made him want to laugh out loud. Still, it was a far cry from House Delacour, where the likes of Houston hardly ever gave him the time of day. The core swooned at all the attention.

Eventually, Alice led him to a suite on the upper floor. It had six donors in attendance, three male, three female, all of them as beautiful and elegant as their immediate surroundings. He had to work hard at feigning disinterest, and as a distraction he stepped up to the perfectly filtered windows and looked down. They were about midway along the Strip, he surmised, and he counted three enormous cranes outside, stretching up toward the sun. Vegas was on a building streak, and new hotels and apartments were springing up like weeds on all sides. As for his new quarters, he assumed they were nothing more than an elaborate jail cell. "Where's Deacon?" he asked when Alice had pointed out the suite's endless features.

"He'll be arriving tomorrow."

Twenty-four hours then, maybe less, and it would all be over. Once again he toyed with the prospect of escape. But the thought of coming face to face with his murderer was too compelling to ignore and his fists balled in anticipation. "So," he began, "am I supposed to stay in here? Are you going to lock the door?"

She appeared taken aback, and he caught the internal struggle in her thoughts as she tried hard not to be insulted. He didn't care. *Teach you to stick me with a needle,* he thought.

"You are free to come and go as you please," she told him. "Sir, this is your home, now. Or at least one of them."

"Ah." He made sure she absorbed his disbelief, and to confound her further he drew off the mask of louche arrogance. "Well, Alice, thank you for taking care of me." He said it like he meant it, and it got him a rare smile which he reciprocated. "I'm tired," he announced. "Maybe I'll rest for a while."

"Of course. And your donors are here to serve your every need."

"Oh, I know." He glanced at the hovering line of humans, caught the eye of one of the girls and winked.

When Alice had gone, one of the male donors stepped forward. "Sir, would you—"

Mark held up a hand. His smile had snapped off as soon as Alice had left the room. "I don't need anything right now," he told them, "except a little peace and quiet, and I don't want to be disturbed for the next few hours, got that?"

"Yes, Sir," they all said in unison.

He felt their eyes and their apprehension follow him toward the bedroom. Halfway to the door, he stopped. His anger was turning him into a prize-winning jerk. He turned around. "My apologies," he told them. "I seem to have lost my manners on the journey here."

"Sir, it's quite all right. We were told you might have lost a number of your companions, and for that we are deeply sorry." It was the male donor who'd spoken before.

Mark stared at him, completely taken aback. They'd all been prepped. They knew everything. Dear God. He wanted to break down, and the need to vent his anger became overpowering. Instead, he gave them a nod. "Thank you," he said. "Now, please tell me your names."

Henry—their leader. Zack and Armando; Leesa, Cherry, and

Cyanne. He embraced each one in turn, felt them all tremble at the touch of his hands. They were afraid of him. Alice, or one of her comrades, must have done quite a number on them and his initial attitude, not to mention his treatment of those poor girls on the plane would have gone a long way to support their trepidation, had it been reported, and he was willing to bet it had.

Obviously, his shitty nature knew no bounds and he realized, yet again, he had some fences to mend. Perhaps he shouldn't have cared, given the circumstances, but in the end it was a matter of pride and a conscious desire to be loved that got him down to work, particularly on Cherry, who seemed to be trembling the most. "Never be afraid of me," he whispered.

They'd take a little more convincing, he decided, as he finally stepped back. "Okay, about that peace and quiet."

"We'll make sure you're not disturbed, Sir," Henry told him.

Once inside the bedroom, behind closed doors, he sat down and attempted to take stock. But there were too many pieces in his head and they caused a ruckus, each one trying to yell the loudest, determined to be heard over the rest—Gilles and Mina, his mistrust of Bryant, Deacon and the prospect of dying all over again, Matthew…

He lay back, twisted and curled up. No Mom and Dad, no brother, no teachers, no friends, no Molly yelling at him, not even Gilles at his side to offer him counsel. Anguish tore through him like sleet, and the sleet became hail and scoured his insides until he felt raw. He couldn't cry, couldn't weep for the others. Instead, all that energy burned like fury and poured into the core, hardening its surfaces, and in his mind's eye he could see it, tough as volcanic rock, heavy on his conscience.

And he realized he was no longer alone.

The girl was with him, down in the hidden vault, in his hiding place, where he thought he was safe. She was watching the core just as he was, made of the same fabric as the object that hung before them. In contrast, he felt fragile, paper-thin. Just one glance and she'd rip him in half. Fear began to crawl on the surface of his skin, but this was his place, his little fortress, and so he summoned the strength and mouthed her name.

"Dimitra." *Don't look, please don't look at me, don't—*

He flinched as her head turned toward him. Glow from the core brushed the tiniest amount of color onto her narrow face. But her eyes remained monochrome, a flat, merciless gray that held him completely in thrall.

"Your pain is hurting them," she said.

"I don't understand."

"For no reason." She shrugged and her attention went back to the core. It was beginning to expand once more.

He tried to make sense of it. He pointed. "It's tricking me. It wants me to feel this way."

"Yes."

"Does this mean Gilles and Mina are—"

She was gone. He was looking at empty space.

He clawed back to the surface in a rush, like a man suddenly afraid of drowning. He opened his eyes. Gilles and Mina were still alive. That's what she was telling him. It was the only thing that made any sense and he was getting all boiled up over nothing. He sat up, slightly disoriented, and rolled his shoulders. How long had he been like this? He scraped a hand through his hair and a smile lit up his features. Bryant must have kept his promise, somehow, either that or Gilles had found a way. They were all still alive, Houston would take care of Matthew, and it meant he could focus on Deacon.

He stood up, walked to the door, and opened it. Henry was hovering close by. "How long have I been out?"

"Just under four-and-a-half hours, Sir. And you had visitors a short while ago, from downstairs. They expressed concerns—"

"But you kept them out?"

"Of course."

Mark grinned. "Good. I'm going to take a shower."

Tiled in gray, marbled stone, the shower cubicle was cavernous, an advantage he discovered as he was joined by Zack and Leesa, both entirely as naked as he was. They caught him by surprise, so that he could do nothing other than stand there while Leesa slipped behind him and got to work, shampooing his hair and massaging his scalp, and while Zack stood before him lathering his torso.

He gave into it, began to relax as two pairs of deft hands scrubbed away the tension in his muscles. He reveled in their company, their irresistible blend of scent and alluring promise of blood, and by the time Zack had dropped to his knees, Mark had a pulsing, hungry erection. He gasped, and his hips jerked slightly as he felt the younger man's mouth sliding forward and enveloping the tip of his cock in blissful heat. He closed his eyes, let his head fall back, felt the water hammering lightly against his scalp while Leesa's firm hands began to knead the muscles in his shoulders. Zack had now brought his arms around him, gripped his ass, and had begun a deep, heady, pull-and-suck rhythm that almost made Mark's knees buckle.

"Slower," he croaked, and "Yes, like that," as the rhythm began to match the somber pace of his heartbeat. He began to breathe, long and slow, and after a little while he reached for the girl, his arm slipping around her slick, narrow waist and he pulled her close against his right side. She was tall, dark-eyed, willowy, and beautiful. He leaned in, kissed her on the mouth.

"Put your arms around me," he whispered, "around my shoulders, closer, that's it," and once she was firmly anchored he let his hand slide around and in between her legs. He squeezed gently and felt her shift and begin to part her thighs. "A little wider, good, that's enough." He began to slide in further, his fingers delicately searching until he was able to push slowly inside her, while his lips brushed the flesh beneath her jaw before traveling to one side of her throat. There he paused for a moment, until finally he pierced the skin. Nice and slow, precise, the incision not too deep. His feet were now slightly apart, his body surrounded and he was penetrating them both. He drew blood from Leesa in lazy increments, used his fingers on her, back and forth, keeping time with Zack's slow, pulsing rhythm while steam enveloped their tangled bodies and the water fell on them with a soft, continuous hiss.

"Thank you," he said, when they were all toweled and dried off. He watched them disappear in a flurry of bows and blushes. He felt energized and slightly dizzy, and his face carried a broad grin that wouldn't let up. In the bedroom, Cherry and Cyanne were waiting for him and they helped him dress in jeans and a distressed, contoured shirt that clung to and emphasized his muscular frame.

"Please, no shoes," he told them. He was beginning to feel like some powerful emperor from a lost civilization, while the core basked on an inflated cushion of entitlement. It was ridiculous but yeah, he reckoned anyone could get used to this.

Reluctantly, he broke away from their attention, and in the sitting room of his suite he strolled over to the window and looked down. Night had fallen and below him the Las Vegas strip glittered and shimmered. He reached up and pressed his fingers against the glass. There were people down there, thousands of them, in a world he was no longer a part of. There. Back to reality. He considered what might very well happen in the next few hours. He was reluctant to delve back into troubled waters, but he forced it and reminded himself exactly where he was and whose company he was currently keeping.

Finally, he would be coming face to face with his killer, and he ran through a few scenarios—what might happen, how he'd react, or act, and what the end result might be—and he figured he had all options covered until he realized he was coming up with nothing. Instead, he discovered this new family connection had kept him blind, had steered him away, had hidden the worst and sheltered him from having to relive and recall the details of his last meeting with Deacon. He thought he'd remembered it all. But he realized he had little more than a hazy recollection and nothing whatsoever to kindle a fire in his belly.

He needed a kicker, something to trigger and reopen the wounds and get back some of his righteous anger. He needed to bleed, and he needed to know exactly what he was up against. He turned away from the window. "I think I'll—"

There was a knock on the outer door.

It was Alice. He told Henry to admit her, and he watched, mildly surprised as all six of his donors nervously lined up.

Pale hair, pale skin, Alice looked as icy as ever. "We've been—a little worried, Sir," she said after a short bow.

"Oh?" He shrugged, slid his hands in his pockets.

"We thought you might have been in pain, in distress at some point. A few hours ago."

It dawned on him, then, what Dimitra had meant earlier and why they'd been hammering on his door, and he barked out a laugh. "What's the matter, Alice? Is my despair spoiling the party?"

"We were simply concerned."

"Really? Well, as you can see, I'm fine. Tell you what, why don't you take me downstairs, then everyone else can see I'm fine, too."

"Of course." She took a step back, then turned toward Henry. "Make sure his—"

Mark stepped in between them, stopping her in mid sentence. "They don't take orders from you any more. They answer to me, and me alone, you got that?"

She pressed her lips together, took a deep breath. "Yes."

"And you can also quit calling me Sir, and start calling me Mark." He looked toward his donors. "And that goes for the rest of you, too. I have a name, and I'd like you all to use it." He saw them nod, watched their eyes flash with uncertainty. He offered a wink to Henry, and on the way out of the door, he gave his shower co-conspirators a smile. All three of them still sported damp hair.

Out in the corridor—

"Tell me something Alice, does everyone here get blown in the shower, or did you tell them to keep me distracted until Daddy gets home?"

She stared at him for a moment, and smiled. "Did you enjoy it?"

"Hell yes, but you haven't answered my question."

"The answer is yes, Mark. Shall I tell them—"

"No. You don't tell them anything, remember?"

"But they're—"

"Mine. And before you ask me if I'm always this much of a jerk, the answer is yes. So my manager was always telling me."

"Your manager." She hesitated. "Your previous life."

He remembered her saying that before and he slowed his pace. "What?"

"I don't want to be impolite."

"As in, impolite when you stuck a needle in my arm when I didn't want you to?"

"I was doing as I was told, and I apologized for that."

"Sure, and that makes it all better. Tell me what's on your mind." They'd stopped walking. Mark curled his naked toes, dug them into the deep-piled carpet. A glance front and rear told him they were alone, and inspired by his sarcasm, the core was pushing, getting him all stirred up. He watched Alice gather herself and attempt to stand up to this high fallutin' third generation pain in the ass.

"You still seem so attached to that life." Her words were finely etched with incredulity. "As though you're reluctant to let it go."

He nodded and a humorless smile twitched across his face. "Yes, and every time I touch a donor I'm reminded of what I lost, of what was taken from me, and how it was done."

"But you're—"

"Deacon's progeny. Yeah, I know."

Her eyes, her ears, her thoughts were all over him, taking on board every expression and inflection. "All this. It means nothing to you."

He shook his head. "Do I sound ungrateful?"

"No. Maybe. It's just—I don't understand."

"He took my life from me, Alice. Let's just leave it at that." He started to walk. "Come, let's go and meet the family."

CHAPTER 27
GILLES

Midway across the North Atlantic, they had passed the southern tip of Greenland and were now dropping toward Newfoundland. Delacour had gotten the message they were coming home, but Gilles didn't want to attempt a real conversation until they had landed. Right now he felt in limbo, alone with his failures and shortcomings, and the loss of his donor.

The cabin was dark. Gevani, Ryan, and Gage were still resting and pushing out bullets. Without the aid of live donor blood, they'd had to rely on an emergency supply, and rehabilitation was proving to be slow and exhausting. In the meantime, Mina was curled up like a cat in the seat opposite, staring at him with reproachful eyes.

"Delacour will know if he's alive," he told her. "As an Elder, he'll feel it, and I'll call him as soon as we land in New York." In truth, he wasn't absolutely sure about that first statement, but right now he felt his best course was to tell Mina what she wanted to hear. He was already regretting being honest. By telling the others about Gannon's identity, he'd created a mental shit storm and had been suffering the consequences ever since.

She nodded, and didn't let up on the stare or the needle-like mental assault.

He tried again. "Look, I'm sorry you didn't know. We both thought it would be for the best, and surely he's of no consequence—"

She leaned forward. "Gilles. You haven't slept with him."

He worked hard at silencing his relief on that score. "And what did that tell you?"

"It told me there's a connection between us. Despite the fact that he's Deacon's..." She stopped, let out a growl of exasperation.

He studied her face. Hurt, uncertainty. So, the tables *had* been turned, then. He'd never seen her fall apart like this, not because of a man.

"And don't look at me like that." She pulled her shawl around her shoulders. "I know what you're thinking."

Gilles leaned back, closed his eyes, felt like he'd been dumped into a vipers nest. Still, this wasn't normal behavior for her, and was so easy to forgive. He sat up straight, looked her in the eye. "What do you want, Mina? Tell me."

"Just don't lie to me anymore," she said. "And don't shut me out. I need to know how he is. That he's alive, at least."

"And if he wishes to remain secretive?"

"It's too late for that." She started to shiver, then her eyes flashed toward him. "There's something about him, and about me. I don't know what it is. It's hard to explain."

He frowned, concerned. "I asked, at the time, if he'd hurt you."

"No, no. Gilles, it was quite the reverse."

"You sure?"

"Yes, I'm sure."

Gilles let it go. The subject was proving traumatic for both of them and he needed to talk to Delacour. "Change the subject?" he offered.

She nodded eagerly. "Yes, let's."

"I've had the jet re-routed to Seattle. Things have been happening over here, too. Come home, Gilles. I don't want to lose any more of you."

After the disconnection, he stared at nothing while his mind got to work. Seattle. Would he ever see the house on the California coast again? Walk along that gentle beach? Delacour hadn't given the slightest hint at the details, but whatever happened, it had been enough to pick up the entire household and move.

"You're not alone," Mina told him a short while later. "We're preparing to head south, to New Orleans." They were in the midst of their final conversation before heading their own separate ways, about to scatter like pigeons before the cat pounced. Gevani was going with her, taking up Goran's offer of temporary sanctuary until he could heal up and arrange passage home. He'd had no choice but to jump on board their jet and head in entirely the opposite direction he wanted to go.

Inevitably, she raised the subject of Gannon.

"Delacour says he's still alive, but as for his whereabouts—" He simply shrugged. Delacour had been vague and Gilles had been too distracted over the fate of the others. He wanted to get back home, wherever that might be, as soon as he possibly could.

Not much in the way of news, but Mina appeared relieved. Gilles said his goodbyes to Ryan and Gage. Both were looking better and he realized he would miss their company. He'd be alone on this next leg of the journey, the only one left, now both donors and Gannon were gone.

Mina gave him a final hug. "I'm sorry for yelling at you, Gilles. Take good care of yourself. Till we meet again." Like it was a given. Just as they both knew things were about to get worse, that they hadn't yet reached the bottom of the curve, not by a long stretch.

The flight home dragged him through a pitching, tumultuous sky and gave him ample opportunity to reflect, and by the time the storm had dumped the jet, bumping and yawing into SeaTac, he was mentally drained and struggling to find the reserves he'd need.

Eleanor was in the vehicle to greet him, a profound look of relief on her face. "Gods, Gilles, it's good to see you. We feared the worst."

He climbed aboard and they embraced. "Did everyone make it?" he asked.

"Yes, although it was touch and go with Houston for a while." She shook her head. "Oh, and I'm so sorry. About Merrill."

He nodded tightly. "She died quickly, I think. I shouldn't have left her alone."

"You were taking care of Mark."

"Yes, and ultimately I couldn't save him, either." The vehicle was beginning to roll across the tarmac and he stared vacantly out of the window. He felt a gentle pressure on his arm and he looked at her. "Yes, I know he's alive, Eleanor. But for how long?"

"He'll be all right."

He tried to stop the litany of blame howling like a gale in his innards. "So, Weiss hit us over here, too? I didn't know he had the manpower."

"Apparently he does."

He sat back, and fought a growing sense of dismay. Blame had been replaced by a staccato list of questions regarding the attack on the House. They piled up, one after another, on and on until he thought his head would explode. He kept a lid on it. Eleanor seemed unsettled enough and he didn't want to make it worse by adding his own fears and questions to the mix. The vehicle was moving out of the city, heading for their new sanctuary, somewhere remote, he guessed, and so he settled and got some rest while he still could.

He broke away slow.

Eric's eyes were closed, his breathing shallow. In contrast, Gilles held back from allowing his own lungs to expand while he fought the siren song of hunger and thirst. It was seductive and euphoric, always attempting to get the upper hand, forever pushing and wanting more.

A moment later, the battle won, he rose slow and easy. "Thank you," he whispered.

"No problem, and I'm sorry about Merrill. We'll miss her."

Gilles watched the donor walk away. He appreciated the sentiment. Merrill had been like a den mother to the others. Her loss would be devastating for them, too.

I shouldn't have taken her with me.

Too late, now. Far too late.

He felt the blood ooze slowly through his vascular system. Under normal circumstances he would be energized and renewed, but the events of the past few days weighed heavy, dragged him down, and he had to will himself to move and go in search of the others.

It was early evening and the atmosphere was cold and damp, so far removed from the dry air of their home further south. Here the rain was omnipresent, drifting in the air, caressing the skin, sliding obtrusively past tooth and tongue with every breath.

Down a short corridor he spied an open door and walked toward it. Outside, the floodlights were on and a few lazy insects danced beneath them. He saw Saleem pulling boxes from one of the trucks. They were still unpacking, having only arrived two evenings ago. Quickly he appraised their immediate surroundings. They were utterly enclosed by forest, shut in by the wide, lower boughs of evergreens, guarded by their tall, narrowing trunks that extended upward, allowing only an intermittent view of the stars above. Gilles stared up at the sky for a moment. No orange glow from the city lights here, and Orion's Belt was quite clear up there in the heavens.

A shout brought him back to earth.

"Hey, when you're done staring into space—" It was Houston, down by the line of vehicles.

He smiled and stepped forward to join them in a human and vampire chain while they transferred the contents of three trucks into the house. It was easy, rhythmic work, and it made him temporarily forget everything and be content in the presence of his companions.

When they were done, he walked into the house with Houston. "It's so very good to see you. And this time I mean it."

"Likewise," answered the big man. "And I'm sorry—about everything, I guess."

Gilles frowned. "A disaster I don't care to repeat. We should never have left the country."

The other man shrugged. "None of us knew what was about to happen." He made a quick gesture toward their immediate surroundings. "But at least we had this place."

They walked along a narrow corridor that creaked and bowed slightly underfoot, and as they passed by a narrow doorway, he stopped in his tracks. Saleem and Tobias Marsh were partially buried amongst a pile of boxes and computer gear, and they were accompanied by a young man who looked so much like Gannon it was uncanny. It was another second or two, after he'd taken in the lesser stature and the fact that he glowed like a donor, that he realized who it was.

Matthew Gannon.

"I was taking him to the range when we got hit," Houston said. "There wasn't much time and I didn't want to dump him on the sidewalk."

Gilles stared. He saw Matthew turn and look toward him, saw his face light up, and watched him approach, hesitant, hopeful. Ah, this wasn't good.

"Gilles."

"Hello, Matthew. I hear Houston has been taking care of you."

"I owe him my life." Eyes flicked toward the other man, but then his attention was back once more. "Please tell me he's alive. Toby says he is, but we were told you were attacked, and—" Matthew stopped. His next breath came out ragged and he appeared to have trouble inhaling the next one.

"Yes, he's alive." Gilles tried to sound reassuring. "And I'm sure he'll be fine, your brother is very resilient." What else could he say? He was hardly about to elaborate on what happened. He glanced over Matthew's shoulder toward Toby Marsh. Of course. Delacour wouldn't be the only one with a mental finger on Gannon's pulse.

He gestured toward Marsh. "What does he know?"

Matthew glanced back there for a moment. "He says—he thinks he's okay, but there was some time yesterday, a sense of loss, pain, like he was grieving."

"Huh," Houston snorted. "They've probably told him we're all dead. Just to stick the knife in, torture him a bit, you know?"

Gilles looked over his shoulder at his colleague.

"Sorry. Only guessing."

"Matthew, he'll be fine. He's third generation, if that means anything to you. His captors will treat him with respect."

"That's high level, important?"

"Yes." He watched Gannon's younger brother take it all in.

"Will I ever see him again?"

"Yes," he lied.

The young man nodded, backed off, and returned to the others while Gilles pushed Houston down the corridor. When they were out of earshot, at the opposite end of the house—

"So, what the hell happened?" Houston began. "Did they just whisk him off in a limo or what?"

Gilles frowned, couldn't help but look exasperated. "No. He was riddled with bullets, trying to stop them from killing us; he had a handgun, a meat cleaver and had a dozen of Weiss's assassins in thrall. Then he collapsed, and Deacon's men kicked the living hell out of him, shot him full of morphine, and dragged him off. That's dragged, Houston. Not whisked."

The big man nodded, all matter of fact. "They immobilized him." His face broke into a grin. "They must have been crapping their panties. Pumped full of bullets and a dozen in thrall, huh? And what was the deal with the cleaver?"

"Don't ask."

"Aw, come on."

"No. You first. What happened to you? Eleanor said it was touch and go for a while."

"Nah, it was nothing like that. I was—" He stopped. His attention shifted outside the window.

Gilles followed his gaze. Delacour was emerging from the forest; he carried a broken shotgun and was accompanied by two male donors. They watched him climb the steps and head toward them.

"Gentlemen." He greeted them with a smile, and appeared unruffled as ever. "We have much to talk about. My office, if you please. If we can figure out exactly where my office is."

CHAPTER 28
MARK

Curiosity gathered around him like a pack of hungry jackals, just as it had inside Miles's club in Los Angeles. Only this time, Christina wasn't on his arm in that beautiful dress, oozing calm and assuaging his fears, and Alice, in fairness trying her best, made a poor substitute. He estimated there were twenty people in the room, an even ratio of men and women, all of them gathered loosely in his immediate proximity. It had started with two, then three, and right now everyone hovered nearby, not necessarily engaging him in direct conversation, in fact some of them had remained silent from the moment of his arrival.

Molly would have told him to man up, that it was part of the job, but he wasn't that Mark Gannon any more; instead this was bizarre and uncomfortable, and he wondered if he was giving off some kind of irresistible scent. Or maybe they were simply waiting for him to perform a party trick or two. If so, they were about to get their wish. The tricks would come, he promised silently, when Daddy arrived.

Another thing sticking in his craw, in addition to Deacon there had been six vampires in that terrible limousine, and no sooner had Alice brought him here, he'd spent the first few minutes hoping he would spot at least one of them. But there had been no sign of recognition, no indications whatsoever. He'd shaken hands with some of the men, gotten the occasional, passing flash of knowledge and, disappointed, hadn't pressed any further. As for the women, they seemed reluctant to touch him and he felt a little more disappointed than perhaps he should have. And after a while the silent scrutiny became too much and, bored and restless, he was about to ask Alice to accompany him down into the casino.

Instead, he sat bolt upright. Seconds passed before he could breathe, and his companions began to regard him with some concern. "Don't you feel it?" he asked them. He saw expressions of incomprehension, while others continued to stare. "He's coming," he hissed.

"But, he's not due until later," Alice began.

"You dare question him?" one of the others demanded.

Movement to his left. One of the males who'd been standing by the window, now on the approach. "He's right." And quickly it began to register among the gathering, producing hushed whispers and a whirlwind of thought.

Mark leapt to his feet, headed out of the room and into the hallway, and on arrival he prowled like a leopard outside the burnished bronze elevator doors, his body keeping busy while his mind was ablaze. Moments later he realized some of the others had joined him. "Alice, go back into the lounge, and take the others with you," he said to his hovering companion.

"But wouldn't you—"

"Just do it." His thoughts became a battering ram and he watched them recoil in discomfort. He kept up the pressure, until he'd driven everyone back inside the lounge and they'd slammed the doors, and left him alone.

Closer.

He began to step back, away from the elevator, panicking, not knowing what the hell he was going to do. In direct contrast, the core, coming alive, pulsing inside, knew exactly. He heard the faint whine of the elevator winch. He felt his gut lurch. Deacon. Oh, God. Oh god, oh god…. Closer still, and the motor changed pitch, and slowed. The doors opened.

Twenty feet away, he could see the elevator was crowded. Six people emerging—four men, two women—followed immediately by another man. He knew every single one of them and he noted with some satisfaction the varying degrees of surprise on their faces. They were expecting to see him. But not like this. The core had him by the nose, was calling the shots, had him balled up in a wad of fury.

But where was Deacon?

There, the eighth and final figure to emerge, taller than the others. He remembered. That was his target. Mark threw his shoulders forward and charged. Just one solid punch to the face. That's all he wanted, and then maybe he'd get lucky, catch him by surprise, get his hands around the throat so he could throttle the bastard. All he needed was for the others to get *out... of... my... way...*

His mental commands raced on ahead, accomplishing nothing. He bowled straight into the four men who'd initially emerged from the elevator, and they landed in a tangled heap on the carpet. He felt their hands grappling for his limbs. He kicked and lashed out, tried to get free, and thought he might succeed until the fifth man walked straight up and punched him hard in the face.

They dragged him upright; he was wriggling like an eel but they had him effectively contained. He looked up, ears ringing and lights flashing in front of his eyes, then grinned at the man who'd hit him. There was no need for another blow to subdue him but he got one anyway, presumably a pure revenge hit for filling the guy's chest full of bullets all those days ago. This time the side of his skull above the jaw creaked alarmingly and he almost blacked out. He growled, tried to stay focused, fought oblivion with everything he had. "Fuck you," he spat. Head down and mad as a hornet, he began to struggle all over again.

He attempted another mental assault, had no idea why the last one didn't work, and that's when he felt the intrusion. Deacon slid into his mind like smooth, polished glass, and Mark's will suddenly became a flat piece of paper that was slowly, inexorably folded in half. Then it was folded in half again, and again, and again. He concentrated, fought it, but eventually the core within him appeared to lose interest and left him to the wolves, until all of his inner strength and sense of purpose were akin to a tiny block of wood pulp, inert and helpless.

"Let him go."

The hands left him, the ones he remembered intimately, that had pulled and torn at his clothes, slid over his flesh, right at the very beginning. He stood amongst them, his balance wavering, and for a sick moment he felt a sense of longing. He wanted them back, because while they had him, he was safe from what came next. They began to move, to part on either side of him, leaving him all alone.

"On your knees."

A calm voice, it almost had the cadence of a request, but Mark dropped to his knees like he'd been given a good, hard shove. He looked upward, into a face his mind had tried hard to forget.

"You know how to address me."

"Yes."

"Good."

The man reached for him and Mark discovered he wanted to scream, but this time it was different. This time, while cool fingers slid along the sore line of his jaw, he leaned into it. There was a connection there that hadn't been evident before, familiar and soothing, natural, inevitable. A soft gasp escaped him. "Father," he whispered.

"You know I need to punish you for this, my son."

"Yes."

"Good. Stand up."

He did so, rising slowly, and by the time he'd regained his feet, the pulpy little mush ball cowering in the corner of his psyche had sprung back, leaving him blinking and startled. Deacon had given him his mind back.

"Let me introduce you," his Father said, while Mark pinwheeled mentally, trying frantically to get all his senses back in working order. "John, Eduardo, Simon, Vaughn, Rebecca, and Carmen. These are the ones who helped create you. You are quite uniquely bonded and for that reason you will be unable to dominate them. They will, however, be loyal. This—" the other man stepped forward "—is Rory. You two have also met before. Rory you will also find difficult to control, purely on account of his stubbornness." Deacon smiled. Rory, the one who'd punched him twice in the face, gave Mark a clipped bow and followed it up with a smirk.

Mark took in their faces, the six of them that had helped kill him, and the other, who had tried at least once, and he began to wonder what 'loyal' meant. Surrounded by all of them, he felt overwhelmed and stymied with confusion and self-betrayal. These were his enemies, they were his family, and seven of them were part of the very fabric of his being.

"Eduardo, Carmen, escort him to his room. Mark, you will stay there until called for. Understand?"

He nodded. "Yes, Father."

He began to walk, a male and female escort on his either side, and the further away from Deacon he became, the better, the more in control he felt.

"Sir, it's so good to meet you finally," Eduardo told him quietly. "We didn't know we would be part of your creation, not until it had already been done."

"Which one of you kicked me off the cliff?"

"I did." It was said in such a conversational manner, it took his breath away.

"And I'm supposed to forgive all that, now?" He shook his head. Anger and confusion were rising like a swift tide.

"You do as you wish," Eduardo told him. "What is done is done."

Mark frowned, looked at the woman. She reminded him a little of Molly, only with slightly fuller lips, and eyes that danced alongside him rather than attempting to bore through his skull. Attractive. "And you're the one who controlled the reins of pain, am I correct?"

She smiled. "It's my gift."

He looked ahead, saw the door to his suite open, and recognized the dependable Henry standing in the doorway. Mark wanted to bolt, to get away from these two horrors, to dash inside, slam the door shut in their faces and never come out. Instead he continued to walk, and on arrival he watched them give him a perfunctory bow, and if he stepped inside the sanctuary of his suite a little faster than usual, he hoped it didn't show.

Behind closed doors, alone with his donors, he dropped to his knees, gasping like a fish that had been abruptly and unceremoniously spat out onto dry land. He fell further, rolled onto his back. He saw Henry and Cherry hovering above him.

"Sir—"

"A minute. Just give me a minute." He closed his eyes. Panic welled behind them, disorienting him so much he felt flipped upside down. Had he still been human he would have no doubt puked out his entire guts. When he finally got a grip and climbed slowly to his feet, his hands were trembling and his head felt fragile like the shell of a bird's egg. He stumbled toward the bedroom. "Zack, Leesa," he pleaded. He crawled up onto the bed and lay there, and when he felt his donors join him, he reached out and clung to them in desperation. He buried himself between them, felt Zack's hypnotic heartbeat right behind him and Leesa's in front, then he concentrated, let the twin beats and their glorious body heat gradually soothe the terrified, screaming banshee in his head.

It was a while before he could attempt the most basic, rational thought, and it all came back to Deacon. He'd been kidding himself, pretending that he'd be perfectly able to stand there before him, master of his own will, if not his destiny, right up to the point where they finished the job and killed him off.

But it wasn't like that. It would never be like that. Not only had he been completely powerless, but when Deacon had reached for him, had caressed him in exactly the same manner as he had on Sunset Boulevard, this time Mark had wanted it. This time it felt good, like a need, a desire, and he also realized that Deacon had no intention whatsoever of killing him. All his beliefs and assumptions, they were all ripped away, and the slender tatters that remained offered him nothing. He was lost, floating in the dark, out of control, and he was terrified. Pain and death, he'd been prepared for that, he wasn't afraid of that. But this…

He shifted onto his back, pulled both donors' heads gently until they lay on his chest, and he realized if he didn't want to go completely bat shit, then he needed to start rebuilding. Leesa stirred, slid her arm across his belly, and he smiled. She was real, Zack was real. He thought about the others, those he'd left behind—Gilles, Christina, Houston, his brother Matthew and his parents. They were still out there somewhere, and despite the shattering, mind-blowing events of the last two hours, he was still Mark Gannon. There was his foundation, right there. Everything else he'd rebuild.

He fell into a doze with his companions, and they gave him maybe another hour before Henry approached and told him in hushed, apologetic tones that he'd been summoned. He nodded and pulled himself from the tangle of limbs. He made sure his shirt was buttoned, and he let Armando run a brush through his hair.

Outside, Eduardo, Simon, and Rory were waiting. All three were in dark suits that blocked out the light and blended with the shadows in the corridor. Had they been dressed like that before? He couldn't remember, he'd been too busy, elbowing and shoving and brawling, trying to get his hands on Deacon.

"Is this necessary?" he asked them. Simon was now crouched alongside, hobbling his ankles with chain-linked metal cuffs.

"Not really," Rory told him with a shrug. "But it's part of the show."

Mark rolled his eyes. He stood compliant, held out his hands, waited patiently while similar instruments were wrapped around his wrists and clamped shut so tight they nipped the skin. He hissed.

"Sorry," Simon offered.

They began the slow shuffle toward the elevator. In the midst of the others, Mark felt like a scruffy prisoner dragged from his cell after weeks of incarceration. He was still barefoot, dressed in jeans, and his cotton shirt was creased and rumpled. Only a straggly beard and the rank smell of old sweat would complete the illusion. Instead, his shirt was still saturated in the blissful scent of the two donors who had so recently lain alongside him and he breathed it all in and smiled.

He fully expected the elevator to go down. Instead, it went in the opposite direction. Another floor, one he had yet to be introduced to. They emerged onto a bare concrete floor lit by flickering fluorescents and quickly arrived at a pair of opened doors. Beyond, Mark's first impression—it looked like a church, or maybe a small lecture hall. Stepped seating led down toward a dais at the far end of a room that contained a large, square, steel frame, and behind the dais, four arched, tinted windows, stretching almost from floor to ceiling.

He had to be helped down the steps. On his way down he glanced to either side, saw a mixture of vampire and donor, all sitting and waiting for him. The donors stared as he passed by, the vampires avoided eye contact completely and their thoughts carried a strong whiff of fear. *Not good,* he thought.

At the base he noticed a stack of panels against the walls, suggesting that the entire seating area could be screened off from the dais. It puzzled him until they pulled him beneath the frame, turned him around to face the audience, and pushed him to his knees. As soon as his knees hit the deck he could see it. Just a miniscule fleck, a trodden-in piece of ash that screamed at him and told him its owner had died on this very spot, had burst into flames like the cinematic vampires in his imagination, and burned to a cinder under the force of daylight.

He let out a gasp and glanced over his shoulder toward the window. Of course, they could shift the tint, fry whoever was chained down here while watching from behind the safety of the screen. Shit. They were going to kill him after all and he hadn't even prepared a speech. His heart couldn't race, and adrenalin could no longer pump through his system. Instead, the core swelled inside. He felt it build, block upon block of quiet, determined rage.

He looked down, tried to stay calm, and he caught sight of something else. Had he been human, he would have been unable to see—tiny molecules of blood, left behind, accompanied by the thin, clawing scent of horror. There were others, here and there, scattered, their voices rising like a demented hell-born choir. The entire dais was a killing ground, awash with the specters of agony and pain, of torture and death. Mark squeezed his eyes shut before the ghosts reached for him, before they locked on to his limbs and dragged him down toward insanity. *Not yet,* he told them, *not yet.* He would join them soon enough.

They had separated the cuffs on his wrists, spread his arms, and hooked each cuff to the frame on either side of him. There was movement on the steps and he saw his own donors, all six of them, being ushered into seats at the back of the room. He hung his head, inexplicably ashamed. The entire House was present, having either been directly involved in the scuffle or having listened to it from behind the safety of closed doors, and no one was allowed to miss the show. Eduardo was standing behind him, and Mark felt the icy touch of a knife blade against his back, heard the pull and tear of fabric covering his shoulders.

"That was a perfectly good shirt," he remarked. He glanced toward Rory and they shared an expression, an agreement on the absurdity of the drama. He was about to say something else when he felt a lump in his throat. It was Father, on the approach. The entire hall became deathly silent while they all waited, until eventually the doors swung wide at the top of the steps. Deacon emerged and began to descend, flanked by Vaughn and Carmen. At the base of the stairway, Vaughn stood aside after offering him a slight bow. Mark figured he should have a wisecrack ready but, truth be known, he didn't have the stomach for it.

Deacon appeared in front of him. "There will be no preamble, my son. You know why you're here."

Mark looked up, swallowed, couldn't summon an ounce of defiance. "Yes, Father."

The man nodded and stepped back and Carmen came into view, dressed from head to toe in matte black Lycra, Purgatory's vicious little yoga instructor. She held a whip in her hand, a good old-fashioned, heavy, metal-tipped cat, and he realized he was going to be flogged like some mutinous sailor aboard a eighteenth-century frigate. She crouched before him and his eyes roamed along her black-clad thighs while he drew in the scent of licorice, blood, sex, and saffron. Her lips brushed gently against his right cheekbone while her free hand spread like a spider and explored the ridges of his abdomen. Her eyes were alive, sparkling with the prospect of hurting him.

"You look magnificent," she whispered. "I promise I'll be gentle."

"Liar," he hissed. He leaned forward, pushed his lips against hers, felt her respond. He slid his tongue determinedly, slowly between her teeth. It felt good, familiar, like he was used to kissing her, and he was sorry when she pulled away.

He saw the others back off while she disappeared to the left, out of his peripheral vision. He closed his eyes. He didn't know whether he should tense up or relax, but hey, it shouldn't be so bad, he figured. She was a woman, a man would be stronger, so this wasn't the worst that could happen, right? Right? All he had to do was get through it. All he had to do was—

Wush…

Shit.

The blow hit him like a train, punched the air from his lungs and slammed him forward, jerking the cuffs so hard against his wrists they bit deep into his flesh. Pain ripped across his back like he'd been cut in half and doused in acid.

Wush…

And so it began.

CHAPTER 29
GILLES

"How many?"

Delacour leaned back in his chair, surrounded by towers of hastily stacked boxes. "Twenty."

Gilles frowned in dismay. "About the same number as the group who attacked the Foundation."

"That could be a pattern," Houston confirmed. "And these guys were well funded and well armed."

Like an army, Gilles thought. "But who are they?"

"I don't know," answered Delacour. "And despite my last clumsy attempt, I think it's time we found out. Quickly." Gilles caught Houston and his Elder sharing a glance.

"What worries me most of all, is they're all human," Houston said.

Gilles understood his friend's apprehension well enough. Humans were never used to fight their battles, lest the more strong-willed became vampire hunters, blew apart the whole notion of secret coexistence and endangered their entire survival. "Weiss doesn't care, does he," he realized. "In fact, if he spawns a legion of crazed vampire killers they'll achieve his objective so much faster."

Delacour nodded. "Exactly. And it will escalate, giving Deacon another good reason to snatch our collective funding and consolidate his power base."

"Well, from what we learned from the Foundation Trustees, Deacon's on his way to doing just that. He already holds some of the major international purse strings."

"Which brings us," Delacour smiled, "to your report."

Gilles settled in his chair. They already knew the bare essentials, now it was time to fill in the details and those areas he'd missed. So he began, gave them his observations on the journey, their arrival, and the meeting the following evening.

"So they were preparing to strike a financial deal with the devil, huh?" mumbled Houston at one point.

"Not knowing the devil already held all the cards," added Delacour. "I suspected as much, which is why I made alternative financial arrangements."

Gilles and Houston stared at him.

"Oh, come now, gentlemen, you're surprised?"

"So, we're not broke?" asked Houston.

Gilles narrowed his eyes. "If our finances were never in jeopardy, was there any need for us to go there in the—" Delacour raised his hand, stopped him.

"Unfortunately yes, Gilles. I know what you lost, and I understand only too well the price we paid. Had I known what was going to happen…"

"I'm sorry." He closed his eyes. His tongue abruptly felt as though it were carved of wood.

"Are you able to continue?"

"Yes, yes. No problem."

"Before he does," interrupted Houston. "Mind if I ask a little more about these financial arrangements? Did we strike a deal with the devil, too?"

Delacour shrugged. "Almost, but not quite. I made an arrangement with Violet Marsh."

"The librarians? No shit?"

"They're running, just as we are. They're scared. They're also considerably wealthy."

"So, they have the cash, we have the muscle?"

"That's about the size of it."

"It's not a bad idea," Gilles added. He pushed the words out, used them to paste over his anger. "Weiss's current methods appear to be divide and conquer. He hit us in London before we could make any significant group plans, and scattered us like leaves in the wind. At least here, we're making an effort to regroup."

Houston shrugged his shoulders. "Whatever. At least I don't

have to worry about where my next rounds of ammunition are coming from."

"All right. Gilles, continue," Delacour said, bringing that part of the discussion to a close. "Tell us about the fight."

"Oh, yeah." Houston began, apparently oblivious. "I want to hear about that." He raised a hand. "Hey—not that I wanted it to happen."

Gilles swallowed his growing bitterness, took in another breath, and began to talk.

"What do you think Bryant meant?" They were now discussing the final events, the part he hoped Delacour could shine some light on.

"About Mark being important to our survival?" Delacour appeared troubled. "I'm not sure."

"Well, he sure as hell isn't strong enough to go up against Weiss, but maybe he'll kill Deacon for us," Houston offered with a grin.

"You think Deacon has inadvertently created his own nemesis?" Gilles thought about it. And it made some sense. "Mark would know the man's weaknesses more than most, wouldn't he?" They both stared at their Elder.

"No." The man shook his head. "It's something else."

"But you don't know what?"

"No. Not yet."

Houston let out a sigh. "Well, whatever it is, it's out of our hands, yes? I mean, shouldn't we be forgetting about him and concentrating on other things, like our immediate survival?"

"Yes, we should." Delacour stood up; Gilles and Houston followed suit. "Very well gentlemen. As I see it, we have two priorities. Our new base of operations with the Marshes, which won't be here, by the way, so don't get too comfortable. I should receive the final details in the next few days. And, I want to put at least half our energies into discovering the whereabouts of Weiss and his murderous little army."

"And what happens when we find him?" said Houston. "Do we get on our knees and beg?"

Delacour grinned. "Yes. That's exactly what we do." And while Gilles and Houston offered one another an uneasy glance, "So, I'll put Eleanor, Saleem, and Tobias on to Weiss. I want you two to make sure everyone stays on the alert, packed and ready to move. We won't have much time once we get the word. And for pity's sake don't let Saleem and Tobias get too comfortable. Cables are already growing through the house like vines."

They bowed, and both waited until their Elder had disappeared down the corridor, before Houston spit it out—

"Where are we heading? Alaska?"

"They do have longer nights up there," Gilles said, only half joking.

"Yeah, and stretches where the sun doesn't go down at all. Great. Our donors will freeze to death."

"At least you get your bullets."

"Huh, we're going to need them, too. A pity we lost Gannon. I'm betting Weiss's troops will show up again, sooner rather than later."

Gilles shook his head. "I never thought I'd say this, but I'm starting to miss him, too."

Houston slapped him on the shoulder. "I'm going outside to check the perimeter."

"Before you go, what was that all about Delacour's last clumsy attempt?"

The other man hesitated, and gave him a hard look. "We managed to take one of our attackers alive. You ever see our Elder torture a human, Gilles?"

"No. Never. I wouldn't think he'd—" He stopped. There had been a willingness to sacrifice Merrill, though, yes? To be seen doing as the others were doing, while pulling that sleight of hand agreement with the Marshes, before anyone else did.

Houston gave him an odd look, suggesting he was picking up his thoughts. "These are bad times, my friend. Bad times."

"Indeed." Gilles watched him go with a sour feeling in his belly.

He spent the next few hours making sure everyone in the house was prepared and ready to leave at a moment's notice. This involved more than one animated conversation with Saleem, whose electronic equipment looked to be multiplying all on its own. He had the donors repack some of the boxes they'd pulled out of the vans, and in some cases stuck back in the vehicles, all ready to go. In the early morning, maybe two hours before dawn, while he was standing in the yard, considering what he might have forgotten, he was approached by Christina.

"Hey." She gave him a hug. "I'm so sorry about what happened."

"Thanks." He embraced her, kissed the top of her head. This was the first real chance they'd had to talk since he got back. "I hear you had troubles of your own."

"We were trapped, Gilles. I thought we were going to die, I really did. They were so quiet, they got really close and managed to shatter a lot of the windows."

"And they attacked at night, too. Same as London. Don't you find that odd?"

"Houston's theory is, they wanted to hide from the cops, and they figured we'd only have half the alarms active, which is true."

"He's playing it down, but I hear a rumor that Houston saved the night."

She nodded. "He wasn't there when it started, and I think he took them by surprise. He had Mark's brother with him. I think he helped, too." She closed her eyes, and clung tighter. "I'm scared, Gilles. What's going to become of us?"

"Well, we're still alive, and we're safe, for now."

"Mark isn't here."

"I know." He'd wondered when that particular subject would crop up.

"Houston told me he got shot, that they beat him."

He offered a silent curse to the trees. "I'm sure he'll be fine, Christina. He's alive, we know that much."

"But for how long?"

"Like I said to—"

Someone appeared at the top of the steps. It was Saleem. He looked panic stricken. "Need help, quick," was all he managed before dashing back inside the house.

Gilles leapt up the steps with Christina close behind. They found Tobias Marsh on the floor of one of the rooms, convulsing and in the midst of a seizure, while Matthew and Eleanor were attempting to roll him into a recovery position.

"What's wrong with him?" exclaimed Saleem.

Gilles shied away from the stricken man's thoughts that stung like hot needles. "I don't know. Eleanor?"

She appeared baffled. "He said something about his back a moment ago."

"Can we take off his jacket?" Matthew asked.

"An electric shock?" Gilles asked. It seemed pertinent to ask, considering their immediate surroundings.

Gannon's younger brother shook his head. "One minute he was standing there, the next—" Beside him, Marsh lashed out and kicked. "Hey. Whoa, easy…"

Saleem was horrified and was frozen on the spot. Gilles stepped past him and reached out.

"Just enough to stop him from hurting himself," Eleanor told him. "Let him move a little."

He nodded and grabbed hold of a leg that had almost connected with Matthew's jaw. He saw Eleanor reach and clasp Toby's pale hand in her own.

Two seconds later, "Oh my. Take off his jacket. Careful," she told them and began to talk softly, steadily, trying to calm Toby down while they wrangled with his clothing.

"Saleem," Gilles ordered. "You see him do anything like this before?" And when he didn't get an answer, he raised his voice. "Saleem."

"No, I—I don't know. He told me a couple of days ago he didn't feel too good. Had bad pains in his chest. But then we had to make a run for it and he seemed fine."

Matthew was hauling on one of the jacket sleeves, and when they'd removed the garment, "What do you mean by not too good?"

"Roll up his shirt," Eleanor said quietly. "Easy."

Saleem looked scared. "I don't know!"

Gilles became aware of Christina opposite him, and she gave him a look that told him to back off. Frustrated, he returned his attention to Toby. They had him on his stomach, and Matthew was carefully rolling up the man's shirt, exposing the flesh on his back.

"Oh God, what is that?"

A series of thin purple lines slashed diagonally across the skin; they faded and were followed by more. A crisscross pattern emerged, only to disappear and be replaced by bolder, angrier stripes, while Tobias continued to twitch and convulse, his hand gripping Eleanor's like a lifeline. Gilles watched, fascinated. "Something beneath the skin, perhaps." He became aware of Delacour, on the approach. The Elder had Houston with him who pushed his way through.

"What the hell is going on?"

"It's psychosomatic," said Delacour from the doorway.

Gilles looked toward Eleanor, who nodded.

"Then who—" he began stupidly.

Christina gasped. "Oh, no. It's Mark."

Delacour's face held a distasteful look. "It's the bond between them."

"Mark? What the hell do you mean?" Matthew had let go of Toby and was now on his feet.

Houston grabbed him by the collar. "You watch your mouth, kid." He didn't let go until Delacour had waved a dismissive hand.

The sickening stripes on Toby's back continued to evolve. Gilles was thankful to see Matthew's attention back on their stricken companion once more. But he looked scared. "What does this have to do with Mark?" he persisted. Gilles merely shrugged, left it at that.

It was a while before the markings ceased to flower. But eventually Toby stopped convulsing and lapsed into a short, stressed breathing pattern. They carried him into another room, laid him on a bed, and tried to make him comfortable. Dawn approached, and Gilles volunteered to stay with Eleanor and keep an eye on him.

During the morning he rested as much as he could while sitting in a chair that had been positioned alongside the bed. He slept for an hour, and on awakening he noticed Toby had curled into a fetal position, that his eyes were open and were staring at him. Simultaneously, he also became aware of Delacour and when he glanced over his shoulder, he saw the man staring down at Toby.

Eleanor had been sleeping at the other side of the bed and was now stirring. She stretched and leaned forward, stoked Toby's hair. "How are you feeling?" she asked him.

"They're not feeding him," Toby whispered, his voice hollow, drained.

"Gilles," Delacour said. "Eleanor will you excuse us for a moment?"

He stood and followed the other man out into the corridor.

"Those two priorities I mentioned earlier," Delacour began. "We now have a third."

He closed his eyes, knew what was coming. He'd been thinking about it all morning.

"I want you to get him out of there, Gilles. Get him out as quickly as you can."

No need to elaborate on whom. "Do we even know where he is?" he asked.

His Elder nodded. "Yes, I know exactly where he is."

CHAPTER 30
MARK

He remained in the pit, his crash pad when things were awry on a conscious level, crouched with his knees under his chin while he watched the core. Was it a trick of the eye, or were tiny slivers of it peeling off and floating somewhere above his head? He had seen it swell up again, watched its boundaries stretch and advance toward him. But now it appeared to have returned to its former size and he wondered if it was cannibalizing itself in order to rebuild him. The energy to repair the tattered flesh on his back and shoulders had to be coming from somewhere, and although he didn't know how it all worked, he imagined a new version of himself, lighter, sunken cheeked and haggard, his back fully repaired but he'd look like shit. No doubt he'd find out when he bothered to go and look.

There was no sign of the girl, although he half expected her to turn up at any moment. He had that feeling, like she was waiting in the dark behind him, ready to step out whenever she chose, a prospect that didn't overly concern him as he was almost reconciled to her being there. In fact, if he were pressed, he'd have to admit he wouldn't have minded her company, for the alternative was to continue wallowing in his pathetic little pond of misery, in which he had already tasted the bitter flavors of self-pity, dismay, stubbornness, despair, and self-admonishment at least three times over.

He also considered he was becoming outwardly unresponsive, uncaring, and blunt-edged after being chewed over once too often by a demon and his sadistic children. Everything seemed unreal, at a distance, or maybe he only felt that way when he was down here.

And maybe he was down here because right now it was the only safe point of view—with the lights dimmed and the sound turned down.

He sensed change and looked up. There was something wrong, up there, out there, he could feel it, and now he had to make the decision as to whether he investigated or not. Easy choice, yes or no, with no idea of the consequences. Maybe if he rose half the distance…

He kicked up toward the surface, drawn inexorably by the stimulus of sound and movement, enough of it now to make him push and crawl those last few momentous inches. He opened his eyes… and he lay sprawled across the bed in his luxurious suite, on his stomach. His back still burned enough to set his teeth on edge, but thankfully there was plenty to distract him.

"Szz…" His first attempt at Simon's name didn't come out so good and so he swallowed, and licked lips that felt cracked and dry. "Simon." He coughed. "Stop hitting him, or I swear…"

Armando was already on the floor, and Simon was about to give Zack another hard backhand across the face. Thankfully, the man did as he was told and Mark let out a ragged sigh of relief.

"You don't understand. They were trying to feed you."

"… because I'm hungry."

"And if they succeeded—then you, me, all of them, we'd be back on the dais. And they—" Simon pointed at all six of Mark's donors, their fear, distress, and anger radiating such delicious heat it made his vision blur with longing, "—would not survive."

"Leave them alone," he muttered. "It's an order."

He dropped back into oblivion, or was dragged there, he couldn't tell. But not all the way down. This time he hung midway, half conscious, but fully aware of the core divesting itself, shifting within, stimulating and feeding, rebuilding, making him whole. He grinned, delirious. *Fuck the blood,* he thought. *I don't need it.* He relaxed, let his head roll back, and he waited.

"How long?"

They'd allowed him to feed as soon as he'd physically recovered. The blood had made him energized and jittery, and because of present company, it was becoming doubly difficult to stay calm. He felt under scrutiny like a lab specimen, and while Deacon looked him over, Mark tried desperately not to recoil. He'd already taken a look at himself—good as new, not a scratch, not even a post-hangover shadow beneath his eyes. It was quite remarkable and added to his continuing bewilderment.

"A little short of five hours."

They were talking about his recovery rate, how long it had taken him to heal up and drag himself out of the abyss. Mentally, he reckoned he still had some ways to go, but no way was he letting them know that. His thoughts remained shielded, a convex barrier, hard as steel.

"And he wasn't given anything during the process?"

"No, despite efforts to the contrary."

"Oh?"

Mark narrowed his eyes, listened while John and Simon tattled on his donors, and he put it on the retribution list. He had all kinds of threats and promises ready, but he couldn't take another beating. Not yet. So he kept his mouth shut and tried to stay relaxed as Deacon approached. The man reached up behind him, rested a hand on his naked shoulder. Mark let out an involuntary gasp at the contact. Again the touch surprised him, and the familiarity and intimacy of it made him despair.

"How are you?"

He felt the hand slide across his shoulder. "I'm fine, Father." *I can lie. I can still fucking lie, you fucking jerk.* Abruptly he became disgusted at himself, reduced to the level of a petulant teenager. Molly had told him once, that despite his attendant narcissism and arrogance, he was one of the least screwed-up people she knew. Obviously his re-creator was about to remedy that. He saw an amused smile flicker across Deacon's face. The man let him go and stepped back.

"Very well. We've taken a look at the body, let's take a look at the mind." He turned toward John. "Are they ready?" After a mutual, silent acknowledgement they all retreated. Confused, Mark was left alone in a bare concrete room with only the flickering buzz of a single overhead fluorescent for company. They'd shut the door—he'd heard it lock. He had a quick look around, confirmed the lack of windows, the low ceiling, and hard floor. No trap doors, no air vents, no way out.

A few more minutes, the lock clicked, the door opened, and people began to enter. He counted five. Rory, three other male vampires he'd met briefly the previous evening, and a male human who just happened to be Henry, his donor-in-charge. All five of them were armed with long, narrow, slightly curved knives.

He looked at the knives and considered his own predicament—bare feet, jeans, no shirt, and empty hands. "Don't I get a weapon?" Rory barked out a single laugh by way of reply.

Mark backed up, tried not to panic. The men lined up on the opposite side of the room. He had seconds, if that, to figure this out. He couldn't dominate Rory, and would be hard-pressed with the others unless he could touch them. The only easy one was Henry, who seemed reluctant, fearful, and just looking at the way he was holding the knife told Mark he knew shit about using one. Rory and the other vampires were another matter entirely.

He flicked his eyes along the line, trying to recall what he'd seen and felt when he'd met them. There. The one next to Henry, the one named Terry, who now stood relaxed but poised, on the balls of his feet.

It was a gamble, but he threw everything he had at the guy, pushed hard, sent one simple mental command. After that, he dived toward Henry's side of the room. His donor raised his blade in a high arc and stepped forward hesitantly. Mark used the only move he could remember from his movie set days. One party trick, *if* it worked. After that, he was fucked and would have no choice other than to prolong the inevitable. He came up under the knife and caught Henry's wrist in the fork of his thumb and forefinger, pushing up with his entire body, blocking the downward sweep. In his peripheral vision he saw Terry break off and make a dive to intercept Rory.

Henry's will collapsed immediately, and Mark gripped and pulled his arm swiftly down to the right, causing the man to overbalance and fall. Reaching down, he twisted the blade from Henry's weak, compliant grasp. "Stay down," he hissed.

By now the other two vampires had arrived and he was wide open. One of their blades slid hard into his right shoulder. A sharp hiss of pain whistled between his teeth, but he now possessed Henry's knife. While he struggled to get a decent grip on the weapon, he brought his knee up and slammed it into one of his attacker's ribs.

After that, it was a free for all, but at least Terry was keeping Rory busy elsewhere in the room. He managed a couple of thrusts with his own knife, while attempting to persuade the other two men to turn on one another. He now had multiple lacerations on his hands and forearms, some of them deep, and they didn't help his concentration. Part way into immobilizing the guy who'd stuck him in the shoulder, the other vampire kicked hard against the side of his knee and dropped him to the ground.

Rory appeared directly and ominously above him. Obviously, Terry hadn't been good enough to keep him away. Mark saw the underhand sweep, felt the blade penetrate, punching upward, inward, going for the heart. He grunted with the pain, his consciousness wavered and everything began to gray out.

"Game over," he heard Rory announce.

Flat on his belly, like a lizard, he could see the bumps and ridges and all the other tiny imperfections on the concrete floor that stretched away from him. He followed the cracks and runnels until they ended abruptly at a familiar face. Henry was dead, his eyes flat and empty, staring at nothing. Taking in the bigger picture, Mark saw the man's head was lying at an odd angle. The throat was torn wide open, the wound still bright red and horribly inviting. Behind the body, Deacon was sitting on a metal chair, waiting patiently while Mark got his act together. His Father's eyes held the look of a cat that had finally got into the birdcage, and there was a slight spatter of blood on his shirt, no contest as to whom it belonged.

Mark attempted to rise. His left knee hurt bad when he placed some weight on it, and looking down at his hands he saw they were covered in thin purple welts, the aftermath of the knife fight. Every breath hurt, every movement made his teeth grind, but he forced himself to crawl until he was alongside his fallen donor. There, he closed his eyes, couldn't bear the horror, the duality of torn flesh and hunger.

"Henry was one of our best," Deacon began softly. "That's why I originally gave him to you. Had you not tried to protect him, had you used him as a shield, you might have lasted longer."

Mark reached out, let his hand trail through the dead man's hair. It felt silky, beautiful, but the scalp beneath was already cold. He wanted to cry, an expression forbidden to him these days. "Why?" he whispered.

"You know why. You seem able to inspire all manner of disobedience, my son, and it is something I will not tolerate."

Of course. They'd tried to feed him. Despite everything, on pain of death, they'd tried. He felt his heart break, felt it crack wide open. Through the gap, another thought emerged, a narrow spike of ice that trailed lazily up the length of his spine. "The others."

Deacon smiled. "They're alive." A polished Italian leather shoe tapped lightly against the corpse. "I think this one will serve adequately as a lesson, don't you?"

"But it wasn't their fault. They did it because they love me." He pulled his hand away. He felt evil, monstrous. He had gathered them close, had told them not to fear him, had overpowered them with his mesmerizing third generation bullshit until they were infatuated and now he saw exactly where it had led.

"Hmm, and now another lesson is learned. Henry has served us both quite well tonight, I think."

Mark looked down at his hands. The welts were beginning to fade. He flexed his fingers. "What is it you want from me, Father?" *What the fuck do you want from me?*

"All in good time, my son."

He heard the chair scrape back, felt a hand on his arm, and with Deacon's help he rose to his feet. Outside, Carmen and Rebecca were waiting and they led him away. He said nothing on the journey. He felt numb, empty.

Back in his suite, his donors hovered uneasily. They were in shock, just as he was. Politely he told them he needed to rest and he shut himself in his room. It seemed safer that way, despite the fact that he yearned for their company. He curled up and actually got part way into persuading himself that his current frame of mind wasn't doing anybody any good, when they came for him again.

This time they plunged him into a tank full of water and drowned him. They waited until his lungs filled with liquid and his heart stopped, then they dragged him out and sat and watched while he choked and struggled to recover. After that, it was a brutal fistfight, and cattle prods, on and on until he reached the assumption that Deacon was trying to break him down and turn him into some kind of automaton that would obey him without question.

When they were finally done with him, he was so crazed and exhausted he could barely crawl back to his suite. This time his hunger was too great. After making sure he had Deacon's permission, he gained sustenance from Zack and Armando and stumbled into bed with Cherry, Cyanne, *and* Leesa in tow. His need shamed him but he was desperate. He couldn't be alone. He was out of control. He was lost. Deacon had hurled him spinning into deep space, where there were no points of reference, no sense of direction, where nothing but madness beckoned.

It took forever, but at some point he managed to claw his way down into the pit. However, even there he couldn't get rid of the heartache. He sat curled up tight, barely aware of the diminutive presence alongside him.

"They're all dying because of me," he told the girl. He didn't need to look upon her face. He knew she had already damned him. He saw her hand reach out and point, and followed the line of her slender arm until it reached the core. Up until now, he hadn't noticed how small it had become. No longer an orb, it had shrunk to the size of a fist, and there it hovered, spinning slowly, thrumming with energy. It looked dense, heavy, built of cast iron.

"This is worse."

He stared, confused, at the face of a girl, into eyes a million years old. Old and unforgiving. He bore her gaze as best he could, and tried not to cower and flinch. He attempted to explain. "I think the rest of it is inside me."

"Yes," she told him. "And you need to die. But not yet."

He wanted to laugh but instead his mouth twisted, bitter and petulant. He couldn't help himself. "Not yet? Why, have you got plans for me, too?"

"Shh," she said. "They'll be coming soon."

He felt her drift away, leaving him alone with the diminished core, but he knew he couldn't stay. She was right, it was already going dark out there in the world and they would be coming. He spent a few more minutes trying for calm and then he kicked for the surface. His eyes blinked open. The room was dark, he heard the three soft heartbeats of the girls close by, became aware that only Cyanne was touching him, her head nestled in his shoulder, her hand splayed lightly across his belly.

He shifted, leaned in and kissed her awake. She smelled beautiful, of blood, salt, and caramel. She regarded him lazily and one of her legs came up, hooked around his pelvis and pulled him in, effectively locking them together. He cupped one of her breasts, brushed the nipple gently, felt it come erect between his fingertips and he heard her moan softly. "Make me forget," he whispered, kissing her below the ear. "Just for a little while."

An hour and a half later he was up, dressed and presentable thanks to Zack and Armando. He gathered them all together, told them where they stood, how not to put themselves in danger, to keep their personal loyalties hidden, especially in front of anyone bearing overly sharp teeth, and hopefully there would be no repeats of the night before. He didn't need to look at their faces to sense their mood. They were like him—defiant yet cowed, wanting to pull at the leash, but fully aware of the consequences. It was a different look than when he'd first met them, and it was all his fault. Inside, he felt a storm brewing.

Minutes later, Carmen and Simon arrived to escort him to Deacon's quarters. Outside in the corridor, Carmen trotted ahead of him.

"We'd better hurry," she began.

Mark drew to a halt. Immediately, it felt as if a ball had dropped, like something had snapped inside and he felt calm and unshackled by consequence. He reached forward, took her firmly by the shoulder and shoved her against the wall, hard enough for a nearby painting to jump and settle slightly askew. He grabbed the front of her shirt, slid her up the wall while forcing his knees between her thighs, pinning her there like a moth right out of the killing jar.

"I will not," he said, glaring into eyes that contained a lively spark of longing, "be told to hurry." He leaned in, allowed one of his extended teeth to graze the skin on her throat, let his tongue dart out and catch the tiny droplets that oozed from the wound. "Not by a vicious little bitch like you." He smiled, locked eyes with her once more. "Do we understand one another?"

She nodded, licked her lips.

He felt Simon hovering close by.

"Mark, Deacon told us—"

He stepped back and let go of Carmen, who dropped and sank to her knees. "Stay down," he told her. "And you—" He gave Simon his full attention. "You fuck. On your knees. Right now."

"Mark—"

"Do it."

The man complied. Mark's face twisted with satisfaction. "Let me tell you something," he said. "If you or any of the others endanger the life of my donors again, it'll be you chained to the dais and I'll be holding the whip." He reached out, hit Simon hard across the face and sent him sprawling. To his credit, the man recovered and scrambled quickly back into his kneeling position. "Do you understand me?"

Simon nodded. "I'm sorry. We were told—"

"I don't give a shit about what you were told. Your loyalties lie with *me*, and you'll do as *I* tell you. Got that?"

They both nodded.

"Good. From now on, you'll call me Sir until I tell you different. And when you're with me, you'll walk two paces behind me. At all times. Understand? And that goes for the others. Make sure they're informed." He shrugged his shoulders, stepped back, could hardly believe what he'd just done. He knew they'd been following Deacon's instructions and that he'd now compromised them, just like he'd compromised his donors. But after what had happened over the last few nights, he found it hard to be sympathetic. "All right," he told them, "on your feet. Let's not keep *Daddy* waiting." He turned and stalked off toward the elevators, not caring if they were keeping pace or not. Hell, if he was up for the pain-in-the-ass Olympics, he might as well go for the gold.

At the elevator bank he waited. The bronze doors slid open and Mark stepped inside, followed by an entourage that now trailed by the requisite number of paces.

CHAPTER 31
GILLES

"What is this?" Houston grumbled. "A reprimand for not bringing him back the first time?"

Gilles shrugged, and continued to rummage through the carryall he'd been given. "I guess I'm just the best man for the job."

"Yeah right, hot shot. I still don't like the idea of you going into that hornet's nest on your own. And what if they've done a number on him? What if he doesn't *want* to come home?"

"They're torturing him, Houston." He gestured toward the bag. "Is this it, everything I need?"

"Yes. And I wish I was going with you. I'd like a chance to take out some of those bastards."

Gilles shook his head. "No. It would just mean more of us ending up dead. Weiss probably wants us all at one another's throats. Makes his job a whole lot easier."

Houston grinned. "Hey, I wouldn't take 'em all out. Just the ugly ones—and Deacon."

The man's attitude was infectious, enough to bring a smile to his face. Not a bad thing, he considered, to shine a little light on current circumstances. He made a final check of his equipment and zipped the bag. "Okay. See you in a couple of nights. Keep your eye on Delacour and the girls."

"You got it." Houston gave him a mock salute on his way out.

Both his Elder and Christina were waiting by the car. Christina gave him a hug. "Be careful," she whispered.

He smiled, déjà vu hitting him hard. "I will," he assured her.

"She means it," Delacour added.

Gilles handed his bag to the driver. "He's important, isn't he?"

"Yes, but not enough to kill yourself for. The first signs of that being a possibility, you get out of there."

"I'll do that." He kept his face blank while recalling London. Not much hesitation there if he remembered rightly. He'd followed Gannon right in, against all odds, and somehow he reckoned this next trip would follow similar lines. Not an unsettling thought he realized. In fact, over the last few hours, a cool anticipation had been growing inside him and gathering speed. He'd need every skill, every shred of experience. This would be a stretch and the trick would be to get out alive. That, and he had to admit, he was curious. Right now his only source of apprehension lay back here, if something happened while he was gone, and damned right he'd be blaming himself if anyone died here while he was off retrieving the Golden Boy.

Nothing more to be done, he gave Delacour a tight, formal bow and slid into the rear passenger seat of the car.

On the way to the airport he attempted to meditate on the task ahead. The location—Las Vegas—concrete, heat, steel, and dust: people in the thousands pressing through casino doors, transient, their faces changing every day, and the city breathing its shifting population in and out, hour by hour, day by day, regularly as if powered by mighty lungs. It would be easy enough to slip into the beat, to move through the flow until he was close. After that, assuming Gannon was still alive, everything would gather speed and become decidedly more difficult.

On a purely objective level he had to admit, he was still puzzled as to why they were putting the man through it. Why go to all that trouble? There were no secrets to be told. No beans to spill. Deacon knew the strength of Delacour's group and every individual within it; Gannon remained the only mystery and neither Bryant's telepathic assertions nor Delacour's vague premonitions offered much to explain those ugly marks on Tobias's shoulders.

It occurred to him that Gannon simply wasn't toeing the line. Deacon was a stickler for protocol and respect, so perhaps they were trying to shift his attitude by any means necessary. And if successful, then what? What would happen if Houston's suspicions turned out to be correct and the man didn't want to come home? No doubt he'd find out in the next forty-eight hours and, Gannon being a stubborn bastard, maybe he could hold out until Gilles got to him. Until the fun really began and it was time to go up against Deacon. That was something he had to avoid at all costs. This had to be cloak and dagger all the way. No direct confrontation. Sneak in, grab Gannon, sneak out. Anything extra and they were more than likely doomed. Deacon's mental strength was immeasurable, Gannon had obviously fallen foul of it already, and he wondered how that initial confrontation had played out. Had Gannon succumbed immediately or managed to put up a fight? Was the family, the heritage, a factor?

He pushed it all aside. Pointless going round and round, juggling with unknown variables. Instead, he went through everything he did know. It would be fully dark when he arrived, with five hours to spare until dawn, and there would be a chance, just a chance he could execute this plan on this very night. He'd brought two sets of protective day gear, just in case, but he fervently hoped he didn't have to use them. As for a practical, detailed escape plan, it was nonexistent. He was working on the fly, and well, maybe it was better if he told himself that's how he worked best, and left it at that.

Just before midnight, and outside it was still hot. The air was dry and particles of sand and grit hung in the atmosphere, kept aloft by a slight breeze. The streets were packed, vehicle headlights glittered between the silhouette of the crowd, all below the blaze of flashing signs and a multicolored array of beckoning lights that drew people like moths to the casinos.

He'd already checked the busy connecting tunnel between hotels, its plush carpet and moving walkways, and now he was heading inside after a quick look at the exterior. He followed the crowd through gilded, sliding doors into the jangling cacophony of the interior. The noise was like a wave, threatening to bowl him over. The heat from the living hit him right in the gut, stirring hunger and longing and it took a moment's concentration to block it all out and pay attention.

He began to move around the perimeter of the casino floor, his step casual, his shoulders relaxed. Right now he wore discreet, smart attire—polished shoes, dark slacks, a slate gray Henley—that clung to his narrow, muscular frame, the color a sharp enough contrast to bring an illusion of warmth to his skin. He walked past boisterous crowds at the tables toward a gathering at the center of the casino floor—some kind of bachelor party, just a bunch of guys in jeans and polo shirts, yelling drunkenly at one another, urging their brothers to empty their wallets as quickly as possible. Although—

He saw two of the men offering a fervent glance toward the room's periphery, as though they were looking for a friend perhaps, or—

A scent of urgency made him change his route, and curious, he picked a quiet spot and waited. There. Another four guys across the room, one of them had nodded toward the gang at the craps table. Gilles didn't linger, but while he continued to work his way toward the rear of the casino, he considered why that particular group warranted his attention. A faint prickling of unease, that was about the sum of it. He switched his attention back to the crowd in general. Right now, human he wasn't concerned with. It was vampire he was looking for.

He continued, between rows of slots, through thin curls of cigarette smoke and the desperate bitter heat that radiated from those sitting mesmerized before the machines. Not far away, three men were striding along the carpet, heading in the same direction. Again he was assailed by an odd disquiet, and he attempted to pay a little more attention as they headed for the elevators. He considered they might well be Weiss's men. Just like those guys back at the gaming tables; like those who'd hit the California house, or the club, or the Foundation. And now a whole list of what ifs rattled through his head, one after another in rapid succession and he knew he'd have to find out exactly what was going on, and do it fast. Because if these *were* Weiss's men—

He realized he was going have to drop out of sight sooner rather than later. He came out of the bank of slots and began to follow the men, saw one of them glance quickly to the right. Damn, he almost missed it. Another tall, thin, dark-haired man standing at a corner by the wall.

Gilles dropped within the protective ranks of slots, kept his pace nice and easy, and saw his opportunity as he approached a dais clustered with foliage that marked and partially concealed one of the exits from the casino floor. There were three people standing there, their backs turned, and so he approached, stepped as close as he could, then pushed—

—sideways, and everything around him abruptly drained of color. Both the dais and the people there appeared insubstantial, sharing space with the image of a wall, stretching ahead and then curling off to the left. The flat plane of carpet beneath his feet fought with the illusion of a stone-paved alley that followed the wall. Gilles had to pause for a moment and go through his usual reorientation.

By now his quarry had reached the elevators and he had to move fast in order to join them. In doing so, he narrowly missed a collision with a woman dragging a rolling suitcase who had absolutely no idea he was there. Not that it would have mattered, but he had never had liked the sensation of walking *through* people.

Alongside the three men, he then had to wait, while around him his memory of the narrow streets of Marseilles' first arrondissement took on life and solidity. It never paid to stand still while surrounded by the shadow of his past, so he shifted slightly, kept the twin view of memory and reality in a state of movement. He smiled as he caught the sharp scent of the dock and the sound of children's laughter, the smell of baked bread and rotten fruit. It all sought to drag him in, pull him away from the brushed metal façade of the doors and his three companions, their body language already beginning to shift. One of them carried a bag that looked heavy and Gilles hoped he'd have the opportunity to see what lay inside it.

The elevator arrived and a group of young women spilled out, their faces alive and full of laughter. It added to the sound of children he could hear in the arrondissement and his mind had to work hard at keeping it all apart. He followed the men inside and positioned himself by the doors as the others moved to the rear. No other occupants. He hoped they'd start talking, but they remained silent as they rode up to the thirtieth floor. It wasn't until they'd stepped out and walked a short distance and entered a stairwell that everything changed. And all at once they became something other than three ordinary guys on a few days vacation.

In the stairwell the bag was dropped and unzipped. Gilles frowned. He wasn't an expert, but the black, short-barreled weapon that sat on the top of the pile looked a lot like a Heckler and Koch

MP7, with more H&K hardware underneath, enough to make the likes of Houston lick his chops.

He caught sight of a ball bouncing across his vision, saw it roll down the street in a view that messed with the stairwell's dimensions. He struggled to focus and decided then and there it was time to move. He had to get Gannon out of there, and fast. Were there security cameras in here? A quick glance around told him nothing. He figured Deacon had to have his own area locked up so maybe they knew what was coming.

He leapt up the stairs, two at a time. Another six floors by his reckoning. Below him he heard the soft footfalls of the three men, cautious but advancing steadily. He'd have minutes, if that.

CHAPTER 32
MARK

"So, you introduced a few rules." Cold eyes appraised him, sank deep and easy through his defenses.

Mark trailed the fingers of his left hand along the back of a chair while he took in his immediate surroundings. The room had a clinical atmosphere and reminded him of a visit to the doctor or the dentist. It could also have been one of those police interrogation rooms they showed on TV were it not for the sink, faucet, and row of cupboards.

"Informality doesn't appear to work too well with this crowd," he replied. He tried to keep his voice level and controlled. Internally he was preparing for the worst, getting ready to dive headlong into his pool of oblivion.

"Rules are good," Deacon said. "They avoid confusion."

He nodded, looked down at a bare metal table and the single chair. They looked innocuous enough, so maybe this wouldn't be so bad. Hell, maybe they were going to sit him down and tell him why they'd been putting him through it for the past forty-eight hours. He glanced over his shoulder. Beside Mark and Deacon, only Rory and John were in the room, flanking the door. John gave him a respectful nod, Rory offered a wry grin, as though he knew exactly what was coming. Mark frowned. "So, may I ask what happens now?" The polite tone of his voice surprised him.

Deacon nodded, smiled. "Of course. We just have a few more tests to perform. Just to make sure everything is as it should be."

Tests.

"And how—" He faltered.

"Come here, Mark. Stand before me."

Two paces. His body complied automatically while his mind jittered and ran through a gamut of possibilities, figuring it was a sure bet pain would be involved. All of a sudden it became a matter of pride that he didn't show the slightest bit of apprehension.

Turn around.

He heard Deacon's voice in his head and obeyed; he remembered the limousine and the pain. He closed his eyes and tried desperately not to flinch as cool fingers brushed the skin on his throat while another hand came around his waist and pulled him backward and, ah shit—

He knew—*knew* the bite was going to hurt. And when it didn't—

Pressure, skin puncturing and giving way, a momentary sting that faded in an instant. Instead of the roaring fire of agony, he sank into a warm, buoyant pool. No pain. None. He gasped, felt his shoulders relax and his balance shift until he was at the point of collapse. All his senses drifted, and by the time awareness finally kicked in, he discovered he was sitting in the chair, the palm of his right hand pressed flat on the table. He felt the cool surface beneath his fingertips and pressure on his upper forearm. When he looked down he saw a blue rubber tie coiled tightly and biting into the muscle.

Deacon was alongside him and he sensed Rory at his shoulder. He frowned, seemed to remember there being someone else in the room. "Where's John?" he began.

A flash of steel in his peripheral vision; the table vibrated hard under the impact. But it was the sound of it that made him shudder, and it took a number of seconds before he'd summoned enough courage to look down. A hand clamped hard against his mouth, very effectively stopping his scream of horror.

"Silence."

The word slithered past his ear as the room spun and he bucked in the chair. He tried to breathe while they held him down. Silence. He tried desperately to comply, and fought hard against the image burned into his brain. He couldn't believe it. He refused to believe it, while the pain and debilitating revulsion told him otherwise.

He shivered and writhed, went through the empty motions of nausea. His head rolled and he caught a glimpse of John holding a butcher's meat cleaver, much like the one he'd stupidly wielded in London. His eyelids slammed shut like traps. He didn't want to see that. He couldn't. Instead, he tried to concentrate on that word, his Father's single instruction. Silence. Maybe if he could just breathe, nice and easy, long and slow.

He felt Deacon's hand relax, and he let out a single, involuntary groan. He couldn't help that. *I'm sorry,* he wanted to say. *I'm sorry.* But it was taking all his effort to stop his body from shaking. Rory's grip on his shoulders began to relax, and for a long moment he just sat there, knowing at some point he'd have to look—to acknowledge what they'd done.

He took another breath, popped open his eyes. And he looked.

It wasn't as bad as he thought, because the cut was neat and clean, severing flesh and bone mid-forearm; there were no gushing jets of crimson and mercifully, the lower section of the limb—his hand, the wrist—were nowhere in sight. But at best, the relief was peripheral. That his right hand and the lower section of his forearm were gone, simply hadn't kicked in to his sense of reason yet, despite the deep red smear on the table, and he figured it was just a matter of time before the screaming really began. As he looked on, he felt the surface of the cut tingle and burn. The sensation made his flesh creep.

His butcher, John, was crouched low at the edge of the table, staring at the wound. His head was cocked, his face registering surprise. "It's almost sealed," he said. "Already."

"Huh, impressive," Rory muttered behind him.

Mark wanted to laugh, while pain played through his body like a harp, every nerve, every muscle, every sinew, taut and ready to bring forth music. He felt Deacon's touch on the back of his head, fingers sliding through his hair, idly caressing his scalp. *Was that good enough, Father,* he thought. *Was I silent enough?* He felt the need to please as acutely as the pain. As for the need to know why the act had been done, he was beyond asking, he didn't care.

Despair beckoned, and he figured his best bet was to dive below and pay a visit to the core, before he lost it altogether in the midst of considering what they might hack off next. An intrusive thought gave him pause, and he felt Deacon's hand stiffening against the back of his head before letting him go.

So, Daddy had felt that, too.

Trouble.

He looked up, slurred his words. "Something's wrong."

Deacon nodded. "Rory, our security is about to be breached."

The man nodded, no questions, and quickly left the room.

"John, see to his arm."

"Yes, Sir."

Mark winced as John slowly unraveled the rubber tie on his arm, fully expecting blood to gush. But apart from a dizzying ache that swelled back and forth like a wave at the seashore, there was nothing of the kind. Either that or he was delirious and just didn't see it. The room dimensions began to sway with the pain, forward and back, forward and back, and he grinned like an idiot. He wanted to shy away from the urgency that tugged at him, he wanted to drop beneath the surface where he'd be content. Instead he was pulled in another direction.

Female laughter in his head. And forget drowning in oblivion. Because now Dimitra was here, a stern, scruffy little goddess, torn dress, tangled hair, crouched and waiting behind his eyes for the show to begin. His perception of her was so intense he thought for a moment he could see her for real.

He fought panic, pushed her away, while the earlier warning grew louder. "Father—"

"I know," Deacon said. "John, get the arm dressed and take him to his quarters, get him ready to leave." He swept out of the room.

Mark sat impatiently as John covered his injury with padding and gauze and gently guided what was left of his arm into a sling. When it was done, he insisted on standing unaided. His injured arm was burning; it felt hot against his torso. "They're coming," he said. "We don't have much time."

"Who is it?" John moved toward the door and held it open.

"Weiss's mercenaries. And we need to collect the donors."

"Sir, there might not be time—"

"John, shut the hell up and do as you're told."

"Yes, Sir."

Mark headed outside, his head pounding, the entire right side of his body aflame. He saw Simon dashing toward him, noted with perverse satisfaction the man's look of horror at Mark's injury before falling in dutifully behind him.

He punched the elevator down button then looked along the corridor. "The stairwells," he muttered. "They're coming up." The doors opened. Just the thought of heading down filled him with apprehension. Something horrible and deadly was on its way up. But not yet. They still had time. He stepped inside, John and Simon followed. "We need to be fast. We have to get the donors down to the lobby at all costs." He watched Simon open his mouth as if to argue and think twice. Mark nodded. One thing less to worry about. The pain was concentrated now, burning like fire at the point where his right wrist should have been. He swallowed it down, tried to forget it, figured there'd be plenty of distractions soon enough. He felt Dimitra, still with him, watching everything unfold with his eyes, and in an attempt to quell his distress, he considered she was simply an embodiment of his pain, or perhaps nothing more than the family ghost—harmless, a pale wraith full of empty threats and promises.

They alighted into a busy corridor. Carmen and Vaughn approached and were openly startled at Mark's condition. Under normal circumstances the scene was crying out for a sarcastic comment, but he didn't have time and his head was currently running through the scenario back in London and all those bodies on the floor. No way did he want all that on his hands again. "The suite," he said. "No wait. You two—" he gestured at Carmen and Vaughn "—commandeer the elevator." He walked on and burst through the doors of his quarters. And again he had to face a wall of shocked stares. He held up his remaining hand.

"No time. Everybody out—now." He herded them toward the hallway. Inside, he could feel it building, the danger. Death was rising, walking up the stairs.

Simon had somehow acquired a pistol and Mark pushed him into the car with the donors. "See them into the main central elevator, send them down to the lobby, then get back here. Move it."

"Wait! Please."

Mark turned and saw Alice running toward him, pulling along two men and three young women. All five donors looked terrified. He acquiesced and allowed her to push them into the elevator with the others.

The door closed on a sea of confused and alarmed faces. Alice then dashed off while Carmen, John, and Vaughn hovered. He paused for a moment. His mind wanted to run on some kind of autopilot, and in the end he let it roll. No time to over-think. Plenty of time later to figure out just how the hell he knew what was going down.

"They're using the emergency stairwells," he told them. "And at some point they're going to block the elevators to these upper floors."

"How many?" John asked.

"About thirty guns."

There were mutters of alarm. "Vampire or human?"

"Human. Where did Simon get that pistol? And where are—" He frowned. He had the immediate future down, but he couldn't remember his companion's names.

"Eduardo and Rebecca. They're downstairs, getting weapons," Carmen told him. "And you should have been in that elevator, Sir. We have to get you out of here."

"No. We go together." He began to move toward the central stairs. "We wait for Simon, then we figure it out together." Still plenty of time, he assured himself. "Come on. Let's go find Rory."

"You shouldn't be here," Rory said. "And you'd better take these." He handed over a pistol and a spare, loaded magazine. "Safety's on, and it's already chambered."

This time Mark couldn't resist. "Going to be a sonofabitch to reload with only one hand, huh?" Deacon was nearby and he made sure his comment was loud enough for him to hear. Father and son had shared a glance a moment earlier, just an acknowledgement, but it was enough to affirm that Mark had made the right decision to stay. All the enmity, hurt, anger, confusion; right now all bets were off. They were fighting for their lives.

Rory didn't take the bait and merely shrugged. "Let one of the others do that for you."

Mark handed the magazine to Carmen, and watched other members of his team load up before setting off toward the south stairwell. There were fifteen vampires in-house, along with seventeen attendant donors, and Deacon had split them up into two groups. They had to get out, at all costs, and it had to be quick and clean, before someone heard all the shooting and called the cops.

Sure. No problem. Mark tried to keep his face a blank slate and his mental brick wall sky high so none of the others could read him, while on the inside, Dimitra sat like a vulture, eagerly awaiting the carnage.

On the approach to the elevators, he slowed, came to a stop.

"What is it?" Vaughn asked.

"Not sure…" He felt a short, percussive snap, muffled, barely discernible. It was followed by two more. "Trouble," he announced. The *UP* light began to flash on the wall.

"Simon?" Carmen asked.

Mark nodded. "Yes, and he's picked up some new friends. Unpleasant ones." He felt sick. This was exactly like London and people were going to get killed. He stared at the floor for a moment. "Okay, Simon and two humans. Vaughn, Carmen, stay with me, the rest of you head for the stairwell. There's more coming up that way."

Had he still been alive, he reckoned his heart would be pounding at double speed and a cocktail of adrenaline would be urging him in no uncertain terms to run for the hills. Instead, he experienced the usual slow metronome, while the excitement, anticipation, terror, and dread had nowhere else to party but inside his head.

He hauled aside his fears of Simon's welfare and concentrated. Only two human assailants and control of them would be easy, well before the elevator doors opened. But he didn't realize until it was too late that his mental commands had fallen short.

He almost made it. He yelled a warning as the doors began to open. He ducked to the left, purely on instinct, and a bullet caught him in the shoulder, spun him backward, and sent him sprawling along the carpeted floor before he had time to raise his weapon. He caught a glimpse of Simon, a bloody, crumpled heap in one corner of the elevator, before everything was swallowed up by the roar and flash of gunfire. In the confusing aftermath, he couldn't remember if he'd fired his own weapon or not.

He rolled onto his good side and shuffled like a caterpillar toward one of their fallen attackers. "Get Simon out of there," he urged. He wasn't the only one who'd been hit. Carmen's usually perfect brown, slender leg bore a nasty wound, but thankfully she was still on her feet. Vaughn was inside the elevator car. Mark could see him, trying to drag Simon out, over the top of a dead male human.

He struggled to remain coherent, while two percussive thuds vibrated through the floor beneath him, and blood, living human blood, filled his senses. He arrived at the second fallen assailant who was soaked in crimson and still very much alive. Mark heard a slight, high-pitched whine coming from black, plastic buds lodged solidly inside his ears. The chest was rising and falling rapidly, lungs desperately grabbing oxygen. Mark leaned against the man, looked down at his face. The eyes flitted before him, danced with fear and pain.

"What are you listening to?" He gripped the wires, pulled out the ear buds. He caught the scent of breath mints, coffee, fear-born sweat, rain and pollution. Hunger beckoned and pulled him sharply toward a wound on the man's upper chest. He drank, quickly, greedily, like the monster the man's eyes told him he was. And with the blood—

Revelation.

This human was, or had been, a donor.

More gunfire along the corridor. He was also willing to bet someone downstairs had upped the ante by calling law enforcement. Carmen reached in and slit the man's throat, and Mark stared as the man twitched and died beneath him. But there was no time to dwell on the act and what he had become, or chew over the horrors of this latest discovery. Carmen hauled him upright. He could feel the blood coursing through him. It felt good, it felt weird, and it increased the burning sensation in his injured arm. The stump throbbed and tightened against the bandage. The sensation made him reel like a drunk, and the recently acquired bullet in his shoulder didn't help.

He leaned against the wall, looked toward Vaughn. "Simon?"

"He'll live, if we can get him out."

"Then let's get him out," he replied. "Block the elevator door, head for the stairwell."

"Can't we get down this way?" Carmen asked. "Reach the hotel core elevators?"

"Too risky. Stairwell has more cover." The walls were beginning to spin once more while his arm pulsed and throbbed.

"They could be waiting for us downstairs," Vaughn told her. "And if they have incendiaries or a flamethrower—"

Carmen needed no further explanation and dragged a heavy table across the hall that proved very effective in jamming open the door. When it was done, Mark helped Vaughn haul the incapacitated Simon while he sent Carmen ahead. He'd given her his weapon. He didn't trust himself with it and besides, with the only available hand pulling the stricken vampire along, he didn't have anything spare to shoot with.

The sound of gunfire was behind them now, coming from the other stairwell. It cranked up the urgency and made it difficult to think, while questions ran blindly and unanswered through his head like frightened deer. Had the donors made it? Why hadn't those men obeyed him? The ear buds? Or maybe it was because he was injured. Maybe losing the hand had simply been too much. Deacon had picked a fine time, he considered. The specter of Dimitra appeared to agree, her manner predatory and judgmental.

They rounded a corner. Carmen was huddled with Rebecca and she beckoned. Here, the noise of gunfire was amplified and set Mark's teeth on edge. Somewhere ahead, he sensed John and Eduardo, deep in the danger zone.

"Well?" he asked.

"Four of us around the corner, against eight of them—and they have better weapons," Rebecca told him in between bursts of fire. "But Sir, they're human, and you can—"

"No, something is stopping me." He took a chance on the ear buds. "I need to get closer. They have something in their ears."

"We can cover you."

"Okay. Carmen, you're with me." It was simple and it was suicide. He watched a look of relish appear on the woman's features. He saw Rebecca disappear toward the shooting. Alongside him, Vaughn was crouched over Simon. "He's going to make it?" And when the man nodded. "All right, get ready to move."

With no wish to begin ruminating over the odds, he breathed a sigh of relief when Rebecca re-emerged and led them toward the battle. He saw John, leaning against a wall, along with two guys he remembered from the plane journey a few nights ago, both of whom had had a lot of fun kicking the crap out of him. And here he was, about to dive into the fray and save all their necks. The irony brought forth a grin, one that widened when he saw the looks on their faces. If he couldn't get through and turn this thing around, very likely they were all dead.

He closed his eyes, shut out the noise and clamor. Eduardo was around the corner and down. Further on, maybe fifteen feet away, one of the gunmen was hiding behind a doorframe. Beyond that, hampered by confusion and jags of pain, he didn't know shit.

Fifteen feet.

That's all the ground he and Carmen needed to cover. Storm the guy, pull out those ear buds, and get him to listen. All with one limb hacked off and a bullet in the shoulder.

Easy.

Sure, it was.

Fuck.

CHAPTER 33
GILLES

He'd already ascended three flights of stairs when he heard the gunshot. The sound came from back on the landing, and Gilles had half a mind to turn around and retrace his steps. Footsteps below had also ceased, everyone silent, tensed, waiting just as he was. Two more shots and the foot patter began anew, and this time it had multiplied.

He resumed his climb, heard vague, hushed chatter behind him that suggested plans might have gone awry. But there was no time to consider if that worked to his advantage or not; he needed all his concentration to differentiate between the concrete lie of the steps and the ghostlike drift of Marseilles' old town, already beginning to solidify and extend beyond his mind's eye.

Another turn, more steps, and at the top of the stairwell, a door. It would be locked, but that was irrelevant while he was ghosting, and so he pushed on, his intention to step through and go directly in search of Gannon. Instead, the shock at seeing who was crouched alongside the door brought him to a halt.

The dull lavender of her dress jolted his perception. Her face and hands appeared as monochromatic as her surroundings, but the garment color, unappealing as it was, drew his eye and rendered her three-dimensional, as if she existed right there at the top of the steps *and* in his memory, which was impossible. As for the pale, mournful features and lank, jet-black hair, once recognized they not only brought him to a standstill, they made his spine quiver in revolt.

He crept closer, the humans on the stairwell still on his heels and closing, but he cared nothing for them at this moment. All his attention lay on the girl, who stood as if to join him. She offered him an impatient expression, as if she had hurried on ahead and had been waiting for him to catch up. At a complete loss for words, he remained silent and did what he considered to be the polite thing. He inclined his head and gestured with his hand. Let the lady go first.

He felt the dissonant shiver of a solid object pass through him as he emerged into a carpeted passageway that culminated in a ninety-degree turn some way ahead. Marseilles was still evident, its richer, more varied textures enhancing the plain walls on either side of the corridor, and, directly ahead of him and sharing this juxtaposition of reality and memory—Dimitra—slender and round-shouldered, utterly three-dimensional.

More gunfire.

She beckoned and he followed quickly as she ducked into a doorway on her left. They entered a small office and immediately crouched low as a deep, heavy thud shook the floor. Their attackers, he assumed, blowing the stairway door. Movement coming from both directions. And more shots fired. He stood, his intention to go back out there, but the girl held out her hand. *Hold,* it said. And so he stayed, crouched low, poised and ready to make a dash outside, while every consecutive second told him his mission, of finding Gannon and getting out of here alive, was slipping from his grasp.

A man dressed in jeans and a polo shirt, bearing a short-barreled sub-machine gun, dropped into a defensive position beside the door. Gilles recognized him as the man carrying the bag in the elevator. He clenched his fists, clung to the vision of the man while his memories grew more coherent around him. He couldn't stay like this for much longer. Surely she must realize that. And yet she still bade him hold.

The firefight seemed endless, until the man abruptly retreated further into the room. Bullets hit the wall and showered the room in plaster and dust. The man gathered himself, and two figures leapt through the doorway and rushed him, slamming into his torso and sending him sprawling. It took only a second for Gilles to recognize one of the attackers, and another to know Gannon was in big trouble.

He didn't waste any more time.

He forgot about Dimitra and twisted sideways, emerging from the invisible cloak his memory had provided, and into the midst of a desperate struggle. Gannon wasn't a trained fighter, he was injured, and his assailant was rapidly gaining the upper hand. The girl with him had managed to retrieve the weapon while Gannon groped toward twin wires at the man's throat, but the human had already half-pinned him.

Gilles stepped forward, reached down around the man's shoulder and swiftly immobilized him. "Do it," he barked toward the startled Gannon. The man shook off his stupor and ripped the cords driven into the other man's ears, just as the guy was trying to break Gilles' lock on him.

Gannon began to talk, a flat, persuasive cadence that made Gilles' skin crawl. He let go of the human and backed away, then watched as the gun was retrieved and a slightly different angle of attack was attained at the doorway. The man was on Gannon's side of it now and would fight to the death.

He shifted his attention to the woman. "Carmen?" He recognized her face, knew her reputation well enough.

"Hello, Gilles." She barely acknowledged him, and her focus remained on Gannon who was pressed up against the wall. Gilles followed her gaze, took in at least one bullet wound and the arm in a sling, but if the man was hurting he wasn't showing it right now. Instead, his attention was on the drab young girl who'd materialized with Gilles and was now standing a few, scant feet away. She had her arms crossed and was regarding him with an expression of mild curiosity.

"You're real," Gannon whispered, bug-eyed with shock. "Oh, shit… oh, shit…"

"Mark," Gilles stepped forward, blocked his view, "we have to get out, quickly." And when he received a look of stupidity by way of response, "Delacour sent me. Come, we have to go."

Gannon reached forward and grabbed his arm. "I can't. Not like this. Not yet. I have to get them out."

Gilles frowned, looked down at the sling. "What did they do to you?"

"Doesn't matter, not now. We need to get everyone downstairs, before the cops arrive."

He turned his attention back to the doorway and considered their best course. "If I go out there and take those things out of their ears, you can do the rest?"

Gannon nodded, still partially distracted by Dimitra's presence.

"I can help," Carmen declared, having a far better command of her wits.

"Okay, then." The man at the door began to fire into the corridor and the noise bit hard into his concentration. "You ready?" he asked them. They both nodded, and so he closed his eyes briefly, took a step back into his gray world, and this time it wasn't the streets of his youth that shared his vision. There was little time to get reoriented and he headed back toward the stairwell, where muzzles blazed and men shouted, while in his peripheral vision the boat rocked and seagulls cried and the air was biting cold.

The aftermath was thick with dust and death, the floor littered with gun casings and other detritus from the fight. Gannon was kneeling beneath him, talking softly to one of the fallen vampires. "I got them out," the stricken man croaked. "I got them out."

Gilles felt boxed in, trapped by the ominous figures of Carmen and Dimitra on either side, while straight ahead, only five paces away, accompanied by six other members of his House—

"Let him through. He's coming with us."

He fought for calm. "No. I'm taking him home." It was like standing in the eye of a hurricane, knowing he was about to be swept up and obliterated as soon as the storm shifted. This was madness and the odds were most certainly against him. In desperation, he took in a few minor details that suggested Deacon might not be entirely invincible. The man's overall appearance was disheveled and there was blood on his gray suit. But there was also a gleam in his eye, much like that belonging to a child climbing off a roller coaster. Like he'd enjoyed all this murder and chaos.

Gannon was on his feet now, unsteady and on the verge of collapse. "I'll go with him," he told Gilles softly. "I don't want any more killing." He sounded tired, wiped out, defeated.

"No. You're coming home."

"His home is with us, now," Carmen insisted. Her close proximity tugged at his resolve but he kept staring straight ahead until, abruptly, his knees buckled.

"I don't have time for this." Deacon stepped forward. The man was inside his head, nothing fancy, just a plain old clash of wills that had dropped him instantly to the floor. But it didn't stop there. Gilles groaned, felt intolerable pain, as if someone had ripped through his abdominal wall and was pulling out his guts.

"Father, stop it. Just stop. Please." Gannon implored.

The agony lessened, dropped away completely. Control, however, remained.

"I'll do as you ask. Please, just leave him alone."

From his position, Gilles watched Dimitra step into the fray, saw her shaking her head. Deacon's mental grip on him was quickly released and he scrambled to his feet. Dimitra raised a slender arm, an action that gave both Deacon and Gannon pause, but not for long.

"Just step around her," Deacon began, his eyes on the young female.

The girl reached out and took hold of Gannon's remaining hand. This time it was Gannon who went down, crumpling like every single muscle in his body had failed him. Those around him gasped and stepped back. Some were looking at Dimitra now with pure, unadulterated fear, and where she touched him, Gannon's fingers were now turning gray and Gilles could plainly see exposed bone and tendon. Fighting his own revulsion, he crouched alongside the fallen man. "Dimitra, please, not this."

But she wasn't paying attention. Her eyes were locked with Deacon's, engaged in an internal standoff, while Gannon writhed, his features pain-wracked.

Seconds later, Deacon's jaw tightened, and he took a step back. He looked furious. The girl let go of Gannon's hand and it flopped back onto the carpet. It looked desiccated, mummified, and its owner let forth a sharp hiss of pain.

"Mark." Gilles shook him.

The man groaned, attempted to sit up. "They're coming," he said.

Everyone began to move at once. Rory arrived, told Deacon he had discovered a safe way down, while Gilles struggled and helped the fallen man back on his feet. Others were pressing in now, as if

Gannon had acquired a brood, one whose members had fear and questions in their eyes, and blind uncertainty in their thoughts.

"Go with Deacon," Gannon told them, lolling against Gilles like a drunk. "Get out of here. Don't forget the donors."

Someone took Gilles' hand for a moment, flesh to flesh, and caught off guard, emotion swelled like a sudden tide, brimming with threats and regret, and he wondered what he was giving out in return as he looked down at Carmen. Something between her and Gannon. Something between all of them and Gannon it seemed.

It was disconcerting to walk amongst so many people, his arm around his bloodied and injured companion, and not draw any attention. But he knew Gannon was working hard at keeping them unnoticed, just as he had contributed to the umbrella of anonymity when they had arrived downstairs, both he and Deacon creating shelter, enabling the entire group to stand aside and be ignored as a team of security guards and local law enforcement raced past, intent on discovering the source of the disturbance on the top floors, although Gilles strongly suspected Deacon had already called up some kind of human support, an interface, one that would deal with the hotel, the police, the mess.

As for the moment of separation in the lobby, there had been a visual show of reluctance. Unfinished business? Gannon had called Deacon "father," had leaked thoughts poignant enough to make Gilles wonder if Houston had been right after all, that this could well have been a wasted journey. Perhaps the outcome of this trip would have been entirely different, were it not for the young girl walking calmly alongside, who appeared determined to keep Deacon and his offspring separated. She had decided to tag along, and right now Gilles didn't have the stomach to argue or ask questions. At least Eleanor would be pleased, and he'd let Delacour handle any potential problems on that score, if and when they got home safely. It wasn't over yet, and he didn't trust Deacon in the slightest.

As they traversed the tunnel between hotels, Gannon's head lolling on his shoulder, feet dragging on the carpet, Gilles compartmentalized the next stages of the journey, tried to highlight all the potential danger spots and come up with a plan to minimize them, while attempting to cope with the heady, mental flood of imagery and other sensory input that arrived via physical contact with an injured, distracted, third generation Elder. Above all, he needed to get Gannon fed, on his feet, and focused.

On reaching his hotel room, he lowered Gannon onto one of the beds, bullied him into ingesting the contents of two blood pouches, and gave him a closer look. There was a bullet still embedded in his shoulder; he didn't need to check the sling too close to surmise Gannon's right hand was missing. As for the other extremity, it looked withered, about two thousand years old. Physically, the man was in stasis, not deteriorating, but not improving any either.

Gilles looked toward Dimitra standing at the window, her arms folded, eyes on the glittering street below. He reasoned he should ask her for help, but what he had already witnessed had frightened him. He didn't understand how, or why, but it reinforced a few of his own ideas about the girl, and why everyone felt so uneasy around her—that she had the potential to kill them all if she chose. Even the mighty Deacon had backed down, so maybe it was better if he kept Gannon out of her reach. One more touch like that—

He heard a feverish whisper. He had to lean in close.

"Mina...?"

"She got out, Mark. She's okay."

The expression of relief was both audible and mental, but the sentiment was brief. "He's using the donors, Gilles. He's using our own people against us."

Gilles stared at him. "How did you—" But the man's face was screwing up, becoming pain-wracked once more.

After a moment, "Now we wait."

He frowned. "For what?"

"For Deacon to be gone." The man struggled to speak. "She's making sure I have no choice."

"I don't understand." He flinched. Dimitra was no longer at the window. She was alongside the bed and was regarding them both. She reached out. Gilles put up a hand to stop her, but Gannon began to rasp.

"It's okay... it's okay."

He backed off and had no other choice but to sit by and watch as she took Gannon's hand once more and gave him his life back.

An hour later they were in the car and heading out of town. Dimitra was by the window, a diminutive, cold presence bearing a teenager's attitude of forced disinterest; Gannon was in the middle, shivering, suffering from extreme discomfort now that his body had kicked into gear and was trying to heal itself, with Gilles at his other side, trying hard not to let his apprehension spill over and get the better of him. Was he doing the right thing in bringing Gannon back home? Even allowing for his injuries, Gannon looked different, sounded different, as if this latest ordeal had changed him in a profound, physical way. As for the man's assertion regarding the donors—

In the end, Gilles decided to stop chewing over it. He brought a small mp3 player out of his pocket, one he'd taken from the body of one of their attackers. He turned it over, examined it, and figured he'd give it to Saleem when they got back. He'd done his job. Mission accomplished. He was alive, Gannon was alive, and it seemed their tiny female enigma had chosen to return to the fold. How she had arrived in that stairwell at that particular point in time would no doubt remain a mystery, but it wasn't his problem. He tried to relax as the car swept out into the desert, despite feeling the weight of the world hovering at his shoulder.

CHAPTER 34
MARK

He raised his head. Moisture had spiked his hair and now shiny drops were trickling down his chin. He'd thought a splash of cold water might have shifted his perception; alas, the man staring at him in the mirror remained a stranger. He tried to relax, but his entire body felt hard, like he'd spent the last ten weeks at the gym on some grueling regimen and had never once let up.

He looked down at his perfect hands and he flexed and curled his fingers. No scratches, no scars, everything accounted for—every nail, every finger, every muscle and tendon, every millimeter of skin—the left arm fully hydrated, the right arm completely re-grown. He wanted to puke and sob with relief.

He focused on his right hand. Six hours, give or take. Everyone had been quite astonished. Yeah. Go him. He'd set the fucking record. As for the left hand, ah—he didn't want to think too much about that, about what Dimitra had done to him.

Instead, he went back to his reflection and attempted to discover what it was that made him, and everyone else, do a double take. He shifted his head this way and that. His face appeared lean, cheekbones a little more pronounced, but not so much that they didn't belong to him any more. No, it was the eyes, he decided. Where they used to mock, or at the very least laugh with him at life's absurdities, they were not laughing any more. Women had always told him he had beautiful eyes, from his grandmothers to his mother, right down to all those girls in high school. Eyes he'd used to great effect over the years in getting what he wanted. But they wouldn't like these eyes. No way. Too cold, too deep. They looked like Deacon's.

He turned away, disgusted by the indulgent self-examination, self-pity, self-everything. He stepped back into his bedroom, pulled the bathroom door a little too hard behind him, and the sound woke Moira, his donor.

"Mark?"

"Shh," he told her, and he sank into bed. He lay back and let her curl against him, let her warmth lull his restless spirit. He told himself although the phrase "at least he was still alive" didn't strictly apply to him any more, it would have to suffice, and he tried to get some sleep.

They were heading further north, and for the last two nights, he'd swallowed his confusion, his anger, his regret, and a tumble of other emotions. Instead, he'd kept his head down and had helped out with the evacuation. He was avoiding Dimitra like the plague, and despite the fact she could appear in his head whenever she wanted to, the physical separation did a lot to keep him sane.

He was also avoiding Matthew. They'd embraced when he'd arrived home, an awkward, brief hug that had enabled him to sense his brother's relief and reproach. Maybe he was being overly sensitive, but it appeared reproach had gotten the upper hand. He suspected it was just the usual friction between them, but his hide wasn't tough enough to deal with Matthew right now. Bad enough that he'd discovered Toby's plight while he'd been away. Delacour had advised him about forming a bond, but he hadn't truly understood until now, and immediately he'd vowed never, ever would he do that again.

As for those he'd left behind in Las Vegas, despite what they had done to him, he felt the need to care. They were family and he was responsible for them. He felt keenly the walls of separation that now lay between them. Had they managed to escape? Were his donors safe? Where had Deacon taken them?

As for Deacon—Father—oh, how *that* concept was messing with his head. He also suspected it was messing with everyone else's. Things had changed. He had changed. Better not to think too hard on it. Better not think, at all.

Unfortunately, his younger brother had other ideas.

They had been traveling for hours. Daylight burned, inexorable beyond thick drapes, the rail carriage rolled gently from side to side and the hypnotic staccato rhythm of the train rumbled up through the floor. Mark was pushed back against his seat, pinned there by Toby and Moira on his either side, both of them rocked into a deep slumber. He basked in their proximity. They were familiar, a distraction, and right now they made an effective shield against the only other occupant in the dimly lit carriage, his brother Matthew.

They were talking about Molly.

"I tried a couple of messages. Delacour won't let me do anything else. I thought maybe you could put in a word, you being the Big Kahuna and all."

"When was the last time you saw her?"

"A couple of nights after you left for Europe. I was with Houston at the firing range when all hell broke loose."

"She'll be okay. And Delacour's right. The less communication, the better."

"Meanwhile, she's still out there, unprotected. Don't you care?"

Mark tried not to grind his teeth. "Of course, I care. Look, how come you're—oh wait, now I see it." A surprise, now he'd taken the trouble to dig a little deeper. "You were sleeping with my manager?"

"Ex-manager, and mind your own damned business."

He shrugged. It was a placatory gesture; he sure as hell didn't want to get into a fight. "It's no big deal. Hell, you got further with her than I ever did."

"No big deal? Quit turning this into a pissing contest, Mark. I'm worried about her. Why aren't you?"

"Okay, okay. I'm worried." He felt Moira stirring alongside him. Toby was already awake. "But with the both of us gone, I'm pretty sure she'll be left alone." Temper still on the rise, he made the fatal mistake of adding, "And don't forget, you both made a choice. Better for her if she had kicked you out."

"So this is our fault? You really are a piece of shit, you know that?"

Aware of Moira and Toby's growing anxiety, Mark tried desperately to relax fingers that had bunched into fists. "Look, I get it. I'll talk to Delacour, we'll check it out, and I'm sure she'll be fine. You don't know her like I do. You don't know the business we were in, or how tough it was. She'll handle it. She isn't afraid of anything."

"She's afraid of you."

"Oh, come on—"

"It's true. Just like the rest of us."

"Okay, now you're really starting to piss me off." He leaned forward and Toby's hand pressed against his shoulder. Moira had already slid away from his reach, and no wonder. He and Matthew were hissing at one another like cobras.

"I don't care. You obviously have no idea what you become when you don't get your way."

"I'll become something worse if you don't shut the fuck up."

"Oh, yeah? What are you going to do? Sink your teeth into my throat?"

"I can do better than that." He felt the core, so much stronger now, burning inside, ready to snap out like a whip. It was Toby who made him stop, his voice distant beyond the roar of Mark's desire to crush his brother's will. Mortified, he sank back and massaged the bridge of his nose with thumb and forefinger. It was a while before he could say anything. "Why are you here, Matthew? Why did you come here?"

His younger brother was pressed back into his seat, as if an invisible hand was pushing against his chest; he looked visibly shaken. "I wanted to ask you about Molly," came the choked reply. "And I wanted to make sure you were okay."

Mark spread his hands; his words came out soft, deliberate. "Well, as you can see. I'm fine."

"I didn't know that. You looked like shit when Gilles brought you in. And I haven't been able to get anywhere near you for two days. I had to get *permission* to come in here."

Don't let me be disturbed. He remembered saying that. Mark closed his eyes for a moment, dismayed. "I'm sorry. I wasn't thinking. And I can't handle a fight with you right now."

"I didn't want to fight."

"I know."

"Look, I'm sorry too, okay?" His brother looked away and stared into the gloomy interior of the carriage.

A smile crept across Mark's face. "Well, at least it's familiar territory." The humor, bitter as it was, quickly faded. "Tell me something. How long have you been afraid of me?" He expected another sharp retort. He also hoped his brother would open up, enough for him to see the truth without having to bludgeon his way into that stubborn, argumentative skull. After a short silence, he received no artifice, no mask whatsoever.

"That time we were at Grandma's, throwing stones, and I smashed a window? You remember that?"

Mark shrugged awkwardly. Yes, he remembered. Now he knew exactly what was coming. His arm draped idly around Toby and he stroked the man's hair. He didn't want to look into his brother's eyes right now, but it didn't matter. Matthew's voice was enough—flat, conversational, it cut him to the marrow.

"Do you remember shaking me and dislocating my shoulder? Making me swear I wouldn't say anything to Dad because even though it was my fault, it would be you that got in trouble, and if I told him then you'd kill me?"

"I didn't mean…"

"Yes, you did. At the time."

"We were kids."

"Yes. We were."

He was growing angry again. He could feel the core's rage creeping into the timbre of his voice and it disgusted him. He glanced down at Toby and saw it all reflected there, so he swallowed it down, like bile, and forced himself to look across the aisle. "And now—"

"I can't let you bully me, Mark. Not any more."

Bully. Shit, that stung. His mouth abruptly felt dry. "I see. And?"

His brother shrugged; he looked miserable. "I'm not afraid to stand up to you any more. And maybe, thanks to me, you're not a total fucking asshole."

He ignored the insult. "I'm sorry. I had no idea."

"I know. But sometimes you go too far, and people break. And you just don't see it."

"Well—you'll be pleased to know I've met my match."

Matthew shuddered. "The guy they're all talking about. Deacon."

"Yes."

"You really think so?"

"I know so."

"And yet you're looking for a way to turn it around. I can see it in your eyes. It's a game, and it's going to kill you."

"What fucking choice do I have?" Mark's hand was a claw on his companion's shoulder.

Toby's eyes were screwed shut. Matthew saw the man's distress and reached out. "I'm sorry." He glared at Mark. "We shouldn't be talking like this."

"No shit."

"I just don't want you to die."

"Matthew, how many times—"

"You know what I mean."

Mark saw tears welling in his brother's eyes, and he felt resentful and distraught. He leaned back and collapsed into his seat. He was wrung out, exhausted. "What do you want me to do?"

"I'm not asking you to run. Just—just be careful, okay? Listen to Gilles, and Delacour, and don't be so full of it. You're not invincible."

"All right. I'll do that."

"Okay, then." Matthew wiped the back of his hand across his face. He curled his legs up beneath him. He looked younger than his years. Thankfully, it appeared to be over.

Mark feigned slumber. He felt Toby and Moira settle against him once more and he listened, until his brother's heartbeat slowed and his breathing softened. He didn't open his eyes until he knew for certain they were all asleep. The carriage continued to roll and rattle as he stared across at his younger sibling. The love he shared with Matthew was strong as steel, and yet it took a fight like this before they would listen to one another. It had always been this way, and probably always would.

He glanced down at Toby, settled once more, his companion's empathic link soaking up all his joy and pain. Did they both know how much he loved them?

They're a weakness, the core reminded.

But the core was wrong.

They were all he had.

CHAPTER 35
MINA

"Mina, I don't like this." They were at the base of the steps leading to the front door of Irena and Charles's Manhattan townhouse, and Martin was staring at the house next door. "You say this one is currently for sale? That it's empty?"

She nodded, but in truth she was barely listening. They'd already tried knocking. Strange that none of the staff had answered. Stranger still, the aroma of blood that had slipped beyond the infinitesimal crack beneath the door, that had sent her involuntarily back down the steps as if she'd been pushed. Goran had figured they had plenty of time. That delicious, awful scent told her otherwise.

"Mina."

She tried hard to pay attention, while panic howled inside.

Martin's impatience cut through it. His voice was jagged and fear-tinged. "Look. The door is open. Could they have gotten into Irena's house through this one?"

They. Them. Whoever had spilled blood and left no one able to answer the door. She tried to think. "The roof terrace. Maybe." She peered down past the wrought-iron stair rail that led to the basement levels of the next house. Martin was right. The door at the bottom of the stairs hung open by a couple of inches.

"And you don't sense anyone or anything?"

"No."

"Then it's our way in."

"Why can't we go around the back?"

Martin shook his head. "It's too dark, too dangerous."

"But I can see—"

"I know. But I can't. And I'm not letting you go in there on your own."

She stared at him. Like entering the house next door was any less dangerous. She raised her eyes and examined the windows. They appeared blank and indifferent and reflected light from a nearby street lamp. "Okay, let's do it."

She pushed him aside, knowing he'd try to go first, but it was chivalry misplaced. If he got shot or stabbed or hurled out of a window, he'd more than likely die, whereas she had a far better than average chance of surviving it. So she weathered his grumble of complaint and descended the steps.

The door swung back easy, revealing a long, narrow room, most of it running the entire length of the house. It looked bare, it smelled of wood polish and new paint, and beyond a blocky kitchen island she could see a curling metal staircase, leading up. Beyond that, the room narrowed to a passage where gray evening light shone from the far end, from a window shadowed by a dark froth of leaves. She sensed no one, nothing. This floor, and the two above it were empty, theoretically safe, and so she headed for the stairs.

Floors of dark, polished wood greeted them at the parlor level, and directly above, a narrow, elegant staircase wound its way up toward the top of the house. Bare walls, no furniture, no carpeting, and every step rang hollow as they ascended the next three floors, no matter how careful their tread.

Cold air and the whisper of a damp breeze greeted them at the top. Still no sign of anyone. Mina crept toward the rear of the house, stepping beyond a glass door that had been left wide open, and out onto a paved roof terrace. Here the sound of the city reasserted itself, and beyond the far wall, past rows of potted ferns and garden furniture, she could see other buildings rearing up, blocky and reassuring, their regimented windows shining yellow and inviting.

Martin was heading toward a vine-covered wall adjoining Charles and Irena's. There was a wooden bench pushed up against it, and a large plant pot had tipped over and spilled tiny white flowers and soil onto the paving. She saw him look toward her, his eyebrows raised.

No one, she mouthed silently. No sense of Charles or Irena, but that might be a good thing. Maybe they had managed to escape and were safely holed up somewhere, despite not answering their phones.

Joining him, she could see the spread of greenery as it crawled and clawed its way across the brickwork. Some of it was damaged, its stems and trailers split or shredded; some of it was snapped and squashed, like it had been torn or trodden.

Martin was frowning. "It was that easy?"

Yes, it was, she thought. Charles's supreme confidence, evident here by the lack of any real security, and her mind's eye caught the broad strokes of movement, of boots and limbs scrambling over this very wall.

"I'm going over," Martin said, and before she could stop him, he'd got a toe in the brickwork and was already pulling himself up and over, adding to the damage inflicted on the vine. She had no choice but to follow.

At the top of the wall the scent hit her and she froze. Blood. Human. There was another stench, chemical, acrid, burned meat, and the latter smell rolled thick as liquid and stuck in the back of her throat.

Martin was already down and moving across Charles and Irena's terrace toward a partially open door. "There's something on the floor, inside."

Not something. Someone.

Mina half-scrambled, half-fell down the wall, and in doing so scuffed the palms of both hands. Vivid memories of London blasted forth inside her head. And now it was happening all over again. The shock of it hit hard.

She pushed past Martin and entered the house's top floor. Her mind had already told her what she would find, but she still felt the need for confirmation. Three strides across the parquet floor and she ground to a halt. The smell was bad enough, but now the scene was spread before her in all its terrible, vivid glory.

Behind her, Martin stepped to one side of the room and flicked the light switch. "Oh God."

She glanced over her shoulder and saw the color drain from his face. "This is how you kill a vampire," she said. Her mouth was dry, her tone bitter. Her eyes flicked toward what was left of Charles. His entire upper torso, his upper left arm, and his head were obliterated.

As for his remains—his pelvis, legs, hands, and forearms—they lay spread on the floor, dissected and cauterized, like pieces of a grisly marionette.

And that wasn't all. Beyond the dead figure of Charles were other bodies. Mina counted three. Two lay sprawled, one was curled up, all had their blood on display, painted garish and flamboyant on the floor and ceiling, soaked into their clothes, or accumulated in thick, silent pools.

Martin was crouched low and had pressed the palm of his hands against the floor. He was breathing slow and deep. "Oh God," he repeated.

Despite the fact she wasn't suffering physically from the shock of what lay before them, it still took her an interminable length of time to move. "I have to find Irena," she whispered. She reached the wall, turned off the light, and began to walk further into the house.

"Don't step in anything," Martin croaked. "Just give me a second and I'll follow you."

She nodded and kept going, her mind pushing through the horror, clawing toward a tiny kernel of hope, that somehow Irena had avoided this. But there was no sign, visually or mentally, of the woman's presence.

Martin was back on his feet, attempting to follow with a leaded gait. "I've never seen anything like that before."

They were at the doorway that led into the upper hall and stairwell. It was pitch black and Mina didn't want to risk the light again, so she pushed him gently against the door.

"Stay here," she said. "It's too dark. Keep your eyes on our exit. Irena might be hiding, so I'll try the floor below."

"Don't be long, Mina. We need to get out of here."

She moved quickly to the stairs and tried not to look too hard at the body that lay sprawled across the treads about halfway down. Instead, she concentrated and sent out a message. If Irena was here, in hiding, and had been successful in covering her tracks, then Mina would have difficulty sensing her presence, unless the other woman allowed it. Irena had always been good at that, and it might well have saved her life. *If* she was here.

She reached the base of the stairs. She could hear Martin above her, his breathing deliberate, trying his best to overcome his body's reaction on seeing the results of cold-blooded murder on the top floor. She tried not to think about Charles stepping confidently toward his attackers, believing he had the means to stop them; three of his staff alongside him, no doubt there voluntarily. And they were all dead.

Speaking of death, another lay on the landing—a woman Mina recognized after frequent visits—on her back, a look of surprise on her face, accompanied by the scent of thickening blood, a miasma of distraction. No time to cry out, no time to grieve. This was just another body to step over.

"Irena." She moved quietly to the next flight of stairs.

Irena, damn it.

Another step down and she stopped, gripped the handrail, and felt the sudden rush of mental contact. She retraced her steps and began to move toward the front of the house, through a door, toward the far side of a bedroom. Now she knew exactly where to look. It was a walk-in closet and she pushed aside a row of garments. Directly ahead was nothing but a blank wall. "Irena!"

The wall began to shift. It was pushed awkwardly aside and now she could see someone crouched there in darkness. No time to be polite. She reached in and pulled on Irena's arm. "Quickly. We have to get out of here."

"Charles," the woman said, scrambling awkwardly through the hole. Cobwebs and dust clung to her hair.

"He's gone, Irena, I'm sorry." The woman had to know this already. She had to.

"But he said he could stop them. He told me to hide. He told me not to worry." She was babbling, her voice was high-pitched and broken. Oh, yes, she knew.

Mina gripped her firmly and hauled her past the bed and onto the landing. "Martin?"

"Almost there." She heard his voice, part way up the stairs. "I heard someone next door. We can't go back that way."

"The front door, then?" This was a blessing, providing they could get out alive. She hadn't relished the thought of dragging the woman past her destroyed companion.

Irena was holding back, pulling at her arm. "Who is that?"

"My donor. Come, quickly now." She heard Martin lose his

footing and mutter a curse. "Sorry. There's a body. I should have warned you."

"It's okay," he said. "Do these stairs go all the way down?"

"Yes."

"I'll keep to the rail then, piece of cake. Don't worry about me."

Light was completely absent. Its access into any vampire house was always severely controlled and this one was no exception, but she didn't want to risk turning on the interior lights. If their human attackers returned in force, they'd be easy meat, and right now darkness was the only defense they had.

They reached the hallway. Ahead lay the front door.

"They're outside, too," Irena's hand gripped Mina's wrist.

"How many?" Martin asked. He had his phone out and the glow from it highlighted his tense features.

"Three," both women told him in unison. "And another three next door," Mina added. "They've almost reached the top of the house. Martin, what are you doing?"

"Contingency. Told you I didn't like this."

"He talks to you that way?" Irena's tone was sharp and accusatory.

Mina said nothing. It was typical of Irena to go old school on her at a time like this. She was about to ask Martin to elaborate when Goran's voice came through on the phone.

"Stay back, we're almost there."

"What's happening?" Irena wailed.

"Ladies, I think he wants us to duck," Martin said.

Mina felt his hand on her shoulder, pushing her down. She pulled Irena alongside her. She could feel the woman's reaction, a disjointed mix of terror and reproach, but there was no time for propriety. Not now. She crouched low, and wondered how her donor had persuaded Goran to come here—

Movement, footfalls, coming from upstairs. "Martin."

"Shh."

Vehicles outside. A short, percussive bark, followed by another and another. Sounds of struggle, confounded by noise on the stairwell directly above them.

"Now," her donor urged. "The front door."

Knowing he couldn't see, she headed straight for the door and fumbled with the latch and the deadbolts. "Are you sure?" It was hard to tell what was going on. Too much input, and fear howled like a storm in her innards.

"For God's sake, woman, move." In moments, he'd pulled hard on the door and was pushing them both down the steps toward a black Lincoln Navigator at the curb. She stumbled across the sidewalk and scrambled inside. She felt Irena fall partially on top of her as the door slammed shut and the vehicle began to move.

"Martin!"

"He's in the next car." It was her Elder, Goran's, voice.

"Sir, what's happening?"

"An attack on the House. Mina, I'm sorry. We've got Danny, and we're getting out, now."

CHAPTER 36
GILLES

The night bore two significant events, and it wasn't the first, but the second that brought everyone to a standstill. The former had been polite and formal, a necessity as Violet Marsh greeted Delacour and acceded rank, metaphorically giving him the keys to their new bolt hole in the Canadian Rockies. As for the latter, which happened immediately afterward, it was late, everyone was exhausted and about to retire for the day, when a slap like a gunshot echoed off the surrounding trees, and Gannon, on the receiving end of it, had to take a sharp step back in order to regain his balance.

"What have you done to my grandson?" The words rang out as loud as the blow.

During the awful silence that followed, Gilles considered that by now, Violet had to know who Gannon really was. But the outrage in her voice spoke volumes. She didn't care. So he loosened up and got ready to move, until Gannon surprised him, surprised them all. In the chill of night, witnessed by both Houses, the man bowed his head and dropped to one knee at the feet of Toby's grandmother.

Alongside Gilles, Houston whistled quietly through his teeth.

They waited, and spent an endless, agonizing moment out there on the wide, stone steps of their new home, until Violet reached out and placed her hand on Gannon's shoulder, who rose and embraced her. Gilles was too far away to hear the conversation that followed, and any outpouring of thought was firmly walled off. When they separated, the tall, blond Adonis and the steely matriarch, there was a collective sigh of relief.

As for the third event, on the following eve…

The arrival of House Goran became a roaring, inexorable tide. Eyes glittered with mistrust, and faces bore a dark wash of fear in the early hours of the morning. Had their latest refugees been followed? Houston, Gannon, and William Marsh headed to the perimeter of the compound in an attempt to find out. Meanwhile their numbers swelled by nine—Goran, Mina, Ryan, and Gage, Gevani and a woman named Irena, a man named Danny who was brought in under duress, and two donors. Everyone was kept busy, accommodating one another, while remaining on high alert.

Currently outnumbered, their precious donors vacated the light-safe rooms and moved into the barn with piles of blankets. Gilles had already moved his belongings into Houston's room and had invited Ryan and Gage to do the same. It would be a tight squeeze, but he was sure they'd all suffered worse. Until they had a ready blood supply available, strict rations were the order of the night. There'd be precedence, of course, based on established hierarchy, and Gilles prepared himself for lean times. Also, there was, he realized, one human who would be completely off limits. And with that thought in mind—

He found Saleem, Tobias, and Matthew talking to one of Goran's donors, a man in his early forties, pale-skinned and red-haired, who somehow didn't seem to fit. Gilles attracted Tobias's attention, and when they were both out of sight of the others, "Where is Matthew sleeping?"

"With us. We thought it would be safer."

"I'm guessing I don't need to spell out what would happen if anyone tries to feed off him?"

"No. I've already warned my sisters, who are quite enamored. And we'll keep a close watch until protocols have been established with our new guests." Toby shrugged, confident the matter was settled to his satisfaction.

Gilles nodded in the direction of the lounge. "Who's he?"

"Dr. Morris. He's a historian, and as you can imagine, he's very interested in the archive."

"Goran's donor?" He attempted to look impressed.

"No. Mina's."

"Ah..."

Nothing more to be said, he left, and a short while later he found

Eleanor in the entrance hall. "It's chaos," she began. "I can't get Mina to share our room. There's something between her and Dimitra, but it's not like we have any extra space. And what about Danny? What on earth are we supposed to do with him?"

Gilles didn't know what to say. Danny was currently under lock and key in the cellar and was a subject he was particularly leery of. Thankfully he was saved by the return of Houston, Gannon, and William, who were now outside, talking to Delacour and some of the others. "Let's go see what this is about," he suggested, sidestepping her question.

Houston was holding court. "There's no one out there, and we double-checked the cameras and trips. But I'm going to need volunteers for guard duty, night *and* day." The Elders were nodding. Gilles did the same. He'd been expecting it. So had Eleanor, who caught Houston's attention and raised her hand to volunteer.

After the meeting, while the others began to disperse, he saw Gannon beckoning. Gilles followed until he was sharing the view of distant mountains beyond the driveway. Gannon's attention, however, was focused elsewhere, so he waited and attempted to figure out what was coming.

It was a more difficult task than it might have been a week ago, because Gannon was different now, and every one of them could feel it. Houston had put it best. "I don't know what Deacon did to him, but right now he's one scary son of a bitch." Gilles had concurred, and it had become a personal battle to treat him as they always had, as just another man on the team and not someone to whom they should now bow and genuflect.

"I never said thank you," Gannon said eventually. "You risked your life for me and I never said it."

"Are you saying it now?"

"Yes."

"Mind if I ask you a question?" This was the first chance they'd had to talk, and he considered it relevant, under the circumstances. "Did you *want* to come home?"

Gannon's laugh carried no humor whatsoever. "You want an honest answer?"

"Never lie to me, Mark."

The other man let out a sigh. "At the time, no, I didn't. It's like they're family, despite what they did to me. It was so very difficult to leave them."

"Deacon has done quite a number on you, hasn't he."

"Yes. He has."

"What *is* he trying to do, Mark?"

After a moment of silence, "He's trying to break me. He just won't tell me why."

"You should talk to Delacour. He's known Deacon a long time."

"He's been busy, and I'm not sure…"

"He'll find time. And remember, you're safe here. No one is trying to hurt you, here." He watched the man struggle and wondered how close Deacon had brought him. How damaged he was. "Just promise me you'll talk."

"I will. Matthew told me I had to listen to you. He gave me hell about it on the train."

Gilles was about to reiterate, until he saw Mina on the approach.

"Excuse me," Gannon said.

He backed off and let them talk. He climbed the porch steps and was about to enter the house when Christina arrived. He watched her expression shift as she looked out into the yard, where Gannon exuberantly held Mina in his arms.

"I knew this would happen. Just not so soon."

"They—" Gilles began. But Christina was already walking away.

He shook his head, pushed aside yet another potential conflict, and began to walk through the house, making sure everything was locked down and ready for the dawn. When he was satisfied, he headed in the direction of his bunk. On this particular morning, Gage and William Marsh had pulled guard duty, leaving Gilles to share a room with Ryan and Houston, who had already settled onto his mattress and was thumping his pillow with a meaty fist.

"This won't be so bad," the man said. "We'll be pulling alternate shifts, so it'll give us more space."

"Good," an approaching voice rang out on the corridor. "It means there's room for me."

Gilles was astonished to see Gannon entering the makeshift dorm, bedroll and pillow tucked beneath his arm.

"You got kicked out of your room?" Houston's face carried a broad smirk.

"I let Dimitra have it."

"That was gallant of you," Gilles said.

"Thank you." Gannon unrolled his bedding. "You make it sound as if I had a choice."

Gilles took note of Ryan's bewilderment at the irreverent banter and couldn't help smiling as he lay back.

"Oh, and put me down for guard duty," Gannon said.

Houston didn't miss a beat. "Already did, hotshot. You're up tomorrow night, with Ryan here."

"I'm not on the daylight roster?"

"You want to switch?"

Gannon barked out a laugh. "No, thanks."

Staring at the ceiling, Gilles felt the others join him, grinning in the dark. He suspected he wasn't the only one basking gratefully in the first light moment since they'd arrived, and it felt good, helped clear his head of troubles, and enabled him to wallow in tentative optimism.

Despite everything, they had survived. He didn't know what form of chaos the next few nights would bring, and perhaps that's how their lives would be from now on, always under threat, while every hour, every minute was a treasure to be savored. But that was fine. The outlook was no longer dulled by certainty, or ironed flat by a burgeoning future that stretched inexorably onward. Right now there was no future, and to Gilles it felt strangely invigorating. He felt the presence of calm, more so than he had in weeks; he was at peace, he was alive.

And Anton Weiss be damned.

CHAPTER 37
MINA

They'd shared only minutes together, two or three, no more. Mutual inquiries and assertions of well-being, hurried and ill-composed, followed by a desperate kiss that threw caution to the wind and exposed far too much pain and delight.

Only minutes, yet it was still too much and the encounter left her fragile and susceptible to the tempestuous breeze that swept through this new sanctuary. She felt battered by it all, although it wasn't just Mark's appearance that had thrown her off balance. It had begun with an abrupt, physical manifestation of the child-mother figure who stalked her visions.

The girl had been outside watching them arrive. Not the ragged little queen of doom on this occasion, instead she appeared like a child, buffeted and dragged along with the rest of them, struggling to cope with the foul storm Anton Weiss had inflicted. And yet, there was no mistaking her. No hiding the fact that part of the storm settled directly on the girl's shoulders, until chaos became order and the unknown became known. Just one look and Mina understood what lay ahead and how real it was. And they wanted her to share a room with this girl?

"It's okay," Mark had told her, his voice soft and reassuring during those hurried moments. "She's made other arrangements." He'd talked as if he knew. As if he and this terrible little girl were already in cahoots. After all, hadn't he been a part of her visions, too? It seemed as if a profound change had recently been inflicted upon him, enough to suggest a future of conflict and strife between them. Nothing good would come of this, common sense warned, despite the pleasure of him being there in her arms.

And now she huddled in a darkened room with her arms around Irena, who was in shock and still coming to terms with the loss of her beloved Charles. There were also two other women in the room, and not one of them possessed an appetite for sleep. She was aware of the slivers of emotion drifting between them: sympathy from Eleanor, mistrust and jealousy from Christina, and from somewhere below, dulled by narcotics, Danny's bitter melancholy sang forth.

No sleep, then. Instead she cradled her ancient companion, rocked her gently back and forth as the woman shook with grief, while her eyes stared unfocussed at a blank wall where a hazy future danced. Shadow puppets that played out images of death and rebirth in the sand. Irrational. Unexplainable. Inevitable.

Her future was all laid out, the path wide and beckoning, and all that was left for her to do was to get up and walk.

About the Author

JANET JOYCE HOLDEN is a writer of contemporary dark fiction. Her novels include *Blood Paternal, Carousel,* and *The Only Red Is Blood*. She also has a number of short stories in various speculative anthologies.

She is originally from the North of England, and has lived in Southern California for the last nineteen years. Her website is at janetjoyceholden.com

CPSIA information can be obtained
at www.ICGtesting.com
Printed in the USA
FSOW03n1156160217
30719FS

9 781941 408674